21st Century Sirens Series

Soul Breather
Blood Sister
Shield Maiden

SOUL BREATHER

TEDMAN

POD edition

This book is a work of fiction. Names, characters, businesses, organisations, places, events, and incidents are the product either of the author's imagination or are used fictitiously. Any resemblance to actual persons, living or dead, events, or locales is entirely coincidental.

Copyright © T Stedman 2015

The right of T Stedman to be identified as author of this work has been asserted by him in accordance with the Copyright, Designs and Patents Act 1998.

ISBN (Print) 978-0-9933098-0-9

Cover Art: Anna Dittmann

Edited by Helen Williams

All rights reserved

A special thank you to my long-suffering children for putting up with their obsessive-compulsive mother, and to my readers, Diane Burke and Sarah O'Brien.

Dedicated to the memory of Craig Wisdom, a rare spirit and a dear friend.

The Royal Families

Of Atlantis
Dubonnetti
Bonaci
Santalini
Florianna

Of Murrtaine
Borge

Prologue

Dubonnetti Estate, west coast of Ireland, eleven years previously

"Get off me you little wankers!" Dante wheezed, from beneath the pile of tangled arms and legs of the bundle that was his four younger brothers.

His father breezed into the room. "Get up Dante. Stop messing around. I've called you here for an important reason."

Dante threw off his brothers one by one. They scrambled to their feet to sit on the leather chairs dotted around their father's study. The last one made sure he let off a noisy fart to prove a point, much to the amusement of the boys. Even Jay, the young friend of the family, smothered a smile, which threatened to break out over his usually serious face.

Dante finally stood to his full tall and lanky height, rearranged his clothes then sloped over to join Jay on the tatty brown leather sofa.

"No Dante. Come here. You need to be standing," his

father said from his perch at the front of his heavy oak desk.

Dante stopped, ran a grubby hand through his tousled mop of black hair, turned and wandered over to his father with a cocky limp. Shit. He'd hoped his father would leave him alone today, as it was his birthday.

The room fell silent. Dante knew they were all holding their breath to see what his father would do next. But instead of speaking he reached into the breast pocket of his blazer and pulled out an old-looking velvet box; the sort that jewellery came in.

"What is it father?" a brother called out.

Christian Dubonnetti didn't answer, but opened the box to reveal a large unusual oval ring. It had an opaque white stone that bulged from an ornate gold setting.

Dante stared at it. He spent as little time as possible around his unfathomable father, so for him to give him such a gift was a big deal.

"Today you are thirteen, Dante. For a prince, that means you have become a man."

More sniggers around the room.

Dante rolled his eyes. Here we go again. His father was slipping into the madness.

"Shh! This is a divining ring. It is ancient from our homeland!" Christian shouted, demanding respect.

Dante shifted his weight uncomfortably and looked at Jay who locked eyes with him as if to steady him.

"Hold your hand out, boy," his father continued.

Dante snapped his head back round to his father. Wary now, he held out his hand, palm up.

Christian impatiently turned it over and took the ring from its box. Dante's eyes widened in horror as Christian pressed the side of the ring and a spike shot out about a centimetre long.

Christian looked deep into Dante's eyes. "Now listen to me, and listen to me good, boy. This ring could be the secret to everything, to you, and to this house."

Dante stared at him blankly, but the rest of the room was deathly quiet.

"You are the eldest son of a family of five sons. It will be in this generation Dante, I know it." Christian's voice raised with his fervour. "The Soul Breathers are hidden somewhere in the world. This ring," and he held it up high, "will tell you when you get near one. It will change colour to turquoise. But if it ever turns to deepest purple, you have found your queen, Dante; your most compatible mate in the world. That is, if you find her before the sons from the other four Atlantean families. Then you will be king, not of just one country, but of the whole Atlantean world."

"She will bring you riches Dante, and such exquisite delight such as you could only dream about. And power, so that Atlanteans and Humans alike will bow down to you. And if ever our forefathers venture back to Earth, then you could have the power and standing to represent us."

Dante looked around him. All he could hear was the old clock ticking. Gone were the giggles, replaced by rapt faces; even Jay looked riveted. They were all actually buying this shit.

His father sensed his distraction, picked up his left hand and slid the ring part way down the middle finger.

Dante knew what he was going to do before he did it. He looked his father in the eye insolently and saw the hint of a smile there. Dante narrowed his in readiness. Then Christian rammed the ring onto his finger ensuring the spike entered the soft flesh between the knuckles.

Although Dante jolted with the pain, he made no sound. He heard murmurs from his brothers and felt the warmth of his blood run down between his fingers and onto the floor.

Something made him glance down and look at the ring. It was swirling with white smoke mixing with his dark red blood until it settled white again.

He looked nonchalantly back at his father and waited to be dismissed.

"Never take it off." Christian snarled.

Dante turned on his heel, as if nothing had happened and strolled towards the door. "Come on Jay, I've heard enough of this bollocks."

The other boy shook the wisps of blond hair from his brilliant blue eyes, got up and followed him out of the study.

But Dante never took the ring off.

Chapter 1

London, present day

The sign was old fashioned. 'The Bluebell' it said simply – pale blue and gold on a polished wood background.

This was the place.

She skipped up the steps, clutching her biker jacket and helmet, pushed through the double-sprung doors into a stylish wooden clad foyer and slammed into the feeling of being hit round the head with a cricket bat.

Whoa! She stopped, gripped her temples, hugged her stomach and grabbed her mouth. Searching ahead for a place to run, the beautiful blue and gold rug in front of her undulated and rippled like a rough sea. Concentrating, she tried to centre her steps on it, fighting the overwhelming need to spew.

She had no clue of the layout of the place as she scuttled through. She leant on the sides of beautiful furniture and the odd anonymous arm, saying whoops, and sorry at intervals. She ran past the lifts on her left and the open double doors to the noisy bar on her right, until her lolloping steps took her to a door with a brass sign on the front meant to look like a woman.

"Thank God."

Falling into the room, she was soon alone as two chattering women left. She lurched over to the sink, clasped the sides and leant over. She spat and heaved. Her mouth watered and her eyes streamed. What was wrong with her? Had someone spiked her drink? Wracking her brains over where she'd been that night she came up with a big fat, unlikely. This was *so* not like any drug she'd ever done.

She realised that trying to work it out was a waste of time and whipped off the red sweatbands she wore on her wrists and plunged them under the cold tap. The water ran over her scarred pulse points and gradually calmed her and cooled her raised temperature, which was causing her head to pound.

Mesmerised by the spot-lit diamonds in the water and its tinkling sound, she stood, gathering herself together.

The door was bashed open.

"There you are, Tia. I said you must be here by now."

She turned and looked over her shoulder at her friend Sian. Not a great friend; more of an acquaintance really; a drinking buddy.

"Flippin hell, you look like shit."

She tried to smile. *You have no idea*. "You say the nicest things. I felt a bit sick, that's all. I'll be out in a minute."

Sian did that thing with her eyebrows, which said, 'Yeah right.' "You're not…you know?"

"Piss off, Sian. You have to have sex for that, remember?"

Sian laughed, "True … hurry up then. We're in the bar. Oh, and don't forget your shades, Tia. Your eyes look well weird." And she went back out.

Tia chuffed a mirthless laugh to herself, turned back and closed her eyes and breathed in and out deeply. The nausea was passing.

She opened her eyes and looked down at the soothing water again. Shit! She grabbed one of the neatly folded white towels on the shelf next to her and rubbed her skin vigorously all over her lower arms as if to rub off the emerging black bands on her skin.

It wasn't working. She looked around her frantically and noticed a redundant hand dryer. Quickly she shoved her arms under it and punched the button and prayed the warm air would magic away the markings.

She stood as long as she dared before her friends sent out a search party again. What possible explanation could she give about her weirdness? She replaced her sweatbands, pulled down the sleeves on her silk top so it almost covered her hands and walked back over to the mirror.

Her eyes were more weird than usual and really dilated. She reached into her shoulder bag for her large shades – her barrier to the normal world – and put them on.

She felt much better. She adjusted her top, put on a bit of lip gloss, picked her jacket and helmet up off the floor, walked out of the loo and turned left into the crowded bar to the safety in numbers.

***

The bar was packed. People had piled in from the surrounding pubs, theatres and restaurants, attracted by a late drink and the cool ambience. Situated where it was in London's West End, it could stay busy till three or four in the morning.

Jay walked in looking crisp as usual in a light grey suit. He was here to socialize with his staff and check everything was running smoothly, as he usually did towards the end of the evening. As he leaned with his back against the bar scanning the heads of the lively crowd, his eyes stopped and backtracked instantly.

She was standing with her back to the far wall with two or three friends. Her hair was honey blonde, falling down to her waist in luxurious waves. Even at a distance her beautiful tanned skin stood out in contrast. She wore bug-eyed shades – probably to cover those large unusual eyes – but they didn't detract from her one bit.

Jay weaved his way through the crowd until he came up next to her.

She smelled fresh like the ocean and looked exotic; even though she was wearing beaten up jeans and boots teamed with a sheer African print top. She somehow looked effortlessly sophisticated.

"Can I buy you a drink?" he said, as he leaned over, flashing his brilliant blue eyes and one of his affecting smiles like butter wouldn't melt.

She turned to look, taking him in from the floor up, and smiled when she reached his face. "Should I know you?"

"No, not really," he replied, "but we have met."

Smoothly, he touched her elbow pointing her to a quieter corner of the bar, "Shall we?"

Amused, she allowed herself to be led and excused herself from the group she'd been drinking with, telling them she'd catch them later.

They stood together and sipped their drinks in sync – scotch on the rocks. She continued to impress him. "I hear Dannyl met a sudden end?"

She squinted at him, searching his face and trying to make the connection.

He enjoyed tormenting her, and took a sip of his drink as he gauged her response.

"Card game. At his club," she concluded, pointing as she said it.

He tipped his drink and nodded, secretly pleased that she had registered him enough at the time to remember him. "I'm Jason. Everyone calls me Jay," and he offered her his hand.

"Tia," she said, shaking his. "Lovely bracelet."

"This was Dannyl's," he said, while he remembered the occasion, letting the stones run through his fingers.

"I know."

"Of course," he conceded, and hoped she didn't harbour feelings for the dearly departed. "Some said it was a heart attack, some said he was killed?" he continued, staring into her face.

She just looked at him and blinked.

"I heard his girlfriend went away for it?" he persisted.

"If you mean did I go away for it, then you'd be right, but I wasn't his girlfriend and I wasn't away long."

"Glad to hear it." He really was. She was being very direct with him, looking him straight in the eyes – a complete turn on, and not without an element of danger. *Oh happy days.*

"Do you always wear sunglasses?"

She laughed at the change of subject as if she'd read his mind, "I am light-sensitive and to be honest, I get bored with people commenting on my eyes all the time."

Jay remembered how arresting her eyes were from the first time they'd met. He snapped into action. "Do you fancy going somewhere more quiet?" he asked, flashing her another smile and half expecting her to say no. *Hey, it was worth a shot.*

"Just for a while; I have an early start in the morning."

His eyes widened – his lucky day – and he gestured the way.

She grabbed her stuff that was bundled on the floor near her friends and followed him through the foyer.

The lift pinged open, and they stepped in.

***

She faced front riding up in the lift. Jay studied her profile. She really was exquisite. He watched her blink slowly behind her sunglasses. Her accent was all South London, but somehow she was separate, rare.

He glanced down at the leather jacket and motorcycle helmet she was carrying and thought she was as hot as hell. "It's not every day you meet a woman who rides a motorbike."

Without looking at him she said, "I wouldn't know." She stepped out of the lift. "I just want to get from A to

B as fast as possible."

She wasn't taking any old flannel and he liked that.

He overtook her and led the way to the door of his suite.

They walked in and she dumped her stuff by the door and headed for the main room through a small hallway. There was no hesitation as she took in his large bed; nothing remarkable, modern maleness.

He loved the large window overlooking the city and thought it was the best part of the room. He watched her make a beeline for it and smiled.

"How does someone your age get all this?" she said, as she let the thin gauze of curtain fall out of her fingers and back into place.

Jay smiled again while he poured two scotches from a decanter. "Why, don't I look the type?"

She sat down and took the drink offered. "I dunno… you look posh on the outside…" She pushed her glasses on top of her head. "But there is something 'street' about you."

"Ah," he grinned sitting opposite her, "There's me thinking I'm fooling everyone."

She narrowed her eyes, "I doubt there is anything you do without realising."

He sat studying her for a minute making up his mind. How far should he push his luck?

"No they're not contacts," she said, pre-empting his next question.

He stood up, "I'm going to take a quick shower." He put his heavy glass down on the table and began opening the buttons of his cuffs and front of his shirt, giving Tia a good glimpse of the heavy black tattoos which covered the length of his arms and his chest, and then he turned, showing that they continued onto his back.

She was left blinking. "You sure I'll be here when you get back?"

He laid his shirt on the bed. "You could always join me?" he said, arching a cheeky brow as he walked towards the connecting bathroom, feeling her eyes on him.

Smirking to himself, he knew he was pushing it, but half the fun was in the gamble, and he always won.

Chapter 2

He wasn't sure what he expected; she was so difficult to read. She might be gone by the time he got out.

Turning on the spray in the wet room he tilted his head back, allowing the jets to massage him. He slowly turned around, put his back to the spray and looked straight into Tia's eyes.

He grinned.

He held his breath as she reached past him and turned the heat dial, plummeting the temperature way down to cold. "I get too hot," she explained, and stepped into him.

His gaze skimmed down over her body appreciatively. He was easily six inches taller than her; putting her at around five feet six.

Her long hair flattened and darkened fast; making her eyes look even bigger, her pupils, huge disks, almost swamped the irises.

Her golden skin began to reveal what looked like unusual dark tattoos around her biceps, chest and rib cage, and also around the tops of her legs and calves. It reminded him of something from his childhood in

Ireland. He shook his head as he traced the ones on her thighs with a thumb and finger. "I like these."

She looked directly up into the fierce spray of water; unblinking and laughing; holding her palms up, "Water!" She exclaimed, as if it were a new discovery, letting the water cascade over her.

Despite the temperature of the water, Jay found himself laughing along with her, as strange as she was; she delighted him and dumbfounded him. He touched her chin as she spat a mouthful of water and grinned at him. Leaning down he put his lips on hers. Electricity shot through him at the contact. He drew back and looked into her eyes.

Reaching up past his head, she grabbed the rail around the shower and hoisted herself up and clamped her legs around his waist.

Yes! He laughed aloud and clasped his hands around her backside and supported her while he took her mouth fiercely; their tongues in combat as they explored a wild, deepening kiss. Cursing, he leant down and kissed and bit her breasts hungrily. Turning his body quickly, he perched her weight on a small ledge and scattered bottles of shampoo and shower gel, letting them clatter to the floor. He pushed her back roughly into the tiles and felt his way down with seeking fingers, and found his way back to her mouth. While not breaking the seal of their urgent kisses, he sought the heat of her and found it instantly, making her gasp. "Fuck," was all he could articulate as her heat seared him. Lust overtook him as he expertly delved and stroked her softness. Impatient, he wasted no more time and pulled her down on to him, aching and waiting.

Both of them cried out as he entered her brutally.

Bewildered, she stopped him and panted. He stopped and breathed deeply with his mouth next to hers. "Okay?" he whispered. His eyes closed, silently grateful for the lull. He needed to get used to her core heat that threatened to end his game before it had begun.

Then, any semblance of his being in control went out the window as she renewed her grip with her thighs like a vice and clamped onto the soft part of his shoulder with her teeth. She dug her nails into his shoulder blades and her heels into his behind and moved on him with strength and purpose. This girl was fit.

Taking her full weight he pushed her into the corner and bit her neck back with a savagery that was rough and urgent to match their relentless rhythm. Glorious noises echoed around the space. Groans, pants and whispered pleas. She was rougher with him than he ever was with any woman and he loved it.

He kicked bottles away from his feet as he leant back against the wall. She reached above her again and pulled herself up and down again expertly and repeatedly.

"That's it," he whispered.

He renewed his grip as his legs shook. When his climax came there was no holding it off. It was ferocious in its strength and he shouted as he came and bit into her shoulder hard, grinding her down into him in circular movements. She cried out at his ear and he knew she was right there with him.

He sagged back into the wall. She flopped her head onto his shoulder. Both stood breathing heavily as he slowly released her down, until her toes touched the tiled floor.

Their conscious thought came back and their hearts gradually slowed, and he became aware of the cold temperature and the disarray of the shower floor.

He put his forehead on hers as he caught his breath and rested his hands on her shoulders. She leaned against him. As his mind was gradually coming back online, he tried to decide whether he wanted her to stay the night, or go.

As if she read his mind, she said, "I must go," and ducked under his arm and out of the shower, wrapping herself in a fluffy white towel.

Okay, he thought, that makes it easy. He frowned as he turned the shower off and grabbed a towel for himself. He wasn't sure if he liked her coming to that decision and followed her into the bedroom where she was already pushing her legs into her jeans.

"Hey!" He reached for her hand and pulled her to him for a hug. "Thank you," he said simply and looked into her fathomless eyes. He noticed they were squinting in the light.

"My pleasure," she smiled, "You were my first." She broke away from him, picked up her boots and tugged them on.

His eyebrows met while he processed the information, not sure he'd heard right. "I'd like to see you again," he found himself saying before he could think any deeper about it.

She looked up from her boots and smiled, "Sure. I'm not sure when though." She fastened her watch back on her wrist. "I leave for the States in a few hours."

"Give me your phone," he said, holding out his hand to her.

"What?" she said, frowning.

"I'm going to give you my number, which I never do," he said seriously, punching in the digits after she handed her phone over to him. "Are you going on holiday?"

"No, work." She said as she threw her bag over her shoulder.

"Can I ask what you do?"

"You can ask," she said, already walking to the door. She bent to pick up her crash helmet and jacket. Then relented, "I'm helping a friend out with some of his horses. He's hiring them out on some film set."

"Ah," Jay nodded as he lent down to give her a last kiss as she'd reached his door.

He found himself kissing her properly instead of the patronizing peck he normally reserved for the dismissal of one of his one-night stands. He straightened and she smiled up at him.

"Later."

"Later."

She pulled out of his grip and crept out of the door and shut it quickly.

Stunned, he walked over to the window and opened it a fraction. He wondered what the fuck had just hit him as he rested his head on the window.

Five minutes later he heard the throaty roar of a motorbike. Then it sped off into the distance.

***

"Get them in then!" Dante Dubonnetti said in greeting as he casually walked up to Jay, propping up the bar.

Jay was his oldest and closest friend. They were more like brothers really.

"Two JD's please Paul," Jay said to the young barman. "What happened to you earlier?"

Dante shook his head, "Fuck knows. It was the weirdest thing. I had to go before I fell over. It must have been one of your dodgy pints." He said in his Irish lilt, his lively slate grey eyes looked sideways at Jay half smiling.

"Fuck off, you arsehole."

Dante grabbed his old friend in a headlock and shook him playfully. "No honestly, I felt like shit, then the minute I got outside and in a cab I felt fine."

He took off his black biker jacket and settled on the stool next to Jay as he always did at the end of the night, just before Jay closed up.

He looked at Jay mulling something over as he stared down, rattling the ice cubes around in his drink. Jay was the quieter one but something was up.

"You look wasted. Bad night?" he said.

"No, not bad," Jay answered thoughtfully, and then shook his head.

"What then, a woman?" Dante poked, the corners of his mouth turned up into a slow smile.

"Do you remember me telling you about a young girl

at Burmese Dannyl's place, over Shoreditch way? It was a couple of years ago." Jay said, turning to face Dante in his chair, "The one I said was stunning".

"The jail bait?"

"That's the one."

"Didn't she do him in?"

"Well I think she was blamed for it … but anyway, yes, that's the one. I was over there playing cards. It was where I won this," he said, and he pulled his sleeve back to show a beautiful and incredibly unusual turquoise bracelet.

Dante smiled indulgently as his friend showed it to him, knowing exactly its significance but keeping quiet. "Yes I remember. What's that got to do with the girl?"

"She came in here tonight, and we … well we hooked up."

Dante laughed. "Fair play," he said, tilting his glass in salute. "Watch yourself with that one."

"Tell me about it. Fuck!"

Dante laughed out loud. "What?"

"I feel played Dant … fucking played!" A look of disbelief was written all over his friend's face.

Dante creased over at the middle. He stopped laughing just enough to order two more drinks. "Will you be breaking the habit of a lifetime and seeing this one again?"

"I think I might have to. My pride demands it," Jay said, flabbergasted.

Still laughing, Dante clinked glasses with him.

Chapter 3

Mark Dubonno was a film star. At twenty-two he was already successful in vampire teen films.

Ready for his next scene, set during the American civil war, he lounged about with several of the young co-stars waiting to be called. All of them were in full American soldier uniform.

Mark was gorgeous, and he knew it, with a headful of blonde wayward hair, pretty girl face, tall and long limbed. His light grey eyes were covered with contact lenses for his role as lead vampire in his latest flick.

Smoke buffeted everywhere to add authenticity to the war-torn camp of canvas tents and piles of guns and ammunition; all ready for the director to call, "Action!"

Mark leaned over to whisper something suggestive to a young female he'd been spending time with between scenes; although he'd already decided he would dump her as soon as filming was over. His attention was grabbed elsewhere. Riding a large Palomino horse bareback and leading two others, the most stunningly beautiful woman ambled by.

His skin prickled as he watched her, mesmerized.

A cowboy hat covered her many long braids, held in a loose ponytail over her multi-coloured, stripy roll-neck sweater. Snug jeaned legs rested relaxed against the horse's sides.

As if she knew he was there, she looked over at him and her eyes physically struck him. Never had he seen the like; the colour a vivid green and wide, almost glowing, like disks.

She dragged her eyes from him.

He jumped to his feet.

"What?" The girl next to him said, alarmed.

"Nothing," he said moodily, "I need a minute."

He walked around the back of a tent and looked at his heirloom ring he always wore on the middle finger of his left hand.

He stared, shocked rigid. "Fucking hell!" he muttered to himself. "My God!" The proof was there in front of his eyes. This ring was green – turquoise to be exact. All his life it had remained an opaque white. His father had always said, "One day son, when you get near one it will change colour."

He straightened up with resolve. He needed a phone right away. The production team would not allow cell phones so he rushed to the catering van and asked to borrow one of the waiting staff's.

He just beamed one of his charismatic smiles and she handed over her phone along with a flutter of her 'come on' eyes. His eyes diverted as soon as the phone touched his hands and he walked away, dialling quickly with his long aristocratic fingers. He put the phone to his ear, "Get me my father, quickly!" he said, and paced impatiently. "Father? Yes it's me, Marco. I've found one." Silence. "I've actually fucking found one."

There was a pause as if his father was sitting down to receive the news. When he gained composure he promised to dispatch two of his brothers to America without delay.

"Yes I'll stay close to her," he promised before he hung up.

He strode back to the others wracking his brains how to ingratiate himself with her, when one of the younger cast members rushed up to him.

"There you are, Mark."

Marco just looked at him – his mind a thousand miles away.

"Are you coming," the boy continued, "Mark?" snapping him out of it.

He shook his head at the boy, not comprehending.

"Tonight."

"Why, what's happening?" Still not really interested, his mind turning cartwheels.

"We are all going to that little club in town."

"Oh, I dunno." He frowned, his English accent coming out the more distracted he was. *Go away you little fuck.*

"You should come, someone said that hot horse wrangler girl from England is DJ'ing there."

He stopped in is tracks. That got his attention.

He looked at Billy and smiled, giving him his full dental impact. "Of course I'll come Billy. Wouldn't want to appear a stick in the mud." He watched the boy walk off excitedly and tell as many who would listen.

As soon as Mark finished on set that day he made a few calls to double-check Billy's information, and it had been correct. She was due to do her set between 12 and 2 a.m. Now all he had to do was to ditch the annoying co-starlet. Her cloying ways had started to grate anyway.

Now he was on to his family's heritage, the sky would be the limit for him.

***

Mark arrived fashionably later than everyone else. Eleven fifty – just in time to get a drink. He found everyone he knew in the VIP lounge just as they were rousing themselves to make their way to the main room. After greeting everyone and getting the pleasantries out of the way he followed them in. He could already feel his hackles rising.

He glanced down at his ring and watched it swirl to the rich turquoise it had been earlier. He looked up and saw her up on the dais by the booth the DJ's stood in. She was chatting animatedly to a couple of huge black bouncer type guys. She was sorting through her records – vinyl, Mark acknowledged.

The place was rammed. It was busier than normal for a Friday night. Everyone had filled the place from the film set, as there wasn't a lot doing in a small town like this.

The MC got on the mike, building up the crowd by introducing her as Queen Ti, House Music DJ from London and Ibiza.

She was already behind the decks with one earphone on, complimenting her swinging braids, cueing her first record. Bug-eyed dark glasses covered her unusual eyes. Vest top and Jeans were all she wore he noticed, with platform trainers to give her small frame some height.

After much dry ice and atmospheric build-up music, she dropped a house tune he remembered his brother playing. The place seemed to erupt. Everyone seemed to be on their feet.

Mark was amazed as he surveyed the room. The place began to jump. The bass was cranked to the level of just right. Dry ice billowed and rose up from the floor. And the clubbers threw themselves into abandon. Even the heavy bouncers shuffled from foot to foot, swinging their arms and glinting gold teeth as they smiled at the musical nectar that permeated the room.

She took the room on a magical journey – building and dropping the music. Clubbers perspired but never sat down. Most of them, he realized, would have never heard a lot of the Balearic beats that shifted their feet. When the tune she was playing broke down to ride its groove, Mark watched with awe as he witnessed the sonic wave which bounced over their heads. She pulled the unsuspecting clubbers to her as surely as if she'd sung from the rocks. And when she had them in the palm of her hand, she held them till exhaustion, playing hard trance, and wowing them with mix after mix. Even he had to admit he was impressed.

Although this girl was here to work the horses, this was obviously her trade. Useful information, he thought, for locating her sisters. Music, he now realized, was going to be the common denominator. Of course they would have been banned from singing – too obvious.

Looking round, he seemed to be the only one immune to her luring power; Handy, he mused, and wondered if she knew what she was doing? Probably not, given how conspicuous she was making herself to fellow Atlanteans.

When her set was over and she put her records away in their sleeves, those around her congratulated her and whisked her off to the bar for a drink.

Billy came bounding up to him sweating like a pig. "Brilliant wasn't she?" he said panting. "Come on, I know her."

"Lead the way," Mark followed along smugly.

When they reached the VIP lounge it was like bees round a honey pot. He followed Billy up to the large crowd, of mainly men, which surrounded her. That was when he knew she was aware of him. She turned and looked over her shoulder straight at him as soon as he was nearby.

"Billy!" she exclaimed, as she saw him and hugged him to her, but Marco saw her eyes were on him.

"You were great Tia," Billy said grinning. "Can I introduce you to my friend Mark?"

"The star? Of course," she said, and smiled, turning her attention to him.

He turned on the full charm offensive, bending over her hand, kissing it like a European prince. The act seemed to off-balance her slightly rather than impress her as she began to make her excuses of early starts and all that.

Just then a large cowboy walked in, and she instantly made her way over to him. He put his arm around her possessively and steered her out of the building.

Mark sipped his drink and pondered to himself. He could be an added complication.

"Billy, let me buy you a drink?"

The younger actor, obviously flattered, accepted at once – even though he was too young for alcohol.

"Tell me Billy, do you know her well?"

"Yeah, we're friends. I've been going and helping with the horses when I've had nothing to do."

"Do you know what she's up to tomorrow?"

"Haven't you looked at your notes for tomorrow yet?" Billy said, shocked. "It's the scene where your character jumps the soldier on his horse, so you'll probably see her there."

Bingo! Mark thought. "I'll look forward to that then."

His broad smile evaporated the minute Billy walked away.

Chapter 4

The stunt was due to be shot at dawn as vampires couldn't be out in the light. Mark was uncharacteristically on time that morning.

After last minute touch ups to his make-up, he made his way to the set.

The director was giving instructions to the two stunt men. One was to ride the horse at a canter and the other was to leap off a tree, knocking him off the horse. The camera would cut and Mark would take the place of one of them to shoot a close up of him ripping out the other's throat.

At this point he could see the girl warming up the horse. She was riding in circles, first one way and then the other. She then rode past the tree with the cameras and the lights to make sure none of it scared the horse, causing him to spook and ruin the take. After she had done this a few times she dismounted and helped the stunt actor arrange his stirrups before he loped off to repeat the run.

Mark watched her amble away in her over-long chaps. He slowly walked over and made sure he would bump into her.

"Hey, nice riding," he said, and held the tops of her arms, and looked into her face.

Confusion briefly flickered across it. "Hello," she said, and took a step backwards, out of his grip.

"Forgive me," he said, and inclined his head. "I just had to come over."

"You're English?" she remarked, regaining her composure.

"Close. Listen, would you like to get a coffee? It will be a while before I'm called, they'll be doing the takes with the horse a while yet."

"Okay, but I need to stand by in case they need me."

"Of course." And he went off to the catering van and brought back two coffees and some biscuits. They both sat down on some camping chairs. "Here, have a biscuit."

"No, thank you." She blew over the top of her coffee.

"Go on, you have a great figure." Pushing the plate back towards her.

"No really, I can't eat that type of food. I have a bad reaction."

Mark smiled, of course she couldn't. "Forgive me,"

"It's okay, you couldn't know."

He stared at her for a few moments. "Was that your boyfriend who collected you last night?"

She squinted while she thought for a second. "Who Cash? No, he's a friend. I work for him here on the film. I've known him for a couple of years." She smiled to herself as she sipped her drink.

"A great DJ and a horse woman?"

"They are my two loves, music and horses."

Mark's brain was going at a hundred miles an hour; how to get closer to her, and give his brothers time to get there to give him further instructions.

"No room for a man in your affections?"

She eyed him suspiciously without answering him.

He was taken aback. Never had he met a member of the opposite sex who was immune to his charms; especially when he was working so damn hard.

"I don't have any time for romance," she concluded, and stood up.

"Wait! Just as friends … of course …" he said, grasping at straws.

"Sorry, I'm going back to the UK tonight."

Shit! "Listen, can I meet up with you if I get some time off? In London perhaps?"

"Perhaps," she said, as she tried to move away from him.

"Before you go, can I get your number? Here, put it straight into my phone." And he handed it to her.

She punched in the digits quickly, looking up as the large cowboy approached them.

"Ready Tia?" he said, eyeing Mark suspiciously. "I think they've finished with us for today."

Mark tried to introduce himself, offering his hand, but almost flinched at the cowboy's expression. "I know who you are," he said aggressively, steering Tia away from him.

Mark was left unsettled. He needed to get rid of the bulldog who was obviously guarding her. 'Protector,' he thought. Must tell his brothers about him.

He strode off to make the call.

**

Tia couldn't believe she had actually called him, and was even more surprised when he revealed that he'd been in LA on business. She had told him she was travelling back and he'd suggested travelling back together.

Tia's heart fluttered when she saw him. He looked much more casual this time in a checked cotton shirt, jeans and boots. None of it was discount store though; all expensive, quality stuff. His mousy blond hair, razor sharp around the sides, was left long on top and flopped lazily into one eye. He leant against a wall; man bag over his shoulder; carry on between his feet.

His face lit up when she approached him; beaming his gorgeous, slow smile, gluing her eyes to his sensuous mouth.

"Hey!" he said quietly, and leant in straight away and kissed her cheek.

Wow. She felt a jolt down to her toes and he smelled great. Clean, expensive and male. She'd never get enough of that.

"Hey!" she replied, trying not to gawp at him too much.

She went to walk towards the departure lounge.

He caught her by the elbow. "This way, I've upgraded you."

She stopped, blinked and processed the information.

"Come on," he continued. "You can't prefer cattle class."

She raised her eyebrows and he put his arm around her shoulders, steering her in his direction.

She had to admit to herself as they snuggled into their first class cubicles, that this was a much preferable way to travel from LAX to London.

"Are you used to all this?" she asked him, as he turned his chair to face her and passed her a scotch on the rocks.

"Yes," he said flatly, with no arrogance or boasting.

"You are a bit like me though."

He looked at her surprised. "Oh, how so?"

"You don't like talking about yourself much either." She watched his small, embarrassed smile.

They were both silent for a few minutes.

Then he reached for another small scotch bottle. "What about if we play a game, where we allow the other to ask three questions?"

She thought about this for a few seconds while she sipped her drink. "Anything?"

"Anything." He flashed that knockout smile again.

"You don't know enough?" She grinned soppily back.

He barked a laugh. "No, I don't know enough."

***

Whether he liked to admit it or not, this one was under his skin and he needed to know more of her and now she knew it. He felt a curious pang of vulnerability.

"Okay then, can I go first?" she said, and smoothed her hand along her thighs. It was, he realised, a habit of hers when she needed time to think.

"Go ahead." He tilted his glass towards her.

"Right … where did you grow up, and who with?"

"That's two questions."

"No it's not...stop stalling."

"Okay," he agreed and laughed. "South East London, and mother.

"No dad?"

"Is that another question?"

"No, no! Ignore that one."

"My turn," he said, and smiled at her. "Same question then."

"Oh ... outskirts of London ... South ... Foster mother and two half-brothers."

He took a slug of his drink making sure he didn't give away any sign of pity. He'd already clocked an air of fragility about her. She hid it well but he didn't want to blow her cover.

"Your turn," he said, and gestured her to continue with his glass.

"I thought you must have had a posh upbringing to run that hotel?"

"Me, no ... Something 'street' about me, remember?"

She laughed at the reminder. "You still haven't really answered the question?"

"Okay ... my best friend's father asked me to work there for him ... My turn, isn't it? Did you kill Dannyl?" It was straight to the point – no point beating around the bush. He needed to know what he was dealing with.

The shock of the question made her choke as she swallowed her drink, "Don't mince your words," she said, laughing.

"What?" he said, laughing along with her. "It's a

reasonable question. Do I need to sleep with a knife under my pillow?"

She got serious for a moment, as if remembering, contemplated the question and looked down into her drink. "Yes… I feel like I did…I mean, I wished it." She looked up straight into his eyes. "Then his heart just stopped."

He wasn't sure how deep her feelings had gone for the bloke, but from what he knew of Dannyl, he was a devious, self-serving egomaniac. He could only guess how she was treated. Instead of pressing her, he looked intently at her for a minute. "I don't think you're dangerous," he said, softly.

Dispersing her glum mood, she said, "You assume you'll be sharing a bed with me then?" She was joking but still tried not to look him in the eye. Her coyness was lovely.

"Yes," he said simply, as if no other option was even possible. Drawing her eyes to his directly and they locked for a long moment.

She shook her head as if to break the spell. "Last question – your tattoos? They don't exactly go with your lifestyle."

He smiled and let her off the hook and considered her question. Of all the questions she could have asked, she had hit on the subject, which was most revealing about him. He debated whether to give her the same old bollocks he gave all the girls but there was something about her, maybe her own honesty and vulnerability. "My best friend made me get them done."

Her eyebrows drew together as if she didn't get it.

"He said the symbols were some kind of ancient spell or prayer or something, from where he's from. It is supposed to keep me safe and give me luck, or something." He shook his head dismissing the emotion and looked into his drink. "I am sceptical."

"That's a really nice thing," she said softly, as if she recognised his bond with his friend. "I mean you have a charmed life, don't you?"

"I guess so," he said smiling. He hadn't really thought about it like that before. "Any way," and he changed the subject. "I have one left."

"Fire away."

"Do you have anyone special in your life at the moment?"

She laughed, "Mm." As if she was nervous about answering.

"Just like to know if I have any competition?"

"Two."

"Two?" He was not expecting that answer and tried not to look too shocked, but strangely for him, when it sunk in, he was not put off.

"They are just friends ... platonic ... but we're close."

He nodded, his brain whirring as he studied her. He nestled back into his chair. The personal questions stopped there. He decided that was enough for one day.

During the rest of the flight they listened to music, slept a little, chatted about films, places in the world they'd like to visit – surface stuff. So the journey passed quickly.

As they landed, she agreed to come to his hotel for a while, before she travelled back to Kent, where he'd learned she lived, but she was cagey about the address.

***

Tia rode in Jay's chauffeur driven car back to his hotel in London. By then it was around midnight. Jay had had her bike moved from the airport to the garage at the hotel on the pretext that she must be tired. That he wanted to spend more time with her gave her butterflies.

As they arrived, her stomach flipped at the memory of the last time she'd been there, it had been steamy to say the least. She grew hot at the thought, wondering if her cheeks were red, giving her away.

When they walked in, Jay held her elbow as they went through the foyer and straight to the lift. He greeted people he knew or worked for him, issuing orders not to be disturbed until the next morning.

They were alone as they stepped in the lift. She gasped as he roughly pulled her to him as soon as the doors closed and was on her mouth in an instant. She complied without thought and melded to him as he pushed her to the wall of the lift and his fingers kneaded her shoulder and her backside. Hers reached into his wayward hair.

As lost in the moment as she was, she still became acutely aware of her core temperature rising dangerously. The doors opened as they reached the top floor. He pulled her with him, not breaking the seal of their lips, slid his keycard down the edge of the door, kicked the door backwards and pulled her into the room.

"Stop!" she managed to say. "Shower!" she said,

craning her neck towards the door she knew led to the bathroom.

He stopped and leaned back slightly so he could look at her face. His face was flushed with want and lips swollen from kissing.

She knew how red she was when he led her quickly to the room she wanted to go to.

When they got inside he turned the dial on the shower and started to unbutton her shirt. "Are you okay?" he asked, while his fingers worked, his expression worried.

"I look that bad then?" She looked up at him wearily while he made quick work of her buttons.

"You are very red."

"Turn it to cold," she said, and quickly walked under the spray.

Jay whipped his own clothes off and joined her. He put his arms around her waist; his eyes all concern. He remained quiet, waiting.

"It happens when I ... you know ... get worked up."

He seemed oblivious to the cold. "Can I ask you a personal question?" he said searching her face.

She nodded, sheepishly, waiting for the blow.

"Was it really your first time, the last time we were together?"

"Yes." She said, quietly. "I've tried a couple of times before, but it never worked. I always overheat ... But last time, with you in the shower, it was fine."

He leant down, picked up her arms and put them around his neck. He kissed her again; deeply and with meaning. He leant back again as if checking she was okay. Then he traced a finger along the dark grey stripes, which had begun to show around her biceps, "These aren't tattoos, are they?"

She shook her head, looking down; damned in the shower and damned out.

"Turn around." He lifted her hair and she knew he was looking at her little brown dots, which appeared from her hairline, down to her nape where they came to a point, and travelled down the length of her spine to her coccyx. Not to forget more stripes, getting darker by the minute, along the ridges of her ribcage from back to front. He ran a finger along them slowly, and lovingly. He didn't say anything and she was grateful, but she felt the silence was laden.

"I have them whenever I get wet … the longer I'm in water the darker they get and the longer they stay. I have no idea why."

He turned her around to face him again, "Do you like being with me?" he said, and stepped closer to her, so she could feel him right up against her, and had no doubt what he wanted.

She looked him boldly in the eye, "Yes I do … very much." She pulled his head slowly down to her mouth again. "I want you," she whispered against his mouth, and he swept her up.

God, she loved the roughness of him. It called to every part of her and pressed all her buttons to 'go'. He travelled down and kissed her as he went. Grazing his teeth and sucking when he got to her breasts, which felt heavy and ached to be touched. Swirling his tongue and drawing into his mouth her nipples. He went from one to the other and then lower. He teased and licked first to one hip and then the other. She hitched a breath when he dipped his head down and reached the juncture of her thighs. He pulled a leg out from under her roughly, and put it over his shoulder. She cried out at the bolt of pleasure at the first contact of his tongue. He kissed, lapped and swirled around her bud. He knew exactly what to do. Thumbs, fingers, tongue.

As it was becoming too much to bear she tugged him from his shoulders. "I want you," she said between breaths, "Please." He moved slowly back up her body still teasing her with his skilled mouth.

When he stood, he stopped still suddenly and looked at her body. Her skin was now paler, almost grey and was emblazoned with its dark bands, even under her cheekbones. Her heart stopped for a beat and she held her breath, not knowing whether he would reject her as too weird. Then he groaned and lifted her on a growl and pulled her down onto him hard. Relief and pleasure surged through her so she thought her heart would burst.

He used the ledge as anchorage as he drove into her, biting her neck and shoulder hard as he went. The instinct to bury himself was strong and overriding, again and again. The rougher he was, the more she wanted.

She felt herself building as she'd done the previous time, but with it was something else – something coming along with it. Whatever it was, it was strong and was ramping her core temperature up higher than it had ever been. Before she could analyse it too deeply, her orgasm hit her, smashing into her, heart and mind; making her gasp his name as she dissolved, causing him to follow in pounding rhythm after her.

Gradually he slowed, along with their breathing, until she slowly unlinked her legs from behind him, and slid down his body to stand.

He leaned his forehead on hers, "Sorry I was rough – you make me crazy," was all he could say between breaths, shaking his head slightly.

"It's okay, please don't apologize." She sidestepped around him on jelly legs and grabbed a towel. Then she passed one to him, which he tied around his waist.

They were both still flushed; their heart rates still up.

"I should go," she said, looking over at him nervously.

He was all rosy-cheeked and gave her his shy smile and she thought, *I'm so in trouble.* She'd never met anyone who excited her like he did.

"That's my line, you know," breaking into full heartbreak smile offensive.

Fuck, she thought. "Really, I should go,"

"Okay," he said, and walked over to hug her.

She put up a defensive hand. "Stop! You'll do it again if you continue."

He laughed, placated. "Okay … I'll let you escape … this time."

She gathered her stuff together and dressed. Her heart sang though. The promise in his last words meant that he wanted it to continue. He'd seen her transformed and still wanted her. *Fuck, I'm in danger of falling for him.*

She gave him a quick goodbye and a promise to be in touch soon.

She zoomed off not to Kent but to Colchester. Her thoughts went from excitement to terror and back again. She needed to get back to America as soon as possible, but first she must see Sean.

Chapter 5

Jay was in a comatose sleep after his long flight and water aerobics with Tia. He was dreaming of manga eyes in an inferno, when the loud banging on his door brought him to his senses.

"Fuck off! He shouted into his pillow.

"Jay, Let me in!"

Jay dragged himself out of bed and staggered to the door in the hallway with his eyes still closed. He glanced at his clock in the hall – 4.30 a.m. – and flung open the door. "Fucking Hell, Dant!"

"Sorry mate!" Dante said, pushing past him and into the hallway; slightly stumbling, off his face as usual for the time of day.

"What are you doing here?" Jay asked as he got straight back into his bed and into the same position he'd left, face down into his pillow. He lifted his head when the thought occurred to him, "I thought you'd been called home to Ireland?"

"Nah, I couldn't face it. I'm lying low for a while," he said, as he held the curtain back and peered out of the large window.

"The 'Kats Wiska's' is lying low?" Jay knew the haunt that Dante would always go to if ever he wasn't in town. "You only had to ask at reception, they'd have given you a room."

"They don't have a stocked bar like you." His Irish accent was thicker than ever when he was drunk. "Besides, I wanted to touch base with ya." He turned and went over to the sideboard.

Jay groaned, "Fucking hell, Dant. I just got off a ten and a half hour flight. I'm knackered!"

"Talk to me man," Dante said, pouring two scotches and shoving one next to Jay's face so it slurped on the bed.

"Aghh!" Jay sat up, giving in to the force of nature that was his best friend. "Why didn't you go home?" he said, rolling his eyes.

"Me dad is in full 'looney tunes' mode." He plonked down into the armchair. "I can't stand it. It makes me want to drink more than usual." He took a large gulp of scotch.

Jay just nodded and resigned himself to the intrusion and the knowledge that Dante was staying for the foreseeable future. "I saw her again."

"Who?" Dante said, settling down for the night; feet up, pillow behind his head.

"That bird."

"What bird?" His bloodshot eyes were slowly closing.

"The one … you know … Dannyl's bird … well not Dannyl's bird, now my bird."

Dante laughed and raised his glass, "I never thought

I'd see the day brother, when you'd find someone you wanted to see again, let alone a girlfriend." His eyebrows were up but his eyes still closed.

Jay shifted uncomfortably, "I dunno about girlfriend?"

"There's hope for us all then," Dante said, trailing off. His feet were now up on the coffee table as he nodded off, glass still in hand.

Jay, who was now wide-awake, reached for the scotch. *Girlfriend*, he scoffed and poured another drink. *I don't want to share her though.*

A frown crept across his brow.

***

Tia stopped just outside Colchester Barracks, got off and leant backwards on her bike, taking off her helmet and shaking out her long hair. She felt it, thinking she must look a nightmare with it still damp. Taking out her phone she texted Sean that she'd arrived, and waited.

She was exhausted now she had stopped. It must be around three or four in the morning as it was still dark.

She had promised Cash that she would check in with Sean as soon as she got back to England, and to be honest, she could do with his steadying influence.

She saw an army vehicle coming out through the barrier. Sean got out the passenger side and jogged towards her. He held up a hand of thanks to his mates in the Land Rover, and then it sped off into the distance.

Sean came up to her and kissed her on the cheek. "Hi babe, give me your keys. I'll drive; you look like death."

Sean was a big guy with strawberry-blonde crew-cut hair, a few freckles and blue eyes. He was off-duty in jeans and a t-shirt, but everything about him shouted military.

She threw him her keys, put her helmet back on and straddled the bike behind him. He revved the bike and screeched away. She nestled into his back and indulged in the warm feeling of safety he always gave her.

They pulled into a travel inn.

"I've booked you a room here," Sean said, as he dismounted the bike, "So you can get some sleep before you ride back."

She followed him in meekly, dog-tired.

Sean grabbed the keycard from reception and escorted her to her room, which was uniform and basic. "Get yourself undressed and into bed," he ordered.

She stripped down to her underwear and slipped under the sheets and threw off the duvet. He sat down on the edge of the bed and stroked back the hair from her face. She closed her eyes and accepted the affection which she'd seen so little of in her life.

His phone beeped and roused her again. He looked at it and put it back into his pocket. "Come on then, what's the news?"

"I've met someone," she said tentatively, and looked at his face and waited for his reaction.

"Okay ... you want to tell me about him?"

"I don't know him that well yet, but I really like him ... I've never felt like this about anyone before ... it scares me," she finished in a whisper.

He pulled her across the bed and into his arms, so he was cuddling the top half of her body. He rocked her as you would a small child. "Just tell me one thing Tia, and it's important. Does he have anything like this?" He drew back and pulled out his dog tags from inside his shirt at his neck, and amongst them there was a necklace with a piece of mounted turquoise at the end. "This stone. Anything like this?"

She looked at it. She'd noticed it before but never thought anything by it. "Yes, he's got a bracelet, but it was Dannyl's. He won it in from him in a card game."

He pulled her back into his embrace. "That's good then."

"What Sean?"

"Nothing. Listen," he said, changing the subject, "There's something I need to tell you as well."

His phone rang and he took it out, looked at it, and switched it off. "I'm getting married, Tia."

She pushed away from him again and looked into his face for confirmation, "Really … Sarah?"

"Yeah, she's pregnant … that's her texting and ringing."

"Congratulations," she said, unsure for a minute if she was pleased for him or not. Although their relationship was not sexual, she still saw him as hers.

"Look Tia, I'm still here for you okay? I'm leaving the army in a few weeks and when I'm settled I'll contact you, but the important thing is that I'm still here." He looked intently into her eyes, giving her shoulders a little shake. "Do you understand?"

"Yes," she said and allowed him to tuck her back down into the bed.

"Sleep now. I'll be here in this chair while you sleep. I've just got to call her before I'm in the doghouse, okay?"

She nodded, smiled weakly and closed her eyes. She lay there listening to Sean's platitudes to the lucky Sarah, and she drifted off into exhausted sleep to his deep rumbly voice.

She was completely unaware when her phone rang and rang. It was resting on the bedside table, buzzing on vibrate.

Sean looked at it for a minute, and then making up his mind, he picked it up, pressed the answer button and put it to his ear. "Hello ... no she's asleep ... I don't really want to wake her as she's shattered ... shall I say who called? ... Okay Jay, I'll tell her."

Chapter 6

The next day Tia had left Sean with promises that she'd speak soon and hopes that he wouldn't get in too much trouble with his girlfriend.

She spent the day at her place in the Kent countryside.

Through friends of Cash's, she lived in a converted loft above some stables. It was a wonderful space. Her space. Precious.

Access to it was gained from a rickety retractable metal ladder, but once inside it was lovely. Its walls were all exposed brick in the one large room. There was a wood burner, a large bed, a multi-coloured sofa, a high back wing chair, a screened off roll top bath – her sanctuary – and a kitchenette in the corner. Fish and vegetables didn't need much cooking. She had permanently set up record decks, and a few fluffy rugs and some quirky Alan Streets originals hung on the walls and completed the eclectic look.

In a great mood after she selected her records for the evening, she put them into her record case and set off for London. Butterflies fluttered in her stomach.

She decided to park near Jay's place first and speak

to him quickly. She hoped he would be up for hooking up later. Then she would go on to the little club she was playing in.

It was about 11 p.m. when she got there. Jay's place was really busy already as she walked through the foyer. She made her way towards the bar; turning heads as she always did with her magnificent mane of hair cascading down her back in large blonde waves over her leather biker jacket. Skin-tight leather trousers, biker boots and visor sunglasses made her look like something out of a music video.

She was about to go into the crowd in the bar area, when the lift opposite pinged open and Jay walked out. God, he looked gorgeous. A dark blue suit paired with the palest blue shirt, left tieless and the top button undone, paired with Italian shoes – yum.

He stopped for the briefest second when he saw her, but smiled a small smile and came straight up to her. He kissed her on the cheek in welcome, but stepped back a pace after.

"Hey!" she said. The tentacles of paranoia crept across her mind from his body language alone.

"Hey, he replied. "I didn't know you were coming tonight?" He looked past her distracted into the busy crowd.

"No sorry, I just popped in. I have to be in Rare Moods in an hour, so I have to go …" As she looked at his eyes she felt the oddest pain in her chest. He was looking at her but he wasn't. It was as though the lights were on, so to speak, but no-one was home. "I wondered if you wanted to meet up later?" She felt lame as soon as she said it.

He looked at her for a second as if he was preparing to say something, and then changed his mind. "It's frantic here tonight. Listen, I'll try to meet you there, okay?"

Before she could answer he was already walking past her. "Sure," she said, quietly and turned and walked out into the foyer again. She turned back briefly but he'd disappeared into the bar.

She continued walking without paying much attention and bumped into some poor person just walking into the place. "Sorry," she said, looking up into his face, "Mark!" She shouted.

"Wow, Tia!" he said, and pulled her into a hug.

"What are you doing here?" she said, completely thrown.

"I could ask you the same question." He looked so pleased to see her.

"I'm DJ'ing at a little place in Greek Street in a minute … you?"

"I'm just meeting someone for a quick drink, then I've a got a late business dinner. But listen … let me meet you later?'

"Erm …" She looked back over her shoulder. *Don't kid yourself girl.* "I'll probably be home by then," she said, turning back to him. "I'm not feeling that great tonight."

"Let me pop round to you then?"

"I live in Kent, it's a bit of a trek." She felt about as much use as a wet weekend.

"No worries, I could do with getting out of town for an hour or two. And to be honest Tia, I've had the day from hell. I could really use some female advice."

She looked at his face and he seemed genuinely upset and his eyes were pleading. "Okay." She wasn't sure whether she was losing her mind or affected by the disappointment she felt in the pit of her stomach, but she told him where she lived.

She said goodbye to Mark and stepped out into the bustling street. Her disappointment in Jay was a tangible weight she kicked along the floor.

***

Mark's heart sang. He couldn't believe his luck. His father had blown a gasket when he'd had to tell him he'd let her go back to England, and now his bacon was saved.

As the doors sprung closed behind him and he saw the reason for his visit step out of the lift and walk across to the bar. He sighed. *Let's get it over with.*

He followed him into the bar area of the hotel his father had virtually given his eldest brother's best friend. He had to admit begrudgingly that he was good at his job judging by how busy it always was.

He could easily see across the crowd being so tall, and there was his useless waste of space brother, propped up in his usual position, next to the bar. His friend, and partner in crime, Jay, stood with him.

Mark said a few, 'Hello, how are you's' to breathless fans who recognised him on his way through the crowd and eventually came to a standstill to the left of Dante.

"Brother, fancy meeting you here …? I might have known this is where you'd be hiding."

"Marco?" Jay acknowledged, lifting his glass.

"Oh feck off, arsehole," Dante muttered in his thickest Irish brogue.

"I had to come here, father wants you home. It's urgent Dante," Marco reasoned, slipping in to his Irish lilt as well which he only did around his family.

"Don't tell me, he wants to crown me king?" he taunted, "Double whisky, Paul. Whatcha having Jay?"

Jay sensibly made himself scarce. He obviously knew which way this conversation was going; he'd witnessed it many times. "No Dant." He held up a hand. "I'll catch you later Marco." He nodded a goodbye, and disappeared into the crowd, glad to escape.

"Listen you pisshead," Marco said, through gritted teeth as soon as Jay had gone. "I've found one, they exist."

"Yes, but you lost her didn't ya?" Dante smirked.

"Yes … no … look, she's here in London. I've just seen her. She'll be at Rare Moods, on Greek Street, for the next couple of hours. If you don't believe me, check her out for yourself.

This is it Dante, time to grow up." Throwing his hands up, he left.

***

Dante watched his brother stride off through the crowd and rolled his eyes. He had the right hump with him, and no mistake. He looked over at Jay who appeared to be busy sorting out a large party who had just come in.

What could it hurt?

He got Jay's attention by putting his hand up and signing he was off, and Jay nodded. Then he jumped in a cab outside, as it was raining, and sidled into the traffic on his way to Rare Moods.

He'd been there before. It was a small, low ceiling place for serious music buffs. Not a cattle market club for picking up girls. He and Jay had discerned the difference many years ago.

When he got out of the cab he was already buzzing. The city lights were a pleasant blur – everything fuzzy, warm and right with the world.

Jay was subdued tonight. He'd have to force it out of him later. For now he was going to enjoy wiping the smug smile off his poncey actor brother's face, when he proved again what a pile of shit all this Atlantean bollocks their father had fed them since childhood was.

The doorman knew him, as most of them did in the trendy clubs in London. He and Jay had frequented them for years as a double act. Most owners viewed their attendance as a good review for their club, so they never queued and were always ushered straight in.

The ambient music clutched at him as soon as he was in earshot. Like a lure it pulled him to the main room just off the bar area.

God, it was hot in here. Low ceilings. He began to perspire and became short of breath. Bloody hell, he felt weird. He grabbed on to a table ledge. Surely he hadn't drunk that much? He shook his head. No, this was different. It was a fucking repeat of the turn he'd had at the Bluebell a few days ago. His heart was jumping and palpitating all over the place. He held out his hands to see how badly they were shaking.

That was when he caught sight of it: his antique ring. The only concession he had allowed his lunatic father was that he wore it continually.

He remembered the excruciating pain when he was first given it on his thirteenth birthday. The ring contained a spike that had to break into the skin when it was first worn, and could only have one owner. The white opal had swirled red before it had settled to its pearly white. 'If it ever turns turquoise son, you have found one,' his father had said. And 'if it ever goes deepest purple, you have found your queen; your most compatible mate in the world.'

He'd listened just like his brothers but only ever thought it a pretty fairy story, never really believing that anything so fantastic could happen, especially to a waster like him. But today – this day – as he looked at his shaking hands it was deepest purple and thrumming.

He looked up and around him. Who could it be?

Overwhelming motion sickness was overtaking him, but he needed to know who it was. She was in the room, but who? He scanned the heads on the dance floor – nothing out of the ordinary. Perhaps she was ordinary.

That was when he saw the commotion.

Three people were in the DJ's booth. Two men were either side of a female who looked like she'd stumbled or nearly fainted or something. But as he shook himself to clear his head he homed in on what she looked like. She must have sensed him because she thanked the two men either side of her, stood unaided and looked over at him. She had sunglasses on but he somehow knew she was looking for him. He stood stock-still and for a second he was mesmerised, until a wave of nausea came over him so strong that he thought he'd spew up where he stood. He had to run to the nearest men's room.

Dante only just made it inside a cubicle when he vomited. When the spasms had stopped, he came out of the cubicle and splashed water onto his face. He felt better though.

He looked down at his hands again and the shaking was better, but the purple in the ring was fading. Fuck!

He ran back out into the club but a new DJ was in the booth. He rushed to the bar? Nothing.

He looked down at the ring and it was white. She was gone. *Fuck! Fuck! Fuck!*

His brain raced. The implications of what had just happened were hitting him like a boxer. That girl whoever she was – was meant for him, and she was beautiful. That meant that everything he'd been told since childhood was true. He wished he'd paid more attention. *Fuck!* He must go home. He must get sober. Detox. He must learn properly who he was. He was Atlantean, for fuck's sake … a descendant from Atlantis … the eldest son of a family of five sons. With a Siren, that made him… king!

That was what she was: a fucking Siren!

Chapter 7

Tia had no idea who the guy was, he was gone as soon as she zoned in on him. All she knew was that it had felt like being hit around the head with a baseball bat just before she saw him. Her temperature had shot through the roof and she was at least thirty feet away. She'd never had a reaction like that with anyone and needed to get out of there fast.

Luckily the guy who ran the place took pity on her; she must have looked rough, and he had let her go half an hour early.

She walked out into the fresh air, took some deep breaths, and began to feel better immediately.

She decided to go home as quickly as possible. She longed for the wonderful incubating feeling of her bath.

Fuck! Mark was coming round. She really wasn't in the mood. Maybe he'd get tied up and not come. That thought cheered her up a bit as she sped down the A20 into Kent.

***

Tia was feeling very sorry for herself when the headlights shone around the room in her loft, alerted her to the car turning around on the shingle drive.

She seldom used her overhead lighting as it hurt her eyes. She much preferred the soft glow of candles.

She'd bathed quickly and put on some fleecy pyjama bottoms and a comfy t-shirt and wound her hair up into a bun on the top of her head.

She'd got very maudlin when she'd mulled over recent events to herself. Sean was abandoning her to marriage. Jay was just abandoning her full stop. She'd seen the brush off enough times to recognise it when she saw it. And now strange men in crowds were knocking her out from a distance. God, she was losing it. She thanked God that she'd just got off the phone to Cash, who had booked her on a plane back to the States the next day. All hands were needed for a mounted cavalry, battle scene.

She dropped her rickety ladder down and called to Mark. She didn't have a doorbell or knocker as she never had visitors. "Come up!" she shouted.

Marco's head came up the ladder through the square hole in the floor. "Hi!" He leant over to kiss her on the cheek. "Nice place," he said, as he glanced quickly around the room.

"Hi! It's not too dark for you? The lights hurt my eyes." *I hope he doesn't think I'm trying to be romantic with the candles. Bugger.*

"No, it's fine really." He held on to one of her hands and pulled her a step closer. "May I?" He stared into her eyes.

She tried her upmost not to flinch away from him, but found it really awkward.

"I've never seen anything like them."

"No-one has," she said shrugging, and moving out of his grip. "Can I get you a drink?"

"Sure, I'll have whatever you're having." He continued to look around at her things. The first time anyone else had seen them.

Feeling completely exposed, she poured them both a scotch and passed one to him. She sat on the fluffy rug next to the fire and leant back on the sofa. He sat on the sofa next to her.

"Bad night?" he asked.

"A bit." She turned to the side and looked up at him. He interested her in the way someone does when you can't work them out, but she didn't trust him. There was something about him that set all her alarm bells off and she wondered what the hell she was doing letting him into her private space.

Marco just lay back and scrutinised her.

Tia was quiet and just stared into her drink. "Sorry Mark, I'm not very good company tonight."

"Don't worry about me. It's nice just to chill out for a bit." And he snuggled back into the sofa. "You are refreshingly different to some of the girls I meet, Tia," he said, after a while.

She sighed. "You know sometimes I think I'd give my right arm not to be."

Marco relaxed and stretched out his long legs behind her, and lay down with his hands clasped behind his head. "Man problems?" He needed to tread carefully. He had to find out how complicated her life was, so no ripples were made should she disappear. He decided to employ all his acting talent on the sympathy front.

"Is it that obvious?" she said, frowning.

"Most people's problems boil down to two things: the opposite sex or money."

"True." She nodded.

"You don't strike me as someone who'd ever have a problem getting a man?"

"Oh I collect 'em alright. The problem is I keep them in the friend category. I don't get close to anyone very easily. And if I do, they're always the wrong ones."

Marco nodded, as he exhaled. "Maybe you just haven't met the right person yet?"

He watched her thinking about his words. He still wasn't sure how much she knew about herself and the world she came from.

"Do you believe we have a person we are meant for then; like fate or something?"

Now she was getting the idea. "For some people, yes I do."

The conviction in his tone of voice made her turn to face him, cuddling her knees to her chest. "You are a romantic I think."

"Who me? Not at all, it's how I was brought up. My brothers and I have had it drummed into us." She didn't have a bloody clue who she was. Astounding.

"Really? Wow, that's unusual, especially for blokes. I'm afraid I find it hard to believe life deals us crap on purpose."

"You should come home with me some day. You never

know, your Mr Right could be one of my brothers."

She laughed, "It's not you then?"

He laughed with her, "No, it's not." His face changed to serious. It had become some sort of perverse game to him to sail so close to the wind with the truth, and her being so totally oblivious, he almost laughed aloud.

"Way to shoot a girl down," she said, with mock anger on her face. She sobered for a minute. "You know you're not at all like my first impression of you."

"Oh yeah, and what was that?

"That you were a vain, superficial, up yourself, prick!"

"Don't pull your punches on my account," he laughed, in shock.

She smiled and bowed her head.

"I think there was a compliment in there somewhere for me?" he said, frowning.

The two of them were quiet for a while.

"Seriously though, why don't you come with me to my family home this weekend, it might cheer you up?"

"I'm sorry Mark. I'm travelling back to the States tomorrow." She smiled at him.

"Work?" His brain whirred to find an alternative.

"Yes, my friend is supplying the horses for the cavalry charge scene."

"The cowboy?"

She nodded.

"What if I come back with you ... I'll have to go back in a few days myself anyway for filming."

"No, I can't expect you to do that."

She was looking surprised and obviously looking for

an out.

"No really, I'd like to. In fact, I was planning on getting away with a couple of my brothers for a while now, and just not got round to it. They could meet us over there?"

"Well ok ... if you're sure?"

"Think nothing of it. I couldn't possibly let you go off alone feeling so low."

Marco was already reaching for his phone. He took details of her flight and managed to get a last minute seat in first class. He upgraded her so she was sitting with him, oblivious to the sadness that crept across her features.

He then texted his brothers:

Tell father am on flight to US with her tomorrow. Get on first available flight after. Meet me there. Expect to bring her home on return. Make arrangements.

He put his phone away. "Just re-jigging a few things. Is it okay if I crash here?" He ignored the fact she looked a little railroaded. He painted an angelic look on his face of him just being a nice caring friend, which he was sure she bought.

"Sure. Won't you need a few things though?"

"No, I'll get what I need at the airport. It's not a problem."

She went to get up and then sat back down. "I almost forgot. You wanted to talk to me about something?"

He looked at her blankly for a second. *Shit.* Then waved his hand across his face. "No matter. I'm over it now."

"Oh well, okay. If you're sure … I had better go to bed then."

"Sure, go ahead."

She grabbed a pillow and spare blanket for him. "I hope you're okay on there?" she said, pointing at the sofa.

"I'll be fine." He watched her as she walked away to brush her teeth in the bathroom area and then climb into bed. He wasn't going to let her out of his sight for a second until she was safely home with him in Ireland.

It was weird; she was actually a nice person, but he wasn't going to let that fool him. Sirens could take a life in an instant.

He let fifteen or twenty minutes go by, and when he was sure she was asleep, he got up and walked softly over to her bed and stood and watched her. She turned over as he stood there. It made his heart beat fast in fear of getting caught, but she was just turning in her sleep.

Her hair was now strewn over the pillow behind her giving him a clear view behind her ear. There, as clear as a bell, was a raised ridge of skin about two inches long. A gill.

Chapter 8

Cash was worried about this one. He didn't trust the guy as far as he could throw him. Now the bastard had talked Tia into staying in LA for a few more days before she came up and joined him to work. To cap it all, she didn't even sound genuinely happy about it. He needed to speak to her himself and make sure she was okay.

Cash had watched over Tia for the last two years. She'd come into his life during some work he'd done with young offenders coming out of council care in the UK. His job had been teaching them the western way of riding. But sometimes showing them how to care for an animal, especially one with behavioural problems, very often helped them with their own.

Tia had taken to it like a duck to water. She possessed a quiet strength and depth of character, and was not afraid of hard work.

He'd offered her a summer job on his ranch in Montana as soon as she was released. Very soon it became obvious that she was different. He couldn't help but shelter her from the other youngsters who worked for him, or anyone else who would pick on her or single her out through jealousy or just plain meanness.

The thing that Tia didn't know about him yet was that he knew what she was, because some of that blood flowed through his own veins.

To prove this, and passed down through generations of his family, was an ancient piece of turquoise jewellery. It was flat like a St Christopher, but had a trident carved into it; the insignia of Atlantis; the birthplace of his ancestors. It now belonged to him.

His grandmother had told him stories of his heritage from when he was a young boy, and how he had a special role in life. That role was a Protector – a lifelong job – as a guardian to a Siren should one ever cross his path.

The very first time she had spoken to him was as clear as day in his memory, probably because of the gravity she had placed on it. He couldn't have been more than about seven years old …

"Come here son, I have something for you."

He ran straight to her as she opened a real old jewellery box. "This was your grandfather's." She took out the necklace from its velvet nest.

"What is it Grandma?"

"Whoever wears this has the most important job in the world."

Cash's eyes went wide. "What job? I wanna do that job," he whispered.

"Turn around." She put the necklace on him. "This is now yours, Cash. This proves you are from an ancient race of people."

Cash's heart beat faster with excitement. "Tell me

grandma." He sat in front of her, cross-legged.

"We are Atlanteans, Cash. There are others like us that have mixed and married Humankind, but somewhere out there in the world there are hidden five beautiful princesses, the purest of all Atlanteans on land. We call them the Soul Breathers. The Humans call them Sirens."

"On land?"

"Yes, son. The purest of all live under the sea in the legendary city of Murrtaine. They are the Murrs who belong to the Borge Family.

"Wow...where do you think the princesses are?

"No-one knows. There hasn't been such as these for centuries."

"What do I do?" Cash asked.

"For each princess, there is a special prince, usually from each of the five royal families of Atlantis and Murrtaine. But there are many princes and they all race to find their princess. Your job is to look after her, should you find one, and make sure she doesn't get into the wrong hands.

"Not let the bad guys get her?"

"You got it."

"What would happen if they did?"

His grandmother sighed and sat back in her chair as if in a dream. "Ever since Atlantis was destroyed, the princesses have been hidden amongst mankind from time to time. But each time the royal families have pursued them, they have killed and corrupted for them, only using them for the riches they could bring or Humans have found them. Never in the whole ten thousand years of our history here has the right path been taken and their power used for the right purpose."

"What's the right path Grandma?"

"Gosh, I don't know son. I'm no seer, but when the right path is taken there will be a king who can lead and unite all Atlanteans, and the Murrs, so that when the other-worlders come again, they won't destroy us like they did last time."

Cash was terrified. "When will they come?"

"No-one really knows, but your grandpa used to think it was most likely when the Soul Breathers came." She looked seriously into Cash's eyes. "Will you take this important job Cash?

Cash stood up to attention, "Yes Grandma. I will keep her safe."

***

Pretty soon after he'd met Tia, he'd become convinced that was what she was. He could hardly believe it had actually happened. He'd dug out the ancient parchment his grandmother had given him, along with the necklace, and in it was an address. The parchment explained that when a Siren was found he should disclose this to no-one other than the person named in the parchment. That was the oldest living relative of the Bonaci Family, located in Ireland for the last five hundred years. This he did.

On tenterhooks he'd waited, until he received a reply. When he'd opened the letter with shaky hands, it instructed him to keep her secret until such a time when she had passed eighteen and male suitors began to pursue her, particularly from the other four royal families. It listed them as: Dubonnetti, Florianna, Santalini and Borge.

The only other help in identifying them other than their names, which could be changed, was a large ring made with an Atlantean stone of unusual colour. The letter ended with the words:

> *The very continuance and prosperity of the Atlantean race depend on it.*

Now when he re-examined the letter he was convinced that the pansy actor calling himself Mark Dubonno was in fact Marco Dubonnetti. He wouldn't have let her go off with any one of the so-called suitors without first checking them out, but this one had snake written all over him. This roused him into action. He quickly informed his contact of what he believed was happening and by whom. Then he picked up his phone and dialled Tia, telling her to get her backside to him ASAP, or she was fired. She could bring her fop actor with her if she must.

He knew she loved him enough to be mortified that she'd upset him, and would come to him straight away.

***

Marco was pissed off. The cowboy was a definite spanner in the works. He'd managed to delay their internal flight to Montana until the next day, allowing his brothers time to get there. But everything rested on his brothers' ability to convince her to go back to Ireland with them rather than go to Montana, and his confidence was fading.

He'd thought of kidnapping her, but the rules clearly stated that marriage to a Siren must be undertaken willingly. Besides, it was pointless anyway because she was quite capable of killing her new spouse even if she didn't know it yet.

It was all really getting on his nerves.

His brothers, Paolo and Antonio, were due to get there five hours after them, which he made about 7 p.m. He'd given them the name of the hotel they were staying in and arranged to meet them casually in the bar with Tia after they'd settled into their room.

He couldn't wait for the reveal. It was selfish he knew, but he couldn't wait to show off such an important discovery.

***

Tia felt tired as she finished getting ready to meet Marco's brothers. She couldn't explain why, but she just wasn't into it.

She decided to wear baggy silk, cornflower-blue trousers over Indian sandals and a long floaty top in a darker blue. Accessorised with chunky ethnic beads and her customary visor glasses, she looked like a film star – all without any effort.

As she walked into the lounge with Marco, she was guided to the brothers already sitting in the comfy chairs.

"Antonio … Paolo?" Marco said, and they both turned their heads as soon as they heard Marco call their names. "May I present, Tia Storm."

Both brothers stood immediately and bowed over her hand like charming princes.

They were both jaw-droppingly good looking and shared Marco's unusual blonde locks and light grey eyes combo. Both were tall, well-built and chic in good suits.

The strange thing was that after greeting her so politely, both of them looked at their rings. They were identical, on their middle finger of their left hand. Then they looked at each other then at Marco and grinned. They really were a strange family.

She couldn't help but look at Marco's hand, and he had one as well. Same hand, same finger, and same stone: turquoise.

"What's going on?" she said, laughing nervously.

"Forgive us Tia. It's a private joke between us brothers. Paolo said, smiling.

"Remember what I was telling you Tia, about our father's obsession with fate and destined partners?"

These guys were weird! "Oh yeah … well?"

"Well what?"

"Any luck yet?"

The three brothers laughed. "Not yet," one said.

***

The four of them arrived at Cash's ranch the next day around lunchtime. Cash had collected them from the airport and welcomed them into his home.

It was a beautiful rustic lodge, with one main room with a huge fireplace and a landing above with all the bedrooms in a row opening onto it.

As soon as Tia got there she asked after Beau, the horse Cash had given her, so he sent her straight out the back to the stable barn to see him. This gave him the chance he needed to speak to the brothers. As he heard the click on the kitchen door he seized his chance.

"Now you can all tell me why you are really here," he said, hands on hips and chin up.

Marco's face looked a mixture of confusion and outrage.

Cash strode up to him menacingly and pointed a finger at his chest. "Let's not bullshit each other anymore. I know you are Dubonnetti," and he looked all three of them in the eyes in turn. "And you know who I am. So am I correct in assuming you are here to make a play for her now she's turned eighteen?"

Instead of answering him, Marco smirked and looked past Cash to the door that led off to the kitchen. Cash followed his line of vision and his heart sank when he saw Tia standing in the doorway. She had a look of confusion on her face, then hurt and betrayal, quickly changing to anger.

"Tia!" Cash shouted, as he saw her turn to run out the way she came.

"Don't come near me, the fucking lot of you," she shouted, already hot-footing it out of the place.

Cash ran after her, shouting over his shoulder for Marco and his brothers to stay put.

As he got to the yard, Tia was already galloping away in the direction of the open fields. Cash shouted for a horse. A lad who'd been exercising his horse dismounted and threw his reins at him. Cash mounted it in one agile leap, dug in his heels and followed her.

He could see her ahead of him riding with reckless abandon, jumping fences and galloping at breakneck speed. He began to get concerned, knowing that the land dropped away on a steep downward gradient ahead, one that she would need to slow down to negotiate safely.

He called but she either couldn't hear or was ignoring him. Then he saw her disappear. She was there one minute and gone the next.

As he got closer, he saw Beau galloping on rider-less. He stopped his own foaming horse as the land fell away and scrambled down the hill to the bundle at the bottom. He took out his cell phone, called one of his stable hands and asked them to bring the pick-up and ring 911. She was unconscious and he couldn't tell if she'd broken anything.

***

Tia didn't particularly trust Mark that much, but when she turned on her heel in the kitchen to ask him if he wanted to come and see her horse, and heard Cash's raised voice accusing him for some crazy-assed, possessive reason; like some kind of misplaced father, she saw red. She loved Cash dearly but when she wanted him to vet her friends she'd ask.

As she jumped on Beau bareback all she could think of doing was putting as much space between her and them as possible. Her head wasn't thinking straight; she didn't even fancy Mark so couldn't understand her own reaction.

As she pelted along the soft green pasture a pang of Jay came to her mind, or rather stung her heart, and she pushed Beau on faster to the steep downward drop. His front legs hit the last piece of turf and she let go; of her reins, of her thoughts, of her consciousness. Smiling, floating, she closed her eyes and raised her arms up …

Chapter 9

The shit had hit the proverbial fan, and Cash had known it would come one day. He was her Protector, and she was a Siren and he had three princes making a play to get her to go home with them and throw her lot in with their family. Now was the time to blow the whole thing wide open.

Her real family had to get involved now. They needed to know about the Dubonnettis, and Tia needed to know who she was in order to make the biggest decision of her life.

Cash had called in his counterpart in England, Sean, for moral support. He had then been told about a possible third he hadn't known about, who Tia had said she liked a lot.

A quick look down the contacts list of Tia's phone told him his name was Jay, and so he called him and explained to him about Tia's accident and that he should come to Tia's bedside. Jay agreed to do this without delay.

Everything was set in motion. Within the next twenty-four hours they would all be arriving.

Among them were her uncle and two brothers.

Cash sat back in his chair exhausted. This should be interesting.

***

Tia had a couple of broken ribs, a broken wrist and a concussion. After an initial assessment she was transferred to a little private clinic Cash had organised. He felt he could control the situation better there given the visitors who would be arriving shortly. Money in the right quarter, he realised, spoke volumes in these situations, and Tia's family evidently had a bundle.

The first to arrive was Sean. Cash shook his hand warmly, and quickly brought him up to speed. He took him through to the waiting room allocated to them, where Marco and his brothers were already waiting nervously. One was having a heated discussion on his phone, which he ended abruptly when he saw the two big men approaching.

As the introductions were made a flustered nurse escorted Jay into the same room. The nurses had never seen such an array of eye candy visiting one patient and whispered about the lucky lady and who she must be.

Jay walked in expecting not to know any one until he clapped eyes on Marco and his brothers. Surprised, he walked straight over, "Marco, Paul, Tony … What are you all doing here?"

"It's a long story, what about you?" The brothers said, looking at each other with shifty eyes.

Cash interrupted just as Jay was about to explain to them his connection. "You know each other? Excuse me, my name is Cash. I called you here."

"Hello." Jay said, shaking his hand immediately.

"This is Sean," Cash said, gesturing next to him.

Jay shook Sean's hand and nodded.

"We spoke on the phone a few nights ago." Sean said, looking intently at Jay.

Jay creased his brow for a second.

"You rang to speak to Tia ... I answered her phone."

"Ah," Jay said, pausing for thought, then nodding in recognition. He pointed at Marco and his brothers. "Their eldest brother and I are close friends; I've known them for years."

Just then there was a disturbance coming from behind them, as nurses scurried around and fawned after a distinguished looking gentleman, and two GQ model-type, dark, young men, with pale green eyes, the colour of apples.

The three stood on the threshold of the room.

"Mr Bonaci?" Cash asked, walking over to them.

He nodded and surveyed the people assembled. "These are my nephews; Thelxiepia's brothers, Dino and Luca Bonaci. You may call me Alfonzo."

He walked in and commanded the room. "Please let me know each of your relationships to Thelxiepia?"

He spoke in a beautiful accent of Mediterranean origin.

***

Jay sat on a waiting room chair watching the weirdest meeting unfold, trying to blend in with the woodwork.

Cash and Sean introduced themselves as Protectors (whatever they were) and seemed nice enough.

The man called Alfonzo then looked at Marco. "Dubonnetti's sons," he stated, as though it didn't surprise him.

Then he slowly turned and faced him, just as he was looking down trying to be inconspicuous.

"And you are?" Alfonzo said, quietly, rolling his R.

"Jay... Jason Gardiner," he said, leaning forward with his elbows on his knees, looking up through his eyebrows.

The man stared at him for quite a few seconds, making him feel really uncomfortable. He seemed to snap himself out of his stare and directed what he was saying to Cash again. "Is she conscious?"

"Yes sir," Cash replied. "She's just in for observation."

"Let us go into her room. She needs to be part of the discussions." And Alfonzo led the way into the room.

Jay stood and followed, not knowing what the fuck was going on. As he walked he noticed all the nurses giggling and whispering behind their nurses' station.

He stood at the back of the room until enough chairs were brought in for everyone to sit around the bed. Alfonzo and her brothers sat at the foot of the bed, the three brothers to the right and he, Cash and Sean along the left.

He allowed himself to look over at Tia for the first time. He hadn't seen her since he'd snubbed her at his hotel a few nights ago. She looked exhausted lying propped up in the bed. Her wrist was in a removable support, and he could see a few bruises and grazes on her face.

She smiled when she saw him. He smiled back weakly. She looked really small in this room full of big males.

Alfonzo spoke when they all appeared to be seated. "Before I explain to Thelxiepia who she is, first I want to make sure all who are here, should be here ... Can everyone produce their talismans?" He paused and looked around.

Marco looked at his brothers and then all three held up their left hand showing their turquoise rings. Jay remembered Dante had one, except his was white.

"Good." Alfonzo nodded, and then looked left at Cash, Sean and Jay.

Cash and Sean both pulled out necklaces with turquoise stone pendants on, slightly different to each other.

Tia looked from left to right in disbelief. Everyone else was looking at him.

He looked around him, "What?"

Marco piped up, "He's Human."

Jay and Tia both looked at Marco with, 'What the fuck', on their faces.

After a moment Tia turned to him, "I think they might mean your bracelet, Jay."

Their eyes locked. He breathed a sigh, then looked at his cuff, rolled back his sleeve and revealed the bracelet with every other link punctuated with a turquoise flat stone. "I won this ... it wasn't mine."

Alfonzo ignored his statement. "Your tattoos, would you mind revealing them to me? We can empty the room if you prefer?"

Jay frowned, shook his head in disbelief, and slowly got up. What the fuck had they got to do with anything? But he started to undo his buttons. "I don't see what this has to do with her?" he said, nodding towards Tia.

"Humour me please…it will make sense in a while."

Jay removed his shirt revealing his lean muscular top half of his body. His smooth skin was covered by heavy, black, ancient lettering and swirls that ran the length of his arms and chest, down to his waist and up over his shoulders.

"Please can you turn around?" Alfonzo said.

Jay stood, a little embarrassed and turned, the lettering and patterns continued all the way down his back.

"Are you aware of the significance of these markings?" Alfonzo asked, as Jay turned back round.

"My best friend gave them to me on my sixteenth birthday. It's a spell; like a good luck thing," he said quietly.

"Your best friend is who?" Alfonzo asked, looking at Marco.

"My older brother; he's not here," Marco explained.

Alfonzo nodded and looked back at Jay. "Your friend must love you very much."

Jay nodded, slightly blushing, as he did the buttons back up on his shirt. He sensed Tia watching him and felt embarrassed that she was witness to his raw emotion. Still, all this must be even more mortifying for her.

As if she read his mind, "What is this?" She demanded, holding her hands out in exasperation.

Alfonzo just held out a hand to silence her. She flopped

back against her pillows with a sulky expression on her face.

"Your markings," Alfonzo continued, "are a pledge. You have the Dubonnetti coat of arms on your arm, and the trident, which is the insignia of Atlantis, on your back. The language it is written in is from there also."

Jay just stared at him. He'd never had it explained to him at all. It was also so typical of Dante to fight his dad his whole life on the Atlantis thing being a load of bull, then plaster him in mystical symbols from the very bloody place he didn't believe in.

"It says you are an adopted son of the Dubonnetti and have the same privileges as a son of that family. So this qualifies you as a Protector of a Siren. You may sit." Alfonzo then pointed at the bracelet on his wrist. "Its owner must have been unworthy."

"You can say that again," Tia muttered.

Jay sat back down. "Siren?" he asked, more of a deflection than anything. His mind was still reeling from the translation of what was on his body. His thoughts were interrupted when Tia's temper started to bubble over.

"Look, it's really nice you all came to see me and all that, but I think it's a bit rich. You two, for a start," Tia said, pointing to her brothers, "fucked off as soon as I was sixteen."

Her brothers sat up straighter with indignation and looked at Alfonzo.

"Calm yourself." Alfonzo said, placating her. "I'm here to explain everything to you today. You have a decision to make and it must be made soon."

***

Tia took a deep breath and bit her tongue and waited for him to continue.

Alfonzo paused, and when he was sure he had her full attention he began. "Your name is Thelxiepia Adonia Damaris Bonaci."

Tia stared at him blankly. *So what!*

"You have four sisters and two half-brothers." And he gestured to either side of him.

Tia's face remained stony.

"When you and your sisters were born, you were extremely rare and special."

Tia rolled her eyes. Jay and everyone else hung on his every word.

"There hasn't been any such as you for five hundred years. You are one of five Soul Breathers or Sirens, as Human folk lore chose to call you."

"Right, that's it! I'm not listening to this crap anymore."

Cash stood up and tried to calm her. "Hear him out Tia," he said.

She allowed him to settle her down. "You don't believe any of this?" she said, searching his face in disbelief.

He looked at her kindly. His expression sobered her instantly. *Fuck, he did.*

Alfonzo continued. "Ten thousand years ago, our ancestors came here from the other side of the solar system, from another world called Atlas, to make a colony. It was a water world." He paused to let his words sink in. "They built a civilization here called Murrtaine. After a time, the architects left and those left behind ventured out of water for short periods, and eventually relationships were made and children were born. The cross-over of species meant a city was built on land, near to Murrtaine, called Atlantis."

"The people of Atlantis were intelligent, cultured and strong. They were able to move around amongst Humans and retained certain underwater strengths, but could not breathe the water like their Murr cousins."

"And so Atlantis appeared to prosper, but eventually emissaries from Atlas returned. They became angry with its inhabitants. They found that they had abandoned their peace-loving culture and traditions and so they passed sentence to destroy Atlantis and cut off Murrtaine from Atlanteans forever to preserve it and its sacred power."

"Those left on land realised that they had nothing more than the Humans around them with which to build their lives, and so pleaded with Atlas to forgive them and unite them as one happy people as they were before. But it was decided that they had become too tainted by the inhabitants of Earth."

"I expect you are wondering where you fit into all this Tia?"

"D'ya think?"

Alfonzo ignored her. "They didn't get away with their crime by just banishment. Each of the five royal families had to give up a daughter to them to return to Atlas. Even the Borge family of Murrtaine was punished."

"Decades turned into centuries and then into millennia and the royal families continued and prospered to this day. But they always remembered the prophecy told to them back then and wrote it down. That the spirits of those five daughters would return. That we would know when they were here by signs. The first of these was when a Prince married a Murr Princess. Your father did this, Tia. Then you and your sisters were born. Five. Then a glut of sons born to princes of all the royal families."

He looked over to Marco and his brothers. "Five born to Dubonnetti. All of them given the rings as you have seen. Divining rings, forged to detect a Siren and ultimately a destined mate. The crucial point we have got to now Thelxiepia, is whose ring will go purple for you?"

Chapter 10

You could hear a pin drop. Most of them had heard the stories hundreds of times; even Jay had heard snippets from being around Dante and his brothers, but it was obviously all news to Tia.

"So I'm like a princess?" she asked.

"You are."

"Well then," she said, in a quiet but simmering voice. "Why the fuck was I brought up in council, fucking, care?" Her voice built in venom and volume as she said it.

Jay had to smile and cover his mouth with his hand, wiping the smile away so as not to get caught.

"I am sorry Thelxiepia … "

"Stop calling me that," she shouted.

"Easy Tia," Cash said, gently touching her on the shoulder.

Alfonzo nodded. "Tia … " he continued. "I'm afraid you and your sisters were so precious to the families that you would have been sought as a commodity. So to ensure fairness to each family, tradition dictated that each family had its chance to secure its own Siren, and so you were hidden in the world."

"What about fairness to me?"

"I do understand that you are upset, but if we had kept you, or even paired you all up as children, the families would have fought each other to extinction. There would never have been peace or unity between the families, which was the whole point. There are also Human factions and government agencies, which know of our existence and would seek to destroy you or use you for their own ends. So to hide you and stop the use of your powers was a way of keeping you safe."

"Powers?" she asked looking around her.

"Were you not kept away from water so you never swam? Were you not forbidden to use your singing voice?"

She nodded, bewildered.

The rest of the room was quiet while they all absorbed the information. None had heard the story explained so fully.

***

Jay couldn't help but remember how Dante had said it was all the ravings of a loony old man, but even he had seen the stripes on his friend's skin when they'd swam in the sea near where he lived which developed the longer he was in the water. Dante's eyes would challenge him to say something about them but he never did. He always just took him for what he was. And he'd seen the same stripes on Tia in his own shower. Yes, there had always been more to it. But he'd never pushed the issue and Dante had always been glad.

"Have you used your powers, Tia?"

She said no, uneasily, looking at everyone around her.

"Anyone?" Alfonzo asked, surveying the room. "It is important."

"I've seen Tia breath under water," Cash admitted, eventually.

"So have I," added Sean.

Tia looked at them like traitors and buried her head in her hands.

"I've seen her control Humans with music," said Marco.

"She sang?" Alfonzo said, shocked.

"No, she DJ's … you know plays records. I could see a sonic wave go over them. She holds them in her power."

Tia looked up shocked. "I do what?"

"Were the Humans around her ever aware of these powers?"

Jay looked between Cash, Sean and Marco, and saw them all mumble, 'no', and shake their heads.

"Interesting." Alfonzo muttered. "This is useful information in locating and identifying her sisters."

Tia looked over at Jay like she wanted the ground to swallow her up. She dreaded him saying anything about how she looked naked, under the shower.

He looked into her eyes and read what she was pleading.

"Jay?" Cash asked. "Anything?"

After a moment, Jay tore his eyes from her and looked at him. "No, nothing out of the ordinary."

Tia visibly sagged in relief.

"The last thing I must ask, and this is for your own safety … has anyone had intimate relations with Thelxiepia?" Alfonzo said.

"Oh. My. God! I don't believe it!" Tia buried her head in her hands again.

Alfonzo looked around the room, starting with Marco.

"No, she's not mine," he said, looking at his ring.

"Admirable I'm sure, but that has never stopped princes in the past."

He then looked at Cash's side of the bed.

Cash shook his head and so did Sean.

"Were you given Elixir as a precaution by your relatives?" Alfonzo asked.

They both nodded.

"And you took it?"

They both answered, "Yes."

"Jay?"

He felt himself blush and then looked up shyly through his eyebrows at Tia who looked at him from behind her fingers.

"I will need to speak to you after everyone has left." Alfonzo said, as a matter of fact, making no big deal out of it.

Jay nodded, and looked at Tia who smiled apologetically.

"Tia?" Alfonzo said, calling her attention back to him. "You have to come to a decision and it must be soon."

"What about?" she said shrinking down into the bed.

"Now the Dubonnettis know of your existence, the

other families will be notified. Also, the risks of Human factions finding you are greater. You must align yourself to a family." He nodded towards Marco.

"What does that mean?" she asked uneasily.

At Alfonzo's prompt, Marco spoke up. "Should you chose to do so, you will accompany me to my family home in Ireland where you will be introduced to my other two brothers to see if you are compatible with either of them."

"Compatible?" she asked.

He held up his ring.

"The prince who wears the ring which turns purple in your presence. You will also know, Tia," Alfonzo added. "There is no mistaking your compatible mate."

She looked back at Jay.

"You cannot take any of your Protectors," Alfonzo said, gently.

"Suppose I am, you know, compatible?"

"Then you will marry him and give your allegiance to him and his family. And as you are the first you will make him king and his family very important in the Atlantean world."

"What about if I'm not, what about if one of the other Sirens were meant to be with his lot?" and she pulled a face as she said the word Sirens and pointed at Marco.

"Then you would be delivered to the safety of your own family who also live in Ireland. There, suitors would present themselves through your family … I have to say though, this scenario is highly unlikely."

She frowned. "Why not?"

"It's complicated to explain today," Alfonzo continued, "but let us just say, that in our world, if someone crosses your path, it's because they were meant to."

Jay saw Tia's eyes stray to his wrist where his bracelet was visible, then their eyes locked for a brief moment.

Then she snapped them away. "What about if I don't want any of this. What about if I want my own life?"

Jay could see Tia's clenched fists and felt sorry for her. She was well and truly backed into a corner.

"I'm afraid Siren princesses never have their own life," Alfonzo smiled ruefully.

"Can I have a moment with Jay please?" she asked.

"Of course."

They all filed out of the room leaving Tia and Jay alone.

***

Jay stood up and walked around the bed. Tia remained quiet and watched him. The only reason she wasn't more shell-shocked at actually seeing him again was mainly due to the overall weirdness of the afternoon's revelations. It somehow paled into insignificance.

"I phoned you the other night," Jay said, as he paused in his pacing and looked at her.

"Did you? I didn't know." She looked down fidgeting with her fingers.

"That bloke Sean answered."

She nodded slowly. Her brain whirred as she fell in when it must have been. "What did he say?"

"That you were sleeping."

She did a quick add up as she watched his serious

face and came up with the answer to why she was shut down the other night. They both remained quiet for a moment.

He broke it first. "Look Tia, I'm not good at relationship crap, okay? I don't really see beyond a couple of dates, you know?"

She looked at him earnestly. "I totally know. I have no gauge whatsoever. I don't even know if what I feel is normal; let alone how to act."

Jay looked at her and a laugh escaped him, which made her laugh. "I suppose you don't."

He walked back round the bed and sat down again, picked up her hand in both of his, and held it to his mouth. "What are you gonna do?" he said, eventually.

"I dunno. What are the two other brothers like? I could deliberately put them off me?"

Jay laughed. "You could. Stephan's just a kid and Dante's a worse commitment-phobe than I am, so it might not take much."

"Mm," she said, pretending to think on it.

"I don't think you have much choice. You could just humour them and go along with it, and when it suits you – just fuck it off." He gestured with his thumb towards the door.

"You're sexy," she said, changing the subject to something more agreeable. She tried to turn onto her side to gaze at him but she winced with the pain in her ribs.

He grinned and blushed.

"Don't do that," she said pulling a pained face.

"What?" he said, laughing.

"You just give me that look and my temperature shoots up."

He leaned in and put his mouth over hers and ran his tongue along her lips. She opened and met his tongue with hers. "I'd better stop," he said, leaving her really red and breathing hard. "I would hurt you. Better wait till you're mended." And he shifted back in his seat.

Just then the door opened and her brother Dino gracefully walked into the room. He went over to Jay and held out his long slender fingers, which held three vials of clear liquid. "Alfonzo asked me to give you these. They are Elixir. You need to drink them five days apart, but drink them and finish the course."

"What are they?" Jay asked, sitting up as he took them from his hand.

"They will help you tolerate her," he said, pointing at Tia.

Jay just raised his eyebrows, obviously thinking of a wisecrack comeback, but decided against it.

"Being close to her could kill you," Dino continued. "She won't mean it, but well … it's up to you, but with no Atlantean blood, you wouldn't stand a chance."

Jay undid the cap and drank the contents of a vial down. He pulled a face and slipped the others in his pocket.

"Good," Dino said. Then he looked at Tia. "Look Tia, about when we left you. We had to, you know? We were called to our family and the rules said we couldn't stay and protect you."

"Okay Dino, I know."

"They bent the rules putting us with you at all."

She looked up at him, remembering the boyish face he used to have. "I'm glad they did, I missed you."

Dino bent down and kissed her on the forehead. "Get better, okay?" and flashed a wonderful set of pearly whites.

She nodded, smiling back.

"We'll see you in Ireland?"

"Yes, I think so," and she looked at Jay for guidance as she said it.

"At least you sort of know this lot," Jay said, helping her.

That settled it. "Tell Alfonzo I will come as soon as I can travel."

Dino nodded satisfied with her answer. "Your Protectors will bring you and stay nearby."

"Thank you," she said, relieved.

Dino held his hand up and closed the door behind him.

"Will you stay and travel back with me when it's time?"

Jay nodded, "Whichever one of them it is, Dante will look after you." He sighed, sitting back in his chair. "It's not like you've got much choice … we'll work something out."

Tia smiled weakly and hoped he was right.

Chapter 11

Tia spent a blissful few days at Cash's ranch after she left hospital. She and Jay took a lot of showers, getting to know each other really well. They even overcame the challenge of sleeping together without her overheating. They found the best way forward was to place a line of pillows down the centre of the bed, and hold hands across the divide. They didn't mind failure. There was always the shower until they had to sleep from exhaustion. But above all, they promised each other to find a way to be together in the future.

Cash had left them to it and gone off and done the necessary work with the horses for the film and left Sean in charge; who complained of a constant need for a bucket, with all the sloshy lovey dovey shit going on.

Sean had arranged for his 'wife to be' to meet them in Ireland, where he would introduce her to this side of his life and hope that she wouldn't constantly see Tia as a threat. They decided between them to tell her that she was a minding job – being a royal and everything. His military background made this really plausible. Tia promised she would pay him, which he didn't like, but he finally agreed when it was pointed out that he would be a new dad, and he had to be employed somewhere.

When Cash returned the sojourn was over, and they all packed up and went to Billings Airport.

They were quiet on the flight. Neither she nor Jay was sure what the future held for them and their fragile relationship.

They flew into London and then caught a connection to Galway. From there, a car met them and drove them for about an hour to a delightful manor house rented for them to be near the Dubonnetti family home.

They weren't given long to settle in when Tia's uncle Alfonzo arrived to brief her on what was to be expected.

She was summoned to the study on her own. It was explained that her Protectors would not be allowed to interfere beyond this point in negotiations. Their job was complete, so to speak.

She walked in and sat quietly opposite her uncle.

"Good evening, Thelxiepia,"

She rolled her eyes at the use of her birth name. "Evening," she replied, as she exhaled.

"I know you must be tired as it is late, so I will be brief. Tomorrow, the Dubonnetti brother who first discovered you will come to collect you and accompany you to his home. There you will be presented to his father, and one by one to his brothers, to ascertain which brother you will be betrothed to. Any questions?"

"Will I be able to come home after that?

"Home? From that moment on, you will be tested and married in accordance with Atlantean tradition. Then that will be your home, as you will be Dubonnetti."

"What do you mean, tested?"

"I'm afraid I can't help you with the answer to that Tia, as it could be construed as influencing the outcome, but suffice it to say, that your authenticity as a Siren must be tested in line with tradition.

"Oh," she said, quietly looking down at her hands in her lap.

There followed an uncomfortable silence as Alfonzo studied her. "Do not underestimate this match Tia."

She stiffened moodily in her chair. The old saying, 'you can lead a horse to water' came to mind.

Alfonzo took something out of the drawer of the desk. He leant forward and passed her a vial of clear liquid identical to what he'd given Jay.

"I thought I was the one supposed to have the powers." She sniped.

"You do." Alfonzo gestured for her to drink the vial immediately.

Huffing she knocked it back in one go and spluttered and pulled a face.

"Your compatible mate will absorb your power and have mastery over you from that day forward. It is the way for Atlantean royals."

Fuck that! she vowed.

"The good news is, that you will be allowed to meet your biological parents after that."

"Oh joy," she muttered.

***

Dante had delighted his father for the first time in his

life, on his return to Ireland. He had presented himself to him in his study and asked him to teach him everything he needed to know, and assured him he was ready to listen and learn.

In his own time he'd jogged along the beach and sparred with his brothers to get his body in shape. He detoxed and lay off the drink and drugs to get his brain sharp. His skin already had a healthy glow instead of the sallow hue of a druggie. And after his extreme reaction at the club he took Elixir so she didn't affect him when he saw her. At last, his father had an eldest son he could be proud of.

Dante watched the house in consternation following the news from Marco that she had chosen them. Well that wasn't strictly true. It sounded more like she had no choice. It was either choose them or another family she knew even less, or hide until the Humans got hold of her, and that didn't bear thinking about. So all that aside, she would be arriving as soon as she was well from a recent fall from a horse.

Marco and his brothers had been sent to secure a rental house nearby to accommodate her Protectors, who would escort her to Ireland. From there, Marco would bring her home to meet the family. Everything was arranged. She was due to arrive the next day.

Dante sloped off to the seclusion of the family library. He was there more often than not these days. He'd discovered he had a real thirst for knowledge. He laughed to himself how he and Jay had breezed through their expensive education, but now everything had meaning, and he'd discovered books, especially the ancient tomes that had been carried out of Atlantis itself.

He climbed the old steps, dusted off a huge volume and brought it down carefully and rested it on the table. Browned and crumbly pages held the same swirls and lettering that covered his and his friend's bodies. He made a pact with himself to learn to read it. He would study all the past generations where Soul Breathers had been on Earth and why each king had failed before him. He guessed all the bloody princess had tried killing each other for whose ring went what colour. He bet it had been carnage. No, he had to do something different, revolutionary even. And have a bit of fun along the way.

He ran his forearm across the tarnished gold and leather cover and saw that it was decorated with five moons circling a planet. Atlas. His heart hitched. Fuck, it was all so unbelievable, but all true. If he ever made it to actually be king, he would be a fucking top king. That he promised himself, or else he'd die trying.

Reluctantly, he put everything away, left the sanctuary of the library and re-joined the rest of his family. Marco's jovial mood was unsettling. Trying to turn over a new leaf was bloody difficult when all he wanted to do was punch his brother in the face. Where was Jay when he needed him? He was off grid for some reason. That bloody girl, he guessed. Oh well, it would be him as well soon. The prospect both excited him and terrified him. He hadn't got her out of his head since he clapped eyes on her.

He hadn't said a word to a soul about the colour his

ring had gone. He was saving it for the meeting – partly to make sure, and partly to wipe the smug grin off Marco's face.

He spent the remaining hours drafting the necessary documents informing the other three families of his betrothal to a Siren, and the proclamation of this special time in history that would unite them in strength and prosperity. Blah … blah. He was getting good at this kinging shit. He could just imagine Jay's amusement watching him. What a laugh they would have.

***

Dante's optimism was short-lived when his father blustered into the study.

"Brilliant news Dante … I can't believe the fortune now showering on our family." Christian said, as he paced animatedly in front of the desk where Dante sat.

"What is it?" He looked up warily.

"Another one Dante, we have another."

Dante's heart began to sink. "Another what?"

"Siren, of course. Your brother Stephan has been keeping one to himself for several weeks."

"Is she his?" Dante asked, hoping she was. He'd got his mind set on the one he'd seen.

"No she is not."

Shit. His brain quickly worked to process the information. She couldn't be his because he knew his ring had already gone purple – that made him feel better. She could be for one of his other brothers or she could belong to one of the other families. Shit, if that was the case, it was risky, but they could try to marry him to all five. As if on cue…

"All five Dante, all the power could not only be in one family, but in one prince."

"Why can't Stephan marry her?" But he knew the answer already.

"No Dante, if all five Sirens don't belong to this family and proven by rings, then I'm damn well not going to hand any of them over to another family. It would have to be a coup. Precarious I know, but we could fight it on the grounds that you were already a proven king. It would be impossible to justify the action for a lesser prince in the same family."

Fuck, his father had already assumed that the Siren would be his. He could feel his new life spiralling down the pan before it had begun. "When does she come?"

"We will test her quickly before the original one is due to arrive. That way if she is an imposter then no harm is done."

"We will make enemies of all the other families, including the Bonaci, if we do this," Dante tried to reason. He knew the only real chance of success in the long run was to keep them all on side.

Christian waved the statement away with his hand. "Any one of them would do the same. I must tell the rest of your brothers."

Dante knew they would all hate him now. He was the prodigal son about to not only get the fatted calf, but the whole herd too. Life just got better and fucking better.

He picked up his phone and dialled Jay. Three rings and he picked up.

"Hello Dant?"

"Thank God, where have you been man? Listen I must speak to you, it's urgent."

"Yeah, me too ... when?"

"I'm kind of tied up tomorrow, day after?"

"Sure ... Dante?

"Yeah?"

"About the girl ... are we cool?"

The line went quiet for a few moments. "Of course mate, I'm pleased for you."

"Thanks, I knew you'd understand."

"Later."

"Later."

Dante clicked the phone off and threw it on the table. He was pleased and a little relieved that his closest friend had found someone special. He hoped that he would too. He'd know either way in the next twenty-four hours. They would either have this cosmic attraction he'd learned so much about, or it would all be superstitious nonsense. Then the new beginning he'd dreamed of would be nothing but grief. One he couldn't run away from or hide in a bottle. Either way he'd have to man-up.

***

Morning came all too quickly for Jay and Tia. They'd woken at dawn and made love with the urgency of lovers whose time was almost up. They stopped only when Tia noticed Jay's lips were blue with the cold.

She cocooned him in towels and the quilt and lay on top of his swaddled body on the bed while she was naked. He looked up at her other-worldly eyes and she stroked back his hair from his forehead as his teeth chattered.

"Look what I put you through."

"It's worth it," he said, through gritted teeth. "I'm getting better since I drank that stuff. Maybe it makes me run colder or something?"

A look of worry crossed her face.

He struggled to free his arms and put his hands on either side of her face. "It'll be okay … I'm seeing Dante tomorrow, so I'll see you, okay? Then I'll have a chance to work something out with him. Whichever one of them it is, they are being pushed into this as much as you are."

She nodded and lay her head down on his chest and they were quiet for a while.

"Come, I'm warm now. You'd better get ready."

She reluctantly slid off him, sitting up with her feet on the floor.

"I'll go and get us some food while you get dressed … don't look too hot," he said grinning.

***

Tia stared at herself in the mirror. She felt so miserable. It was the first time in her life she'd been truly happy, with the man of her dreams and a relatively healthy sex life (well almost), and it was all about to be taken away from her to marry a complete stranger.

In a wilful temper, she stood and set about dressing. She took out her tights and ripped them in several places. She dug out her old black Dr. Martens boots, the shortest denim micro-mini known to man, and a thin white shirt with a black bra for underneath. Then she braided some of her hair and back combed the rest, tying it all to one side with a scarf. She black-charcoaled her eyes, and popped a lump of bubble gum in her mouth to complete the look.

As Jay walked in with a tray, she turned around. "Ta dah!" she said, popping a bubble.

He nearly dropped the tray. "You look like a St Trinian on acid!" His eyes were wide trying to take it all in. "If you're trying to put him off, you'd have been better dressing as a librarian. He's the original 'Rebel Without A Cause'. You're playing right into his hands," he said, laughing.

She flopped down to sit on the bed hopeless, and put her head in her hands. "My life is over."

Jay put the tray down, came around the bed and pulled her up against him. "Give him hell, okay."

She looked sadly up at him and nodded. "You think it will be him don't you … "

A knock at the door interrupted their locked eyes. Sean's voice came through it. "It's time, Tia."

"Coming." She called behind her.

"You haven't eaten," Jay said, quietly.

"I don't think I could anyway," she said, swallowing the lump in her throat.

Jay walked her out of the room, along the landing, and to the bottom of the stairs.

Her uncle was in the hall waiting for her. "Jay can come no further, Thelxiepia."

Panicking, she turned into Jay's chest and clung to him. He allowed her this, kissed her cheek and whispered, "I'm still here. It's okay."

She felt her eyes prickle with tears. She daren't look at him, in case he saw and thought her a wimp.

Alfonzo held out his hand in way of a prompt. Marco was waiting by the open door, impeccably turned out.

Eventually, she turned within Jay's arms, without looking at him, and put her hand in Alfonzo's. He led her down the hallway, past Cash and Sean, who both wished her luck.

She noticed a pretty blond woman standing next to Sean. "Sarah," she said, absently. The woman smiled sympathetically. She wondered what Sean had told her.

Alfonzo made no comment about her dress as he escorted her right up to Marco. He held up her arm and offered it. "The Royal House of Bonaci gives its daughter to the Royal House of Dubonnetti."

Marco bowed deeply. Tia felt like she was in a dream and would wake up in a minute. Her face must have looked like she'd been smacked in the gob with a wet fish.

Marco continued. "You honour us," and he took her hand.

She felt every one behind her eyes boring into her back – but mostly Jay's. The urge to turn around and have one last look at him was unbearable, but she knew if she did she'd fly back into his arms, and they'd have to drag her out the place kicking and screaming. So she put her best DM forward and walked out of the door to a waiting limousine – leaving the house and her old life forever.

Chapter 12

Marco led her into the hallway of the ancient grey stone house. Inside everything smelt old; she supposed from all the old wood and creaky floorboards. A grandfather clock ticked reliably in the corner steadying her beating heart.

Deep down she felt a deep sense of foreboding, as if she was being led into a Lion's den. Marco looked so smug and happy that she felt uneasy rather than comforted. It was as if he was up to something.

"Come meet the folks," he said, as if she'd popped round for tea. He led her into a large sitting room with a cheery fire in the grate. There was a grand piano in the corner, two large leather sofas facing each other, with a polished dainty table at one end topped with a vase of freshly cut white flowers. She didn't know what they were.

Marco let her look around while he called for everyone. She wished her heart wasn't thumping so.

The two brothers she knew entered the room. They walked up to her and welcomed her like old friends, kissing her on both cheeks. She noted them both raising an eyebrow at how she was dressed. *One to me!*

She knew the moment he got there; she felt the hairs on the back of her neck rise, her stomach fluttered and she felt dizzy, but she managed to hold it together. She tried with all her might to resist the urge to look around but curiosity got the better of her.

Framed in the doorway like an old portrait he stilled, and then walked gracefully into the room. He was nothing like his brothers. His hair was long, to his shoulders, jet black and wavy. His brothers' was blond and short. Their eyes were light grey, his were dark like slate.

The only similarity between them was that they were all tall –over six feet – but he was taller. He was lean, looking great in an open necked black shirt over trendy black trousers. *Wow*, was the only word that came to mind. He exuded sex appeal. She found herself hyperventilating and perspiring. *Fuck!*

Marco, she realised, could hardly contain his glee standing next to her. "May I present my brother, Dante?" And held his arm out towards him.

Dante just stood in front of her looking into her eyes. She tried desperately to hide her reaction to him, but failed miserably. His eyes danced with mirth. He was not the sensible austere would-be king she was expecting, even though Jay had warned her.

She watched his eyes glide over her body and meet hers like a co-conspirator. He reached for her hand hanging limply at her side and rubbed his thumb back and forth over the back of it. Then, wide-eyed, she watched him take it to his mouth and kiss it with lips barely containing their amusement. Her body bloomed for him as if he'd licked it. His big ring glinted in the light, exactly the same as his brothers, except purple. Electricity shot to her toes, amongst other places she refused to acknowledge.

"Pleased to meet you Thelxiepia," he said, grinning and showing off perfect white teeth.

I'm fucked! He was knockout. She'd been hoping that he'd be like a little gnome or something that she could be friends with. But this guy ... she couldn't decide whether he reminded her more of a gipsy or a pirate. His thick Irish accent only made him seem more rakish. She wondered why his brothers spoke perfect Queen's English and he didn't: the rebel in him, she decided.

"Tia! Please call me Tia." She found herself saying. *Per ... thetic!*

He stepped to the side as an older gentleman stalked into the room. The father, she guessed. He was tall, slim and greying, with not the slightest look of frailty about him. He studied her shrewdly making no hint of his disapproval at her obvious lack of respect in her dress.

He picked up her hand. "Thelxiepia! Welcome."

She watched his eyes dart to Dante's ring and then he smiled at her, drew her hand to his mouth and breathed over it. He fixed his eyes on her like a cobra. "I am Christian Dubonnetti."

She fought the urge to shudder. "Hello," she said.

"Where is Stephan?" Marco said, breaking the evil spell.

"He is with the young lady already in the pool. Her name is Joselle." Christian said.

It struck her what an odd thing to say that was.

He put his arm in the small of her back. "Shall we join them Thelxiepia? It's time to meet your sister."

How strange it was that Alfonzo hadn't mentioned that she would be meeting her sister today.

***

When Dante saw her he thought her breathtaking. He drank her in before he walked into the room. Her act of rebellion in dressing the way she did only appealed to him all the more; fuck, he'd have done the same thing. No shrinking violet would hold his attention.

She obviously hadn't connected him to the first time he'd seen her at the club. Thankfully the Elixir prevented a repeat of his physical reaction to her.

His ring, which had been a part of him for years, vibrated on his finger. He'd come to realise it was telling him it was changing. So by the time he brought her hand up to his mouth to kiss it, he didn't need to look at it to know it was purple. The proof was there. She was not only one of the Sirens he'd been told about all his life, but she was his. The most compatible person to him in the whole world; whatever compatible meant – supposedly a perfect match for him to marry. Whatever it was, she would bring power and riches to his whole family.

He felt a little sorry for his father now. He'd given him a really hard time over the years, calling him a raving lunatic most of the time, when all he'd been doing was telling him the truth.

Now he followed behind everyone as his Siren was led off to the basement and the underground viewing area.

It had always reminded him of one of those large zoo aquariums where dolphins and whales were kept. Except this one was in his home; no wonder he'd thought everyone was mad. Well, he had to start embracing these differences to the Humans they lived amongst. *Fuck! It was so alien.* He found himself laughing at his own pun. God, he was losing it; sobriety was crazier than being drunk these days.

The viewing area was damp and dark; originally the old cellars. He felt a stab of guilt at the barbarity of the test as they walked down the stone steps. His father had told him the old stories of Witches being tried in the seventeenth century using ducking stools; much the same as the one they had here. They were really testing devices for water-breathing folk. Some they found would have been Sea Witches living among Humans, but on rare occasions, they would in fact be a Siren, who could lead men to their doom or to great power and wealth.

Although he felt guilty, he knew deep down that fascination would win over, and he would watch to see if she died under the water. Besides, his turn would come.

***

She was led along a corridor, through a wood panel in the library wall and down some dimly-lit spiral stairs. It was just like an old Hammer Horror movie. She could already smell the dampness and the water.

At the bottom of the staircase, they came into a small

room with one whole wall to the right made of plate glass, with an old metal frame around it. It was lit from behind like a large fish tank with blue water from floor to ceiling. The whole feel of the place was like a dungeon; it was so dark and old.

She put both her hands on the glass and peered into the water. "Christ, is there a person in there?"

"That is your sister, Joselle. You will meet her." Christian purred. "She didn't find the test easy, so you will be a comfort to her."

Bastard. The poor creature was cowering on the bottom looking terrified.

She looked around at those assembled with her. Paolo and Antonio looked at her guiltily. The one she hadn't met yet; she assumed he was Stephan, looked upset and angry. He was apart from everyone, pacing like he wanted to punch a wall. He was so young; he couldn't be more than about seventeen or eighteen.

Christian interrupted her thoughts. "My servant will take you to the pool surface so you may join her."

She looked at him, her eyes heavy lidded with contempt at how he sugar-coated something so heartless and cruel.

All her life she had hidden her ability successfully; now she had to show it to prove who she was. The irony wasn't lost on her. She took a deep breath, resigned herself to the test and stepped out of her boots, tights and skirt. She pulled her shirt over her head until she was only in her underwear.

She didn't understand the impulse, but she turned to

the dark one, hovering quietly at the back. "Can you hold these for me? I don't want them to get wet." It felt a lame thing to say, but for some reason he didn't seem to be part of the madness.

"Of course," he replied, and took her things.

"I won't be able to speak for about an hour when I get out … just so they know." She found herself explaining.

He nodded.

***

Dante watched her follow the large bodyguard in her bra and knickers, looking so small and fragile like a doll. She disappeared up the narrow staircase next to the pool, which led up to the surface.

It had surprised him that out of all those present, she'd passed her clothes to him and explained that she would lose her voice, even though he was no less guilty than the rest of them in condoning what was happening to her.

He admired her courage and wandered how bad her life must have been to have honed such a strong spirit to take all this in her stride.

***

At the top of the stairs it looked like any other indoor swimming pool, but she could see at the deep end there was a six square feet of much darker water. This must be the gap in the floor where it dropped away into the tank that could be viewed from below.

The chair with restraints was mounted on a metal frame on a miniature crane type mechanism, which would swing out over the pool, and then lower into the deeper part.

"You don't need to strap me in the chair, I can get into the pool myself."

The bodyguard thought about it for a second and then nodded.

She jumped in and put her head back and wet her hair. The guard watched her the whole time. "You must swim down into the tank," he said.

She nodded and dove down. She realised there was a glass top to the tank with a hatch. She guessed the guard would close it over her when she went down; terrifying for anyone not confident in breathing under water.

Gradually she swam down looking for the girl. She had quite a capacity for holding her breath and could have probably completed the test on just one lungful of air but she knew what they'd brought her here to see, so she decided to get it over with.

She circled her arms so she sank slowly to the bottom to a kneeling position. She made sure she was facing the black expanse, which she knew was the pane of glass. Nothing much was visible through it except a few dark shapes and dim lanterns.

She concentrated and slowed her pulse down and gradually let the water into her lungs, closing her eyes as she did so. Her gills opened with a jolt and she opened her eyes and resumed her search of the tank.

There she was, huddled in the far corner, small and fearful. She had white blond, straight hair, and her frightened wide eyes were the palest cornflower blue, with large dilated pupils.

Gradually she moved closer so as not to scare the girl. Soothing her, she stroked her hair and used encouraging gestures to get her onto her feet.

She pulled her up to the glass and banged roughly on it with the heel of her hand, and then she pointed her thumb upwards and signalled to get them out.

***

Dante watched riveted as she swam to the bottom of the tank. The moment she let the water in was obvious and fascinating. He watched as she slowly opened her eyes. Her pupils had become huge; transforming her face to an otherworldly beauty.

When she'd smacked the glass he'd seen enough. "Let her out."

His brother Stephan agreed with relief. "This whole fucking thing is barbaric, get them out of there."

Christian conceded. "Very well. See that they don't leave the house, otherwise they will have to be confined here."

Both Stephan and Dante rushed up the steps to the pool surface and helped the girls get out of the pool. Tia was helping the other one get the water up out of her lungs, which she did with a lot of coughing, retching and gulping of air. Tia expelled hers quickly and efficiently.

Dante wrapped a towel around her shoulders and she looked at him gratefully with still transformed disk-like eyes. She squinted; the light obviously hurt after the darkness of the water. "Come with me," he said. "You'll be safe in my room."

Chapter 13

She allowed him to lead her, vaguely aware that Stephan was following with the other girl – her sister. She could hear him whispering affectionate words, which she couldn't make out.

Her heart ached for Jay. He seemed a million miles away. Empty and low, she put one foot in front of the other.

When they reached his room, her overnight bag had already been delivered there. It was a large room dominated by a large bed. It had a chaise lounge under the window and a door leading off to what she guessed was an en-suite bathroom, to the left of the bed.

She stood in the middle of the room and waited.

"Please feel free to shower the pool water off. It's just through there," he said, pointing towards the bathroom.

She nodded, picked up her bag and headed straight for it. Shit, no lock on the door, so she couldn't barricade herself in. She slumped onto the edge of the bath. What was the point? He was to be her husband and soon. She wasn't unaffected by him though, probably because he was Jay's best friend. She was bound to like someone that Jay liked.

She showered quickly and brushed her teeth then dressed quickly into some slouchy baggy trousers and a t-shirt.

When she came out someone was delivering a tray with breakfast stuff on it. Dante thanked the woman, who looked like a maid, took the tray from her and put it on the bedside table.

"I didn't know what to get you so I ordered a few things. There is some hot lemon and honey for your throat," he said, offering her a steaming mug.

She looked at him bewildered, swallowing the lump in her throat and shaking her head as if to snap herself out of it.

"It's okay, I know you can't talk."

Wow, no-one had ever known what she needed before. The hot lemon soothed as it went down and she closed her eyes as she drank. She could sense him watching her the whole time.

"Please sit, I doubt you ate much this morning."

She sat on the edge of the bed and looked at the tray. It had a mixed selection of fruits, croissant, poached salmon and scrambled eggs. She looked over at him. She must have looked bewildered as he spoke unprompted.

"Intolerance to meat is common in our people."

She didn't know why she had such a lump in her throat but she did. She picked up a croissant, nibbled and fought back her emotion.

He smiled at her kindly. "Look just eat what you want and sleep a bit. I bet you didn't sleep much last night?"

She shook her head and thought of her night in Jay's arms with a bone-deep ache.

"I'll just sit over here." And he pointed to the chaise lounge. "I can't leave you alone but I can give you some space until you wake. Then we can talk."

She nodded gratefully again.

After nibbling on some of the food, she curled up in a ball on the bed and faced him. Her mind drifted as she ran her eyes over him. He watched her back as if he was allowing her to examine him. Never in a million years would she have put him as Marco's brother. He was sexy and dark and mysterious. Marco was fair, cunning and vain.

Her uncle had told her that all the royals were related, making her his cousin. So this guy was the one of the purest bred Atlanteans – after her uncle she'd met.

Was he so different from other men? She was certainly physically attracted. A pang of guilt stabbed her after that thought. Still, I'll see Jay tomorrow, she thought, as her eyes slowly closed.

***

Her mind came online to gravelly male whispers. It took her a second to remember where she was. God, she had gone right off into a deep sleep, which was unusual for her.

"You're awake!" Dante said, after closing the door. "That was Stephan, we can meet with them later if you want so you can get to know your sister."

She sat up and grabbed the water left next to her on the bedside table and swallowed a large mouthful. "Thanks.

What's the time?" She said, between glugs.

"1.30 p.m; you've been out a couple of hours. Do you want to go for a walk? I can show you about the place."

He seemed really friendly. She supposed it was better than staying cooped up. "Okay," she said, and stood up and began rooting around in her bag for something to put on.

"Here," he said, chucking a grey sweatshirt at her.

The act of familiarity made her pause. "Thank you," she said quietly. She held the oversized top up against her and then pulled it over her head. It went half way down her thighs and smelled totally of him. Citrusy and male. *Stop!* She tried to shake the feelings it evoked. A pain hit the pit of her stomach again.

"Come." And he held the door open for her.

She pulled her trainers on and quickly walked past him out of the room and without looking at him.

Thankfully, he led her down a back staircase so they wouldn't see anyone. It took them through the kitchen where he greeted a cheery Mrs McNally, the cook. "This is Tia, April." He said, warmly.

The cook did a little bob at the knees, "Miss."

"Hello." Tia replied.

"Come Tia, lets go outside."

When they got outside, "Is she … you know, Atlantean?" Tia asked.

"Everyone who works here is." He led her down some stone steps and onto a large lawn, which swept down to a river. They walked slowly and quietly.

Tia pulled leaves off the odd bush as she went, deep

in thought.

"You can ask me anything, you know," he said, after a while, and looked at her and smiled.

She was trying not to like him so much. "That was cruel this morning," she blurted. "Not for me, I mean, but the other one." Her face was stony.

"I know, it was cruel for you too." He grew serious. "But if it's any consolation, the worst test is to come and it's for me."

She looked at him shocked. "What do you mean?"

He stopped, turned to her and picked up both her hands in his and looked deep into her eyes. "They will marry us within twenty four hours, Tia. Do you know what it entails?"

She shook her head and looked at him with concern.

"I can't help you, it's against the rules. But I think it's safe to say that we both go into the water and it will be up to you whether we both come out."

"What?" she said, in horror. "No-one said anything about hurting anyone."

"It's part of the ceremony. If I live it means you have accepted me."

She let go of one of his hands and they continued to walk. He was as much a victim in this as she was.

"What's all the ring business about?" she said, in an attempt to lighten the mood.

He held up his hand so she could look at it closely. "All Atlantean princes are given these. They are called divining rings; forged to tell us when we get near a Siren."

"Yours is a different colour to your brothers'."

"Only when I'm near you. It is white when I'm not and so are my brothers'. It sounds really corny when I say it out loud but it shows me you are the most compatible as a mate."

Her eyebrows drew together. "What's that supposed to mean … genetically, sexually, mentally?"

He laughed ruefully. "Good point. I haven't the foggiest."

"Because I'd hate to disappoint you but I've not been that great in the … you know … sex department."

"Neither have I."

"You haven't?" she stopped walking and searched his face.

He shook his head and sighed. "No, there has always been something missing. When I have managed to get it on, I had to drink gallons of alcohol, which is fuckin' counter-productive, you know, to bring my core temperature down, and I had to take cold showers, and shit like that. Then I end up drinking more because it all feels … you know … wrong somehow?"

Surprised, she studied his face. "You're like that? I get so overheated I can fit … try that for embarrassing."

He nodded and laughed. "That makes sense. Don't you see Tia, it's all supposed to take place under water for us?" he said, and took hold of her by the tops of the arms.

She was quiet as she looked at him and thought about it. God, it all made sense. "So the purer your blood …"

"The more you'd need to do it under the water," he

finished for her. "And you are half royal Atlantean and half Murr."

"I see," she said, and resumed walking again. "Tell me about the Murrs?"

"They are our cousins, the Borge family, and their descendants. I haven't met any yet, but they live under water; as crazy as that sounds."

"Can they walk on land?"

"I think for short periods, I think that's where the tales of mermaids come from."

"Oh," she said, letting the new information sink in.

Just then Marco trotted up to them on a large, lively, chestnut horse. "Why, it's the love birds. Spoken to Jay yet, Dante?"

"I'm seeing him tomorrow," Dante replied.

Marco's horse jogged and spun round eager to be off. Marco gave a huge grin to Tia, laughed and then galloped off.

"Your brother is such a dick. Thank God I'm not destined to be with him."

"I knew I'd like you," he said, as he playfully bumped into her and smiled. "Let's find Stephan."

***

They found Stephan with Joselle, having tea in the large conservatory. It was bright and warm with plants everywhere, and comfy chairs arranged around a white wrought iron and glass table. They both looked up as Tia and Dante entered from the garden.

"Stephan," Dante said, "can we join you?"

"Of course," Stephan said, and held out his hand

towards the empty chairs at the table.

"Joselle, isn't it? This is your sister, Tia," Dante said, as he pulled out a chair for Tia to sit.

She smiled in way of thanks.

Tia looked over at Stephan and Joselle who hadn't let go of each other's hands. Tia studied her. She was so pale. She looked as though the colour had been sucked out of her, and so delicate like she'd brake; nothing like herself.

"Where'd they hide you?" she said.

"Pardon?" Joselle said, in a thick accent.

Tia looked at Stephan for help who translated in English. "She asked where you grew up?"

Joselle looked at her. "Russia. I was put in a strict dance regime with Russian Ballet company," all rolling r's.

Tia just nodded.

"You?" Joselle asked her back.

"Foster care … London," she added.

"What about music … how it come with you?"

She looked sideways at Dante for help.

Dante thought for a moment. "Sirens were used in the past for their luring singing voice; that's why you would have been banned from singing. She was asking if your gift with music came out another way?"

"Oh … I'm a house music DJ," she directed back at Joselle.

Dante grinned.

"House DJ?" Joselle looked at Stephan again.

"Night club music."

"Da, da," Joselle said, with understanding. Then looked from Dante to Tia, "You are fortunate," she said, with a sneer on her face.

Tia sat up a bit pissed off. "How … what do you mean?"

"You have purple ring and will marry." Joselle looked back at Stephan and held up his hands and kissed them.

"Listen," Tia said, "I only just met him. I'm in a relationship with one of my Protectors." It sort of came out involuntarily; she felt sorry the minute she'd said it in front of Dante. "Sorry," she said looking at him, "I didn't mean to be insensitive."

"Protector?" Joselle asked, looking back at Stephan.

"Don't you have any?" Tia said, surprised.

Dante laughed slightly, his eyes narrowed. "Well how many do you have?"

"Three."

Dante ignored Joselle's question entirely, but turned in his chair and stared at Tia. He was vaguely aware of Stephan answering her as he continued to watch Tia closely.

"What is Common Atlantean?" Joselle persisted.

"For fuck sake. Not royal!" Dante said, loudly, starting to lose his patience – still looking at Tia. "I didn't know you were in a relationship?" he said, lowering his tone to almost a whisper.

Tia's brows met as she just looked at him confused. "Marco didn't tell you?" She could feel herself starting to panic.

Dante closed his eyes, sighed and shook his head.

He was oblivious. That meant he had no idea it was Jay. Oh my God. Jay thinks he knows. Her face flushed as the implications hit her.

"What's the matter?" Dante said, his voice low.

"Oh nothing … I thought you knew that's all." She looked around at the three sets of eyes on her. "Why can't you two marry then?" she said, trying to change the subject.

Joselle held up Stephan's ring hand, "No purple ring, only green."

"No, hang on," Dante interrupted, steering the conversation back. "How serious is this relationship?"

Fuck, he was starting to look angry. "I … I'm sorry, I thought you knew."

"That fucker, Marco," he said through gritted teeth, glowering at Stephan. Then he stood so suddenly that he knocked his chair over backwards.

Tia saw the anger boiling up in him. She was shocked and a bit scared; not that she hadn't seen her fair share of violence in her life, but she felt severely out of her comfort zone.

She was grateful when Stephan came round the table to shield Joselle and try to calm him down. They were all complete strangers to her. She didn't know what he was capable of.

"He probably forgot or didn't realise Dante," Stephan reasoned.

"Oh, he fucking realised alright – the prick."

His reaction was terrifying. She didn't understand the whys, but she sure as hell wasn't going to tell him who it was. "He knows I'm going to marry you. It's okay," she reasoned.

Dante stopped his train of thought, narrowed his eyes and looked over at her in disbelief. "Tell me this ... how can I trust you to save my life, when you want someone else?" He broke away from Stephan's grip on his upper arms and strode back out into the garden towards the house.

"It's okay, I'll go," she said to Stephan, and ran after him.

"Dante. Dante!" she called.

She was forced to run past him and in front of him to stop him and put her hand out onto his chest. "Stop, please."

He used his weight to step right in to her personal space as if to test her, and glared down at her. His eyes seemed to smoulder as they bore into hers. He grabbed her upper arms and put his mouth on hers in one swift move.

The move shocked her but the hand she had pushed into his chest gradually weakened. Slowly she allowed him to pull her to him. His arms went around her back and hers slipped around his waist.

She knew she should stop it but her body seemed to take on a life of its own. She found herself parting her lips allowing him to take advantage and push his tongue into her mouth. Not gently but invading; defying her to stop him, and God help her she could not. Just as she thought she could muster the strength to pull her hands back around and push him away she found them reaching up into his beautiful soft wavy hair and pulling him to her tightly.

It was he who broke the contact of their mouths for a moment to look into her eyes. He was breathing deeply. "Do you feel it building in you?"

She did, but how did he know? That glow in her chest that got hotter and hotter. Her face was on fire and so was his. She ran her fingers over the perspiration on his brow. "We are the same," she said, in wonder. For so long she had felt a freak. So totally alone, with nobody to share her experience with, or who could understand an ounce of what she felt. But this man felt it all.

"I won't let you die." She whispered, and she meant it at that moment. How could she lose the one person who could understand her so totally?

Dante grabbed her by the hand and began walking so fast, towards the house, that she was forced to run to keep up with him. "Where are you taking me?"

He continued to walk fast. Her eyes were wide with fear as they came through the kitchen. Never had she seen such pent up anger – not even in her spiteful foster mother.

Mrs McNally turned from what she was doing and let out a small yelp, and jumped back with her hands up as they stormed through her kitchen.

Dante paused on the threshold. "Tell my father we are in the pool now April, do you understand?"

"Right away sir!" she replied, all of a fluster.

As they came into the wood-panelled hallway, Marco was walking out of the sitting room with a newspaper under his arm. Dante flew at him like a banshee.

Tia screamed, "No, Dante!"

He ran at him and smashed him up against the wall so violently that it cracked with the force. He wedged his forearm under Marco's jaw, restricting his breathing. "You'd better shut that fucking hatch man, do you hear me? Because, if I come out of there alive, I will fucking kill yer!"

Paolo and Antonio rushed out of the sitting room, grabbed Dante's arms and pulled him off. Dante's eyes remained riveted with hate on Marco, who grabbed his coat off the hat stand silently and made his exit out of the front door. Dante was left glaring at his other two brothers.

Paolo spoke up, "We didn't tell you, because we couldn't see how it would help; you being on the wagon and all. What difference would it have made?"

Dante spat with contempt. "Y'all want me dead," he said, pointing a finger.

Tia's gradual backing away was halted when he picked up her hand again and pulled her towards the basement stairs, and the viewing room.

When they got to the damp room, he threw the switch on the lights that lit the tank and the pool house at the top of the stairs.

"Come, it's time to put your money where your mouth is," and he pushed her roughly up the stairs.

She tried to reason with him with apologies and pleas of how she thought he knew, but it fell on deaf ears.

"Undress," he commanded, as they got to the top of

the stairs.

"What?" she said, in a weak voice.

"Get in the fucking pool,"

"No!" she said, sick of being pushed around.

He nodded at her menacingly and began stripping off – shoes, socks, trousers and t-shirt until he was buck-naked. She couldn't stop her eyes skating over every inch of him.

Human-style tattoos covered the majority of the top half of his body, but she recognised the Dubonnetti coat of arms on his arm and the trident emblazoned on his back. The pictures were scenes of the sea; mermaids nestled amongst intermingling swirls and arcs. Every flourish stabbed her heart with a memory of Jay.

He stalked slowly towards her. Her core temperature shot up betraying her. *Fuck! Fuck! What was happening?* She wanted to fight him off but found herself pulling off her trainers as she watched him approach.

"Everything," he said, as he got to her, and helped pull the sweatshirt off over her head and then her t-shirt.

He ran a finger gently over the lace of her bra. "You can take this off here, or it comes off in the water, it's up to you."

Almost hyperventilating, she unclipped the clasp and peeled it away.

His face flashed red and hers did in response.

"I'm burning up," she said, in a whisper.

"So am I ... come," and he pulled her into the shallow end where they could wade in.

They stood waist deep in the water facing each other.

The water was cooling and soothing, but their cheeks were still flaming red.

"Why do we heat up like this?" she asked, her throat feeling like it was closing up.

He trailed a finger slowly down her cheek and down to her breast. "Our bodies are building up to it."

"Up to what?"

"I can't tell you. It's an instinct ... I guess we'll find out together."

"Have you ever breathed under water?" She asked.

"Never."

She swallowed, realising the enormity of what was about to happen and the trust he was putting in her.

He leant down and kissed her mouth slowly and reverently this time, and she didn't fight him. When she thought of Jay, she somehow felt that he was nothing to do with this. This was totally separate and necessary. "I love him, Dante," she said, and looked into his eyes so he knew she meant it.

"But you want me." He ran a thumb along her jaw.

"Yes," she whispered, shutting her eyes and swallowing down her shame. "Yes I do." At that moment, she thought, she'd never wanted anything or anyone so much in her life.

"Let's do it then." And he swam towards the deep end and she followed.

His brother Antonio came up the steps and Dante nodded to him.

Tia guessed he was to close the hatch after them.

Dante took a deep breath and dove down and Tia

followed him. They heard the clang of the hatch being closed soon after. She pulled him to the bottom and he swam over to the glass and knocked with his knuckles and they heard a knock back. She supposed witnesses were needed. It was a marriage after all. *Fuck, this was it.*

Chapter 14

Quickly she allowed the water into her lungs; she didn't want to waste time. She needed her wits about her in case everything started to go south.

When she felt the bubbles start to rise from behind her ears, she pulled Dante down so he was sitting on the floor. She set about calming him down. Panicking was not a good thing down there. He was big and she was small; damage could be done and then he definitely could die. They sat and sat. He had a longer capacity for holding his breath than the average Human, she realised. She watched in awe as he produced similar markings to her own. But still he sat.

When they'd been there about ten minutes, Tia started to mime to him to let the water into his mouth. He shook his head and resisted. She had to think quickly and decided to sit on his legs and clamp her own behind his back and hold each side of his face with her hands. She tried to communicate with him through her eyes: *calm down, let it in; just let it go, relax*. She stroked his face, his forehead and back.

He began to shake his head wildly, fighting the

inevitable intake of water.

Let it in, she willed. *Relax.* She nodded slowly.

He let out a silent cry and squeezed his eyes shut. She felt the worst person alive as she gripped her arms around the tops of his so he couldn't push her off. And for a few moments she fought with him with all her strength She was about to have to give up, he was so strong, when he started to push and pull weaker and weaker, until he eventually stopped and went limp.

His eyes were open but unseeing. His arms just floated in the water.

Dante … Dante … she thought, shaking him.

She looked behind his ears. All she could see was a faint red line like a scar – no gills to speak of. God, how long did she have? Panicking, she wracked her brains. What did he say about building up and up?

On impulse she thought of CPR – the kiss of life – and put her mouth on his.

His lips were slightly parted so she pushed her tongue in and blew slowly and went with her gut. God, if he died, Jay would think she killed him and hate her.

She concentrated. The feeling she remembered always came from the centre of her chest. She imagined it there growing and growing, bigger and bigger, travelling up her chest into her throat, through her mouth, into Dante's and down into his heart.

When she opened her eyes Dante was glowing. First he was red, and then orange. His face glowed brightly and then his chest. She continued to repeat blowing and kissing, blowing and kissing. She felt him jolt, then jolt again, and then his eyes opened. His arms came around her and she threw her head back in relief and triumph.

She didn't intend for it to go so far. To be honest she didn't think past keeping him alive for Jay and she would have hated to lose the surprising affinity she had discovered in him already.

Then when he clamped onto her after she'd saved him and swam with her to the secluded part of the tank, all sane thought just evaporated with her underwear. She knew he was a gorgeous bloke, but this attraction between them was ridiculously off the chart. And God, after his essence first entered her, so he was inside her body and mind, there was no hope of going back. She was totally fucked. He had her fair and square and so she was pulled in, hook, line and sinker.

***

The feeling was like being kicked in the chest – not once but twice. When his eyes opened he was hit with such an immense feeling of euphoria, it was like main-lining joy.

Hey, welcome back! She was in his head.

He was aware of jets of air behind his ears and the feeling of rushing in his heart intensified, followed by an erection such as he'd never had in his life before. When he saw her throw her head back an instinct took over and he bit down on her neck and sucked. *Fuck! Where did that come from?*

He wound his legs around her and swam with her to the far end of the tank where a dark glass wall was positioned for privacy and soft seaweeds grew on the floor like a soft bed. He swam with her there with his lips on hers. Good job she didn't need to breathe.

As they entered the cordoned off section he pushed her into the corner so she couldn't move. She wasn't resisting him; it was just that he felt all-powerful and he was a man possessed. She had saved him, chosen him, wanted him above anyone because no other could share this feeling with her but him. He was hers and she was his, irreversibly; it felt perfect. He wasn't sure what passed between them or what it was called, but in that moment he understood her to her core – her feelings, her intentions and her fears. She could project the thoughts she wanted him to hear, and he wanted to reciprocate. He wanted to reach that place in someone – in her – and not deny that instinct deep inside him any longer.

He kissed her slowly, solemnly; his hands moved all over her, gradually moving down between her legs.

I want you, he heard as a whisper in his head. He wished she could hear him as well. His fingers stroked the heat of her and groaned at the strength of feeling he had already for her; so different from any previous fumbling attempts with Humans. This was who he was meant to meet his whole life.

He jolted when she touched him in impatience. She stroked and pulled him to her.

Now, he heard her say.

Without preamble, he positioned himself with her legs around his waist and he pulled her slowly on to him to his full length. He filled her completely. He began a slow rhythm, building and building in strength and speed; the feeling in his chest grew in symmetry. The power of the sensation was enough to bring him to his knees if it wasn't for the water holding him in a caress.

She scratched his back deeply and pulled him to her mouth. He felt a sharp pang and tasted the metal tang of blood as she trapped his tongue with her tooth and breathed the wonderful glow into him again.

He pushed into her and retreated faster and harder. She was so pliant, but she gripped him hot and tight. What he felt was indescribable – out of this world – and tipped him so far off the edge he thought he'd never stop falling.

The weight in his chest became unbearable until the sensation was like bubbles travelling upwards into his throat and then his lips. He understood, yes. He wanted it to leave him and travel across their tongues and into her. Over it went.

She looked startled initially, but it quickly dissolved as the white glow permeated her face and he could feel her drift in ecstasy as she let go. Her muscles pulsed around him in an orgasm that milked him on and on.

This is how it was meant to be, Tia, he said, as he moved over her.

Fuck, yes, oh yes.

They could now communicate telepathically. Her life's essence had gone into him, and he had gathered every part of himself and it had flowed into her, and it knew exactly where it was going. Like a migrating bird instinctively knowing its way.

It had been the perfect communion of body and soul;

complete intimacy on every level. The very thing they'd always missed with every other joining.

Carefully he laid her on the floor. He was so grateful they'd had this privacy. As he lay with her in his arms, he didn't want another living soul to spoil this special time together.

He promised her she would be his queen and he would take no other.

It did feel like a marriage – one of the spirit.

***

Jay went up to the bedroom after Tia had gone and sat on the bed. He had to get a grip. Dante was his best friend and would know how much this one meant to him. It didn't stop him wanting to punch a wall though.

There was a soft knock at the door.

"What?"

Cash's voice came through the door. "Sorry man, but Alfonzo wants to speak to us before he goes."

"I'll be right down."

Jay walked into the study and nodded at Sean and Cash who were already there. Alfonzo sat at the heavy desk and Dino stood next to him.

"Please take a seat Jay. I want to take this opportunity to thank you all for protecting the eldest daughter of the Bonaci family and bringing her safely to her destiny, which is of the upmost importance to the Atlantean nation."

"She will be married in the next few hours and presented as queen to her mother and father tomorrow at the wedding celebration and you will be expected to attend."

They all remained silent.

"You will be expected to remain her Protectors for life, and will be retained financially by the family. That will be all." Alfonzo nodded at Cash and Sean, which they took as their dismissal. "Jay, please stay for a few moments."

The two men shuffled out the door. Cash touched Jay on the shoulder as he left.

When the door closed behind them, Alfonzo resumed speaking, "It was hard to see her go?"

Jay gave a small almost imperceptible nod. Where was this going?

"The Bonaci are grateful for your sacrifice and would like to reward you and welcome you as part of their family going into the future."

Jay didn't say anything, he didn't really understand what was being said to him and willed him to just get on with the golden handshake.

Alfonzo threw a large brown envelope across the desk, which Jay leant forward and picked up. *Here we go.*

"Open it."

He did as he was told. "The deeds to the hotel?" He looked over at Alfonzo in confusion.

"Yours." Alfonzo lounged back in his chair for a few moments. "We know you have a position of privilege within the Dubonnetti family, but we think, and I think you will agree, that this will be difficult to maintain once Thelxiepia is married to your lifelong friend and brother, so to speak."

"Dante and I will remain friends." *He will know she's mine.*

"And that is commendable, but having discussed this with Christian, Dante's father, we have agreed that you will be offered the same privilege with the Bonaci."

"Thank you, but I'm sure it isn't necessary."

"Think on it, you can let me know tomorrow. A point to note: The Bonaci has a large corporation, which will be worth billions now that our Siren has been located. We would like to appoint you as CEO as the public face of Bonaci."

Jay sat there dazed, trying to take in the new information. He was kind of expecting some sort of pay-off to disappear out of Tia's life, but welcomed into the fold he was not.

Alfonzo rose from his chair and Dino helped him gather his things. He stood still at the door.

"Make the right decision Jay."

Jay nodded without looking at him.

Chapter 15

They weren't sure how long they'd been in the water but guessed it was a long time when Dante's skin on his fingers started to crinkle. Time to face the music.

Finding the hatch open, they swam through and waded out of the shallow water holding hands. As soon as they were out of the deep water Tia coughed and spat the water out of her lungs, and projected for Dante to do the same.

She rubbed his back and sympathised with him for the searing pain that always came as the air replaced the water, through the windpipe and over the vocal cords, which was why speech was difficult for a while.

When Dante's eyes cleared, they noticed a beautifully made up day bed with blood red petals strewn over it and the tiled floor. Freshly-cut flowers had been arranged everywhere making the whole room smell fragrant.

Tia put her hand over her mouth overcome with emotion. Never had she had all this attention. Dante hugged her smiling, *hey look, Mrs McNally thinks of everything.* He walked over to a small table with a single red rose in a tiny vase. There was a Thermos which he opened and sniffed, *Hot honey and lemon.* The rest of the tray was covered in an array of salads and seafood, iced champagne and two flutes.

Two fluffy robes were folded neatly on a chair. Dante passed her one whilst rubbing his hair on a towel. *I think my first proclamation should be that you have to be naked.*

She looked at him slyly, *what all the time?*

He drank her in, appreciating every inch; *I'd never tire of seeing you like this.* He picked up her hand and twirled her around so he could see every angle of her transformed skin.

Her belly ached with a rush of emotion. He liked her strange markings and all the differences she'd tried to hide all her life. And my, did she like his.

She sat heavily on the bed munching on a juicy peach. *Seriously, what is the first thing you're going to do?*

He dropped his eyelids. *Sleep with you on that bed, and when we get too hot … get back in the water.*

She lay back against the pillows giggling. *Your wish is my command.*

He leapt on top of her.

***

When Tia and Dante finally emerged it was to congratulations from all the Dubonnettis – except for Marco who had curiously gone missing.

Telegrams from all over the world had arrived from Atlantean prominent families and dignitaries. Tia was overwhelmed with all the well-wishing. She glanced over at Dante and got the impression that being the good guy was new for him too. *God, that gorgeous fiery, passionate man is mine.* And her breath hitched in her chest.

She tried her damnedest not to think of Jay. She'd been sort of caught up in a whirlwind up until now. But as she looked at everyone's happy faces, especially Dante's, she felt the worst kind of traitor. Shit, they were both beautiful in her eyes, and yet so different. The fact that they were such close friends just compounded her feeling of self-loathing.

Dante's father interrupted her thoughts. He looked drunk and deliriously happy when he greeted her as his beloved daughter. He still made her skin crawl. Thankfully Dante whisked her off to his room to escape his family and to get ready for their wedding celebration.

They spent the next couple of hours getting ready, just the two of them. She allowed him to cheer her up and in doing so realised what great company Dante was – always witty and entertaining.

A magnificent gown had been hung in his room for her. She'd never seen anything so beautiful; moss green silk to go with her eyes. "Do my DM's go with this?" she said, in all seriousness.

That look came in his eye. "You can go feckin' barefoot for all I care," and he pounced, pushing her down on the bed. *Shit. What chance did she have?*

***

Dante couldn't ever remember being this happy. They arrived at the Bonaci family home, which was more like a castle. The driveway was long and the entrance was grand. Liveried servants came out and showed the Dubonnetti clan into a hallway as antiquated as their own.

Sebastian Bonaci met them there and greeted them warmly. He shook hands with Christian, then Dante and lastly, when his eyes rested on Tia, he pulled her into an embrace, which she accepted woodenly. "My beautiful Thelxiepia. How your mother and I have longed for this moment."

"Hello," was all she could manage.

Dante put his arm around her back after their coats were taken.

"In love already." Sebastian said, in his Mediterranean, sing-song voice. "Please follow me. We do not live in this part of the house."

They followed him further into the hallway to a panel, which opened revealing a lift. The lift doors opened and they all stepped in. "This castle was cut into the cliff side." Sebastian explained. "It enables us to have easy access to the sea and my wife's family; that is your mother, of course, Tia," and he inclined his head towards her.

As they stepped out the room appeared dark, but a party was obviously in full swing. The lift was at an angle, so as they turned and looked around to their right, there was a small flight of marble stairs leading to the largest most unusual room they had ever seen, cut into the very rock and all black.

When they stood at the top of the steps and looked to their left, the room had a huge window the size of a cinema screen, the length and floor to ceiling of the vast space. The window was lit outside and had fish, rocks and seaweed like a huge aquarium. A second take made them realise it was the sea. They were below sea level.

The centre of the room had a beautiful carved marble fountain. Black chandeliers hung at intervals over the high ceiling. Comfy sofas, chairs and coffee tables were arranged all over the room like a gothic hotel lounge.

Overall it had the feeling of an old horror movie – equally it would make a great nightclub – but tonight it made a really cool wedding reception.

They all walked down the steps into the main room and began to get noticed. People came up to the royal couple one by one to congratulate them.

The first were Cash and Sean, who hugged Tia fiercely. They shook Dante's hand having never met him before. They announced who they were, but Dante was preoccupied looking for the third; the one he really wanted to meet.

Her brothers and her uncle were next. They led her towards the fountain where a beautiful, scantily clad woman was standing. She was taller than was usual with long blond locks tumbling over her blue green dress. Her skin was so white that it had a bluish tinge. Her eyes were large and brown like a deer.

Tia's mother, Dante thought. Both he and Tia were in awe of her, as neither had met a genuine full-blooded Murr before.

She curtsied low and gracefully before them. Dante bowed.

"May I introduce to you my wife, Naomi?" Sebastian pulled her in closer to him. "Alas my wife has no vocal cords but can communicate by projecting her words to you, and can hear your replies both spoken and thought."

My dearest child.

Dante pushed Tia closer to her mother causing her to almost trip into her. She leant in giving her a patronising pat on the back. "Mother."

She knew when Dante hid a smile by looking the other way. He then decided to save her, saying, "Thank you for this wonderful celebration. We look forward to getting your advice and discussing our future plans with you, but perhaps another time. Right now we would like to celebrate," and he kissed Naomi on both cheeks, which pleased her greatly. The old Irish charm worked every time.

"Of course, Your Highness." Sebastian bowed low and stepped backwards. Dante could get used to this shit.

As they went to walk away, Naomi stopped Tia with her hand as she went past. *Just a small private matter, Tia. Sometime soon, you will become overwhelmed with a need to be under water. Please do not ignore it, but seek me out. I will tell you what to do.*

Tia smiled uneasily, having no clue what she was referring to. Before she could question her further, Dante whisked her off to the nearest servant carrying glasses of champagne. She quickly forgot about it as Dante offered her a glass. "We need a drink."

***

Where the bloody hell was Jay? He'd been texting and phoning him on and off all day. He could do with his grounding influence right now. In the meantime he had to do all this king stuff. Endless cousins and officials from every branch of every Atlantean royal family were presenting themselves to him. It was such a yawn. Most of them he hadn't seen since childhood; if at all.

The only ones of special interest to him were the three really tall cousins dressed completely in black. They were introduced as princes from the Borge family, which meant they were Murr. Vionne, Dax and Caan bowed low. Dante gauged that Vionne was the oldest and would become Lord Advocate one day of the city of Murrtaine. That much he had learned. One to watch.

You'd better believe it! he heard in his own head.

"Fuck!" he said, shocked.

Yes, we can read thoughts, not just projected speech, Vionne replied and grinned.

Dante laughed, liking him right away.

Tia, oblivious of the internal conversation, smiled looking from one to the other.

Dante excused them from their cousins and moved them along. He had been keeping an eye on Tia the whole time and sensed, despite appearances, her growing anxiety and preoccupation as time wore on. He supposed it was through the new bond they shared.

She was looking for him. He'd sensed her melancholy a few times since he'd known her and guessed she was thinking of him. *Shit.* He'd strongly hoped that he'd wedged himself into the other guy's place in her heart, but watching her scanning the room, he wasn't that confidant.

"I'm just going to say hello over there, babe," he said, allowing her the time she wanted on her own. He kissed her cheek. "Will you be alright?"

"Sure," she said. Dante was sure he spotted relief, or did he feel it? He wasn't sure.

He walked away, chatting to guests, never taking his eye too far from her. He watched her start to move through the crowds till she found Cash. The two of them collected Sean on the way, and the three of them went to the lift.

Dante quickly caught on to them. He said a hasty goodbye to the people he was talking to and pushed quickly through the crowd to follow.

He let them get in to the lift and got in the service one, a few feet away. When it opened, it was further down the corridor in darkness. He walked slowly towards the voices and stayed in the shadows.

"Why didn't you make him come with you?" he heard Tia accusing her Protectors.

"He insisted on getting his head together, Tia." He heard Cash reply.

A phone beeped.

Sean checked his phone. "It's him. He's just pulled up."

Chapter 16

Tia went to rush outside. "No Tia." Sean grabbed her arm. "Stay inside."

She exhaled impatiently but did as she was told. She stood back smoothing down her dress, making herself look presentable. *Shit.*

Then Jay walked unobtrusively in through the big porch doorway. Dante could have cheered. *Thank fuck!* He was just about to walk out of the shadows to greet his best friend, when Tia ran and threw herself at him.

Jay caught her in his arms, buried his face in her shoulder and neck, and breathed in her scent.

Dante watched in disbelief as his friend kissed her like you read about; like they needed a fucking room.

No, this was not fucking happening. He was shaking his head to wake himself up as he walked out of the shadows and into the light.

Cash and Sean correctly read the situation instantly and faced Dante with their hands out, ready to halt his progress.

Dante noticed the second Jay opened his eyes and saw him. He broke his kiss and called him. No shame or guilt; like a, 'hey mate, there you are'.

"Jay, no ... Jay!" Tia said, trying to pull him backwards towards the front entrance.

"What? It's ok ... Tia, it's Dante," he said, not understanding at all.

"Jay, he doesn't know."

"What? What do you mean?" Jay said, frowning, trying to free himself from her grip.

"He doesn't fucking know!" She ended up shrieking at him.

Jay turned back to look at Dante, confused.

Dante felt a mixture of incomprehension, anger and then pain, while he struggled to get a handle on what was happening in front of his eyes.

"Dante. We spoke. You knew about her. We were cool, remember?" Jay said, looking back and forth between him and Tia.

Dante was shaking his head trying to compute; to fathom what the fuck was being said to him.

Jay tried reason again. "Marco and your brothers were in the States. I was there. They knew. I spoke to you afterwards?"

The extent of Marco's omission was starting to hit Dante in waves. "Your girl worked with horses, mine's a DJ," he said lamely, grabbing at straws.

"She does the horses with me," Cash said softly.

In his desperation Dante turned his attention to Tia. "I talked of Jay all the time and you knew?"

"I didn't Dante. I mean, I thought you knew about me and Jay, right up to just before we went into the pool, then I daren't tell you," she said, pleading.

Jay spun her round roughly to face him. "You went in the water with him?" He said jabbing his hand out towards Dante.

Dante interrupted, "Jay, she had no choice, man. It's part of the marriage." A thought popped into his head as he said it. "Hang on, who did you save my life for, you or him?" And he pointed back to Jay.

Tia started to back away from both of them. "For us both," she said, in a small voice.

Sean had seen enough at this point and pushed in front of Tia, right up in to Dante's face. "She's fucking innocent, leave her alone. For fuck sake, you're all innocent." He pushed Dante back in the chest.

As Dante eyeballed him, coiled and ready to go, about an inch from Sean's face, Jay pushed in between. "Stop! Let's cool down."

Dante pushed apart from all of them, grabbing an unopened bottle of scotch from the sideboard. "Just keep away from me the fucking lot of yer."

***

Jay looked around at them all and went to follow Dante.

"Jay?" Tia whimpered.

"Do not let her in the room," he said, ordering Sean and Cash and pointed as he walked past.

They both nodded.

Jay disappeared down the corridor. A door opened and slammed and then the door opened and slammed again.

"Oh my God!" Tia said, rushing into Cash's arms.

"Help him."

Sean shook his head. "Don't worry about him. He can handle himself. Believe me, I know what I'm talking about."

***

Dante was sitting at the desk in the library pouring a large scotch when Jay walked in. He closed the door and pushed a heavy sideboard in front of it, not wanting any interruptions.

"I hope you brought another bottle with you," Dante said, throwing the contents of his glass down his throat in one go and pouring another straight away. "Just go home Jay, okay," Dante said, looking up with hopelessness in his eyes. "I'm about to get fighting drunk."

"I can't," Jay said, flopping into the chair opposite Dante. "I mean, I am home, sort of."

Dante drew his eyebrows together in confusion.

"You're looking at the new son of Bonaci, CEO of the Bonaci Corporation and owner of The Bluebell boutique hotel; well, that is if I say yes."

"Fuck, when did they offer you all that?"

"Just after Tia left yesterday to go to you."

Dante thought about it for a moment. "They knew this was going to happen."

"I reckon they did. Alfonzo had talked it over with your dad and decided my previous relationship with Tia meant my existing circumstances was unworkable … whatever that means. They pitched it as a reward for services rendered; above and beyond the call of duty."

"Bastards."

"You know this was all your brother's doing?"

Dante nodded and simmered as he opened another bottle he'd found. "What happened in America?"

Jay leant forward with his elbows resting on his knees. "Cash called everyone who knew her when she'd fallen off her horse. Your brother had been sniffing around. I got there, and there was the three of them: Marco, Paolo, and Antonio. I couldn't believe it." He titled his head towards the door. "The two out there were there. Alfonzo turned up with her brothers. Then he explained to Tia who she was, and made her decide whether she was coming here. She didn't have much of a choice, Dante. Christ, I pretty much talked her into it, saying what an okay guy you were." He shook his head at how naive he'd been. "I stupidly assumed Marco would tell you about it straight away."

"I hit the roof when she told me she was in love with one of her Protectors … No wonder she didn't want to tell me it was you." Dante said, swilling his drink.

Jay's head reeled at the words; she was in love with him. *Fuck!* He shook himself out of it and pushed it to the back of his mind. "What happened in the water?" he said, cutting to the chase.

Dante stood up, grabbed a glass and poured a drink for Jay.

Jay shook his head. "What happened?" he repeated.

"Okay …" Dante drank Jay's drink and scratched his head, not knowing where to start. "You know how we test a Siren?"

"Yeah, I think I do. You make 'em stay under water to

see if they can breathe, don't ya?"

"Yes, well in a marriage, the man; and it has to be a prince, you know, pure blood, has to be trapped with her to the point of drowning."

"Fuck!" Jay leant forward, changing his mind for that drink.

Dante poured it for him. "And then the Siren has to decide whether she accepts him by either letting him die or breathing her life's essence into him. This kick starts his gills, enabling him to breathe under water and saves his life."

"Bloody hell! You had to do that?"

Dante nodded

"Was you scared?"

"Fucking terrified. She told me she loved her Protector about ten minutes before we went in."

Jay stifled a laugh, which made Dante laugh.

Dante threw his glass smashing it against the wall and put his tired head in his hands. Jay knew all too well when Dante mixed alcohol with head-fuck you got trouble in boatloads.

"I'm a fool Jay, she told me she loved someone else over and over and I ignored it … I got carried away and mistook her doing her duty for caring … you know? We fit … I thought we were the same … I thought we were …" Dante got up kicking the chair and knocking everything off the desk in a rage of self-recrimination and humiliation.

Jay sat still, calm and cool, but every muscle in him twitched in readiness. Dante drunk and in a temper was an unpredictable thing; a lot like an injured animal lashing out at anyone.

"You!" Dante said, pointing at Jay while he stalked towards him.

Jay stood quickly. His chair fell over backwards.

"Mr fucking calm. The first girl you've ever fucking liked and I've taken her." Dante said, laughing. "It's fucking priceless. We've fucked a cast of thousands, and the only one that either of us actually likes, is the same fucking girl. You couldn't make it up could you?" Dante leant on the edge of the desk to help him stop laughing. Then looked Jay ominously in the eye in all seriousness. "I'll never give her up Jay; we are bound now and it's permanent."

Jay imperceptibly shrugged, his face equally serious. "So what you saying?"

Dante flew at Jay, grabbed him around the head and took them down to the floor; breaking a chair to pieces. They rolled around in the fragments. Jay used all his strength and speed to avoid Dante's punches. He couldn't believe the strength in him.

Jay managed to punch him twice in the face, catching him in the eye and the mouth. Then he managed to get to his feet. Dante followed.

Someone was battering on the door. Then shouldering it - moving the sideboard inches at a time with every bash.

Dante pulled an oil painting off the wall and threw it at Jay across the room, then launched himself at him again. The momentum pushed the pair of them into a glass fronted display cabinet, showering glass and wood everywhere as they fell onto the floor again.

"Fucking stop it, Dante!" Jay said, breathing heavily, sitting on his chest.

Both men had cuts on their faces and skinned knuckles. Dante had a split lip and a black eye. Jay's cheekbone was swollen and he had a cut above the eye. Both were trying to catch their breath.

Jay eventually stood up and held his hand down and pulled Dante up.

"I won't give her up Jay. It's impossible now." Dante said, spitting blood onto the floor.

"I know." Jay said, still breathing hard with the exertion.

"What now?" Dante asked.

Jay walked right up into Dante's face. "I'm gonna go … but you fucking know I'm her Protector. A job for life, and if she comes to me of her own free will, I won't turn her away. Do you hear me? And you …" He almost touched Dante's nose with his. "You won't stop her."

Dante nodded slowly, eyes narrowed. "Deal."

Jay turned and walked towards the door just as Sean and Cash managed to push the oak chest far enough for them to squeeze into the room. They looked around at the damage; at the state of Dante and then the state of Jay.

"Make sure you tell her I'm still here for her." Jay said, over his shoulder on his way out.

Tia was standing with her back to the wall in the hallway, tears streaming down her cheeks as he walked by.

Jay made sure he looked down at the floor – not able to look at her. He walked briskly past her and out of the front door.

Tia slid down the wall, hugged her knees and wailed.

***

Dante poured the remainder of the second bottle of scotch into a glass and plonked into the chair behind the desk; the only one not smashed to pieces. He felt his face for damage, winced and looked at the blood on his fingers, and wondered where the hell he'd go from here.

The two Protectors had gone out of the room to see to Tia who was understandably very upset. He heard her brothers' voices outside as well. *Shit!* This was a fuck-up of mammoth proportions.

He looked up as his father pushed around the door, which was still partially obstructed by the chest Jay had put there. Fucking hell, he was all he needed.

"Jay's been then," his father said, scooping up any salvageable ornaments off the floor.

"You knew he was with her and never said a word," Dante accused, disgusted.

"Because you are such a fucking sap Dante, you would have refused to marry her," Christian shouted at the top of his voice and threw a china figurine, which bounced off the arm Dante used to protect his head. "That boy's worth ten of you."

"Once a waster always a waster," Dante replied, draining his glass. He'd heard it all before.

"When are you going to be a man," Christian spat.

"Be a king," he added at a shout.

Dante was about to come back with some juvenile comment when he heard Tia in his head. *Dante ... Dante. You are king. Always remember that. I pledged to you in the pool and I meant it. You have the power of my spirit always, so use it.*

Christian was going red from shouting, infuriated at Dante's apparent lack of response.

Quickly Dante's mind came back to his father.

Tia slipped into the room, and Cash, Sean and her brothers followed her. Her eye make-up was all gone from crying, he noticed. She came up to him and put her arm around his back in support and stood under the arm he put around her in a daze.

Dante looked back at his father. "I am king," he said quietly.

"Show it then," his father hissed.

Dante focussed his mind with every fibre of hatred in his being, for this man who had mentally and physically battered him for years, and brought him to his knees.

Christian's hands went to his throat while he choked, as if to remove an invisible noose. Dante went and stood over him. "I am king," he said, low and furious, pointing a finger. "You will address me as, Your Royal Highness. And if you ever raise your voice to me like that again, I will kill you." He let go of his mental hold and Christian sagged onto all fours, breathing and gulping for air.

Dante walked up to Tia, picked up her hand and led her towards the door. All Christian could do was meekly watch them go. Dante stopped at the door and faced

Cash and Sean. "She won't need you anymore tonight." And then he turned to Tia's brothers. "Please tell your father, that we thank him, but could not wait to go home and be alone."

Dino and Luca nodded and bowed.

Dante held Tia's hand, squeezed it, and walked through the hallway and out into the night with purpose.

***

When they got back to the Dubonnetti home, Dante went to walk up the main staircase to his old room.

"No Dante, let's sleep in the pool house," Tia said, laying a hand gently on his arm.

He looked at her hand and slowly turned and looked at her.

"We can do anything we want now you are king. We don't even have to live here if you don't want to."

"We?" he asked weakly.

"Of course, we."

He allowed her to lead him back down the stairs and in the direction of the basement in a daze.

When they reached it, "Lock us in," she said.

He did as she told him in confused silence. When he'd finished locking the entrances she was already sitting on the bed and taking her shoes off. Taking his cue, he began undoing his cuffs and shirt buttons. He eyed her with suspicion. "What is this, damage limitation?"

"There were no winners tonight, Dante, we were all losers," she said, wearily.

She wasn't wrong. He nodded with a deep sigh and put his silk shirt neatly over a chair.

She winced looking at his cuts and bruises. "Lay down," she said. "Let me get something for those."

She walked over and wet some hand towels in the shower under the cold water and dabbed one over the bruises on his chest and used another to clean his cuts. "To think I was worried about him earlier," she said, as she dabbed his split lip.

He flinched slightly. "He can take care of himself."

"You didn't use your power?"

"I'm not really used to it yet, and to be honest I'm not sure what difference it would have made."

"Have you fought with him before then?"

"All the time when we were kids," he said, smiling to himself. "My father used to bring him to play with us when we were small. I used to push him around getting him to do stuff I wanted him to do. But when he'd had enough, he'd punch me in the face and scrap with me like a navvy." He laughed at the good memories.

He got serious again. "Why did you help me, Tia?"

"I am married to you," she said, sounding a bit wounded. "I meant what I said when I pledged myself to you." She looked so genuine looking into his eyes. "And when your dad said that if you'd known you wouldn't have married me, and not been king, well, I thought, that's true, you wouldn't."

Dante sagged and his eyes shrank away from her.

"No, Dante," she said, making him look at her again. "That makes you a strong person, not weak. And then I thought, if this Atlantean nation – whatever it is – needs a king … well then, I thought you'd make a good one."

He looked at her with something like adoration at that moment.

"I never lied to you Dante. My feelings for Jay haven't changed. But, nor have they for you either." She bent down and planted the gentlest of kisses on his mouth and then either side of it and above each eye so as not to hurt him. "Come lie with me in the shallow end."

He grimaced as he stood up. His bruises had begun to come out around his ribs. She undid the button and zip on his trousers and helped him out of them. He undid her dress at the back and she pulled it over her head. She took him by the hand down to the shallow end, which you could paddle in, only a few inches deep. She helped him lay down and splashed him all over his body and then lay next to him and held his hand. They both looked up at the ceiling like a couple of kids watching clouds.

"He made me promise to tell you he's always there for you, if you need him," he said, without looking at her, not wanting to see her response.

She turned her head to look at him for a long moment. "You are a good friend, Dante," she said, eventually.

"Am I? I don't feel it." He felt the worse kind of traitor at that moment, but he wouldn't have wanted to be anywhere else in the world.

She turned onto her side and ran her fingers down his chest, barely touching him, down the trail of downy hair from his naval to his growing erection.

***

She allowed her finger to gently go along it. Around the

top, down to the weights underneath, to the inside of his legs and back again. She could see the flush already in his cheeks.

"You managed to do it with him?" he said, quietly.

She knew the question had to come eventually, "Yes, but only him."

He nodded as if this satisfied him.

Without saying anything else and wanting to cure both their hurt, she leant on her elbow and took him into her mouth. Then she began to slowly lick the route her finger had taken earlier. It felt necessary to worship his body in this Human way, although she knew, as she manoeuvred herself over him, looked into his fevered gaze and sank her body down onto him, that it would never be enough for them. "Open your mouth...I don't want to hurt you."

He parted his lips. His eyes never left hers.

While she still rode him in a gentle rhythm, she began a steady blow into his mouth. The light blossomed in his face like a flower opening to the sun. He groaned in ecstasy as his orgasm crept over him with a growing force. He gasped her name and she followed him over and over, on and on, relentless.

Chapter 17

Forgetting his aches and pains he pushed her into the deeper water to support their weight. He grabbed her hips roughly and re-entered her from behind. He wanted to control every part of her; completely encase her with his body so she could never escape.

Just when she would need to allow water into her lungs to breathe or pass out, he pulled her head to the side and reciprocated with his essence so she was forced to gulp in every particle of him, over her tongue and into her being. He pushed her forcefully on, owning everything.

An act of Human love was soon buffeted and bruised into something alien, but as necessary to them as breathing. It was a need that they could only satisfy with each other; both understood it like a solemn oath.

***

If you could bottle this feeling you'd make a fortune, Tia thought, as she luxuriated in the soft bed with Dante half on top of her, breathing into the crook of her neck.

A silk sheet covered their lower bodies and she wasn't too hot. Maybe because his body ran a few degrees cooler than a Human, as hers did. Wow, a first. She felt mellow and comfortable; the words, 'most compatible mate', echoed in her head.

Her perfect honeymoon night was only marred by the memory that Jay had gone and she didn't know if she'd ever see him again or whether Dante would allow it. She swallowed the lump in her throat that appeared whenever she thought of Jay.

Then she looked at Dante's sleeping and gorgeous body so wonderfully in tune with her own. God, it called to her with a power just as strong as any Siren and the attraction was growing exponentially. But he would need careful handling. He was passionate and unpredictable and used to always getting his own way. Pushed from pillar to post all her life, she valued her freedom more than anything else.

She felt him stir, especially below the waist. He knew what buttons to press with very little movement at all. Gyrating his hips and biting her shoulder was enough to ramp her temperature to over a hundred. She was covered in an instant film of sweat.

"Again," he said, as he lifted her arms above her head moving his lips down her body before too much heat was generated.

When he saw her skin at her hips flush red, he sat up scooping her up with him and walked to the pool.

"I need food, Dante." She pleaded from his arms.

"After." And he jumped straight in the deep end with her.

She had no time to even let the water in her lungs before he put his lips on hers to breathe into her mouth.

Shocked with the charge of electricity she went limp. Along with the overwhelming euphoria came an understanding of him: want, need and love eternal. It simply took her breath away. Such honesty and emotion was humbling and she melted to him as she found she always did, finding her rhythm with him under the water. Breathing life into him and him her, over and over, through every inch of the pool, at the surface, on the floor, until they were weak from hunger.

Three days they kept this up.

Mrs McNally brought them provisions through the garden entrance several times a day to keep their strength up. "How are ya lovely honeymooners doing?" she'd ask, every time she brought in a tray.

Tia couldn't help get caught up in the constant love and body worship that Dante showered on her, morning, noon and night. She certainly never had to question how he felt. Even without the bond he was ever passionate and demanding.

On the third morning the sun streamed in through the bank of windows and French doors that led onto the garden behind them.

Dante woke up and smiled his devilish smile, which was always a prelude to something wickedly naughty.

"Can we have breakfast outside today, Dante? It's beautiful outside."

He groaned. "We haven't got any clothes down here though."

"Come on, you can put your suit trousers on." She jumped up and slipped the green silk dress over her head that she'd worn to the party three nights previously, with no underwear on.

"You think you're safe in that?"

"I have no idea what happened to my knickers."

"Well, at your own risk," he said, as he swung his legs over the edge of the bed.

He phoned Mrs McNally in the kitchen to bring them some food.

Tia was already throwing the double doors open and breathing in the beautiful day. The garden was like a picture book, with flowers and shrubs and daisies in the lawn. She sat on the grass, cross-legged. Dante joined her, in just his suit trousers, and lay next to her with an arm around her backside.

Mrs McNally came along with a tray. "Well, this is an improvement honeymooners. You've made it twenty feet. Perhaps you'll make it up to the house tomorrow," she said, smiling at them.

"Sarcasm is the lowest form of wit," Dante replied, in his thickest Irish accent to parody Mrs McNally.

"Oh, I'm just kiddin ya, my lovelies. It's grand you've found each other, just grand. Ah, here's Master Stephan to join you, and Miss Joselle." Mrs McNally spread the picnic blanket on the grass, left the tray and went back to the kitchen.

"Stephan!" Dante, said, in greeting. "What's bothering you?"

He sat on the grass sombrely with Joselle, who gracefully sat next to him.

Tia noticed Joselle eyeing her messy appearance

disdainfully. She didn't blame her actually, as she hadn't put a brush through her hair for three days, and it had been wet and dried more times than she could remember. The ache between her legs made her think it was worth it and she smirked to herself.

Dante caught on to her smugness, and bored with his brother already teased her telepathically. He warned her of what he wanted to do to her as soon as they were alone. She answered him playfully and pointed out he'd have to catch her first and she'd have to tie a knot in it. This made them both giggle.

"Dante…Dante?" Stephan shouted, bringing back Dante's attention to him. "For fuck sake Dante, listen to me, this is important."

"Sorry Stephan," Dante tried to keep a straight face. "We can talk to each other in our heads, that's all … I wasn't listening. Please say it again."

"Really?" Stephan replied, almost longingly, obviously unaware that this was even possible with a Siren. His face got serious again. "Look Dante, Joselle and I want to be married like you and Tia. I demand to have the same as you." He sounded like a petulant child.

Dante sat up showing genuine concern. "It's not that easy Stephan, you know?"

"Why isn't it, you're the king aren't you? I've read the books. There has been some generations where all the Sirens married into the same family."

"That only happens when the rings in that family all went purple for each son … yours didn't for Joselle."

"So, why can't I just keep her?"

Tia giggled.

Dante tried to keep the smile off his face and failed. "She's not a puppy Stephan." He pulled himself together. "It means she has a mate out there in one of the other families."

Stephan looked sideways at Joselle. "What about if she knew where her sisters were?"

They were all silent at the bombshell.

"You do?" Dante said, eventually.

"Da," Joselle said. "We have connection. We are close."

Tia just stared at her absorbing what she said. This girl was supposed to be her sister and she felt nothing. She'd put it down to all the events over the last few days but now hearing her speak of a connection with her other sisters, why didn't she have that? Was there something wrong with her? Instead of growing on her, Joselle was starting to severely piss her off.

Dante looked at Tia and then back again. Deep thought creased his brow. "No Stephan. As soon as her uncle found out, he'd have to notify all the families. What you are suggesting is against the rules."

Tia didn't know why she was so relieved at his answer but she was.

"What could they do if we just married them first anyway?" Stephan said.

"Oh I don't know Stephan. That would cause some major fucking agro, wars even."

"What if we all married you?" Joselle threw in. "We pledge, but have our own partners."

Tia looked at Dante shocked. He looked like he was

actually considering it. Shock was quickly turning to horror. She got up and stomped back towards the pool house, the unzipped back of her dress flapping behind her.

"Look at state of her," she heard Joselle say as she left.

She felt a little better when Dante followed her trying to placate her. "Look babe, we have to consider all the options that's all. The power of the five is what any king needs."

She knew she was being irrational. "You want a fucking harem, is that it? I won't stay for that, Dante."

He pulled her to him and put his chin on the top of her head. Fuck, she hated that he knew she was bothered.

A few minutes passed while he held her like that, thinking. "I want you to release Jay as Protector," he said, out of nowhere, quietly into her hair.

"What has that got to do with anything?"

"Are you that cruel, that you would keep him tied to you all his life? We live long lives, Tia."

He was affectively bartering with her and it pissed her off. She turned in his arms and poked her finger into his bare chest. "Never! Do you hear me? Never will I release him." And she went to turn and stomp away from him.

He lunged and turned her back to him, trapping her in his arms.

"Let me go Dante, You can't control me," she gritted out as she fought.

He put his hand in her knotty hair and pulled her head back roughly. He stared angrily into her eyes. She saw and felt his want and frustration.

"I will use my power," she threatened.

"Don't pull the power card," he said, beginning to smile. "Your power is now my power, so against me, you have no power."

She struggled, wanting to scratch his eyes out.

He crushed her to him tighter so she couldn't move. "When I have your sisters' power, I will be more powerful than all of you. It is your whole purpose in life," he said, in triumph.

Way to make a girl feel like shit. She pushed her hands up between their bodies and began pummelling him with her fists. He grabbed her wrists looking like he enjoyed this new interaction. He put his mouth millimetres from hers. "When will you understand Tia, that you will never be free of me?" And he kissed her forcefully, crushing her lips and her body under his rough fingers; ripping off the thin dress, which had already fallen off one shoulder, revealing her breast.

Her struggles lessened and lessened as she realised this would always happen as he held her traitorous body prisoner and held the key to taunt her with. He only released her when he'd wrung an orgasm out of her some time later. Satisfied she was his slave, he relented and stroked her forehead, worn out. "I will make it so my brothers marry the others ... I can only handle one she-devil."

***

After two weeks, Dante was gradually starting to learn what it was to be king.

The Atlantean nation was spread across the Earth,

haphazard and disorganised. Blessed with fortune, which his father referred to as the Chi that few of them deserved, Earth's Atlanteans were greedy and acquisitive, lacking honour and the old values.

Chi came from the Orb and went back to the Orb as part of life's never ending circle. It was a mythical energy force rumoured to have come from Atlas with them ten thousand years before. The ancient jewellery they all carried had a piece of the orb and so it was believed that the Chi came to them. The old saying, 'money goes to money' comes from that very truth.

Dante was learning that Atlanteans weren't satisfied with riches, they wanted power and prestige. It was the only thing they really respected. And if they were ever to give an account of themselves to Atlas then they needed a great leader and to be a great leader Dante needed the power of the five Sirens and the standing that having them gave him.

Although it was illegal for him to effectively marry off the other princes' Sirens, it had never done the nation any good in the past sticking to the rules. When they had actually managed to secure their own, which had been rare, they had battled each other for supremacy, never agreeing on who should be king. But he was first and had found his Siren, so that put him ahead of the game. This time, in this generation, he had to box clever; bending the rules if he had to.

He vowed to himself as soon as he had the time, he would become an expert in Atlantean history and law so he could be a step ahead of his competitors and make full use of any loopholes.

In the meantime, he had secretly struck a deal with Joselle. In return for her bringing her three sisters to him, he would allow her to stay to be with his heartsick brother Stephan. But getting them there without anyone finding out was the important thing at the moment. Apparently, they'd been spread across Eastern Europe, but according to Joselle their sisterly bond was strong and it brought them together when her ballet had performed in Moscow. They'd stayed in touch ever since.

Tia thought it was a whole load of bullshit. She said she felt nothing for Joselle or anyone else for that matter. He didn't dismiss her instinct but thought it was probably the green-eyed monster and secretly enjoyed her being jealous. And besides, if they were imposters, surely Joselle would be spending her time kissing ass, not making an enemy of Tia.

The main problem he faced was getting them to Ireland as none of them had Protectors. That he thought was strange, considering Tia had three. Then he laughed to himself thinking, trust her to surround herself with men who all adored her.

This was the reason he paced to and fro in the study. He was mustering up the courage to pick up the phone. He hadn't had the bottle to do it until then, and he nervously dialled the number.

"Jason Gardiner," Jay said, confidently.

"Jay?"

"Is that you Dant?"

"Yeah man, you okay?"

"Yeah, I'm okay."

"Where are you?"

"I'm in London."

"The Bluebell?"

"No, I'm at the office, sorting stuff out, you know?"

"Oh yeah, you took the job then?"

"Yeah."

Things were awkward. Dante had so much he wanted to say but knew he never would, and he knew Jay internalised everything. The original 'Mr Cool'. "Listen Jay, I need you to do something for me."

"Like what?" Jay said, his voice flat.

"I have found Tia's remaining three sisters."

"I see…what do you need from me?"

"They have no protection and I need to get them home. I need to get them to throw their lot in with me before Alfonzo finds out about them."

"So what's that got to do with me? I have a slight conflict of interest, you know?"

"I know mate, but you are literally the only person I can trust. Can you get to Ireland?"

"Like when?"

"This weekend … I'm getting Tia to send Sean and Cash over with the plane to bring them back from Moscow. They only want to meet in a public place, so I'm hiring a local nightclub. I need to keep it secret so I can't use the Honourable Guard."

"What the fuck's that?" Jay said.

"Can you believe it? They are an underground unit of soldiers trained especially to look after the royal families, particularly the king and queen.

"Nice." Jay sounded impressed.

"Yeah, except if I use them, then Alfonzo knows about it."

"So let me get this straight. You want me as bodyguard for a load of Russian birds?"

Dante laughed, "Well…"

"Will she be there?"

"She ain't happy about any of it so I'm going to keep her busy DJ'ing. Sean and Cash should be okay looking after the Russian lot, so it is Tia I want you to keep an eye on really."

The line went quiet for a while. "What you gonna do, kidnap them?'

"I'm hoping it won't come to that."

"Fuck Dante, you've got me doing some crazy shit in your time."

"This is serious though Jay. This isn't being my wing man with twins, it's securing my bid for the crown."

"Are you going to marry them all?"

"No, I will get my brothers to marry them, but pledge loyalty to me."

He could hear Jay sigh. "Does Tia know I'll be there?"

The line was quiet for a beat. "She won't do it unless you are there."

Chapter 18

Tia had received a request to call on her from her mother Naomi. Blast, what did she want? Then she remembered the intriguing comment Naomi had made to her at the wedding reception, so she accepted the request out of curiosity more than anything.

Christian had loaned her the small sitting room to receive her for privacy and she waited anxiously for her arrival.

Eventually there was a quiet knock at the door, and she straightened in her chair as a servant showed the tall, unusual woman into the room.

In she glided and sat in the armchair opposite her. She nodded and blinked slowly as she sat very still. There was nothing Human about the woman at all. She couldn't help but stare at her. She was deathly pale. Her bone structure was good, but too angular. Her hair was long and lustrous, as was her own. But there the similarities ended. Her eyes were larger than hers and brown and her limbs were long and willowy. Scantily clad, she got the impression that clothes were worn more for convention than warmth. Her blood was probably even cooler than hers.

Tia snapped herself out of staring and leant forward in her seat to pour the tea.

Good day to you…

There was a pause.

Tia. As if her mother was remembering the name she preferred to be known by.

"Hello Mother." Tia replied with a frown at how weird it sounded. "Where is father?" She almost laughed at how ridiculous it was.

Naomi's expression didn't change at all. Nor did she move a muscle. *He is talking with Christian. He is allowing us some precious moments together.*

Tia put the teacup near her mother and sat back and sipped her own. There was a fat gaping silence between them. What should she say? Where have you been all my life? She decided against that.

Instantly a picture of a young mother clutching a tiny baby to her breast, flashed into her mind. It was so sudden and so vivid and strong it took her breath in shock. Had she read her mind?

Eerily, Naomi nodded and more of the pictures flowed into her mind like a slide show. Love and togetherness were the feelings that came along with it. Tia instinctively knew the baby was her. It was her mother and father sharing a moment of great love between them.

The pictures ceased as quickly as they came, and she came back to normal, but everything seemed dark as if the light had been taken. She put her hands up to her cheeks and felt that they were wet with tears. "What just happened?"

Naomi smiled. *We Murrs have no language of words. That we learned from Humans. We communicate through a series of mental pictures that we project with feelings. I merely sent you how I felt when you were born.*

Tia stared at her, still shell-shocked. They were much more powerful than any words. "You loved me then?"

Naomi blinked slowly and smiled. *Of course child, but I had no choice in giving you and your sisters up. I was devastated. I don't think I would have got through the long years if it weren't for your father.*

Tia swallowed hard and nodded, surprised at the depth of emotion she felt. She had grown hardened to the imagined set of parents she'd had since childhood.

You are sad child, I feel it.

Tia could feel her eyes glassing up.

Tell me, or can I roam the corridors of your mind?

Tia shook her head vigorously. There were some things even an estranged mother shouldn't see. She began cautiously. "I met and fell in love with my Protector before I met Dante … and now … everything's a mess."

Naomi nodded sagely. *Do not be too hard on yourself child. The fact that you succumbed to your husband is no crime, despite loving your Human.*

It felt like it was. "But I love Jay, I really do. How can I enjoy being with Dante the way I do knowing it hurts Jay?" She blurted. "It's as if I love Jay when I'm with Jay, but I love Dante when I'm with Dante."

Listen to me Tia. You have to stop trying to think like a Human when you are not. You fell in love with your

Human in a very Human way.

Tia arched a brow, but waited for her to continue. Being outed as an alien wasn't that comfortable to listen to.

Then you were forced to get in to the water with a male who genetically matches you perfectly. So not only does every cell in you welcome him, but for the first time in your life, you have met someone who can return your love in the natural way of your kind. I should say you do well to hold any feelings at all for your Human, especially as your bond with your husband only grows stronger with time.

Fuck. She allowed Naomi's words to sink in. She felt less of a tramp though.

Naomi stood. *I sense your father is ready to leave. Remember I am here for you daughter.*

Tia stood as well. "Thank you … for coming." Tia said, awkwardly.

Naomi touched her cheek gently as she floated gracefully towards the door. She stopped on the threshold. *Your love for your Human is on borrowed time Tia. Soon Dante will overrun you completely.* She closed the door and left the smell of fresh flowers behind her.

Tia flopped back into her chair, her heart and mind racing on what she'd learned. She'd been so preoccupied she hadn't even asked her mother what she'd meant the other night.

***

The night of the party came. Tia was dreading it and looking forward to it equally. She had an uneasy feeling about the impact these sisters of hers would make on her life. She'd always thought that having a sister would be nice, like a close buddy. So no-one was more surprised at her own reaction to them than her. But on the other hand, Jay would be there. He would keep an eye on things. Her stomach flipped at the mere thought of him.

Guilty, she looked over at Dante sitting next to her in the chauffeur driven car. He was holding her hand and looking straight ahead with purpose. Probably turning over in his head all the possible ramifications of the evening.

She let her eyes roam over him. From his beautiful profile to his body just made for sex; correction ... just made for sex with her.

His clothes were smarter these days; tailored suits, but always a bit edgy and always teamed with some sort of flamboyant shirt; a trademark of his. And lastly the large purple ring on his left hand, so much a part of him; a symbol of her.

Her mother's words were still in her head and she wondered if Dante was aware of the power he would hold over her. Everything in her screamed against the injustice of it.

"You okay?' he said, breaking the silence.

"Yes ... I'm not looking forward to tonight." Partly true.

Dante squeezed her hand and leant sideways giving her a chaste kiss on the lips. "Don't worry babe, it's just a necessary formality. It'll soon be over."

She nodded, not convinced.

They pulled up outside the club. Dante's brothers

pulled up in the car behind them with Joselle. The other sisters had arrived the day before and were installed in the house rented for Cash and Sean; the one she had stayed in when she first came to Ireland. She didn't like that either. Why couldn't they get their own Protectors?

They all got out of the cars and were ushered into the club by bouncers employed by Dante.

The party was already buzzing. Dante and his brothers all looked like male models; although Dante was a little more rock 'n roll. Joselle looked demure in a beautiful floor-length silver gown.

Tia looked down at herself. She wore battered bleached jeans and an army shirt with the sleeves rolled up. Her hair was in a loose ponytail, she had put on her customary visor sunglasses to cover up her eyes that were worryingly getting worse – possibly because of the amount of time she was now spending under water – and she clutched her record case in her hand.

She had argued with Dante over what she would wear, which had resulted in her going for the tattiest thing she could find in defiance. She had to put her foot down to safeguard the smallest of freedoms.

They stood on the threshold of the main room of the club. Tia surveyed it and found Jay's eyes in an instant. He looked away and resumed helping the technician on the DJ's dais. When he looked back and gave her his shy smile and blushed her heart fell into her boots. *Fuck!* She felt exactly the same for him. She had wondered if Dante had supplanted him in the time she had known him, especially after what her mother had said, but no can do. She didn't know if that was a good thing or not and sighed ruefully.

Jay's mixture of shyness, confidence and aloofness, as well as his banging hot body was as irresistible to her as it always was. Her sense of foreboding intensified.

Dante cut across her thoughts. "Tia. It's time. They are all in the VIP lounge."

"I want Jay to come in with me."

He looked at her in silence for a beat then raised his hand to beckon Jay over.

Tia was amazed at the emotion on Dante's face as he pulled Jay into his body for a hug. She would never fully understand the dynamics of their relationship. She watched transfixed as Dante whispered something intimately close to Jay's ear and Jay nodded. Then Jay came and stood behind her. Every cell in her back lit up like a Christmas tree at his close proximity to her. Her heart thumped.

Dante glanced at her before walking on towards the VIP lounge. *Fuck! He can read my feelings.*

Her heart stopped when she began to walk and Jay leant forward next to her ear and asked if she was okay.

She nodded, allowing herself a quick glance at him.

"Glad you've dressed up for the occasion!" he added.

She smiled nervously. "You know me."

She couldn't look at him longer than a second and faced front as her face burned at the memory of the last time she'd dressed inappropriately – and how they had felt then.

Her train of thought halted when they entered the

VIP lounge. Joselle pushed past her rudely and rushed into the arms of her sisters who sat on a group of sofas around a low table.

Cash and Sean stood behind them, propping up a small bar in the corner.

Joselle got up again and motioned for her sisters to do the same. Dante stepped forward and called his brothers to stand with him. Tia was pushed into the background.

"Okay?" Jay asked again, at her ear.

"Yeah … I feel nothing for them though. Is that normal?"

Jay shrugged, keeping an eye on the show playing out in front of them.

"Your Royal Highness. Please may I introduce my sisters?"

First to come forward was a girl introduced as Genevieve. She had loads of blond hair glacier blue eyes and a good figure poured into pale blue, long, hugging gown.

The next was Cocoa. What kind of a name was that? She had straight red hair with a fringe, brown eyes, and was wearing a masculine black suit – expensive though. Lastly, there was Tamsin, classy looking with a severe black bob and wearing a short black cocktail dress. All three were good looking, but nothing like each other and most of all, nothing like her. Was that likely?

Dante kissed each girl's hand, and each one bobbed a perfect curtsy. *Give me strength.* The girls were almost stepping on each other to get to him.

He then called each brother over in turn and

introduced them. All the while he looked at each of their rings. Turquoise everyone; none went purple. *Yes!*

Then the moment she'd been dreading, Dante called her over. She felt Jay come with her. Relieved, she stood into his body heat as Dante introduced her as their eldest sister. Each one looked her up and down, not even hiding their obvious shock and disdain.

Jay squeezed her arm to steady her. Situations such as these always made her want to play up to the label given her. To Dante's credit he pulled her to him and introduced her as his new wife and kissed her on the cheek. She felt like shouting, 'In your face,' and giving them the finger, but restrained herself just in time. Besides, she wasn't sure whether he was reinforcing her position so the sisters could see or staking his claim for Jay's benefit.

"Hello," was all she managed to squeeze out. "Can I go and set up now?" She said, looking up at Dante like a small child.

"Go," he said, like a parent worn down. "I'll stay here and get them paired off with my brothers."

She heard him call Sean and Cash over so she rushed to them first. She kissed and hugged them quickly, then heard Dante say to them, "No-one leaves."

They both nodded.

Grateful to get away, she sloped back through the partygoers with Jay.

***

She introduced herself to the resident DJ who was playing just before she went on.

He was a tall, wirey, guy with a ponytail. "Hi, I think I heard you play at The Ministry?" he said.

"Yeah? It would have been a while back now."

He kissed her on the cheek and said he looked forward to hearing her set.

She sorted through her records to get an idea of a rough order she would play. It all depended on the crowd though, what her final set would be. "I need the ladies room before I go on," she said, to Jay.

"Come on. I'll show you where they are... The Ministry? Me and Dante could have been there," he said, while they walked.

"I doubt it. I would have felt it if Dante was there," she said. *Fuck!* She glanced at him and could have kicked herself when he looked away.

Cursing herself, she followed him out to the cloakroom and down a staircase into the basement where the toilets were. When they got to the bottom she pulled him aside, under the stairwell. "How are you?"

"I'm good thanks," he said, smiling down at her, giving nothing away.

"You're working for my father, Dante said?"

"Yeah ... I'm your new adopted brother," he said, looking awkward down at his feet.

She reached up to touch his face with her hand and lifted her glasses to see him more clearly.

His brow creased in concern. "Your eyes Tia. Are they okay?"

"They're fine. It's when I go under water. The more I do it, the less they go back to normal, that's all."

He stepped back out of reach from her touch, as if coming to his senses. "I can't afford to have any feelings for you, Tia. It's not what I do," he said, quietly.

"I have feelings for you still." Her voice was small.

He just stood there silently, not saying anything further, a long gaping silence.

"Do you want me to release you?" she said, eventually. Her eyes were glassing up, to her annoyance. She shook her head to get a grip on herself, then braced herself for his answer.

"I said I'd always be here for you and so I will." His gaze was intense.

She nodded, relieved. "Come on then, I'd better go on before I punch one of those stuck-up cows."

He just smiled and held out his arm for her to go first, relieved to be off the hook.

Fuck! Fuck! Fuck! She felt like she'd been kicked in the guts. Through all Dante's tantrums, the punched walls, kicked furniture, shouts and demands; he couldn't hide how he felt. And that she found strangely comforting. But Jay, she had no clue. She had no rights to him she knew, but it didn't make it hurt any less. He wouldn't leave me though, she thought, and clung on to that like a life raft.

Chapter 19

Dante watched her do her thing from the back of the room. He hadn't had much opportunity before and was too curious to miss the chance. How cute she looked with the big earphones on over one ear; the way she rode the music and picked her tunes totally absorbed. Flipping and picking records quickly, playing short samples, knowing when to play the record through. She was amazing.

He glanced over at Jay. It was the first time Jay had seen her in action and he could tell he wasn't unaffected, as cool as he was.

The crowd was buzzing. You could tell the Humans straight off. They were the ones who'd been whipped up in Tia's music and threw themselves around and couldn't sit until she let them. The only ones who resisted the pull of the music were those royals present, and Jay, who, having drunk Elixir, was immune.

Each time she lost herself in the rhythm and the music dropped, she would pulse her power, which rippled invisibly over the clubbers' heads. But he could see it like a ghostly cloud. After watching her a while, he concluded that she couldn't help doing it. The biggest revelation to him was that he could feel her do it deep inside him and filed the knowledge away.

He looked over at her sisters all dancing gracefully in the crowd. Each one had latched on to one of his brothers according to plan. Stephan and Joselle were smooching in the corner.

Yes, tonight had been a success. He couldn't afford to let the grass grow though. He needed to get them to his home tonight, test them and get them married off tomorrow. Then he could announce it to Tia's father and uncle so his full recognition as king could be proclaimed worldwide. He was already king in name, but until all the Sirens were accounted for he didn't feel secure. Now he was in this world, he was realising it was an uncertain, dangerous place.

***

Dante and Jay were in the viewing room back at Dante's family home. Each girl had been tested and all seemed to have passed with flying colours.

Dante had hoped that after witnessing it that Tia would have warmed towards her sisters, but she hadn't.

"They have no markings," was all she could say. "They are nothing like me."

"Except they breathe under water," Dante reminded her, and she flounced off and left him and Jay alone.

"Tia is not very enamoured of her sisters," Jay commented after she'd gone.

"Ah, she'll get used to them over time."

They were quiet for a while, both looking into the blue

of the tank.

"I'm sorry Jay."

Jay turned to face him with his hands in his pockets. "Why? You belong together."

"Still, I am sorry."

Jay nodded and turned back to the tank.

"If it's any consolation, I'm jealous of you," Dante said.

Jay choked down a laugh. "Why would you be jealous of me, you're king, for fuck sake? You've managed to find your destined mate and marry her."

"But that's just it Jay, I'll never know if she's attracted to me or whether it's just some hocus pocus, destiny shit. You, on the other hand, she loves, even though the odds are stacked against you."

He scoffed. "What about if the ring just picks out your most compatible mate for reproduction or something like that? And it is nothing to do with love. You must have something she wants?" and Jay laughed, making Dante laugh.

"I'm a sex god; and you know that," Dante said, indignant, and they both laughed like old times.

"Should your brother be in there with her?" Jay said, pointing at the tank.

"What?" Dante said, walking over to see what Jay was looking at. "What the fuck? That's Stephan and Joselle. He's trying to get himself hitched. Little fucker. I'm going to kill him when he gets out."

"What's he trying to do?"

"Watch … when his air supply runs out, she'll breathe into his mouth and bang! They're married," Dante explained.

Jay shrugged. "No hassle I suppose."

They watched shoulder to shoulder. It was obvious when Stephan had run out of air and he began to struggle.

"Come on?" Dante urged. He banged on the window. "Breathe for him you stupid bitch! I'm going to have to go in if he doesn't breathe in a minute. The stupid cow is killing him ... Fuck! I'm going up. Call everyone!"

Dante shot up the stairs to the pool house.

***

Jay ran up the stairs to the main house and called for anyone to come. He followed them back down as everyone rushed past him up to the pool. He watched the tank in morbid curiosity, only dragging his eyes away when Tia came into the room and stood next to him.

They watched Dante swim down and push Stephan up through the hatch and saw legs and arms grapple and pull Stephan out of the water. Then they couldn't believe their eyes, as amongst the bodies swimming above the hatch there appeared to be females. They then swam through the opening, shutting it as they went through. It was clear then that the four females were Joselle and her sisters now locked in the tank with Dante.

"Can he breathe?" Jay asked. Panic was rising in his voice as he looked from her to the tank.

"He can do it on his own now," she said, stony-faced.

Jay didn't understand the look on her face. Distracted he turned back to the scene playing out in front of them.

First Joselle came up to Dante and took hold of each side of his face and looked as though she was leaning in for a kiss. Then Cocoa did the same. She then swam backwards to allow Genevieve and Tamsin to repeat the process. Each time Dante's arms went around them in an embrace as they approached him.

"Son of a bitch!" Tia said, low, like a growl.

"What? Should we get him out?" Jay said, in complete confusion.

"He can fucking drown for all I care."

It was obvious to Jay when Dante realised that Tia was watching him, as he looked straight at her. Tia turned and walked away holding her temples. "Get out of my head," she spat.

"You okay?" Jay said, coming over to her.

"He's trying to speak to me in my head." Tia looked up at Jay, "Take me away from here Jay. I never want to come back."

After checking her face to make sure she was deadly serious, he said, "Come on then, let's go now." Then when they got to the hallway upstairs he asked, "Do you need anything?"

"No! Just go." She continued to hold her head.

They could hear echoes of voices, bangs and crashes of what sounded like a fight coming from the pool.

Jay took out his phone and dialled a number as he led Tia out of the house to his car. "Sean? Yeah, I'm okay… look, meet me with Cash at the airport … now … yes, I have her with me … yes, the Bonaci jet." He put his phone back in his pocket and put her in the passenger side of his car. He watched her continually holding her head as if in pain, "Tia?" he checked again.

"I'm trying to block him out."

The further away they got the more she let go of her head. "It's better the more we get away," she said.

"Are you sure about this Tia? It's not too late to think about it."

"No I'm sure, Jay … take me away."

Chapter 20

As Tia wanted to get as far away as possible, their course was set for America and Cash's ranch in Montana. There, Tia could take a break and recalibrate her future.

Once they had got up in the air Jay picked up his phone ready to dial.

"Who are you ringing?" Tia asked in panic.

"Your uncle."

"I won't go back."

"I've got to tell someone, Tia."

She shrank back in her chair.

"Alfonzo? Yes, it's Jay. Sorry to ring you so late but something has come up which couldn't wait … Tia asked me to remove her from the Dubonnetti house tonight … We are all on the plane to Montana … Dante has four women he believes are Tia's sisters … He tested them tonight."

The others on the plane were all quiet, earwigging on the conversation.

Jay took the phone away from his ear. "Your uncle asked if you still pledge your allegiance to Dante?"

Tia pulled a face while she thought. "Yes, but I don't

want to live with him."

"I see … yes, I'll tell her … Okay, you're welcome." And he clicked off his phone.

"What did he say?" Tia asked.

"Surprisingly, he said you did the right thing by going, I did the right thing by taking you, and you'll never believe this?"

"What?" everyone said.

"They can't be Sirens; at least one of them can't"

"Bloody hell!" Tia said. "How does he know that?"

Everyone sat forward to listen.

"He knows exactly where one of them is, and who she is meant to be with."

They all looked at each other amazed at the revelation. "What's he gonna do?" Tia asked.

"Your uncle said he's going to leave Dante in his own mess for a while to teach him a lesson, and then when he is ready he will take over and teach him to be a proper king and get him away from his family."

"Blimey!" Was all Tia could say.

***

After the excitement had died down, Tia sunk down into her chair and wallowed in the latest mess that was her life. *God, I've been in this Atlantean world for five bloody minutes and it's already turned to shit.*

Dante was still in her head but he was bearable now, as she put some distance between them. She looked over at Jay on his phone and laptop simultaneously. It struck her how poles apart her two men were. Dante demanded her attention twenty-four hours a day, and yet could do something like this. And Jay was always out of reach – perhaps that was his appeal; the unobtainable. But she didn't really believe that. Her thoughts continued to meander as she looked out the black screen of her window.

Eventually she looked around and realised that Sarah, Sean's fiancé, sat in a chair across the way, was saying something to her.

"Oh I'm sorry Sarah, I was lost in thought. Yes, I'll live. How are you feeling? Sean told me your happy news, congratulations."

Sarah looked pregnant even though she could only be a couple of months along. She hadn't been noticed in all the kafuffle but Tia assumed that the poor girl had been dragged along purely because she happened to be there and Sean couldn't very well leave her behind.

"Yes I'm okay, a bit tired. I've got a while to go yet."

It was good for Tia to talk chitchat and take her mind off her problems.

Sean came over and rested a loving hand on Sarah's bump and kissed her on the cheek. Sean got called away to look at something so Sarah came over and sat closer to Tia. "You know I hated you when I first knew Sean."

Tia was a little taken aback at her candour. "I can bet, always calling him at odd hours."

"I thought he had a relationship with you," Sarah continued, accusation in her eyes.

Tia sensed this was something Sarah needed to get off her chest. "Sean is a friend. Cash is a friend. There has never been anything other than that." She hoped that satisfied her. Then tiredness so strong began to sweep over her. She wasn't sure how much more she could handle – not today anyway.

"I suppose I just resented that he would drop anything to go to you."

Tia looked at Sarah's eyes and guessed the unsaid words were that, she still does.

"Sarah, I'm really grateful and so is my family, for the sacrifice you and Sean make. And we'll make sure you are all really looked after; especially your new addition." She laughed as she said it trying to lighten the mood, but she made a mental note to have a chat with Sean about his circumstances. She hated the thought of him being unhappy in his service to her. She needed all her friends now.

***

Tia was exhausted by the time Cash showed her to her old room at his ranch.

"Come here girl," Cash said, in his lovely accent. He pulled her to him in a bear hug only he could give her.

She let him envelop her and breathed in his scent, all lovely, manly and safe. He felt like the father figure she'd never had. He just swayed and held her.

"Where's Jay?" she asked, eventually.

He sighed. "I put him next door." He pulled back to look at her face. "You still feel the same about him?"

She nodded and looked down ashamed. "I know I have no right, but I can't help it." Tears began to stream down her face. It was like a dam breaking and she began to sob. She didn't know if it was the hurt from Dante's betrayal, or Dante being so hurt, or that Jay was so distant, or the lack of sleep, or the whole bloody lot.

Cash just continued to sway with her as he said, "Shh," every so often.

***

Jay closed his eyes as he heard Tia's sobbing through the wall. He'd acted on impulse when she'd asked to go, but now he'd got her away he wasn't sure what he was meant to do with her. He was sure she'd be fine here with Cash. He could go back to London and carry on his corporate work for the Bonaci Corps, but the thought of walking away from her now she was free was going to be difficult for him, which simply wasn't logical.

His phone rang. *Shit. Dante. Fuck.* He may as well get this over with. "Hello?"

"Is she with you?" He sounded ruined – his voice almost gone.

"Yes," Jay answered.

There was a silence for a few moments.

"Can you tell her they jumped me Jay? I didn't plan it, it just happened."

"Look mate, I was standing with her, she saw what she saw. It's none of my business … I doubt it was just that." His old friend surprised Jay. He didn't rail or swear at him or threaten him. He sounded like the shit had been kicked out of him. But Dante did everything in a big way, so it stood to reason that if he fell in love then it would be hard.

"Will you tell her?" Dante asked.

"Of course."

"And look after her."

This really cut Jay to the quick. Dante was usually so selfish …"I will."

The phone clicked dead. Jay looked at the dead phone, as dead as his childhood friend. That guy had gone forever. With a heavy heart, he put his phone away.

***

Every time Jay went to leave there seemed to come up a reason to stay. He'd barely said a word to her, but leaving her felt as hard as saying goodbye to your record collection or that favourite leather jacket. It just wouldn't happen. And so he watched her mope about.

Every day she would get up early, ride and help out with the horses. He would lie in his bed –not a morning person. She would take a book and sit on the swinging chair on the veranda. He'd work on his computer and on conference calls.

Cash tried his best, give him his due, to organise dinners or barbeques to get Tia to loosen up. But she'd just grab something and take it to her room like a teenager. Fuck, he didn't know what do with her or what she wanted.

That evening, he sat, kicking back with a beer with Cash and Sean. Tia had gone to bed as usual and Sarah had gone too, as she was still in the first stages of pregnancy and got really tired.

I'm going back soon, I want Sarah to have her check ups at home," Sean informed them.

Jay and Cash both nodded, as it seemed the natural thing to do.

"I wish Tia would perk up before I go," Sean said, directing his gaze at Jay.

Jay looked sideways at Cash who was giving him the eye as well. "What?"

"You can't think of anything?" Cash said.

"Fuck knows. I'm beginning to think I did the wrong thing in taking her from Dante."

Cash and Sean just rolled their eyes.

"What?"

Cash got up and grabbed another beer for each of them, then plonked back into his chair. "You never told us how you met her … I mean, it still amazes me how the fates work." He pointed to Jay's bracelet. "You were best friends with the future king and you cross paths with a crooked Protector, win his talisman and come into the path of a Siren." Cash whistled and shook his head. "That's some crazy shit right there."

Jay raised his eyebrows in acknowledgement and nodded. He had to admit that the coincidences that landed him in the Atlantean world were adding up. He took a deep breath and exhaled loudly. "It was a couple of years back," he began, "I used to play a lot of cards. You see I had really good luck. I mean, I used to tell myself I was a clever poker player, but now? I'm not so sure." He smiled ruefully at Cash and Sean who got his drift.

Dannyl lived over in Shoreditch, East London. He had a little dive with a basement and bar. It was done out tacky – you know, like a Copa-cabana. I got there late, this particular night…

***

The game had already started. Dannyl had specifically invited Jay as he'd taken all his money at another game the month before.

He followed the black bouncer down the concrete steps, into the basement, past the little beach bar covered in bamboo. That was when he first saw her. She looked about sixteen years old, but she was beautiful even then. She was busy putting away clean glasses when she first flashed those eyes at him. They stopped him in his tracks. He'd never forgotten it. He had to snap himself out of his stare before he got caught out. You never let Dannyl know you liked something – especially if it was his.

Jay sat down to the game.

Dannyl was a rubbish player, so Jay had to let him win a few rounds so he could keep his temper and save face. But every so often Jay had to take another peak at the girl who worked away as unobtrusively as she could, until she was eventually finished.

She took a last lingering look over at the poker table as she ascended the stairs and Jay couldn't pull his eyes away.

"You like my woman, Jay?" Dannyl said.

Shit! Captured. But knowing Dannyl he'd clocked him all along. He decided to brazen it out. "What's not to like? She's beautiful," Jay said, not missing a beat. He regretted showing his hand. He wasn't sure what Dannyl would do to her after when no-one was around.

"Hands off Casanova," Dannyl said.

The others round the table chuckled.

"She's just a baby."

Jay bowed his head slightly. "I wouldn't dream." But he knew Dannyl didn't care two shits how old she was.

Jay lost patience after she'd gone and cleaned Dannyl out soon after. All he had left was his jewellery and the club they were sitting in.

Deciding to leave Dannyl on good terms after his whipping, he just took his jewellery. He put the bracelet on and wore it ever since ...

***

"Now of course it seems that was meant to happen all along," Jay said, coming back to the present. "Why, I have no idea."

Cash and Sean both looked amazed.

"Did you see her again after that?" Sean asked.

Jay shook his head. "Nah. I sent out a few feelers to see if she was okay, but it wasn't long after that we heard Dannyl was dead. I figured she was all right then. It wasn't till months later I heard that a girl had been arrested for it. I didn't have a clue it was her though. I didn't see her again until she walked into my hotel a few weeks ago."

"Shit," Sean said.

"What?"

Sean looked at Cash

Cash understood immediately. "It was around that time that Tia got arrested."

"What, you mean it could have been over me? Do you know what happened? I never asked her, and she never volunteered the details when she touched on it," Jay said.

"The guy was the worst kind of bully. You were right. He didn't care how young she was; easy to control, having no-one to look out for her. Fuck, it was supposed to be him." Cash said, pointing at Jay's bracelet again."

Jay's heart began to sink as he could guess what came next. "What did he do?" he asked, bracing himself.

"She didn't tell me much. She's closed mouthed about most things in her past, but she did tell me that when he wanted to take something out on someone he would tie her up and beat her."

Jay closed his eyes. He'd suspected as much, but hearing it put into words … "Did she kill him?" He hoped she did, and made him pay.

"Well, she isn't sure really, but I think she did." Cash looked at Sean, and he nodded in agreement. "You see, she didn't know of her powers then. She said one night he tried to force himself on her, and when he tried to kiss her, she said he froze, keeled over and died. Just like that, his heart failed. But instead of running, she called an ambulance and the police got involved and she ended up getting arrested. And with no-one to fight her corner, she ended up in a youth remand centre, which is where she crossed paths with me," Cash said, smiling.

"How do you think she killed him?" Jay asked, more curious than anything.

"Just as they can breathe their spirit into a person, they can take a spirit away … when he locked lips with her, it was the kiss of death, literally."

Jay sat back and absorbed the info. It all made sense,

and his mind flashed back to what Dino had said to him back at the hospital, when he'd first given him Elixir.

He ran the stones of his bracelet between his fingers. Something, somewhere, had delivered this bracelet into his hands, so that when he met Tia again he could look after her. It was astounding. If you thought about it too long it would blow your mind, what with all the other implications of Dante, and the Dubonnetti, and everything else. He dragged his mind out of its tailspin. "You always knew what you were?" he said to both Cash and Sean.

"Pretty much," they both replied.

"And you weren't tempted," Jay said, though narrowed eyes.

Sean looked at Cash, who answered first. "Of course we were tempted. But we knew what we were, and what she was, and it would have been foolish to have even contemplated going there … It was easy for me to take on a more fatherly role."

"What about you?" Jay said directly at Sean. He noticed how quiet he'd been.

"He's right … I never went there. Look, shall we get back to deciding what we are going to do to perk her up?" Sean said, obviously not comfortable with the conversation continuing in that direction.

Jay continued to look at Sean a while longer, but decided to let it go … for now. He sat quietly sipping his beer until he felt the two other men staring at him again.

His eyes moved from one to the other when he realised

they were waiting for him. "Look the only thing she likes is music and horses."

"That's all?" Sean said.

"Horses ain't doing it," Cash added, swigging his beer.

They were like a bloody double act.

A thought struck Jay. Today is Tuesday. He could probably get them here by the weekend. "Do you have a barn that's empty, Cash?

"I do."

"Can you get a few people together for a party this weekend?"

"Sure I can." Cash saw where he was going.

Jay got up. "I've just got to order something online. It must be here before Saturday."

Cash and Sean clinked beer bottles.

***

They arrived on Friday. Jay and Sean spent ages faffing, trying to put them together. They eventually enlisted an electronics whiz that Cash knew. Finally, by the Saturday morning, they were ready.

They couldn't fully test them without giving the game away, so Jay prayed that everything worked.

"Go get her," Sean said, when they'd finished.

Jay found her curled up with a book on the swinging sofa on the porch. She looked so small and fragile at that moment. As if she were wasting away with melancholy.

"Tia!" he said, as he walked up to her.

She instantly shut her book and sat up. She looked on tenterhooks.

"Can you come with me? I want to show you

something."

"Okay," she said, warily, as if she didn't like the sound of it.

Fuck, he hoped this worked. He was at a loss if it didn't.

He led her to the barn and threw the sliding door across. She walked in and looked at the bunting and balloons and hay bales arranged like seats, that he, Cash and Sean had spent hours arranging.

Cash and Sean grinned and held out their arms to present the surprise.

"Record decks!" She shrieked

"Surprise." They all shouted.

She burst into floods of tears.

***

She just stood like a baby with her hands over her eyes. She felt arms go round her – mmm, Jay's, and snuggled into him crying all the more as the floodgates opened.

"Fuck. Tia, I'm sorry. I thought you'd like it. I wouldn't have done it if I'd known."

"I love it," she said, between hiccupping sobs.

"You what?"

"I love it … it's the nicest … thing anyone's … ever done for me." And she wailed again.

"It's okay." Jay breathed a sigh of relief as he looked up at Cash and Sean. "She likes it."

She completely milked the opportunity to wrap her arms around Jay; it had been so long.

Cash and Sean came over. "Come on soppy," Sean said, laughing. "You've got to play tonight, Cash has arranged a party."

She looked up at Jay for confirmation. He just looked down at her and nodded.

"Records?" She shouted. "What am I gonna do without records?"

"It's okay, I've ordered a selection of some of the ones I've heard you play – Sean helped. And I put in a few I like."

She wiped her eyes and nose with the back of her arm. God, she must look a sight. "I'd better practice." And she broke away from Jay's arms and began to ooh and aah over the crisp new twelve inches. She slid them out of their sleeves and treated them like they were precious. Soon she was cuing up and practicing in a world of her own.

The boys left her to it.

"Bass. I need more bass," she shouted, as she dropped in a break beat.

***

The night was a great success. Some of the older stable hands were even two-stepping to a dance classic by Masters At Work – much to Jay and Sean's amusement.

Lots of alcohol was being consumed and everyone was having a great time, even though, for the most part, those invited had never heard a lot of the music before. But as usual, Tia had her crowd in the palm of her hand, to do with what she would.

Jay watched her with awe. Her skill was astounding. He couldn't believe that he hadn't known this part of her for so long. Music and rhythm was obviously at the very root of her being, and he could have kicked himself for not thinking of this therapy earlier.

He watched as Cash managed to get her to play some old country music for the old folks, as he called them. She must have took pity on them as she gave in and played some records that Cash handed to her, and he could tell she'd never heard of them.

Cash then took to the floor with a lovely flame-haired lady, who came in once a month to do his books.

Sean, he noticed, was whispering and laughing while he sat on a hay bale with Sarah, taking the load off.

Jay shuffled his feet awkwardly, with his hands in his pockets when he saw Tia making her way towards him.

"I've handed over to Jeff," she said, in way of explanation.

"You wanna drink?" he asked.

"Yeah, a long one."

They walked over to the improvised bar, rigged up by Cash. Just a few kegs with some pretty fairy lights around.

"You played my favourite song," he said.

"Oh really, which one?"

"*Heaven.* The Chimes."

"Aah, so you're old school. I saw you moving to that. You're a sexy mover."

Jay felt himself blush. "Oh I just shuffle around."

"No. Understatement is cool. Less is more, you know?"

He laughed and looked into her face. She was radiant tonight, and he felt the familiar pull towards her. He also noticed that they'd subconsciously stood closer and closer into each other's personal space. He kidded himself it was because they couldn't hear, but they sipped their drinks at the same time as well. "Do you reel me in like you do your audience?"

She looked up at him wide eyed and shocked. "Why, is it working?'

He laughed.

"What?" she said. "Seriously, I don't know what I do to people."

He felt suddenly reckless. "You do something to me," he said, quietly, leaning down so his face was mere inches from hers. "You really don't know what you do to me?"

Her lids lowered as she stepped in so her lower body touched him. "I know what I want to do to you."

The electric atmosphere was cut when Cash walked up to them with the lovely Miranda on his arm. Jay and Tia instantly sprang apart, but Cash had definitely noticed and flashed a knowing smile at him. Jay just scratched his head nervously.

"It's breaking up about now. I'm going to go in and make some hot chocolate if you want some?" Cash said.

"Sure." Jay said. He looked at Tia. "You can sort out your records tomorrow."

"Yeah, good idea. I'm knackered. Thank you both for a lovely surprise." She kissed them both on the cheek.

They all walked together across the yard to the main house and drank hot chocolate in the kitchen.

Sean and Sarah had already gone to bed. Cash was next to say goodnight.

Jay and Tia looked at each other wide-eyed when

Miranda followed him. "The old dog," Tia whispered, and laughed.

They found themselves alone. It was quiet for a few moments. Jay broke the silence. "I've got to go back to London in a couple of days."

"Oh."

"I'll probably take Sean and Sarah back."

"Okay," she said, nodding.

"Your father is assigning the Honourable Guard to stick with you now you're alone and Sean and I have a lot on."

"That's the army isn't it?"

"So I understand," he said, quietly.

She stood up, and so did he, not knowing what to do with himself. He sensed her disappointment.

"I'd better go up," she said, awkward all of a sudden.

He nodded. "Tia?"

"What?" she said, a little too quickly.

"Nothing. I'll come up as well."

They walked up the staircase and along the long landing with all the bedrooms in a row. Her door came first. "Thank you … for tonight," she said, not looking at him.

"You're welcome. You seem happier," he said, leaning down kissing her on the cheek.

She didn't look at him anymore and slipped in to her room.

He stood there for a moment after she had gone in, took a deep breath and went next door to his room.

***

She shut the door and leant on it, shut her eyes and took a deep breath. Why did he still have such an effect on her? She thought they were going to kiss. No, it was obviously one-sided. He must have been toying with her earlier.

She kept replaying his words over and over: 'you do something to me'. She was getting hot at the thought of what it meant.

She kicked off her shoes and stepped out of her jeans and then switched the shower on, dial set to cold.

There was a rap at the door.

Chapter 21

Her heart thumped in her ears.

"Who is it?"

"Jay."

"Come in." She could barely get the words out her heart was beating so wildly.

He stepped into the room and shut the door. His face looked hot and fierce.

He stalked towards her not saying a word.

"Jay?" she said, with a trace of fear.

In one fluid move, he stalked towards her and pulled her into the mother of all kisses. Fuck, it was a toe-curler. It only took her a millisecond to acclimatise to the turnaround of events and meld to him. God, she'd missed him.

The kiss became urgent and quickly he started to pull her shirt up over her head and she did the same. Then she undid his belt and pulled down his jeans, which he stepped out of.

"Shower," he rasped, walking her backwards towards the waiting, running shower.

Their actions were frantic.

He pushed her under the shower, but she wanted to enjoy him. She'd starved of him long enough. She needed to feel him, smell him and at that moment, taste him.

She kissed down his neck, down his tattooed chest and down lower and lower until she was on her knees.

Her hands were everywhere – stroking him, scratching him, cupping him. She put her mouth over him and swallowed the length of him and he groaned aloud. He leant back on the tiled wall to steady himself. She grazed him with her teeth to drive him wild then covered them with her lips to slide faster over his silken skin. She took total control while he lost his hands in her hair. "Ah fuck, Tia," he said, pulling her up – not wanting it to end too soon. He kissed her roughly and turned her quickly to face the wall to spread her legs with his foot like a cop. He could wait no longer and plunged into her deeply.

She cried out with the sensation of invasion and fullness as he began a pounding rhythm immediately. He spanned his fingers around her small waist to keep her braced against him. She revelled in the feel of his chest on her back as it tantalised her skin so sensitive to touch.

His hands roamed her back as he pounded into her and she knew he was feeling her markings. They were now in their full glory. She could tell by his caress that he totally got off on them. And the knowledge drove her to the brink.

He groaned her name and she felt him pulse inside

her. Every spasm of muscle drove her further and until she sighed and came along with him. Milking every last sensation she worked herself, gyrating and ringing as much out of him as she could. He leant forward and bit her shoulder, trapped her and reached down to touch her bud gently and urged her in small circles. Feeling him encasing her in his body was like coming home. Emotion threatened to bubble up in her chest. She half sobbed as she cried out and came again, but he was merciless, continuing till she could stand it no longer and she grabbed his arms and they both collapsed and panted against the wall.

Eventually she turned around and saw that his eyes were still closed. Still catching her breath she said, "I didn't ever think you would do that again."

"I tried not to," he said quietly, leaning his forehead down on hers.

She ran her thumb along his flushed cheekbones, "Don't ever try not to again."

"It's pointless," he said, and ran his tongue down her body.

***

A couple of hours passed until they were sated, exhausted and, in Jay's case, cold. Tia tucked him into her bed under the duvet, turned up the air con for herself and lay on top of him naked. She couldn't bear to be apart from him now that she had him.

Once he was warm his arms enveloped her while she lay on his chest with her legs between his and they fell into exhausted sleep.

Tia couldn't remember the last time she had slept so well – not since with Dante anyway. But she refused to think of Dante. She simply convinced herself that, had duty not forced her into it, she never would have left Jay in the first place.

She slept so soundly that she even slept through her alarm to go and feed and muck out the horses. That was probably the reason Cash knocked on her door to see if she was okay when he'd finished doing them himself.

She was a little embarrassed when Cash knocked again later asking for Jay. "Jay, Alfonzo just rang for you and asked me to give you an urgent message."

"What is it?" Jay answered in a croaky voice.

"The Honourable Guard is turning up today, in time for you to go back tomorrow."

Tia looked at Jay's face with disappointment as she realised he was going.

"What time are they coming?" he said, looking back at her as if he read her thoughts.

"Around noon."

Jay looked at the clock. "In an hour," he said to Tia. "Thanks Cash. We'll get up."

Tia didn't say anything and went to slide off his body, resigning herself to the fact that their little interlude was over, and he was going back to England.

"Hey?" Jay said, and stopped her sliding away. "Talk to me?"

"I didn't know you were going back so soon?"

"I have to go back some time," he said, holding her chin while he ran a thumb over her lips.

"Everyone's going to know we slept together," she said, blushing.

"Fuck 'em! The hints they've been dropping Tia, I should think they were amazed it took us so long."

She laughed. He was always so restrained and intense, that any little bursts of his personality were rare and precious moments to her.

"Doesn't anything bother you Jay? Don't you ever get scared or angry or anything like that?"

He looked at her strangely, smiling, with his head at a really cute angle. "Everyone does Tia. I just choose not to dwell on that stuff."

Before she could say any more, he got up with one fluid movement and pulled her with him. "Come on. I want you to scrub my back."

And just like that he'd smoothed her melancholy away, or under the carpet.

***

A little later and they were fresh from their shower, eating breakfast and drinking coffee in Cash's kitchen.

Sarah and Sean had gone into town to do some last minute shopping which left Cash and Jay to welcome the Honourable Guard.

Jay wasn't sure how he felt about it. He'd never knowingly met any other Atlanteans other than the Dubonnetti's and Cash and Sean, as he and Dante were only ever on the fringes of Atlantean society while they were growing up.

He imagined they were like secret service types; like bodyguards or something.

"They're here." Cash said. "You'd better come and meet them."

Jay picked up Tia's hand and led her into the large lounge. Cash threw open the front door and asked in two of the biggest men Jay had ever seen. Brick shit houses came to mind. They were easily six feet five, but built with it – all muscle and testosterone. They looked military in tight black t-shirts and black baggy pants, but nastier.

Jay, never one to be intimidated, made sure he looked them both in the eye as he shook their hands. He'd already worked out which was the one he would deal with, as the other avoided eye contact as much as possible and remained silent. But he wasn't lured into assuming he was weak.

Cash showed them to seats and Tia got up to make some coffee. "No need, thank you," the leader guy said. "I am Marius Santalini, and this is my brother Keenan."

"Jay." he said abruptly, looking at him directly, waiting.

The guy just smiled at him showing some of the biggest canines he'd ever seen.

Jay's eyebrows rose in acknowledgement, but he said nothing. *Fuck, Dracula on steroids.*

"I understand you are Human?" Marius continued. "With no Atlantean blood?"

"What's that got to do with anything?"

"I am just trying to understand what a Human is doing with a royal Bonaci Siren?"

Tia's sharp intake of breath was audible at the obvious

dig at Jay.

Cash shifted his weight uncomfortably, like everything was going downhill fast.

"Why don't you stop posturing and get to the point. And while you're at it you can explain what a royal is doing here sporting a fucking fat divining ring, in the presence of a royal Bonaci Siren?"

Cash put his head in his hands. Tia put her hand to her mouth. The quiet one actually paid attention and looked up and actually hissed through his canines at that. "You have nothing to fear from me. I have my own Siren."

Tia gasped. "You have? Who? My real sister … what's her name?" she said, in a rush.

"Tia!" Jay reprimanded.

The two men looked astonished at the way he spoke to her. The one called Keenan spoke directly to Tia. "I was brought up with my Siren. It was a special dispensation given to the Honourable Guard, as it is our job to ensure the secrecy and safety of all the Sirens. It was my family who placed you all in the Human world when you were babies."

"Wow," she said. "Can you tell me about my sister?" She looked at Jay asking his silent permission.

He didn't like their interaction with her. He couldn't put his finger on why but bit down the feeling. She looked back at Keenan.

"She is similar to you in height and build, but has dark hair and green eyes, but more Human looking than yours."

Jay rolled his eyes.

The one called Marius was watching him closely.

"Can I meet her?"

"I am afraid not she has disappeared."

Jay tuned back in at that point. "You are guarding her but lost your own?" he said, not believing his ears.

"Jay!" Tia scolded.

"No, it's a fair question," Keenan replied on a sigh. "It's complicated." And he explained briefly how they had both been brought up among Humans just as Tia had been; how they had been in a children's home together until she was eighteen. Then how they arrived in America hoping to make a new life, where he was to be told who he was and accepted into the Guard. But before they could go to his family she disappeared from a nightclub where she was working and he hadn't been able to find her since. That was a few months ago.

"Is she a DJ?" Tia asked. "I'm a DJ."

Keenan smiled at her. "No. She is a club dancer. She loves music, and her options were limited coming from where we did."

Jay had heard enough and wanted to get to the point. "So you are not interested in her in that way?" he said, nodding his head towards Tia.

"No I am not." Keenan said, very definitely.

Marius, who had been quietly studying Jay, turned his attention to Tia. "You married the king?"

Jay saw Tia squirm at the question and began to feel annoyed. "She did," he interrupted.

Marius looked back at him. "You were his best friend

and brother in the Dubonnetti family?"

"I am." Keep going arsehole, pressing my buttons.

Jay subconsciously clenched his fists and his jaw ticked under his skin. Tia started to look nervous.

"Now can we take it down a notch boys?" Cash said, trying to diffuse the atmosphere.

"Why don't our guests just cut the crap and get on with saying what they want to say." Jay said.

"Okay … if we're going to put our lives on the line guarding her," Marius said, while he pointed a finger at Tia, "We need to know why a Siren married a royal prince and then ran off with his best friend – a Human."

"Who employed you, Dante or Alfonzo?" Jay asked, squinting his eyes.

"Alfonzo."

"Then come on, cut the bullshit, you know what I am to Dante and to her."

"Keenan, perhaps you could take Tia for a stroll and talk to her about her sister?" Marius said.

Keenan inclined his head. "I would love to."

Tia smiled enthusiastically and looked at Jay for permission. He nodded.

"I'll show you the horses," she said.

As soon as they left Cash made himself scarce, and Marius got down to business. "Okay, now we can speak freely."

Jay waited.

"Alfonzo wanted to know whether you and Tia had resumed your previous relationship?"

Jay let out a sigh and resigned himself to this inevitable

line of questioning, "I think you already know that we are close."

"What would you do if she made the decision to return to the king?"

"I would not stand in her way."

"You have to know that a Siren with a strong prince is the preferred outcome?"

"As I have said to Dante himself, if she and he are happy together then I wouldn't stand in their way. But, if she comes to me of her own free will, as her Protector, I wouldn't turn her away because of any loyalty to my friend."

His honesty seemed to satisfy Marius who mentally logged away what Jay had said. "Is there anything you wish to ask me?"

"Yes. Have you seen Dante recently?"

"I have."

"How is he?"

"He is like Keenan. Living with something missing. He is a mess at the moment, but Alfonzo will tutor him and he will come good eventually. Alfonzo sees something in him. And he is the rightful king by first pledge from a Siren."

Jay listened to what he said. It wasn't a surprise to him. He could just imagine how Dante would have hit the bottle with a vengeance, except he hadn't had him to do it with. He'd lost two people. Then again, when Tia went back to Dante, he would as well.

Marius smiled at him. "I must confess, when Alfonzo told me that Dante had adopted you in to his family and

Alfonzo had done the same, I did wonder what kind of Human held so much sway on Atlantean noblemen that they would want to honour him to such an extent." He nodded to himself. "I will send a message to Alfonzo and Dante that the Guard accepts the charge, Tia Storm, into their care.

Jay nodded, not sure what he should say.

***

Tia moved along the barn petting each horse in turn. Keenan followed her along the line. She still couldn't believe the size of him. He was about a foot taller than her with biceps the size of her waist. "Are you all as big?" she said, glancing at him as she rubbed a velvety nose.

He blushed a little. "We grow into this size. We are regular size as children and adolescents."

"How come?"

"They reckon that we were the first Atlanteans to leave the water and lived on a diet of blood to survive."

Her eyes went wide as she felt her own teeth. "So your teeth … you're vampires?"

He laughed. "Not anymore."

He was a lovely looking bloke, she decided. How lucky her sister had been to grow up with her mate. Perhaps, if she and Dante … She squashed that thought. "Never?" she asked.

"Only at puberty and when we join with or marry our female."

That sounded hot. "So that makes you big?"

"So it seems," he said, flashing a lovely smile with fangs and all.

"Does she breathe water ... my sister?"

"No, not that I know of. Did you?" he asked.

"Yes. I discovered it by accident. I was in care as well you know."

"Yes. We know where all the Siren are ... well, all except mine." He lowered his eyes in shame.

"You'll find her." She said, touching his arm. "I can't wait to meet her ... Will you marry her as soon as she comes back?"

He nodded. "Yes, I hope so. But I'm not sure if she'll have to pledge to the king first, or how it's going to work."

Her face clouded over. "I see." The horrible memory of Dante and the other girls swarming around him like parasites in the tank at Dubonnetti's invaded her.

"The Human has a death wish," Keenan said, interrupting her thoughts.

She smiled. "Who Jay? I've never known anyone like him."

"You love him?"

She nodded and moved along to the next horse.

"Then you will have a rough ride in this world, being a Siren."

"I'm beginning to realise that."

"Still he's got guts, I'll give him that."

"Dante told me they fought all the time."

Keenan flashed another fanged smile. "Well, anyone who keeps Dante in line can't be all bad."

She laughed, deciding she liked Keenan. "Will you be staying from today?"

"Marius will let me know when we go back in – unless he's chewed up your Protector," he said, breaking into a laugh at the horror on Tia's face.

Chapter 22

The two guards were introduced to Sean as part of the Santalini royal family, and stayed from that day. And he was introduced to them as yet another of Tia's Protectors. But they understood why they had been assigned when it was explained that Sean was an expectant father, Cash had to work his ranch and Jay had the Bonaci Corporation to run. Besides, bodyguards had to be a part of life now as she was a queen, whether she was estranged from Dante or not.

The day loomed when Jay was to go back to England. He paced in Tia's room on his phone, always talking business. Tia lay back on the pillows watching him with a towel around her after enjoying another session of lovemaking like it was going out of fashion.

Jay switched off his phone and turned and looked at her. Her markings were still vivid and her pupils still dilated. They made him feel like jumping her all over again. He fucking loved them. But the thought of her going back to Dante and the very words Marius had spoken that afternoon were still ringing in his ears. Of course she would go back, it was as inevitable as breathing.

He missed his best friend like a right arm, and longed for old times when they would laugh and get into scrapes together, but he knew those times had gone forever. Even if you took Tia out of the equation Dante was a king and needed to start acting like one and not someone in a rock band. He laughed out loud at that thought.

"What?" Tia said.

"What?" Jay repeated, absently. He shook his head and snapped himself out of his memories. "Nothing. Listen, do you want to come with me when I go back tomorrow?"

Her eyes lit up. "Really? Yes of course I do." She jumped up and flung her arms around his neck. "I thought you'd never ask."

He put his mouth and nose into the soft crook of her neck and breathed in deeply, resolving to enjoy the blessings of the right here and now and not over-analyse everything.

"What made you decide?" she asked, pulling away grinning at him.

"I'm having some new deep baths put in to the top floor of The Bluebell."

Her breath hitched then her eyes narrowed. "How long have you been planning that?"

"He whispered next to her ear. "Since the first time I had you in my shower."

***

Tia left with Jay the next day, accompanied by her guards, which were now to be permanently assigned to her. Days moved into weeks, and weeks moved into months, which Tia referred to as their golden time. She went everywhere with Jay. London, New York, Paris. You name it, wherever Bonaci business was, Jay would have to go and she was always on his jet, at his hotel and in his bed. They were the happiest times of her life – except those brief days of honeymoon with Dante, which she refused to revisit in her memory banks.

Jay was proving to be a huge asset to the Bonaci Corporation; pushing them to new heights and prosperity. He had become a formidable businessman.

She knew he always sought news of his oldest friend, often getting updates from Alfonzo. They found out that Dante had begun to put his house in order. He'd kicked out all his wives and concentrated on the Dubonnetti family business, which was coming up alongside Jay's on the map.

Jay was pleased, she could tell, but they never discussed him. It was so typical of him to be so generous in his goodwill towards Dante, that she loved him all the more for it.

But despite spending all her time with him, he'd never once said he loved her. They had a strong physical relationship. She had no complaints there. But emotionally he remained distant and aloof. She warred with herself, craving emotional intimacy with him on one hand, but also welcoming the space Jay instinctively gave her as well. Shit, she didn't know what the answer was. She reasoned that no-one would want to spend as much time with someone and for so long, if they didn't have feelings. And perhaps he didn't like to visit them any more than she did hers for Dante. And so she pushed her feelings of isolation aside.

After several weeks away and six months after leaving Dante, they came back to Jay's hotel in London. It was to be no holiday though, as he had some big takeover he was working on which was going to take up all his time over the next few days.

When they arrived back at The Bluebell Tia felt restless and longed to get some downtime with Jay, but knew better than to hassle him for it.

Feeling like a spare part and a tag-a-long was becoming a habit these days. "Do you mind if I nip down to Kent to my place while you're so busy?" she pitched to Jay. She hadn't been out of his, or the Guards' sight for months.

Jay looked at her while he thought about it from behind his laptop. "I don't see why not," he said, eventually, "How long are you thinking?"

"Oh not long ... couple of days? I just want to check on it. I haven't been there for months."

"Okay babe, when are you going?"

"I might go now. I can get the train down and get my bike so I've got it up here."

"What about the Guard?"

"Oh Jay, I would like to be in my space alone. Please Jay."

He beckoned her over, curling a finger. She obediently walked over. He put his laptop aside and pulled her onto his lap. He looked into her eyes for what seemed like an age as if searching them for something. She held her breath. *He's going to say it. He's going to say it.*

Then he just pecked her on the lips. "Go," he said, "before I get you all hot and messy."

She smiled and felt a small disappointment pain hit the bottom of her stomach, but swallowed it down. "Okay then … I'll be off."

He didn't look up any more.

She closed the door of the suite with a lump in her throat, sniffed and stomped to the lift. You've got to stop kidding yourself girl.

***

The Kent countryside whizzed past as she stared out of the window of the train. She'd forgotten how beautiful and green it was. There was something so permanent and honest about the land. Although most of her DJ'ing work was in cities, the countryside held her heart.

Cash had always joked with her that if neither of them married they would grow old together on his ranch. She sighed at the warm fuzzy feeling that thought gave her – so calm, serene and uncomplicated. It still wasn't beyond the realms of possibility.

Before long she'd jumped out of the train and into a cab, which she directed down the old windy lanes to a dirt track and onto the gravel in front of her barn. Her heart lifted the minute she saw it.

She paid the cabbie and ran across the yard. Her ladder was down, which was strange. Maybe she left it down when she was last here?

She bounded up the steps, flung her bag down and went to walk into the living room area of her loft and stopped dead. There, sitting as bold as brass, was Dante, in all his terrifying, sexy glory.

"Fucking hell!" escaped her lips.

He was sitting forward on the sofa with his elbows on his knees. "Hello babe."

He wasn't the cocky, immature, charmer she had left all those months ago. He seemed to have filled out. He was unsure and serious and devastatingly good-looking. *Stop!* she had to say to her own line of thinking, and shook her head to regain her senses.

"Aren't you going to say anything?" he asked.

"How did you know I'd be here?"

"I spoke to Jay today."

"Oh." She felt uneasy, then disloyal – weird.

Then a thought suddenly struck her. "Jay doesn't know this place, no-one does ... except?"

Dante nodded. "Yes, the delightful Marco took great pleasure in rubbing my nose in the fact he'd been here."

"What an arsehole. I knew straight away it was a mistake giving him my address."

"Ah, no bother, I enjoyed rubbing his nose in the floor to get the information out of him. So thanks for that." He smiled at her. The old glint in his eye was still there.

"You haven't changed that much then?" she said, playfully accusing him.

"I'm sober, single and sensible now," he said, in his wonderful Irish accent, still with a grin on his face.

Not willing to succumb to the charm, she asked, "What happened to the old ball and chains?" emphasising the 's'.

He laughed at that. "Gone. All of them. I should have taken notice of you." He got serious for a second. "They weren't Sirens, any of them. You kept saying you had a funny feeling about them, but I wouldn't listen," he said shaking his head. Then he looked back straight into her eyes. "They jumped me in the pool that day."

Tia rolled her eyes and exhaled.

He was trying to keep the laughter out of his voice at the absurdity of what he was saying. "It's true, they were Sea Witches."

"Sea Witches?" she scoffed, with very little belief in what he was saying to her. "More like Sea Bitches."

Dante laughed, "I know. I think they thought you were muscling in on their gig. The fucking annoying thing was that they could breathe the water but no power passed to me that day, nor any other day. But by the time I knew something was up, you'd already gone."

She tried not to be affected by him and eyed him suspiciously, "Why would they do that?"

I still haven't got to the bottom of who sent them, but they were just lower-class Atlanteans trying to make a bit of fame and fortune for their family. I don't think they expected to keep up the pretence for long. Whoever was behind it used them to buy some time to find your real sisters. I was too stupid to see it." He shook his head and looked down at his hands, annoyed with himself. "Then he looked up at her earnestly. " I lost you because of it, most of my brothers won't speak to me and Stephan wants to kill me."

She looked a bit confused at all that.

He must have read it on her face. "Joselle is blind. My fault. Stephan now hates my guts."

She softened a bit and came and sat nearer to him. "What happened?" she said, in concern.

"Although she wasn't a Siren and couldn't breathe for me or give me power or anything, she had what Witches call the second sight."

She shook her head, not understanding.

"Well …" He looked a bit shifty. "When I wanted to find out what you were doing, when our mental bond was growing weaker, if I gave her a small sample of my blood and she drank it, she could see you and tell me about you. Whether you were happy and whether you had …" he stumbled his words and swallowed as if the thought were very painful to him, "bonded with anyone else."

She thought about it. "Breathing you mean?"

He nodded.

"How does that blind someone?"

"The more you use the second sight, the more normal sight dims." Then he didn't look her in the eye. "I did it a lot."

She was quiet. Her mind was racing. Eventually she looked at him. He was just looking at his hands – still wearing the ring. "What do you want, Dante?"

He stood up and started to walk around the room as if it was difficult to say what he wanted to say. In the end he just stopped and turned towards her and took his hands out of his pockets. "I just want to hang out. I want to take some time out from being a king – being an Atlantean. I dunno being an arsehole. I just want to do what normal people do, if only for a little while?" The fact he was in pain was written all over his face.

"Why me?" she found herself saying, lamely.

"You have only ever known me as a king and an Atlantean, but I was normal before that, Tia; before I knew you."

Then he thought about what he'd said for a moment and added, "Well I was still an arsehole, and a drunk, and took gratuitous drugs. But that was normal in my circles, honest." He couldn't help himself from laughing as he finished what he was saying.

She found herself being charmed by his honesty and hopeless sense of humour. "Oh fucking hell, Dante!" she said, trying not to laugh. "I did not see this coming, not in a month of Sundays."

"Oh, what d'ya say? Let's go mad. We can just go off on holiday; clubbing in Ibiza, or I dunno, boating in Venice, whatever you fancy." He was kneeling at her feet and gently shaking her by the tops of her arms.

She was grinning back at him almost getting caught up in his whirlwind when the laughter drained out of her face. "What about Jay?" she said, utterly deflated.

Dante stood up and walked away from her, then half-turned back with a calculating look in his eye. "If he knows you've bumped into me, he will be expecting it."

"I don't understand. What do you mean, he will be expecting it?" she said, standing up as well.

"We have an understanding." Dante said, quietly.

"What understanding?" A deep feeling of unease

crept over her.

"That whoever you want to be with, we have to accept it. And not, you know, influence the outcome."

"What? When did you arrange this?"

"When we were alone in the room at your father's. The night of the wedding celebration."

She went quiet trying to compute the information. "God, you two are priceless, you know that?"

She stormed past him to go to her bathroom.

"Where are you going?"

"For a bath ... alone!"

"What shall I do?" he said, at a loss.

"You can ring the shithead and tell him what you just told me ... and then you can make arrangements to go to Timbuktu for all I care ... I can't believe the two of you have it all sussed. And I ... I can't fucking believe it." She built in anger and volume. "I can't believe that I've carried around all this guilt when the pair of you are still fucking mates." She banged and crashed her things and ran herself a deep bath. She lit candles around it and put Grover Washington Junior's Limelight on loud to drown everything out. She undressed and submerged, opened her lungs and let her gill bubbles sooth her to the beautiful lulling tones of the saxophone.

***

That went well. Dante grinned to himself.

He didn't get through to Jay. He just sent a text message:

Bumped into Tia. Gone to Italy for a few days. D.

He clicked his phone off. His jet was already primed

to go. He'd decided on Italy as he had a nice little villa down there – with a huge pool.

He smiled. He wanted her back with every fibre of his being. He was going to love her so well she wouldn't want to ever leave him.

Chapter 23

After keeping Dante at arm's length all night, threatening to stab him if he came near her, they boarded the Dubonnetti plane late morning.

No longer impressed by the jet set lifestyle, Tia was quiet and moody all the way to Italy.

Dante smirked to himself, confident he'd wear her down, and sooner rather than later. Now he had her away from Jay, and on her own, he could employ his whole arsenal of charm.

They landed at about 4.30 p.m. at Milan Malpensa airport, and a driver took them the forty-five minute drive to Lake Como where his family's villa was situated.

As soon as they arrived Tia snapped out of her mood. "Dante, wow!" She ran from veranda to veranda looking at the lake and the gardens, cooing and 'aahing' as she went.

Dante just stood and watched her run around. "Do you want to go for a walk? It's starting to cool down at this time of day, and then we can go for something to eat?"

"Yes!" she said, running up the stairs before realising

she didn't know where she was going. "Which room?' she stopped and asked.

Dante had followed her up. "Any one you want," *as long as it is with me.*

She ran into all six bedrooms and settled on the one with a beautiful balcony and view of the lake. She threw open the doors and went out. "This one," she whispered.

"Come, let's go out," he said quietly, next to her.

She flung all the stuff out of her bag with no care for her belongings at all, much to his amusement, as he was meticulous with his own clothes. It struck him that he knew so little about her. He watched her settle for a loose halterneck maxi dress and gladiator sandals, which strapped up her leg.

Dante tore his eyes away to choose some cooler clothes for himself. Baggy navy trousers, Italian sandals, of course, and a loose cotton white shirt left untucked. With his long curly hair and Ray-Bans® on his head holding it back, he could easily pass as a local. In fact he spoke fluent Italian.

The evening was balmy and the air was fragrant as they followed the footpath that meandered through shady trees and shrubs next to the lake.

They could hear a party with chatting people and indiscernible music at a distance. Dante tried to hold her hand a few times but she pulled it back with a firm, "No … it's a slippery slope Dante."

That made him really laugh. "You think you can keep that up?" his eyes twinkling.

"Stop that!"

"Stop what?" his face all innocence

"Sending out your pheromones or whatever it is you do."

That made him double over. "No-one makes me laugh like you; accept maybe Jay." Which sobered them both.

"Where are you taking me?" she asked, changing the subject.

"There is a lovely little alfresco place up here that has music and dancing."

"Really?"

"I thought as we have never been out together …"

"Oh, I suppose not … I wouldn't have pegged you as a dancer."

"No? We were in nightclubs from the age of fourteen."

He didn't use Jay's name this time but it was very hard as all his memories included him. Instead he tried to get her to talk. "Tell me something about your life?"

"Like what?"

"I dunno, like … how did you start DJ'ing?

"Okay … I got a job just washing dishes first of all in a night club in Shoreditch when I was sixteen. The guy who owned it used to let me play on the decks during the day when no-one was about."

"Was that Dannyl's place?"

"Yes. How did you?"

"Jay!" They both said in unison.

"Look," Dante said. "Shall we just make a pact that it is okay to talk about him?" He was a major part of both their lives so there was no point in pussy footing around.

"Okay." She smiled shyly. "Tell me something about

you?"

"Okay ... Me and Jay had a DNA test as soon as we were old enough to see if we were brothers."

"Really?" she said, touched. "Nothing?"

"No ... we had some crazy notion that there had to have been a reason why me dad brought him round to us from an early age, so we assumed he was his dad."

"How did you both take the news when he wasn't?"

"I told Jay I still reckoned me dad was shagging his mum."

Tia put her hand over her mouth in shock and stifled a giggle. "Dante ... what did he say?"

"Nothing. He just beat seven bells out of me."

They both laughed. The tension between them was gradually dissipating as they neared the restaurant.

When they arrived it was quaint and small with little circular tables with candles on each one. There was a trellis with plants growing all around and over their heads, and coloured bulbs strung across the latticed beams. It was just beautiful.

The music was chilled and soulful.

Dante spouted impeccable Italian as they were shown to the best table. "What do you want to drink, wine or whiskey?"

"Why wine or whiskey?" she asked, creasing her brow.

"Well, wine goes with the food. I know you like whiskey, and it would help lower our body temperatures," he said, with heavy-lidded eyes. "Or we could go for getting shitfaced and have both?" he added, lightly. "I'm easy."

This made her laugh. "Whiskey." She said, shaking her head.

He ordered the drinks and food in Italian and then explained to her that he had ordered a selection of seafood for them to pick at.

She nodded and appreciated that he took her limited diet into account.

"Was eating hard growing up in the Human world?" he asked, genuinely interested.

"Looking back, I think they must have told them I was allergic to meat as I was never given it and went to school with notes and stuff."

"I'm sorry you had to go through all that, Tia." He smiled at her. She blushed and just looked down at her hands. He suspected he didn't know the half of what she went through.

The lull in conversation was broken when a whole bottle of Irish whiskey was brought to their table, then a carafe of local wine with their food, which looked perfect.

Tia began to loosen up and Dante enjoyed finding out about her for the first time. He realised that she was really a very solitary person, allowing very few people to get close to her. He felt very privileged to be in that small circle.

"What will you do after this holiday?" she asked.

"I'm going to help my cousin find his Siren."

"Keenan?"

"Yes …" then he remembered that Keenan was part of her Guard.

"Will he marry her ... or how will it work ... you know ... the king shit?"

He laughed. "I'll be honest with you Tia, now I know more about it, I think all the Sirens will be pledged to me but have their own partners. Does that make sense? It is the power of the five that's needed to hold the throne."

"Doesn't pledging mean marriage? Will Keenan mind that, him being a prince and all?"

"Probably, but the only way I could see to stop the infighting between the princes would be for them to sit on the council and have a hand in government. The marriage is just in name only."

"He looked the jealous type to me."

Dante smiled a wicked grin. "Like me." And he took a sip of his drink.

The music got livelier and Dante stood reaching down his hand towards her. "Come on, let's dance." And he pulled her to a tight bunch on the small dance floor. They moved towards the back where they could be obscured and put their drinks down.

***

Sunshine Anderson's *Heard It All Before* came on and Dante began to move. Tia was amazed at how easily his body moved to the music. Again he tried to hold her hands. "No!" she kept saying firmly with her index finger up. "I won't get hot Dante ... No!" and he laughed and continued dancing. But gravity kept moving them into each other and his body would come around hers, all but touching. It was uber-erotic.

A small man collecting glasses gabbled something to

Dante in Italian and Dante replied laughing.

"What did he say?" she shouted, over the music.

"He told me to hold on to the beautiful girl."

She blushed and turned her back and continued dancing as Faith Evan's *Love Like This* played. He pulled her close for this song. He pushed his knee between her legs to part them, and pulled her low onto his leg. He placed her arms up around his neck and he linked his around her waist, and then moved with her. He bent his head down to her cheek and they moved together.

With his lips tantalisingly close to hers, she let herself go and her body went with his. He felt wonderful. She was his to command and she gave herself permission just for the duration of the record. As it wore on he pulled her in closer and tighter – so close that she had to hoist her long skirt up, showing her strap-covered legs. When her body was in close proximity to his it owned her. She couldn't explain her physical reaction to him. He was like an overload of the senses.

Both of them were hot after the music ended and both were at a loss for words and had to gather themselves together.

Dante threw down some Euro's on their table and picked up their carafe to take with them. "Come. Let's walk." And he picked up her hand and she didn't fight him this time.

It had become completely dark as they walked, but pretty lights twinkled all around the lake.

"Here," he said. After taking a swig of the carafe, he handed it to her.

She took it from him. "Are you trying to get me drunk?"

"Yes. I have no scruples."

She laughed, choking as she drank having laughed mid-swallow. The drink went down her chin so she was forced to lean forward to let it drip on the floor.

"You need to wash that off," he said, laughing at her.

"You are not getting me in that pool, you know, Dante."

"What about the lake?"

Her eyes went wide and he copied her making fun of her expression. He took the carafe off her then swigged from it again and threw it down. He picked up her hand then the other and pulled her to him. He pushed her arms up around his neck, so he could hold her tightly around the waist. He put his nose and mouth into the soft part of her shoulder. "I've never enjoyed female company like I do with you, Tia," he said, breathing her in. "Come into the lake with me?" he whispered, and ground his hips into her.

Fuck, she didn't pull away. Her resolve was eroding. "Dante I ..."

"Don't think Tia. Just go with how you feel. I know you feel it too." He ground his hips into her again. He left her breathing heavily.

Before she could make another protest, he bent down and picked her up and began to walk along a small jetty with her.

"Dante ... Dante!" She shouted, "Don't you dare!"

"You should never dare me, Tia." And he kicked his

sandals off and jumped in holding her.

Her squeal was smothered as they entered the cool dark water. It wasn't deep, and they could touch the bottom. It came up to Dante's chest and lapped over her shoulders.

More evening strollers walked by and looked over at them and laughed at them standing in the water fully clothed. She spat the water out of her mouth and hit him in the shoulder. He held it dramatically saying, "Ow! What?" Then he stifled her barrage of abuse by pulling her in quickly for a kiss. But he was gentle and loving.

When the kiss finished she looked up into his eyes, which appeared to shimmer like the surface of the water. "I promised myself I wouldn't do this anymore."

"You shouldn't make promises you can't keep," he said, honestly, knowing as well as she did that any denial of the pull between them was futile. So he bent forward and kissed her again.

He was melting her and she lost herself in the kiss for a moment.

He broke away. "That day Tia, when you left, would you have left even if it hadn't happened with the girls?"

She studied his face for a few beats and decided not to lie. "Yes."

He breathed in deeply. "That was basically what Jay said. Can you tell me what I did wrong?"

She touched his cheek gently. "We hardly knew each other Dante, and it was so intense. I couldn't breathe."

"Is that what Jay does, give you space?"

She went to swim away from him. He swam around

her heading her off. "Please Tia. Then I won't mention it again."

"Look," she huffed, and then composed herself, "the two of you, you're poles apart."

He just stared at her, waiting for her to elaborate. "Tell me."

"I won't talk about my relationship with Jay with you, Dante."

He looked exasperated, obviously thinking Jay had some magic formula.

"You are you, and Jay is Jay. That's it."

"Come on Tia, how is it even possible?" The volatile Dante temper was starting to show.

"Oh here comes the old Dante ... okay then let's do this." She said, her temper starting to match his.

"I'm waiting ..." His face was fierce.

"Okay. Where there's a will there's a way." She tried swimming away again.

He pulled her back by the arm. "What's that supposed to mean?"

"We have a full sexual relationship, Dante." She emphasised her words slowly, especially the word 'sexual'.

He swam in close to her and pulled her between his legs and touched her face, searching her eyes. "Then why are you here Tia?" he said softly. "I know this will be the way with us as long as we live," and his hand pulled her to him by her backside while he kissed her hard.

Somehow she mustered the strength of will to push him back. And the hurt in her eyes was not outrage but pain, in that he was probably right. She knew the minute she admitted that to him she was lost.

"Please Tia, I can only do this king shit if you're there for me."

"But I can't be there Dante, I'm with Jay. It's always been Jay." Fuck, he looked as though she'd just stabbed him in the gut. She fortified herself by remembering that he'd probably never been turned down so brutally – fuck, probably never been turned down.

His face, hardened towards her. "Even if we are not together, we need to renew the pledge so I can absorb your power every few months."

"As you will with all my sisters." *Yes mate, I'm hardly special.*

The will to argue seemed to have gone out of him. "Yes."

"I will do that, as I promised I would." A pang of sadness hit her so strongly and she looked down into the water. She would have rather he ranted and punched and screamed with frustration than this resignation. It was much easier resisting someone you were angry with. The fact was he was totally right about her. She was holding out. She did melt in his arms, and he would know it the instant she breathed her innermost emotions into him.

He sighed, "Come on then, let's do it now so you can get back to him." And he sunk slowly beneath the water.

Chapter 24

They weren't just quiet on the way back to the villa because their throats were sore. There just didn't seem much else to say. They had shared each other's essence in the lake and the bond meant they knew exactly how each other felt, but that didn't seem to alter things a jot. The evening had lost its magic and Tia's heart felt heavy and she knew it was her fault.

Even though breathing for each other gave immense physical pleasure, it always came with the cost of complete understanding. It just broke her heart. Dante's love was a fierce, tangible thing and the strength of it frightened her. She was truly sorry she couldn't be with him, but that part of her that needed to be free, needed Jay with a yearning that Dante would now understand.

If she could have rolled them into the same person she would have. The truth was she loved them both, if that was possible. But Jay fascinated her – in the way that she could never really know him. And her darkest fear: that he would no longer want her, or that she would end up some kind of Stepford wife. Dante now felt it all …
Fuck!

As they neared the villa Dante stopped and projected, *don't go in,* and he turned to face her. *I won't leave you alone if you do. I'm going to get the driver to take you to the airport.*

She swallowed hard and nodded – it was probably for the best. She wasn't sure how long she'd hold out with him anyway.

I'm going to get your stuff and put you straight in the car. Don't move! He ordered.

She watched him walk briskly up the path and take out his mobile phone, texting as he walked. He couldn't wait to be rid of her now. She felt like crying.

Five minutes later he came running back down. *This way.* He led her out to the front of the villa where a car was purring by the curb. He spoke roughly to the driver, holding his throat while he gave instructions, then walked back round to where she was standing and opened the back door for her to get in.

She got in bewildered at how such a turnaround of moods and events could happen in one day. He leant in and kissed her tenderly on the lips, which didn't tally with his actions. *Jay is landing in thirty minutes at Malpensa, you'll be safe then.*

She nodded lamely. But as the sleek car pulled away and she watched Dante's back walk quickly the way they came, she couldn't help but wonder what a strange thing it was to say.

***

Dante had walked along the path as lost in thought as she was. Thank God they couldn't read minds but only project speech, because he wouldn't want her in his head right now.

Fuck. The love she felt for Jay and he was such a cold, hard, bastard. That was his secret. It wasn't the attack that would win fair lady but the retreat. So as hard as it was, it was what he must do. It made sense when he thought about it, she'd been pushed from pillar to post as a kid, so the last thing she needed was him ordering her about.

As they neared the villa his thoughts stopped dead as he stood stock-still. The lights were all on in the villa and they'd gone out while it was still light.

Quickly his brain rallied and he made the decision to put her straight on a plane and get her out of there. It didn't feel safe and if he gave her any clue there may be danger he knew she wouldn't want to leave him to face it alone. So he made up the excuse –not too far from the truth – that she needed to go for her own good.

While he'd walked up to the villa and told her to wait for him, he'd texted the driver and then Jay and explained there was trouble, and that he wanted her out of there ASAP. He made sure he told Jay she was unaware and untouched. Dante didn't want Tia to have any grief she didn't deserve if he thought he'd been all over her.

He'd sneaked into the house, crept up the stairs, grabbed Tia's bag and shoved all her stuff back in it. He made sure her passport was there, and crept back out.

A text buzzed from Jay.

In air. Will divert. Land thirty minutes.

He breathed a sigh of relief.

He'd heard Stephan's voice in the villa and someone else he didn't know. He hadn't a clue what he was doing there, but he sure as hell wasn't there for a social call, so he was relieved when Tia was safely off in the distance in the car.

***

Tia's heart sank as she arrived at Malpensa. Jay's plane was there, engine running with the steps down.

Her car drove out onto the tarmac. The driver came around and undid her door and informed her that Mr Gardiner was expecting her. Oh joy. She thanked him quietly and got out the car with a feeling of dread. Probably more from guilt than what she would say to him.

Slowly she climbed the steps, unsure of what he would say or do.

'Hello Miss!" The cheery steward said, as she stepped into the plane.

Jay was sitting in his armchair, laptop open, phone to his ear as normal. When he caught sight of her, he put his phone to his shoulder. "Strap in, we're leaving straight away."

She just stood and blinked and watched him resume his call. After a moment she did as he asked in a daze.

He ended his call, closed his laptop and looked over at her. "You didn't think to let me know yourself you were fucking off yesterday?"

Thank fuck he was Human. She was beginning to think he was a cyborg. Anger suddenly flashed through her. "I thought everything was cool with your little arrangement." She flashed him a mirthless smile.

He smiled back arrogantly. The bastard actually smiled a patronising smile at her and played dumb. "And what arrangement was this?"

She felt like screaming at him but kept her voice level. "You know, the deal you made with Dante ... the one where if I went to either of you of my own free will, then you'd both be cool about it?"

"That one," he said, still smiling. "You're wet."

She was just about keeping a lid on her temper. "I've been in Lake Como seeing the sights," blinking and enunciating every word.

He smiled at her sarcasm, re-opened his laptop and continued his work.

"Aagh!" She shouted, and threw her bag at him with all her strength.

He just dodged back in his seat as it sailed past and didn't even look back at her. Just clicked away on his keyboard.

I'm starting to dislike you Jason Gardiner.

***

Dante made sure when he re-entered the villa he made a lot of noise. "Honey I'm home!" He shouted out, but his throat was still gravelly and sore.

When he walked into the living room Stephan was sitting on one sofa and a bulldog-looking older man was on another. "Brother!" Dante said jovially, "You should have phoned ahead. I haven't got a thing in."

"Where is your bitch?" Stephan spat.

Dante dropped the sarcasm and looked at his watch. "Getting on Jay's plane about now."

Stephan stood up and his sidekick followed his lead.

Dante's nerves were on high alert but he tried to look impassive and a little drunk, as Stephan would expect him to be.

"That's a real shame," Stephan said, grimacing. "I was looking forward to giving her the same treatment you gave Joselle."

Dante held a placating hand up. "Look Stephan, about Joselle. I am really sorry about that. I promise I will do all in my power to get her sight restored. The Murrs have advanced medical technology, so I'm sure they could come up with something."

But Stephan was in no mood to be placated. "You're sorry ...you're fucking sorry," he screamed. He looked at his friend, who took his cue and strode forward. Dante readied his stance and assessed his opponent as probably Human as he wasn't that tall.

Thankfully years of sparring with Jay had turned him into a respectable fighter, if not with Jay's flare, he was effective.

The guy broke into a run and Dante dodged him at the last minute, using the fool's weight and momentum against him and pushed him into the wall. As he smashed into it Dante kicked him hard in the kidneys.

The man grunted and turned and began swinging punches, which Dante weaved and bobbed away from. He continued this while he gradually moved backwards, picking up furniture as he went and throwing them at him or using them as a shield.

The bloke just wasn't tiring. He glanced over at Stephan at the same time, as he was a slippery bastard, and he wouldn't put it past him to hurt him while his hands were busy.

Fuck. Just as he glanced over Stephan pulled a small grey handgun out of his pocket and held it out towards Dante's moving body. "Think about it Stephan," Dante reasoned, while he continued to fight. "A murder attempt on the king is a death sentence for you."

"No-one even knows I've been here; it's just an aggravated burglary. Such bad luck."

Dante was going to have to think quickly. As powerful as he was with Tia's power, he couldn't stop a bullet. And he didn't want to alert her to his predicament unless he really had to.

The indoor pool … his strength was in the water. He allowed the bloke to get in a lucky shot that pushed him backwards through the double doors that led into the indoor pool. The lights were off – even better. When he reached the edge of the pool, he dodged a swing, twisted and pushed the man over the side and dived on top of him before Stephan could aim his gun.

He opened his lungs immediately and swam low while the man scrambled about in the water looking for him. He struck like Jaws and pulled his legs down into the deep end. He made sure the man's face remained under the surface and just held him and waited.

The man kicked and fought and tried to roll into a ball, anything to get a hold on Dante. But he was as slippery as an eel and dodged his clawing hands and held onto his leg on and on.

Dante prayed Stephan wouldn't have the guts to dive in to help his friend. The gamble paid off as the guy's struggles lessened, until they stopped all together and he hung there as if suspended in the water. His arms and legs were open and his eyes bulged.

Dante kept to the edges of the pool. The fashion of black tiled pools made it look like a black hole from the surface, especially in the darkness. He swam slowly around the edge, watching the silhouette of Stephan as he skulked around the pool slowly, trying to spot him.

When Stephan finally stood still, Dante seized his chance and lunged up out of the water, grabbed Stephan's ankle and pulled it from under him.

Stephan screamed. His head cracked on the tiled floor even though his elbows hit the floor first. Dante took no chances and dragged him in. He snatched the gun from his hand and put his hands around his throat and squeezed until Stephan's eyes nearly popped out.

He looked into his brother's pleading eyes. His conscience warred with his logic. If he killed him he would be justified under Atlantean law. Stephan could be executed after this any way. Instead, he released his throat, picked him up, and threw him out of the water, so he rolled and skidded along the tiled floor.

Dante got out in one fluid move and stalked over to his spluttering, bleeding, pathetic excuse for a brother. Dante pushed him down with his foot and wedged it hard under his chin, almost choking him again. He didn't speak because he couldn't but his meaning was clear in his eyes. 'Get out of my sight,' and he took his foot away.

Stephan scrambled to his feet and ran out of the house.

Dante leant down onto his knees and took some deep breaths. As soon as his voice came back he would phone the local police and inform them of a terrible armed burglary, where he was forced to defend himself, and a man died.

He flopped down to sit on a sun lounger. *What a fucking night!*

***

Twenty-four hours later, Tia and Jay walked back into The Bluebell. Jay had had to complete his business in the Balkans before they could come home, but very little had been said between them.

Tia was tired, unhappy and confused. Jay walked in and headed straight for the lift. Tia walked past him into the empty function room, grabbed a full bottle of vodka from an optic and went over to the decks. She plugged herself in and set about drowning her sorrows to a beat for as long as she could stand up, and she was well practiced.

Jay had made no effort to find out what was wrong with her, instead, he entered the lift when it opened, and went up to bed.

Tia finished the vodka by about 4 a.m., turned off the decks and decided she fancied a swim.

She went down to the basement and stepped out of the lift. The smell of chlorine hit her nose. The lights were dimmed as it was the middle of the night, but that suited her and the mood she was in.

Hiccupping, she slithered in off the side in just her underwear.

Briefly she wondered if someone would come in, then thought, fuck it, and opened her lungs and swam. Round and round, faster and faster making her own, personal, whirlpool. She was drunk and maudlin and felt she must be the loneliest person in the world. I have two men – how can I be lonely? Evidently I can.

She would have loved Jay to come to find her and ask her how she felt, just once. Then she contemplated reaching out to Dante with her mind but squashed the thought when she remembered how quickly he had wanted rid of her. No, just like when she was a kid, she only had herself to rely on. Besides, everything was her own fault; she knew it was.

She wasn't sure how long she had been in the pool but decided it was a good idea to go up to her room before her hangover hit. She didn't even have a bloody towel.

Her feet splattered over the tiles and into the lift, leaving footprint shaped puddles. God, she must look a sight; pissed alien coming through! Good job no-one was up yet as she was fully transformed and would scare some poor early swimmer.

She let herself into Jay's room and dropped her clothes on the floor as soon as she got in, knowing it would really annoy him. Then she padded around the bed until she just stood there, just looking down at him.

He didn't open his eyes but just pulled back the quilt

for her to slide in, which she did.

"Fucking hell Tia, you're wet." Still without opening his eyes, he leant back and reached down the other side of the bed and produced a towel he must have left there earlier and dumped it on Tia's head. She huffily put it under it.

Within a few moments she felt Jay's arms come around her waist and his legs behind hers, red hot with body heat. Soon his breathing became soft and even and she knew he'd gone back to sleep, but she couldn't. He was making her roast but still, it didn't make sense. She'd drunk enough vodka to knock out an elephant.

After what seemed like an age, and not wanting to wake up Jay, she remembered the new bath. Stealthily, she got out of the bed and went into the bathroom, without turning on the light, and the loud extractor fan, and began to run herself a tepid bath.

She filled it as full as she dared and got in and fell into a troubled sleep. She dreamed of Jay trapped behind a glass partition where he was shouting but she couldn't hear him. She really wanted to, but it was like TV with the sound switched off.

***

Jay woke and felt the bed next to him. She wasn't there. Where the fuck ...? He could have sworn he'd felt her get in the bed last night. Where the fuck was she now?

He went into the bathroom, checked himself in the mirror and used the loo. When he glanced over to the new sunken bath he noticed it was full of water.

He flushed the toilet and edged closer, not knowing

what he'd find. There, sound asleep, was Tia, just lying there under the surface. Her eyes were half open and fully developed black markings covered her whole body. *Fuck.* What should he do? Should he just leave her? He could see bubbles so he knew she wasn't dead, but it was something he'd never seen her do before. In fact, he'd never seen her under water or this transformed before.

He came to a quick decision. He'd go for his run and wake her if she hadn't woken by the time he got back.

Forty-five minutes later he was sitting in the bar with a coffee and a newspaper, still in his sweats. He was blowing over the surface of his cup when Dante walked in. "Bloody hell. What happened to you?"

After he'd asked the barman for an orange juice, Dante explained to Jay what had happened with Stephan, after he'd put Tia in the car.

"Fucking hell, Dant. You've got to start having some sort of protection now." Jay looked him over and came to the conclusion that apart from some facial bruising, skinned knuckles and, by the way he was standing, a couple of cracked ribs, he seemed okay.

"I had to kill the guy, Jay."

Jay just pulled a 'what could ya do' face. "What happened to Stephan?"

"I just roughed him up a bit and let the little shit go."

"You know he'll come back at you."

Dante nodded and hugged his ribs hissing. "I know what you're saying, but he's my brother."

Jay nodded and they both sipped their drinks.

"Did you tell Tia what was happening?"

"I didn't get a chance mate, after throwing her bag at me, she hasn't said a word since."

Dante creased his brow. "I didn't do anything apart from the breathing thing Jay. You didn't have a go at her did you?"

Jay didn't even answer him. He so wasn't gettting into anything with Dante.

Dante lowered his voice. "You know that I can feel what she feels when she does that to me?"

"Spare me." Jay said, holding up a hand.

"No, hear me out … She loves you Jay. I know. Why do you shut her out like that?"

"Dante, I'm not doing this with you." And he went to get down from his stool. Then he hesitated. "Except? When I woke up this morning, she was asleep in the bath. It's the first time I've noticed her doing it. Is it normal?"

Dante frowned while he thought about it. "Do you mind if I come up and see her?"

Jay shrugged. "Come on then," and they walked out and rode the lift in silence.

***

Dante walked quickly into the room and straight to the bathroom. Jay followed. They both knelt down looking at her under the water.

"She's still in exactly the same position."

"Fuck, she's fully transformed Jay. How long has she been like that?"

"She got in the bed wet about six this morning. That was the last I knew."

Dante looked at him a long moment while his brain worked. "I'm going to try and talk to her telepathically, okay?" He thanked God they'd recently renewed their bond.

Jay shrugged. "Try."

Tia, he projected quietly. *It's me Dante. Please wake up. I'm worried about you ... I got in one hell of a fight when you left last night.* Still he got no response from her. *I made you go because I knew there was going to be trouble …. You understand don't you?*

"I've never seen her like this." Jay interrupted. "You know, breathing under water. And her markings have only ever been faint before."

Dante turned around and fixed him with a hard look. "This is what she really is Jay. This is what Atlanteans are." He said it forcefully to drum it into him, hoping it would make him handle her differently. He stood up. "What's going on with you Jay?"

Jay squinted his eyes like he wasn't sure he understood what he was getting at, and not sure he liked where it was going.

"Do you know how lucky you are?

"I dunno Dant. Why don't you tell me?"

Dante saw Jay was getting agitated but persevered, even though he knew Jay was spoiling for a fight. "She is one of only five that happens only every five hundred years, or so."

Jay pulled a 'what' face.

How he didn't smack him one he didn't know. He took a breath. "She loves you … she wants you," he said, jabbing Jay in the chest with his finger.

Jay's smug smile looked back at him. "You sure you're not just sore because she didn't want you?"

Dante threw his hands up in the air in exasperation, and almost walked away but turned back. "That's just it Jay, she does want me. We are a perfect match on every level," and he held his divining ring up for him to see. "I know she feels it, because when she breathes herself into me and me her, it is a rebounding growing attraction that we can't help, no matter what we do," he laughed bitterly. "And she still said no to me Jay. Do you realise how much strength and willpower that took?" Dante smiled, shaking his head; allowing his words to sink in with his friend.

He sighed, gave up and leant down, reaching into the water behind her head and began to push her forward. "Help me sit her up."

Jay helped and between them they sat her forward. Dante gently rubbed her back, all the time talking telepathically to her.

Suddenly she seemed to become aware and looked around her in fear. She saw Dante and began coughing violently. He continued to hold her arm while he rubbed her back until her lungs were empty and she began taking large painful lugs of air. He pulled her to him.

Jay stood there with folded arms and a frown like he was unsure what he should do or make of it?

Tia, are you okay? Dante projected.

She nodded then grabbed her head. *Head's killing me ... aagh. I drank a bottle of vodka last night. I feel sick.*

Dante smiled at her. *I'm the only pisshead round here.*

She pulled him to her in a tight hug that nearly broke his heart. He closed his eyes accepting the embrace as the most special thing in the world.

Jay fidgeted. Dante noticed before he got carried away. "Tia, I'm going ... Jay's here. If you need me – anything at all – you can think me," and he pointed to his temple. "And I'll know ... or you can just ring me."

This made her laugh and grab her head again. She smiled and nodded.

Dante stood up. "Come and take your woman Jay."

Jay came around the bath, swapped places with him and steadied her.

"Look, there's loads of shit going down at the moment," Dante said, pushing his hands into his jean pockets. "I've got to help Keenan find his bird and strengthen my position. There's even a rumour that the US government has a Siren, but that hasn't been verified yet. You two have got to sort this out, okay?"

Jay nodded, then looked at Tia who was holding her mouth like she was going to throw up. She stood up and then began to push them out of the bathroom in case she was sick. They gave her space and Jay walked Dante to the door.

"Sort yourself out with her, Jay." Dante said.

"I get what you're saying."

Dante paused as he went to go out of the door. "Because I will take her off you if you don't." And he walked out.

Chapter 25

Dante's words had sunk in with Jay. Although he'd spent the last few months with her, she'd really taken second place to his work. Her own life had been put on hold and she'd gone everywhere with him, demanding very little for herself. His treatment of women wasn't that great at the best of times, and of course she was not a regular woman. Dante had rammed the point home that she wasn't even Human. He supposed that as he'd been around Dante and his family most of his life, he took all the weirdness for granted. But hearing it from Dante, and seeing Tia lying under the water the way she did, it was time to get real and either give her what she needed or pack her off to Dante, who could.

Fuck, Dante's whole position would be safer with Tia by his side. He really did owe his friend a lot. The least he could do was to stop acting like a kid and man up.

He came to sit next to Tia who was lying on the bed, groaning.

She just croaked, "I feel like shit."

He laughed and pushed her hair back from her face; her beautiful strange face with its black stripe under each cheekbone and eyes wide and black with stretched pupils and splintered irises, showing nearly no white at all. It was the face that had affected him so utterly from the moment he'd first seen it.

He leant down and kissed her gently on the head. "I'll make it up to you, Tia."

She gripped his hand with hers and gave it a weak little squeeze. "I'm just going to have a nap first."

And he smiled.

***

A few hours had passed with Tia out cold. Jay came and checked on her periodically. Eventually she stirred. Jay was sat just a few feet away from the bed. "Hello, sleepy head."

She blinked, trying to get her bearings.

"Better now?"

She nodded, sat up and looked around for a drink. He got up and passed her a bottle of water, which she glugged.

"Listen, I've been thinking."

She stopped mid-swallow.

"Would you like to go to Cash's and see your horse for a while?"

"On my own?" she croaked.

"Do you want to go on your own?" he said, leaning back and steepling his fingers.

"No." She said, shaking her head, bottle still in her mouth.

"Then we'll go later today," he said, coming to sit next to her on the bed. He leant forward and took hold of her chin. "What was last night about?" He said it gently, but waggled her chin a little in reprimand.

Her eyes tried to look away from him but he pulled her chin back so that she couldn't ignore him. "I promised Dante I would sort things out with you." His look was genuinely concerned.

"Dante was here?"

Jay sat back. "You don't remember?"

She shook her head. "I thought I dreamt him."

He took the comment on the chin, like a physical blow. That she would think Dante came to her in her dreams to comfort her … He sucked it back. "I don't think I've spent enough time with you lately. My mind has been elsewhere."

She studied his face, offering no argument.

"Will you let me make it up to you?" he continued.

Her eyes welled up and she pulled him to her by his neck. He knew her well enough to know she didn't want him to see her cry. Despite her efforts he felt her sob. "Hey, talk to me?"

She sniffed. "I'm sorry I went off with Dante." And sobbed again.

"Shh." He stayed quiet and willed her to say what was really bothering her.

"Sometimes …" She stopped, deciding against what she was going to say.

"Come on. Tell me."

"Sometimes I feel like you hate me."

Jay just stayed in exactly the same position with his face next to her neck. "Go on."

"I have no clue how you feel. Ever."

He pulled back and looked intently into her eyes.

"I think you hate me for how things have turned out with Dante." She looked down, ashamed.

"No, no, it's nothing like that," he said and pulled her back into his arms and then arranged her so she could sit in his lap. "It's just me. I'm hopeless, I've realised, with anything to do with demonstrating ... feelings." He blushed and shook his head with embarrassment. "I do miss the way it was with Dante, but that's not your fault." He made sure he looked her dead in the eye so she knew it was the truth.

She nodded weakly as if she wasn't sure.

"Sometimes Tia ... what I feel is so intense ..." He was having trouble putting his emotions into words. *Fuck.* He'd never needed to explain himself before. Never wanted to. He tried again. "The only way I can deal with it ... is to close everything down. Does that make sense?"

"Like stuff to do with me and Dante?" she said, rubbing the top of his hand, which was resting on her knee.

"Especially the stuff to do with you and Dante ... I've said enough"

"Thank you Jay," she said, solemnly.

He looked back at her surprised. "For what?"

"For opening up ... even if it was just a bit." And she put her index finger and thumb together to emphasise how small.

He pulled her up with him to stand. "I'll order

something for you to eat. You can get ready and then we'll go. I've got a surprise for you once we're up in the air." And he rubbed her cheek with his thumb.

Her eyes went wide. "What is it?"

"You'll have to wait and see." And he kissed her.

***

As they boarded the Bonaci jet, a young stewardess, smart and cheerful, came and took their bags and jackets. "Your special items have been delivered sir," she said discretely to Jay as they sat down.

"What special items?" Tia said. Her eyes glittered with excitement.

Jay wasn't given to shows of romance or grand gestures so she truly had no idea what it could be.

"You'll have to wait until we are at thirty thousand feet."

"Should I get pissed or not get pissed?" She joked.

He laughed. "Alcohol won't hurt. But stop trying to wheedle it out of me because I won't tell you."

Tia felt like it took forever for the plane to get up in the air and for the seat belt sign to go off. As soon as it did she crept over to him and sat on the floor between his knees, put her head on her folded arms and looked up at him.

"You'll be the death of me," he said, smiling down at her. "Come on, its time." And he held out his hand for her to take, and led her to the cabin towards the back of the plane. It was seldom used because he was usually working.

He pushed open the door. "After you," he said, holding

out his hand to urge her inside.

When she walked in the air felt chilly. "Air con?"

He nodded, smiling.

Inside was a beautifully made bed. On a small table was a vase of flowers, a bottle of champagne in ice and next to it four huge grey plastic sacks. "What are they?" She said, pointing at them.

He hefted one up on top of the bed, took out his penknife attached to his keys and slashed the sack along the top. He then let the sack fall over, pulled it from the bottom and tipped out the contents all over the bed.

"Ice cubes!" she said, understanding slowly dawning on her.

"We've got four bags," he said, grinning, and walked slowly towards her.

She was surprised but happy. "I've never done it on a bed, out of water, or in the air." She laughed. "The mile high club."

Jay smiled an almost sad smile. "I thought you might want to see how we mere mortals do it."

She nodded and tears welled up in her eyes.

"Don't," he said, wiping her eyes with the pad of his thumb. "Okay?" he asked, after a moment.

She nodded.

His nimble fingers made quick work of her buttons as a flush had already appeared on her cheeks. He quickly shucked his own clothes and laid her gently on the bed. Then he cupped his hands and moved the cooling ice all around her, sprinkling it gently over her chest and stomach and then lower down.

Her eyes were glued to him throughout the slow erotic process. She breathed heavily, finding it the most sensual thing she'd ever experienced. Watching him go to work all business was foreplay in itself.

He picked up an ice cube and put it in his mouth and bent over her on all fours. He put his mouth over hers and pushed it in and kissed her while he swirled it around, cooling their tongues while the ice got smaller and smaller.

He took another piece, held it in his fingers and ran it along her brow and down to her jaw, oh so slowly, and down to her neck across her hot pulse.

Then he pushed her arms out wide and slowly glided a piece of ice along each side of her arm and watched in fascination as the black rings surfaced and disappeared as the ice went over them.

He put another in his mouth and travelled and kissed down from her neck to her breasts, leaving a tingling coolness wherever his lips touched. A totally attentive lover, he dragged the ice in handfuls, conscious of keeping her cool the entire time.

He gripped one nipple with his lips and allowed the ice cube in his mouth to swirl around the hard pebble with his tongue chasing it, driving her wild. And then repeated the process the other side.

Lower he went with the ice.

He looked at her from between her legs, always keeping eye contact as he gathered ice on her body again and dipped his head, making sure when his tongue touched her delicate folds it was ice cold. He teased and tantalised as he moved ice next to her heat-radiating core with his mouth.

She groaned with want. Never had she felt this aroused.

He put his hands in the ice and touched her gently. Exploring, entering and feeling, he allowed himself this slow prelude for the very first time with her.

She reached down and pushed her fingertips through his hair and then moved them down, digging her nails into his upper arms when the sensations became more intense. "Please, Jay."

Slowly he replaced his tongue with his fingers and kissed his way back up her body, never rushing, stroking her with cool hands. He was everywhere.

"I want you now," she whispered, when his ear came next to her mouth. She gently nipped his earlobe.

He turned his mouth to hers and kissed her fully and passionately while he arranged his weight between her legs and pulled more ice between their bodies.

He held his weight on his arms and nudged at her. She bloomed for him, wetness pooling instantly as he gradually pushed further and further, so different from their usual rushed, frantic love-making. As if he'd read her mind, he pushed into her on one hard thrust. She cried out and grabbed him to her and moved with him as he began to rock, gently at first until he built in power and pushed her legs up over his arms to bury himself as hard and as deep as possible. Everything felt more forceful and more overwhelming; she gasped at the sensation.

She was trying not to be noisy but when she caught sight of a new tattoo over his left shoulder she cried out again and her orgasm enveloped her and robbed her of reason.

Emblazoned with a coat of arms was her Atlantean name in bold old-fashioned black lettering.

"Jay," she cried.

He pounded harder and cleaved to every part of her when he knew she came. It was new; so hot and wonderful. She began to feel herself float again. He throbbed inside her and gasped with his own release.

He sucked her neck and moaned. She stretched out her arms and rested her wrists in the cool pools of ice on the bed. She knew she was dangerously hot.

When he let his sated wet body drop his full weight on top of her, she whispered to him to turn onto his back.

He did as she asked and flopped onto his back and lay there catching his breath. She got up and grabbed another sack, scored it with her teeth and nails while he lay languid and propped up on pillows watching her.

"Which was my present?" she asked, bringing the bag closer. "The ice or the tattoo?"

His face looked serious for a moment. "The ice was for you ... the tattoo for me."

She put her head to one side, not understanding.

"I wanted something to connect you to me." His eyes were large and soulful. "Something permanent."

Blown away by his first demonstration of any kind of love, she felt awe and then guilt. When she was with Dante, she left something of herself inside him forever when she breathed for him, and he did the same for her. Jay didn't have that.

She made up her mind and crawled slowly up the bed until her lips were mere millimetres away from his. "I want to give you something of me," she said in a whisper, kissing him gently.

He nodded imperceptibly.

"Did you drink all your Elixir?"

"Yes." he said, sucking in her lip and nibbling it.

"You understand what it means? It's forever."

He nodded and kissed her again harder with his hands gripping her waist hard. "Do it," he said, pulling her down on him so she could feel how turned on he was again.

She exhaled as she allowed herself to sink down onto him and envelop him. Heat flashed through her like a furnace. "Ice!" she cried.

He pulled the bag nearer, tipping it all over his chest between their bodies, hitching a breath at the shock to his system.

"This will warm you," she said, putting her mouth to his. "Open for me." Her tongue parted his lips.

He breathed heavily, his chest moving up and down.

She closed her eyes and delved to the depths of her being – to the heart of her. She felt it rising up and up it came till she felt it tingling on her lips. She let it flow only for a few seconds and watched his face glow red, then orange and his head fall back in ecstasy and his eyes roll back. She leant up and watched it journey down into his heart where he would feel the rush.

She knew the instant he felt it. His hands gripped her waist hard and he shouted, his face in ecstatic pain. He ground his orgasm into her, on and on, wave after wave.

"Ah Tia!" he moaned, into her shoulder, biting her skin as another wave hit him. "Fuck!"

She just lay still and let him hold onto her until the shudders became wider apart and eventually stopped.

She pushed him back gently onto the pillows and sat up. His face was red hot and his eyes bloodshot. "Bloody hell Jay, you look terrible." She took a pillow out of its case, put a handful of ice in it and held it to his forehead.

He looked at her with glassy eyes.

"You feel my heat. I'm sorry Jay, I shouldn't have done it."

"Shhh!" he said, too weak to move. "Tia, it was fucking … I dunno, the best buzz. It was mind-blowing. And I felt you … everything you feel … for me." He looked at her with awe.

She smiled weakly and dabbed his hot body and face with the ice bag. *I love you.* She projected straight to his mind and he grinned a heart-wrenching grin.

***

He heard her voice as clear as a bell. He tried his best to reply but it either didn't work or he was too weak.

"It's okay Jay, I think it needs to be a two-way thing for you to be able to do it back." She reassured him and stroked his face.

Yes, that was probably it. But the knowledge the act they just shared gave him was humbling. He could even feel her worry for him now and wished he had the strength to envelope her in his arms. What had started as a present for her, ended up as the most sacred gift to him. She was now a part of him forever. It was a marriage of sorts. He totally got it now.

He wished he didn't feel so shit. He had hoped he'd feel better as time wore on but the truth was he was feeling worse and worse. In fact, the urge to throw up was getting really strong. "Babe, I'm gonna ..." and he held his mouth.

Tia leapt off the bed and grabbed the champagne bucket. He spewed into it and felt wretched. His stomach griped and his head swam.

She tried cooling his wrists and lay him gently back down flat. But his teeth were chattering and his body had begun to shake violently. "Oh Jay, Fuck! Fuck! Fuck! What have I done?"

Everything went fuzzy then black.

Chapter 26

Tia grabbed Jay's phone and hit Dante. It rang and rang and went to answerphone.

She left a message:

"You probably know what I've done, I'm a stupid, stupid cow. He's burning up, being sick and now he's unconscious. I don't know what to do Dante. Please help."

She looked back at Jay. No change. She tried Cash next. He picked up. She explained roughly what had happened. He cursed and said he would pick them up and try to reach Alfonzo who would probably know the best thing to do. She thanked him and went back over to the bed.

Jay was on fire. She swaddled him with as much ice as she could and sat in misery watching him. "Dante, please help," she thought, over and over.

***

Cash had taken no chances and had an ambulance meet them at the airport. The paramedics had come from the same small private clinic where Tia had convalesced after the fall from her horse.

He'd primed them that Jay had an exotic virus which recurred from time to time after spending a lot of time in Africa in his childhood. He figured it was a safe fabrication. Plus Human doctors would be treating him as a Human and wouldn't notice anything untoward; well he hoped they wouldn't.

The paramedics carried his stretcher and loaded him into the ambulance. Tia wanted to ride with Jay, so Cash, anxious to speak with her, told her they must speak as soon as she had a chance when they got to the hospital. Preoccupied, she agreed and hopped in next to Jay.

Jay was soon settled into his private room. Monitors beeped all around him. He was on a drip and was packed in ice in an effort to bring down his sky-high temperature. He was stable for the time being, so it was a good opportunity for Cash to go out into the corridor with Tia.

"Have you managed to get hold of Dante?" she asked.

Cash shook his head. "I spoke to Alfonzo though, who said he would contact the Guard in New York. They'll bring a booster supply of Elixir. He said he was confident that it would sort Jay out, and if he lived through this, he should have a much stronger constitution. The next forty-eight hours are crucial."

"Thank God." Tia said, closing her eyes.

"There is more Tia ... the shit seems to have hit the fan in Ireland."

"What do you mean?"

Cash sighed deeply, as if mustering the strength. "Dubonnetti has disowned Dante."

Tia looked at Cash in disbelief.

"Apparently, Marco has found letters proving that Dante isn't his son. So Marco is now arguing that he is now the oldest son."

"But not of five. Doesn't the law clearly say that the king will be one of five, just as the Sirens are one of five?" Tia added.

"That's what Alfonzo said. He said it was an illegal claim, but Dubonnetti is counting Jay's adoption to make it five. Oh, and one last thing – a girl has turned up with the Guard, believed to be one of your sisters."

"Bloody hell. Keenan's?"

Cash nodded. "Not confirmed yet … And lastly, your uncle sent us a warning. On no account must you go off unescorted. He's had certain intelligence that a government agency is planning to snatch a Siren."

"What do they want me for?"

Her naivety was touching, "What's it ever for, Tia? Because you're different … Leverage. Power. The important thing is to stick together, okay? The one piece of good news is that Sean and Sarah have had their baby – a little boy – and they are coming on a commercial flight. Should be here later today."

"You should have told them to take some time together, Cash."

"I did, but you know what Sean is like. He can't miss anything."

***

Jay's dreams were turbulent and Technicolor, always with Tia trying to reach him whilst he could never hear what she was saying. He tried to wake up but sleep kept taking him down over and over again.

He was sure he kept hearing Tia tell him she loved him, and was sorry. He tried to respond but the effort was just too much – like in a nightmare where your legs won't move no matter how badly you want them to.

Now everything was just black.

Jay ... Jay!

He was looking around him in the blackness for Tia, but it wasn't Tia. It was a male voice. *Dante?* he thought. *How can he be in my head? I must be dreaming. Delirious again.*

No Jay, it's me. Really me. It's weak because I'm a long way away.

Dante?

Yes mate.

How is this even possible? He still wasn't convinced he wasn't losing his mind.

It's through your new bond. I am talking straight to you because I can't get there yet Jay, all kind of shit's gone down. Now listen carefully mate, because you and Tia's lives depends on it.

But I'm sick Dante. Useless.

I know mate, that's why I'm here. Pretty soon Keenan and the Guard will turn up with a booster supply of Elixir for you. Now I don't know if we can trust him yet. He has his Siren back and he may decide to take all five, as the Guard know where they all are. Do you understand?

Yes but ...

The Elixir he gives you may be fake, so that you don't

make it and he gets access to Tia.

What can I do Dant?

You've got to beat this Jay.

I don't know if I can.

What's happening to you is like a kind of DNA invasion; that's the only way I can explain it. Instead of physical traits, all her emotional, spiritual and philosophical ones are trying to join with yours at a genetic level. You're feeling so shit because your body is fighting it like a virus invading your body. You've got to find a way to let it go Jay. Just gradually shut yourself down and give in. If Keenan comes through then no harm's done, but if not, you're gonna have to beat this Jay, otherwise she'll be gone.

Then everything was black again. *Did that really just happen? It was incredible.* But what he heard was plausible though. Did it make sense to give in, or fight more? Did he want her in every cell of him or not? Yes he did. That was the whole purpose of the fucking exercise. His body just didn't know it yet.

He decided to start from the feet up, and began to concentrate like he'd never done before.

***

Tia had walked out of the hospital room to get a coffee. Sarah, Sean and the baby had arrived an hour before and had just left to go back to the ranch with Cash. It had been a long tiring flight for them. Cash said he was coming straight back and had given her strict instructions not to go anywhere. Like she would actually want to be anywhere else.

Her thoughts were interrupted by a noise that started

as a rumble, and then began to sound like heavy boots – a lot of them. There also seemed to be a lot of activity with the staff. Should she hide? She decided to pick up a magazine and look inconspicuous, in the same way a child hides under the covers. She sat cross-legged and pretended she was reading.

Her thumping heart was as loud as their boots when they marched into the room she was in. A pair stopped right in front of her. She was too frightened to look up.

"Tia!"

She recognised that voice. Slowly she let her eyes rise up the huge black-fatigued legs, muscular, black t-shirted stomach, chest, and then face. "Keenan," she breathed in relief, and jumped up and threw her arms around his neck.

He leant down slightly to allow her to reach him, but put her away from him shyly a moment later. He obviously wanted to get on with the business of why he was there.

He reached into his jacket pocket and pulled out a clear vial. "Please Tia, give this to Jay. Speed is essential."

She took it from him quickly, and went to take it into Jay's room but her progress was halted when a nurse came over to protest. Keenan and another guard barred the nurse's way with an arm. She started to threaten to call security and got really annoyed when Keenan just smiled without even bothering to reply.

Tia took the opportunity to rush into the room and shut the door. She uncorked the vial and went up to the bed and felt Jay's head. She wasn't sure if it was wishful thinking but she could have sworn he felt cooler.

She slid her hand behind his head and tilted it forward slightly. She put the tiny vial next to his lips and was about to trickle it into his mouth, being really careful she didn't lose any of the precious liquid, when his arm came up lightening-fast and grabbed her by the wrist. She yelped in fright at the sudden move. "Jay, it's okay. Keenan brought this for you," she coaxed.

He stared at her then allowed her to feed him. She wasn't sure if he was aware or not, but he took down the whole vial.

The door had opened and closed behind her as Keenan came into the room. "Is he okay? Fuck! He's awake. Did he take it all?"

"Yes," she replied.

Jay slowly closed his eyes again.

Keenan gave her another vial. "Give him this in twelve hours time. He must be very strong."

"What do we do now?" she asked, looking up at Keenan.

"We wait."

***

The night wore on and Jay appeared to be sleeping peacefully. His fever had broken at long last and the doctors were confident that he was out of the woods.

Cash and Sean had come and gone again, safe in the knowledge that four of the Guard, including Keenan, remained.

Tia hadn't moved from Jay's bedside. Keenan nudged her shoulder and handed her a cup of hot chocolate from the machine in the waiting room. Then he went and sat in an armchair in the far corner of the room. The lights were dim and made him look menacing in the half-light. "You love him very much?"

"Yes," she sighed. "I never thought it was possible to care for someone so much."

"And Dante? That must be really difficult for all of you?'

"Yes it is." She looked away from him so he couldn't see the emotion on her face.

"What about you?" she said, changing the subject. "Any news?"

"She has turned up."

"That's great." Then, reading the look on his face, "Isn't it?'

He shook his head then leant forward with his elbows on his knees. "She has no memory of me."

"What? How can …"

"I don't know. But she has no clue who I am." And he shut his eyes and shook his head as if in pain.

"Bloody hell Keenan, I'm so sorry. Doesn't anyone have any ideas?"

He sat back in his chair in a 'fuck knows' pose. "Some say a strong vampire could have erased her memories. Some have said an alchemist could have given her something. Either way, without knowing her connection to me, she could be taken by anyone." He stood and walked to her side of the bed. Sitting still was too uncomfortable.

Tia picked up his hand and gave it a squeeze. "And

you came here to help us despite having all that to deal with? Thank you."

"Hey!" he said, looking past her at the patient.

She turned her head and saw that Jay was blinking and trying to sit up. "Easy," she said, passing him a glass of water from the bedside table.

He made short work of it but dropped the empty glass on the bed, and pointed his index finger at Keenan. "Get the fuck away from her."

"Jay!" Tia scolded, shocked at his outburst. "He's here to help. He brought the Elixir for you."

"I don't fucking care. Step back!" Venom dripped from every word and hatred sprang from his bloodshot eyes.

Tia was gobsmacked. "Jay. What's the matter?"

Jay fumbled in the sheets and found the glass he'd just dropped with his other hand. He smashed it on the corner of the bedside table and held the piece of glass in his hand like a weapon.

"Easy tiger!" Keenan said, half laughing with incomprehension, his hands up in submission.

"Jay, you must still be delirious!" She reasoned.

"No I'm not." And he pointed the shard at Keenan. "He's got his woman back ... he knows where you all are. He's here to snatch you."

"Where on earth did you get that from? He's been with me ages waiting for you to get better ... alone!" she said, shaking her head.

Keenan grinned. "I'm going to ignore that insult and put it down to post-traumatic paranoia." He laughed.

"If I didn't know better I'd think that slippery cousin of mine had been putting ideas in your head." He turned to Tia. "I'll be outside. Give you some time." He grinned at Jay again and shook his head as he walked out of the room.

Jay flopped back on the pillows.

"You owe him an apology Jay."

Jay looked troubled, like he was trying to work something out. Then he looked at her square in the eyes. "The Elixir didn't save me Tia …" he said, coming to a conclusion. "It was Dante."

Chapter 27

The concentration needed to think project the distance to Jay was exhausting, but he daren't leave to go to America, not now.

Dante had come to the conclusion that his life was in a cement mixer; loads of crap and more being chucked in the mix all the time.

He'd thought it was weird when Stephan turned up at home bold as brass, with no shame whatsoever after their last altercation. The next thing he knew he was being summoned to his father's study. It felt the same as it did when it had happened umpteen times as a kid. His father had beaten him down physically and emotionally time and time again, until Dante grew enough in size and temper that he didn't dare. Most of the time Dante was off his head on drink or drugs or both anyway, so his father just ignored him.

He thought they'd turned a corner since he'd become king and taken over the family business, and started making them some real money. But hope of that quickly evaporated when he walked in and his father engaged his usual sneer of disgust.

His father threw a bundle on the desk of what looked like letters tied together with a red ribbon.

Dante looked at them and then his father and waited for him to get to the point.

"They are letters to your mother." Christian said.

Dante shook his head. "I don't understand."

"From her lover."

"What's that got to do with …?"

"From your father." Christian drooled the words.

Dante was left opening and closing his mouth like a fish.

"Duke Ormond Delissi … my first cousin."

"How did …? Why now?"

"Your brothers found them playing billiards. Bashed the wall next to the fireplace, and out they dropped. She couldn't have removed them before she died," he said, absently, as if lost in a memory long gone.

Dante's mind was racing a mile a minute. "What do you want me to do?" Dante asked, simply. What else could he say? There must be some point to his father – scratch, Christian –bringing him here, and it wasn't just to chew the fat.

His father stood up behind his desk, like an old-fashioned judge about to put his black cap on and pronounce the death sentence. "You will leave my house with only the clothes you stand up in, and never return. You are not, nor ever have been, my son." And he flopped down in his chair as if the air had been sucked out of him.

Dante wasted no time with recriminations. He

reached towards the desk and picked up the letters, stuffing them into his jacket pocket. He decided that further words were pointless, and he walked out of the room and out of the house without a backwards glance.

"The great king has fallen," Marco scoffed as Dante strode past, but Dante was too preoccupied to hear, let alone rise to the bait.

***

Dante trudged for two and a half hours in the pouring rain to reach Ballygowan Castle – home of the Bonaci.

He didn't know where else to go with not a penny to his name and his mind still reeling. He knocked on the big old oak, porch door, and hoped to God someone would hear, as they lived below ground.

It was nearly dark and he didn't know what he would do if Sebastian, Tia's father, didn't take him in.

His mind kept going over all the implications; whether or not he was still king; whether Tia was still his wife; where he stood legally with Royal Dubonnetti Industries; whether the Bonaci would turn their backs on him – that he decided was pivotal.

He knocked again. Then he remembered his mobile phone and took it out of his jacket. Thank God he had it on him. He dialled Alfonzo, who answered quickly. "Let me in, Alfonzo. I'm at the door."

A few minutes later a butler opened the door. Dante didn't wait for any pleasantries and pushed passed him.

"Master is below, sir."

Dante nodded and pushed the lift button.

***

Dante stood dripping in front of Sebastian, Tia's father, and Alfonzo, her uncle. He explained the story as far as he knew it and took the letters out of the inside pocket of his soggy jacket.

Sebastian said nothing but rang for a servant. *Shit, he was going to get shown the door.*

The servant came immediately. "Please get his Royal Highness a towel, and make a room ready for him."

The servant bowed and left the room. Dante breathed a sigh of relief and closed his eyes in thanks. It appeared they were prepared to take him in.

"We will have to consult the ancient tomes on this, but I think the fact that a Siren has pledged to you is still a position of strength," Alfonzo explained.

Although Dante was relieved, he was still confused. "What about me not now being one of five sons?"

Sebastian looked surprised that Dante knew anything of what the prophecies said. "But you are," Sebastian said, "on your mother's side. And she was as royal as Dubonnetti."

"As is your father, Delissi," Alfonzo added, and Sebastian conceded a nod.

"Have you heard anything from Tia?" Dante asked, anxious to know whether she and Jay were okay.

"She is well." Sebastian said, smiling. "Keenan is with her. He telephoned recently to say that Jay had regained consciousness." He stifled a titter into his hand. "So much so that he threatened Keenan with a makeshift weapon minutes after waking up in his sickbed.

Dante couldn't keep the smile off his face. "Really?"

I bet he fucking did as well. God, what he wouldn't do to be with him right now. "He was probably worried Keenan would take Tia now he has his own Siren back. He may have got wind of what was going on over here," he said, trying to sound more serious.

"Possibly, but Keenan is loyal, as is all the Guard. He also has his own problems." And Alfonzo explained to Dante the troubling revelations related to Keenan's Siren's lack of memory.

"I think the important thing to do next is to consult our lawyers regarding your fortune and your access to finances tied up in Dubonnetti business dealings. He cannot leave you penniless. Your mother was a rich woman in her own right. Then we'll summon Keenan with my niece as soon as he's comfortable about it. If we can pledge a second Siren to you, the other family heads will capitulate, provided we offer an incentive."

Dante nodded, grateful for everything they were prepared to do for him. "Thank you … Thank you both." And he meant it with his whole being. They had shown belief in him where his former family never had. "And for helping my friend, and my wife."

"No need to thank us, dear boy. They are a son and a daughter of this house, as you are now, through marriage. The rightful king; one of five, first pledged to a Siren." Dante swallowed back a lump in his throat and nodded.

"Now you are away from the poor influence of Dubonnetti, we would like to start your real education to be a great king – one worthy of Atlas – if you accept us as mentors?"

Dante closed his eyes, filled with emotion and gratitude, and then looked at them earnestly. "I'm ready."

***

Jay was kept in hospital for another day and then was discharged. In fact, the staff were amazed at how quickly he had bounced back after being so gravely ill. But he hadn't just bounced back, he felt different, stronger, quicker and more alert. He couldn't explain it.

More good news was that his body temperature for a Human was now low – very low. He tested out his theory the first night he was back at Cash's ranch.

Tia was busy arranging their bed as she normally did so they could both get some sleep, when he leant down and stilled her arm. "Don't do that tonight."

"What … Why?" she said, not understanding.

"How would you normally sleep if I wasn't in the bed?"

"Naked. Just with a sheet."

"Then I want us to try it like that tonight."

"But?"

He smiled at her. "Humour me?"

She did as she was asked and they both slid between the sheets after undressing. She lay on her side with her head on her pillow and he on the other facing back at her.

"Come here," he said.

"But we …"

He leant over and pulled her to him. Then he arranged

her under his arm, tucked in with her head on his chest and leg across his.

She looked up at him. He kissed her forehead. "How do you feel?"

"I feel fine."

"Not too hot?"

"No," she said, obviously surprised.

"It's what I suspected."

They snuggled together and he nuzzled her hair.

"I'm sorry for making you sick, Jay. I'll never do it again. I promise."

He lifted her chin so he could look into her face. "But you must Tia."

She shook her head and tried to move away from him. "I can't risk losing you. I could live without anyone except you."

He was touched at what she said and smiled and pulled her back to him. "I know it made me sick, Tia, but what it gave me was … indescribable. I believe if we're careful, I could get stronger every time, as my body gets used to it."

"Can we just get you better first?"

He held her tight and relished the novelty of it. "I warn you Tia, I'm getting better very fast." And he squeezed her.

***

Tia made sure she got up very early to do the horses, the next morning. She didn't want to take any chances with Jay, sexy and naked, waking up next to her.

She was having breakfast in the kitchen with Cash.

Sean was jiggling the baby in his arms waiting for some formula to warm up, when Jay walked in wearing worn jeans, no top and bare feet. I can't look, Tia thought, and crossed her legs.

He walked straight over to where she was sitting on the breakfast stool, put his arms around her waist from behind her and kissed her neck.

Heat flashed into her cheeks. She tried to put her hands up to her face to hide it.

"Hey Sean," Jay said. "Congratulations man. What's his name?"

"Ronnie."

Jay smiled and nodded. "Nice."

"He's been a little toe-rag all night though."

"Fancy a spar in a minute ... wear some of that stress off?' Jay asked, with raised eyebrows.

"Yes." Sean said emphatically. "Yes, I bloody do. Give me five." And he hurried off with the baby's bottle to find Sarah.

"Can we use your barn Cash?" Jay asked.

He nodded. "Sure."

"Jay!" Tia scolded, swivelling around in her chair.

He smiled his shy smile.

Irresistible. "Aagh." Realising that there was no point in her saying anything else, she turned back around.

"Come with us. You can put some music on while we work out."

"You're supposed to be taking it easy."

"And I will. I promise not to break Sean's nose."

Cash barked a laugh. "Stop trying to turn him into a

sissy Tia."

She looked daggers at Cash, which made him laugh all the more.

"Okay, I give up." And she held her hands up in surrender.

They all trooped into the barn. Tia went over to her decks, still set up from her last visit. She fired them up. "What do you want then?" she shouted.

"Plug in my MP3. I fancy something aggressive," Jay said, smiling at Sean.

Tia went to Jay's collection of drum 'n' base.

Jay paced like a panther while Sean took off his t-shirt. Tia was trying not to look. She knew Jay was capable but he was only twenty-four hours out of hospital. Sean was a soldier and fully trained in hand-to-hand combat.

"I'll umpire." Cash said. "But I want to spar the winner."

"Okay by me." Jay said, already low in his stance, circling with Sean.

Tia found herself having to look on in morbid curiosity. It looked like a mixture of boxing, martial arts and wrestling. It was quick and surprisingly very evenly matched. Every jab and kick was blocked; very little got through on either side.

***

Jay felt fantastic. He felt in tune with every sinew and fibre in his body. He felt an instinct a millisecond before Sean decided where he was going to hit or kick next and he could pre-empt it correctly every time.

"Let me have a go," Cash shouted from the side lines.

He was already unbuttoning his checked shirt revealing his huge bear-like chest. Jay was tall but very lean. Cash was a big cowboy who could wrestle steers to the ground.

Tia put her hands over her face.

"Have a bit of faith, Tia!" Jay shouted to her.

Tia shook her head.

Again Jay got low. He knew he'd have to use Cash's weight against him, as he was probably twice his. Again he managed to dodge every lunge. His speed was amazing; everyone was noticing it. He even found he could use his peripheral vision and his ears, which made his intuition perfect.

Jay was aware when the four guards, including Keenan, entered the barn. Keenan leant back and folded his arms and watched the show in front of him.

Jay and Cash were sweating. Jay hadn't enjoyed himself so much in ages. It felt as though his body was a machine that could do anything. Eventually he and Cash touched knuckles and called it a draw. Both were breathing heavily but wore huge beaming smiles.

Jay turned around to Tia still smiling. "See, I'm okay."

Tia shook her head and put another record on.

"Not bad for a Human," Keenan said, from the edge of the barn. He was studying Jay's array of Atlantean tattoos for the first time as he turned around to him.

"You wanna have a go?" Jay said, with a straight face.

"You have fought twice already, it wouldn't be fair." Keenan replied.

"I don't mind if you don't." *Yes you fucker. Let's have it.* Jay paced round in a circle as Keenan pulled off his black t-shirt and removed his watch.

Tia noticed the new challenger, switched off the decks and came over to them. Cash pulled her quickly to the side with him and Sean, out of harm's way.

Jay got low again. Keenan looked massive in comparison. His hairless chest and back rippled with knotted muscle and the Santalini warrior tattoos moved with him like a warning.

"What say we make it interesting and use a weapon?" Keenan offered.

"No!" Tia shouted, but quickly shut up when she heard Keenan say she had no faith in her man.

Cash chucked over two broomsticks. "That's as sharp as you're getting."

They both caught them and got down in their stances.

"This is cool." Sean said, and took out his mobile phone to record it.

From the first bash of sticks, it looked and sounded like lightening. They used them like quarterstaffs, blocking with the staffs held wide and striking like they were long swords. They turned, twisted and smashed above each other's heads.

Jay was in the zone. Fuck, he felt like he was Neo out of the Matrix, his reflexes were so fast. He knew Keenan was toying with him at first, but when he really started to see him as a worthy opponent, he turned it on and Jay was ready for him.

Today he was putting his stake in the ground to show Keenan once and for all that he wasn't to be messed with.

Before long, Keenan managed to beat Jay back against the wall and pinned him with his stick across his neck. He grimaced as he spoke showing Jay his fangs. "What about something a bit more close quarters?"

"Anytime," Jay bit out.

One of the other guards who were standing nearby took two daggers out of a holster under his jacket and quickly passed them to Keenan.

Everyone went to step forward to shout their protests, but the three other guards barred their way. "Let them continue," one said.

When Keenan released Jay from his hold, Jay dropped his staff and took one of the daggers from Keenan whose grin was totally saying 'you're mine now'.

"This is how we spar," Keenan said, returning to the centre of the barn.

Jay followed him – not intimidated in the slightest, but completely focused, – passing the dagger from hand to hand to feel its weight.

Keenan lunged forward. Jay spun out of the way, kicked out a leg and tripped Keenan up so he went to the ground. Murmurs around them sounded as Jay leapt on him and they rolled over and over in the dirt. Keenan managed to throw him off and scramble back to his feet.

Keenan lunged again. This time Jay went to the floor and used his foot and Keenan's momentum to throw him over the top of him. But Keenan wasn't easy to dupe for long and began to read his moves and became harder and harder to throw, until eventually he unbalanced Jay and used his weight to pin him with his dagger to his throat.

They both stared into each other's eyes, breathing heavily. Jay couldn't move – not a millimetre. All the spectators dared not breathe.

"I could have killed you in the hospital and I could kill you now," Keenan said, in a gritted whisper that only Jay could hear.

Tiny swirls of blood entered Keenan's ice blue irises, turning his eyes red for a second. Then they dissolved, leaving his eyes clear again.

Jay watched wide-eyed while his breath hacked in and out of his lungs, and his brain worked hard for an out.

"You don't give up do you, even when you're pinned?" Keenan said, as if he'd read his mind.

Jay remained silent.

Keenan smiled, sat back onto his knees, and as he stood he offered a hand down to Jay to pull him to his feet. Jay used the hand offered but remained quiet and thoughtful as he walked back over to the group of Cash, Sean and Tia.

Keenan walked back over to him as he pulled his shirt back over his head. "Have you sparred with daggers before?"

Subdued, Jay shook his head. "Would you teach me?"

Keenan nodded, turned and walked out of the barn with his Guard mates.

Sean and Cash clapped Jay on the back.

Chapter 28

Later that day, a letter arrived by courier with the royal Dubonnetti seal on it, addressed to Keenan. Cash passed it to him as soon as he'd signed for it and closed the door.

They were all sitting on the porch escaping the heat of the afternoon with a beer.

"Do you think it's from Dante?" Cash asked, as he handed it to him.

"I doubt it ... this should be interesting." Keenan snapped the seal and read it quickly in his head and then closed it and put it in his back pocket.

Everyone looked at him expectantly as he took a swig of his beer.

"Well?" Jay asked.

"Well what?" Keenan replied.

"You're not going to tell us?"

Keenan sighed as if he were calculating what he was going to say. "It's from Marco Dubonnetti, ordering us to bring you two," and he pointed to Jay and Tia, "back to them in Ireland, and bring my own woman while I'm at it."

A sad silence fell on everyone. They waited again uncomfortably. They all came to the conclusion that it meant Dante had been deposed as king. When they eventually realised that Keenan wasn't going to be forthcoming with any more information, they slowly dispersed to do other things or to the privacy of their rooms.

Cash called Tia to help him apply a poultice to a skittish colt, and left Jay and Keenan alone. As neither were big talkers, there was a gaping great silence between them. But Jay wasn't going to be intimidated into talking crap any more than Keenan was, so the pair just carried on swigging their beers. Jay eventually broke the silence. "Do you want something stronger?"

"Sure," Keenan said, draining his bottle.

Jay went into the kitchen and grabbed a bottle of Jack Daniel's and a couple of glasses and came back out on the porch. "You know I won't let you take Tia to that prick!"

Keenan laughed. "You are always so confrontational. Do you know that?"

"What can I say …you bring out the best in me."

Keenan tilted his glass as if to say cheers. "Look, I'll tell you this much, the Guard is a royal family. We will not be ordered about by some poncey boy you could knock over with a strong gust of wind. We have long traditions and honour."

"What are you gonna do?'

"Speak to Alfonzo for a start. I've got a feeling it's a bluff to get us all there."

"What, and you think Dante is still king?'

"Exactly."

"Where do you think Dante is?"

"Let's find out." Keenan took his mobile out of his pocket and hit Alfonzo's number. "Alfonzo?" He explained what was in the letter he'd received, and that it had been sent with the king's royal seal on it.

Jay felt he was a good judge of character and although Keenan ruffled all his feathers most of the time, he was proving to be an okay guy. He'd come through a few times now.

"Yes he's with me now," Keenan continued. "Okay, I'll tell him." And he ended the call.

He looked at Jay. "Dante's still king. He's now living at Ballygowan Castle. This letter," and he pointed to his back pocket, "is an act of treason."

"What are they gonna do about it?"

"They're planning some strategy to bring all the families together for some meeting. Because of the Sirens being Bonaci, and the Bonaci backing Dante, I think he's safe … for the time being anyway."

"Good." Jay said, relieved, and he poured them another drink.

They were quiet for a while again.

"You know I thought you were a traitor to your friend when I first met you?" Keenan said, sitting back in his chair more relaxed now.

"I know," Jay said.

Keenan smiled. "So you've known Dante all your life?"

"Pretty much."

"And you are fucking his wife?"

Jay just looked at him in warning. "What is this …you trying to pick a fight now?"

"There you go again … I'm just trying to understand. You seem close to Dante, even now. I'm supposed to be guarding the lot of you. I sort of think it's important to understand the dynamics of this relationship triangle; whatever it is."

Jay sat back in his chair and downed his drink. "It's a fucking mess." He sighed. "It could have been less messy, if it wasn't for Marco Dubonnetti."

"I don't understand?' Keenan said, confused.

Jay went on to explain the short version of the story. How he and Tia had met long before he or she knew what she was, or even who Dante was in connection with her, and Marco's part in fucking them all over.

Keenan quietly listened. "So he is your closest friend. You both love the same woman, through no fault of either of you, and you are all tied together permanently.

"That's about the size of it."

Keenan digested the information for a second and shook his head in disbelief. "Lacy; that's my Siren, was my best friend; the closest person to me. There were no family for us growing up- only each other."

"Was?" Jay asked, frowning.

"She doesn't know who I am … not a clue."

"Fuck!"

"Yeah … exactly. So I've got to find a way to get her to remember me before some bastard takes her off me."

"Like Marco?"

Keenan looked at Jay with pure hatred on his face. Jay saw the eerie red swirls enter his eyes again and disappear and guessed they were to do with anger or something.

"I would gut him like a pig before I gave her to him."

Jay understood that sentiment and poured them another drink. "The thing I have learned, mate, is that it all happens under the water. And it don't matter if they force them in there or not. When it comes down to it, it's just the Siren and the bloke, and if she doesn't accept him … it's curtains."

Keenan nodded and clinked his glass with Jay. "You're right."

It was a strange meeting of minds, but as the two of them drank their Jack Daniel's, a new understanding and allegiance was formed.

***

The next few days were busy on the ranch. Cash wanted to get his hay cut, baled, and in his barn before the weather hit. So as well as the extra hands he hired, everyone pitched in and helped do the heavy work.

Tia enjoyed helping with Sarah to bring out cool drinks and food, especially as it gave her ample opportunity to perve on Jay's stripped-to–the-waist body hefting the hay. All it needed was some Barry White in the background for the complete sensory package. Jay totally thrived on any sort of physical activity.

The sun was going down as they put the last few bales in the barn. All felt the satisfaction of a job well done. Everyone's face beamed as Mrs Ross, the housekeeper, rewarded them all with a huge spread to celebrate on the back porch.

All the men swarmed over the food, piling their plates high. The mood was jovial. Beers sprouted from barrels filled with ice, and were grabbed by everyone as they passed by.

Tia enjoyed watching Jay interact with everyone and thought how much he'd fitted in and relaxed since he'd been ill. She'd managed to avoid sexual contact with him since, but seeing him sunburnt and happy, her resolve was dissipating by the minute.

She was vaguely aware of the phone ringing in the house while she was gazing at Jay. Then Mrs Ross came out and she dragged her eyes away to watch her go up to Keenan and whisper something discretely. He nodded, stood and went into the house, so Tia turned her attention back to Jay who was sitting next to her making short work of a plate of ribs; something she could never try.

He sensed her watching him and looked sideways at her. "Am I making a pig of myself?" he said, with that adorable lack of confidence she'd grown to love about him.

"Not at all," she said, and leant into him to kiss him on the cheek. "I was thinking the outdoor life suits you."

He pushed his plate away, washed his hands in the finger bowl and sat back holding her hand. "Yeah, I've really enjoyed the last few days."

"Could you ever see yourself living this life?"

He half-turned his body so he could look at her

properly and smiled. "Why, are you propositioning me?"

"Oh yeah," she said, inching closer to him and wishing they were alone.

As she was about to throw caution to the wind and out and out snog him anyway, Keenan came back out from the house, having changed his clothes, put his keys in his pocket from the table and announced to everyone he was going.

The mood sobered instantly as everyone sensed there was something wrong. The three other guards were already on their feet.

Jay quickly stood. "What's up mate?"

"Christian and Marco have turned up at our HQ in New York. That was my eldest brother Marius," he said, nodding his head back towards the house. "They have been trying to win him and my uncle over to accepting Marco's claim to the throne by throwing in with them."

"They won't will they?" Jay asked.

"I doubt it, but I'm sorry I have to go. Lacy is there. They'll want her to pledge to Marco, and there's no fucking way I'm having that."

Jay was already taking out his phone. Tia eavesdropped him making travel arrangements while Keenan apologised to everyone. They were just concerned for him and told him not to worry about anyone else.

Jay ended his call. "My plane is at Billings, take it."

Keenan shook his hand. "Thank you man, I won't forget it. I will take two of my men and leave one with you."

"That's fine," Jay said. "Me, Cash and Sean are capable

of overseeing things here. Just go mate."

Keenan thanked everyone and took a hasty goodbye. Worry and anxiety were written all over his face. How he loved her sister. She really hoped they worked things out, and for the first time she really longed for a sister; something she'd never had before.

***

Tia was subdued for the rest of the evening. When at last she and Jay got into bed, he asked if she was okay.

"Oh, I dunno," she sighed. "I was thinking about Keenan that's all, and how horrible everything is for him at the moment."

Jay nodded, while he lay on his back and looked at the ceiling with his hands behind his head.

"I know it's been hard for us," Tia continued. "But I'm sort of glad that I've done my pledging already. It sort of takes me out of the game, doesn't it?"

Jay pulled her to him. "I still don't trust what they're up to, Tia ... I think we need to be careful."

She turned onto her side to look at him. "How do you feel about the Dubonnetti's, you were sort of part of the family weren't you?"

"Yeah, but it's always been me and Dante really ... His dad used to just bring me there, that's all. I had no bond with him or anything. I used to feel angry at the way he treated Dante most of the time."

They lay quietly in each other's arms for a while.

"Can I ask you a question Tia?"

"Of course." There followed silence. She looked up at him when he didn't speak.

"Aagh," he said, sitting up, pushing his hand through his hair in impatience with himself.

"Come on, out with it," she said, not letting him off the hook.

He looked at her as if debating with himself. "Have you been avoiding me?" he said, his cheeks bursting red with embarrassment. He tried to pull away from her, grumbling, "I'm not used to talking this kind of shit."

Touched, she sat up and grabbed his face in her hands and looked deep into his eyes. "I've been letting you get better."

He looked at her a long while, with that calculating look she knew so well. "I've been sparring every day with Keenan, working with Cash, I'm as strong as an Ox, Tia." He pulled out of her hands as if he'd convinced himself of something and sat on the edge of the bed.

Tia could feel everything spiralling out of her control. She knew how hard it was for him to talk anything remotely resembling feelings. But deep down she was terrified about losing herself to her true nature and hurting him again, perhaps killing him this time.

"I can't feel you in me anymore …" he said, over his shoulder.

"Wouldn't you rather I was like a regular … you know … Human girl?"

He turned around frowning, his face a picture of disbelief and anger. "Have you any idea how many girls I've been with … Have you?" he shouted, making her jump. He almost never ever got angry. That was always Dante's department.

"No," she said, honestly.

"Fucking hundreds. Me and Dante were super dogs, the pair of us. And not one did I want to see more than a couple of times…Almost everyone I've mixed with in my life was Atlantean, even though I didn't know it … then you came along…" he said, more quietly and pulled her up into his arms with his mouth in her hair. "I'm so shit at all this. You were so … I dunno, independent and beautiful."

She held her breath hoping he would say the magic words. When they weren't forthcoming she sighed. "You don't have to be an alien to be independent or beautiful," she said, exhausted.

He remained quiet and still. She could almost hear his brain ticking over what she'd said and knew exactly what he was thinking: Dante.

She looked up at him.

His blank face was painted on.

"Don't you fucking dare," she whispered.

He squinted his eyes but said nothing.

"I'd do anything, do you hear me? Anything, to be a Human like you and make love with you like a Human girl."

"That's not what I want," he said, his face like thunder.

"Oh yeah! What is it you do want? Break the habit of a lifetime, Jay, and tell me how you really feel. No holds barred …" She was goading him in the heat of her temper, pushing him in the chest with her fingertips, playing with fire.

Before she knew what happened, he'd put a leg behind

hers and tripped her onto her back on the bed, and he was on her like a flash, an arm either side of her head. His face was red and hot. "I want you to stop seeing me as a weaker sub-species Tia, and start looking at me as a man ... then I might stop feeling like you'd be better off with Dante."

He was breathing heavily, trying to get a rein on his temper. It was a side of him she'd never seen before. Mr Control. But she'd heard him loud and clear, and he was right. In loving him so much she was guilty of emasculating him. But no matter what she did, he was physically weaker, and there wasn't a damn thing she could do about it.

He sprang away from her and paced the room while she slowly sat up. "I'm sorry Jay," and she buried her head in her hands. "The fact is, we can't change what we are."

He stopped pacing and looked at her, his head was hung low and defeated when his phone rang. Their eyes both went to the bedside table. He walked over. "It's Alfonzo. I'd better take this."

Tia looked on in concern as Jay spoke to Alfonzo. Not really listening to the words but registering him curse now and then and agreeing at intervals. Then he ended the call.

He put down the phone and looked at her. "When the plane is back in a couple of hours, I must go to London."

"What's the matter?"

"The Dubonnetti's are trying to take over the Bonaci business, buying off shareholders –probably for a proxy vote. I need to be there, Tia."

"Shall I come with you?"

"No, it's safer here. You have Cash and Sean as well Reeve from the Guard."

Her heart sank at his rejection. She scolded herself that he had a lot on his plate and she shouldn't get on his case, but she couldn't shake the feeling that it was a convenient brush off.

She watched him shower quickly and pack his small flight bag efficiently without looking at her once. The old, cold Jay was back, with walls up and everything. "Please don't leave angry with me," she said, eventually, hoping to break through.

He sat heavily on the bed and pulled her to him.

"I love you Jay, so much."

He put his mouth on hers and brushed his lips across it, and whispered, "Then you know what I want."

She breathed in. He was freshly showered, smelling of soap, male and sexy. Heat fired up in her like a generator. She fought every instinct in her to blow gently into him her essence, all the while hyperventilating and panting. She knew he was deliberately pushing her to it. Dirty tactics. It would be so easy to give in. She burst into tears shaking her head, "No!" And she scurried away to the other side of the bed.

He took a second to get a hold on himself again. Then he grabbed his bag and left without a backward glance.

Chapter 29

There was no sleep for Tia following Jay's departure. The next day she helped Cash silently with the horses. She supposed he knew Jay had gone because he hadn't questioned her mood.

When she'd finished she grabbed a bagel from the kitchen, asked Cash if she could borrow some of his vinyl and went to her decks. The last thing she wanted was to play anything reminding her of Jay – pretty hard when he'd bought the bloody things for her.

No, 'Love hate love', by Alice in Chains, was more where her head was going. She curled herself into a ball on a couple of hay bales and listened to the suffering that mirrored her own, in the soulful rasp of Layne Staley's voice.

She was so lost in thought that she didn't notice Sean come in through the sliding door till he stood right in front of her.

"Do you want some company?" he asked.

"I'm not much fun today, Sean."

"Come here," he said, opening his arms.

She immediately stood and rushed into them, and

her floodgates opened. He just held her. She was glad he didn't ask her to talk about it, as she didn't know how to put into words that the man she loved more than life itself, loved her for all the differences that could kill him. And because of that she was in this hopeless, no man's land of misery.

She was so wrapped up in herself and Sean's arms, with him stroking her hair, that she didn't notice Sarah enter the barn and stand watching them on the threshold.

Eventually she coughed.

Tia looked up from Sean's chest as he turned around.

"Sorry to interrupt," Sarah said, dryly, "but Antonio Dubonnetti has just turned up here, and Cash said for us all to come inside."

Tia hurriedly wiped her eyes. Sean put his arm around her shoulders and gently guided her out of the barn. Sarah's face was hard and blank.

***

When they all came in to the large living room it was to a commotion. Reeve was holding Antonio up against the wall, pressing his forearm into his throat, and Cash was trying to pull Reeve off and coaxing him not to break his windpipe.

Sean immediately went into the thick of it, eventually getting Reeve to stand down so they could at least hear what he had to say. Sean started them off. "What are you doing here, mate?"

Antonio rubbed his throat and tried to get his breathing back to normal. "I've left them," he managed to rasp.

"What do you mean, you've left them?" Cash asked.

"I wanted no part of any of it." Antonio continued.

"Why here though?"

"I couldn't think of where else to go. I was forced to go with them to New York, so I gave them the slip there and got on the first plane here."

Tia thought he sounded pretty convincing. She remembered back to their first meeting and thought then that he and Paolo weren't really like Marco.

"There is no way they can win," he went on.

Cash and Sean looked at each other, then Reeve, and tried to come to a decision.

"I say chuck him out," Reeve said.

Cash took out his mobile and dialled Alfonzo. He picked up and Cash explained the latest development. He then passed the phone to Antonio. "He wants to speak to you."

They heard him repeat all the things he'd said to them. "They are going for another Siren."

The room went silent.

"I'm not sure where. I think Humans have her …Yes, they are trying to ruin the Bonaci." Then he passed the phone back to Cash. "He wants you again."

"Okay," Cash said after a while. "He can stay," he said, clicking off his phone.

Moans and murmurs sounded from person to person. Cash called Mrs Ross and asked her to make up another room and Antonio followed her upstairs.

When he had gone Cash turned to everyone. "Alfonzo said probably best to keep our enemies close."

"He doesn't believe him then?" Sean said.

"Well, he didn't really tell him anything he didn't already know, so the jury's out I think. Just keep your eyes open everyone and remember who he is, okay?"

Everyone nodded.

***

Later that day, Antonio found Tia on the porch. "Do you mind if I join you?" he said, in his impeccable English.

"Go ahead," she said, putting her book down.

"Jay is in London?"

Tia nodded. "Yeah, your lot are trying to take over the Bonaci Company."

They were quiet for a while. Tia studied Antonio's face for any signs of guilt. Nothing.

Antonio broke the silence. "So you chose him over Dante in the end?"

"It wasn't like that Antonio."

"Still, it must be hard though?"

"You have no idea," she said, ruefully.

He pulled something out of his jeans pocket, and then pushed it across the coffee table towards her.

She leant forward and picked up what looked like a plastic strip of pills. "What are these?"

"I got them from a contact who trades with the Murrs."

"What are they for?"

"These are nigh on impossible to get hold of ... they use them for when they go on land for any length of time. They supress Murr characteristics."

"Why do you need them?"

"I don't much ... I thought you might find a use for them." And he looked at her knowingly.

"For what?" she said, feeling uneasy.

"Any time ... you know, you don't want to look or act like a Siren. Pop one of them ... instant Human." He sat back, pleased with himself.

Alarm bells were going off in her head, but still, she couldn't help thinking of the argument she'd just had with Jay. This could be the answer to all her prayers. But, she wanted to think about all the implications first.

"No worries if you don't want them?" and Antonio leaned forward to take them back. Quickly making up her mind, she snatched them up. "No, I do want them. Thanks."

***

The summons arrived by courier late the following day. It officially requested Tia to attend Ballygowan Castle for a royal presentation of two of the Sirens to all five of the great royal families of Atlantis and Murrtaine. God, she would meet a real sister at last. She felt a pang of excitement at the thought.

Everyone invited would have to sign a charter accepting Dante as king. Hopefully that would put an end to the Dubonnetti's attempts to discredit him. She wondered how Dante was getting on. Her mind had totally been on Jay lately, and he had been fighting for his life too. It was sad for him that, out of his whole family, Antonio would be the only one attending to represent the Dubonnetti House.

Tia would attend with her Protectors. She decided

that she would use the opportunity to build bridges with Sarah and asked her to come as her special guest. Sarah was delighted with the invitation, but then shrieked in horror that she didn't have a thing to wear.

"Don't worry Sarah, neither do I. We've got tomorrow. Maybe we could have a day shopping, what do you say?"

Sarah thanked her and so did Sean. He smiled at Tia in gratitude, immediately reading what she was trying to do.

While everyone sat and chatted after dinner, talking Atlantean politics, Tia said goodnight and went to bed early. She took a shower and lay in her usual position – naked in the bed with the air con on high.

She wasn't sure how long she'd been lying there letting her mind wander, when she felt a wonderful familiar warmth spooning around her back and down the back of her legs. Then there was a light kissing of her cheek, neck and shoulder and that unmistakable smell – oh so familiar. But it wasn't Jay. Her mind was so sluggish, she must be asleep.

"Dante?" she said, to herself. "Am I dreaming?"

The wonderful kissing like feathers continued, and soft hands moved along her legs, to her hips and softly along her arms.

No, it's not a dream. The Irish lilt drifted to her ears.

"Are you here?" she said, drowsily.

No, I'm not here either. Not really. It's just a psychic social call to check if you are all right.

"Are you taking advantage of me because I'm asleep?"

A little chuckle by her ear, *No, just a pleasant*

coincidence. His hands continued to run all over her.

"Jay is in London."

I know, babe.

"We argued."

Jay? Impossible.

She felt Dante's smile next to her skin as he kissed her shoulder.

"Well, as much as Jay could argue."

You can't really blame him, Tia.

"What? You know?"

It's not rocket science ... Once someone has experienced the Siren's breath, they would have to have more.

"Even if it could kill him?"

You are what you are. It is what he loves about you.

Her mind leapt to the tablets Antonio had given her, but she squashed the thought before Dante could sense it. "What if I could change that?"

You can never change what you are, Tia, which is why you will always come back to me.

She wanted to tell him he was wrong, but it was impossible. He was all over her, overwhelming and consuming. The feeling was so strong it was like an intense sexy dream. When she opened her eyes she was there, in her mind's eye, in a black room, on a bed, with Dante, softly lit, in its centre.

You see your stripes, Tia? In your mind's eye, we are always Atlantean.

Surprised he'd actually appeared in her mind, she looked down at his arm, with his large ring and the thick black stripes over his forearm and bicep moving over her thigh; blending in with her own thick black stripes. His hand moved over her soft stomach and he ran his fingers along the stripes on her ribcage as if to emphasise his point.

He cupped her breast in his hand and she found herself arching into it. His lips moved to her ear. *Let me comfort you Tia, just for a little while, as only I can do.*

She began to pant as his lips came near her own and she turned her head to brush his. She knew if she kissed him she'd be lost. It had been so long. She stilled. *We are not in water?*

It isn't physical Tia. It is our psychic bond. You can allow yourself this ... surely.

Before she could analyse it too deeply, she found herself pushed onto her back and his mouth was on hers, parting her lips and invading her with his tongue. Then he moved down and was all over her; hands and mouth, everywhere.

Control was fleeting as she threw her head back and totally gave in to him. He laughed in triumph as he felt her body slacken and open to him, and kissed her with no mercy. He wasted no time in hammering home his advantage and dipped his head with no preamble and put his mouth straight between her legs and buried his tongue. "Dante!" she cried, loudly. He drove her near to madness and brought her to ecstasy in moments.

He crawled back up her languid, boneless body and came back to her contented face and kissed her tenderly and lovingly.

She felt bereft and groaned, wanting all of him.

I have to go, he said, his slate grey eyes soulful and serious. *It takes such enormous concentration for me to cover this distance ... remember you are never alone ...* and his voice was getting softer, and his face began to fade, flickering like a hologram, but there was such love in his eyes. *Not alone, not really ...*

Her hands reached for him but there was just a fine mist, which soon evaporated. After a moment, she sat up and switched on the bedside lamp. She felt her cheeks. They were wet with tears. Her body was still thrumming from her orgasm. She felt confused and heavy-hearted.

She got out of bed and went to the bathroom. She had definitely had a sexual experience.

She would kill Dante when she saw him. But the second she had the thought, his sheer cheek made her smile. She could never stay angry with him for long.

A loud bell interrupted her thoughts. It was coming from outside. She ran to her window that looked out over the yard. She could see orange in the sky in the distance. She opened the window and stuck her head outside. People were running everywhere. "What's the matter?" she shouted, but she could already smell the acrid smoke. The hay barn was alight. She threw her clothes on and ran downstairs.

Everyone was up and out helping to douse the flames. In the distance she could hear the fire brigade. But despite everyone's efforts, Tia could tell that the whole lot was ruined.

The real job now was stopping its spread to other buildings. They all worked their socks off throwing water from any receptacle they could get their hands on; smothering little fires with wet sacks. They worked to the point of exhaustion until all that was left was a stinking smouldering, smoking pile. Nothing resembled the sweet smelling rectangles they'd stacked the day before.

Tia had been really impressed with Antonio. He'd busted a gut along with everyone else. No he was a good guy, he'd proved it.

Eventually, after hours, they trouped into Cash's kitchen; bedraggled, dirty and smelling like a bonfire. Cash had thanked the firefighters and come inside and sat with everyone else, heartsick at his loss. Thousands of dollars of animal feed had gone up in smoke. Tia felt desperately sorry for him.

Mrs Ross, always the angel, was busy making drinks and breakfast for everyone. Tia took a drink to Cash and put her arms around his neck and sat on his lap like a little girl. No-one took any notice, as it was normal for them to have such a tactile relationship. "Cash, I'm so sorry," she whispered in his ear and kissed his cheek.

"Stuff happens Tia ... I just don't understand it. They're sending an investigator later today."

"Shall we say we can't go to the presentation?" she asked.

Reeve spoke up. "We can't afford not to be there, timing is crucial at the moment."

"No, we'll work through today, even if I just come for a couple of days. I'll make sure we get you there." Cash said, and squeezed her.

"We still have to have something suitable to wear?" Sarah said.

"Sarah," Sean said, pulling her back by the arm.

"No it's okay," Tia, said. "We can still go shopping can't we? There's not a lot we can do here."

"There is no-one to accompany you today." Cash said, wearily.

"I can." Antonio offered. "I won't be much use."

Tia looked at Cash and Sean for permission.

"Okay," Cash must have come to the same conclusion as Tia, when he said, "Watch her like a hawk."

"Of course," Antonio said, inclining his head.

Chapter 30

Although they were all dog-tired, Tia and Sarah showered and dressed, ready to go out and get something resembling a gown fit for a royal presentation. The wonderful Mrs Ross offered to have baby Ronnie for Sarah, freeing them up to try stuff on.

Antonio appeared looking like a supermodel. No-one would have believed that he'd been up half the night fighting the fire with everyone else. He was turning out to be a really good guy.

Tia kissed Cash and Sean goodbye and they jumped into Cash's old pick-up and set off for Billings.

Sarah, Tia realised, was quite good fun once you got her away from Sean and responsibility. They all traipsed into every half-decent shop. Antonio always managed to find a comfy chair and rabbit to someone on his mobile phone. Then he would nod or shake his head when either of them came out of the dressing room to parade in whatever outfit they'd tried on.

Eventually, Sarah went for a lovely black to the floor number with a plunging V at the back. Tia, who really wasn't a dress person, had found it really hard. But Sarah convinced her that a purple asymmetric sleeveless dress was perfect. "It will match Dante's ring," Sarah added.

Tia told herself that it was nothing more than a PR exercise at the end of the day. Not a show of her undying love for Dante. She didn't want Jay thinking that – no way.

***

Antonio finished his call as they paid for their dresses. "Let's get a coffee shall we, and take a well-earned rest? I saw a nice little place just around the corner."

Both girls agreed a pick-me-up was just what the doctor ordered and trailed after him to the shop he'd spotted. They flopped into their seats and Antonio got the coffees in.

As they sat and sipped their drinks, Tia thought how quiet they all were. Everyone's knackered she guessed. They'd been up most of the night. She was lost in her own thoughts when a familiar voice spoke from next to her. "Hello Tia. Long time, no see."

She blinked before turning her head slowly in disbelief. "Marco?"

He pulled up a chair.

She looked over at Antonio and Sarah, but their faces were blank and were continuing to drink their coffees as if a friend had just joined them for a lunch date. Everything felt really odd; like a bad dream. "What do you want, Marco?" she said. No point beating around the bush.

"Nice to see you too …" Marco said, eyebrows raised, as if he was surprised at his reception. When she didn't say anything further, he continued. "I want you to come with me and pledge to me as king. Then you'll be free to go on with your life … with Jay isn't it?"

"I've already pledged to your brother, you know that."

"Half-brother. And he's no longer king, Tia," he said, blinking slowly with annoyance.

She swallowed. "That's a matter of opinion."

He grabbed the top of her arm and squeezed it hard; hard enough to make her wince. She looked over at Antonio and Sarah for some kind of back up. Everyone appeared to be frozen in their seats; their eyes looked away, and Sarah was going red. *For fuck sake!*

"I could take you by force," Marco grit into her ear, so other patrons didn't notice anything was wrong.

She turned her head to him, squinting in hatred. "You could, but then you'd have to take your chances with me in the tank. How do you rate your chances, Marco?"

He let go of her arm with a rough push. She rubbed where he'd held her with her other hand.

"No matter," he said. "I was hoping I wouldn't have to do this."

She felt a sharp scratch on the side of her neck. She had time to look at Sarah, then Antonio and everything faded to black.

***

Dante's lawyers had earned their money and unfrozen the fortune which had been allocated to him from his mother on her death.

The bid for the Bonaci Corporation had crumbled when Jay and Dante joined forces and fought back by doing exactly the same thing with Dubonnetti Industries, which put Dante firmly back at the helm.

The crisis meant that Dante and Jay had spent a precious couple of days together, almost like the old days. Dante had accepted bodyguards as part of his new station in life and took them as seriously as Dante could. But his juvenile side made an appearance whenever he and Jay challenged them to sparring sessions to tune up their fighting skills, which was constantly, much to the annoyance of their lawyers and accountants, buttoned up in their stiff collars and expectations.

The night they saved their companies they got really pissed together, just like old times. They made the guards join them; even though they were supposed to go back to Ireland to get ready for the presentation and for Dante to greet his guests the next day. Jay insisted they spend the night at The Bluebell, which Dante thought was a grand idea.

The night ended with them both sitting on bar stools at 4.30 a.m. like they'd done so many times before. The two guards clapped them on the back and said they'd had enough and were turning in, to which they were called lightweights.

When they were alone, Dante broke the silence. "Have you spoken to Tia since you've been here, Jay?" he said, looking into his drink.

"No, I've been busy. And no, I'm not going to talk about it Dante."

Dante held up his hands in mock surrender. "Okay, okay. I was just gonna say that I couldn't blame you for wanting to do it again, is all."

"You spoke to her?" Jay said, looking sideways at his friend, with half-closed suspicious eyes.

"Yes ... but I guessed anyway. It wasn't hard."

Jay turned to face him on his bar stool, interested all of a sudden. "When did you speak to her? You've been with me the whole time."

"This morning ... in bed. It was a psychic thing, like the time I spoke to you when you were sick." Dante couldn't stop the grin creeping across his face as he said it and tried to hide it by taking a sip of his drink.

"You bastard!" Jay said, who read the situation bang on, and slowly shook his head. And Dante knew he had and found it all the more funny. "What?" he said, in all innocence.

"I should fucking drop you where you stand, you fucker!"

That made Dante roar with laughter and he put his arm around his old friend's shoulders. "What do you expect when you leave her unattended?"

A barrage of expletives left Jay's lips, which tickled Dante all the more with their increasing baseness.

He was still laughing and holding his stomach when he answered his phone. His face dropped immediately. "We'll leave right away ... call the Guard in New York. We'll meet them there." He ended the call and picked up his money and keys off the bar.

"What?" Jay asked, getting off his stool ready to go.

"She's gone Jay ... she's fucking gone." He was already walking out into the foyer, and ringing the two guards.

***

As they sped through the empty early morning streets on the way to the airport, Jay simmered. Dante swore to himself as thoughts came to him.

"Antonio was supposed to have been minding her. Fucking Antonio! What's he gonna do?" Dante ranted, looking at Jay in exasperation. "They were out buying bloody frocks for the presentation."

"There was a fire you say?" Jay said.

Dante nodded absently.

"Do you know what I'm starting to think?"

"What?" Dante said, looking at him.

"This whole thing, Keenan going, me getting called here, Antonio turning up, the barn catching alight... it was all to get her alone and unguarded."

"Yeah," Dante thought about it. "Everyone picked off one by one ... It was weird how the takeover just crumbled like that."

"Mm, it had served its purpose."

They both nodded and sighed.

"What exactly did Antonio say?" Jay asked.

Dante relayed the version of the events, as told by Antonio of what happened in the coffee shop.

"What I don't get is the other two?" Jay said, shaking his head. "Doesn't add up."

"Antonio reckoned that Marco wasn't interested in them."

"Did he say it was Marco who's got her?"

"He's not sure."

"He's back at the ranch right?"

"Yeah, Cash and Sean have him."

Hatred didn't even cover the look that crossed and settled on Jay's face. His deathly white pallor was even scarier than when he went red and quiet. *Fuck!*

***

When Dante and Jay arrived at the ranch it was early morning and the place was a hive of activity. People had been arriving all through the night from various locations. The kitchen was filled with huge guards making themselves cups of coffee and sandwiches as they squeezed through from the back door.

They shook hands with Cash and Sean as they walked into the large living room, which was just as crowded. It had now become centre of operations.

They noticed Keenan and a small beautiful girl with him. She had dark hair, similar colour eyes to Tia, and was very striking. She looked nervous and averted her eyes from everyone. Dante and Jay walked over to him. "Tia's sister?" Dante said, straight away, smiling at her.

"I thought it was safer to bring her with me."

Dante agreed.

Keenan introduced her formally to Dante and then to Jay. She gave an unsure smile and got behind the cover of Keenan's body.

"No change?" Jay asked discretely.

Keenan shook his head.

"You can tell she's her sister though, can't you?"

They all agreed.

"What's the plan?" Keenan asked.

"We think they planned to take her all along." Jay

said.

Keenan nodded. "Distractions? Makes sense."

"Where's my brother?" Dante called to Cash, a little way off from him, in the throng of people."

"I'll go get him." And he went up the stairs. He came back in a few moments. "He's gone." And held out his empty arms.

Dante looked at Jay. "He was in on it." They said simultaneously.

Dante motioned for Sean to come over. "Where is your woman? Has anyone spoken to her yet?"

"Yes." Sean said. "She's very shaken up though."

"Do you mind if we have a quick word with her?

"Come on, I'll take you to her."

They followed Sean up the wooden staircase, and along the corridor of bedrooms. Sean knocked quietly on the door to their room. He put his head around the door jam and called her quietly to come outside, so as not to wake the baby. She looked like she'd been crying.

Jay took the lead after looking askance at Dante, who nodded. She didn't know Dante that well, so it made sense that a familiar person had a go. Besides, he wouldn't put it past Dante to try to shake it out of her.

"I just need to ask you a couple of questions Sarah, okay?" he said, gently.

She nodded and dabbed her eyes with a tissue.

"Whose idea was it to go shopping?"

"Tia's." She sniffed.

"Okay. Did Antonio volunteer to take you?"

"Yes. Everyone was busy because of the fire. And Cash

said we still had to go to the presentation."

"What about the coffee shop. Who picked that?"

"Antonio."

He looked at Dante. "What happened when Marco turned up?"

She explained everything they already knew, up to the point when someone came up to Tia and then she collapsed.

"What I don't get is why you both sat there and didn't do anything?" Dante butted in.

Sarah's face puckered ready to cry again, "I'm so sorry … Antonio whispered to me to sit quiet, and said Marco would just talk to her and then go."

Sean pulled Sarah into his arms and looked daggers at Dante. "That's enough. You can see how upset she is."

Dante turned away in exasperation.

Jay continued softly. "What do you think happened, Sarah?"

She sniffed. "It looked like she was injected in the neck with something." She looked nervously at Dante.

"The people who were with Marco. What did they look like?" Jay said.

"They looked military. Definitely. I'd know them a mile off," she said, straightening up.

"Thanks Sarah." Jay nodded at Sean, who took her back along the landing to their room.

"What do you think?" Jay asked Dante.

"It sounds as though, he asked her to pledge to him, and when she said no, he went to a plan B …handing her over to the Human authorities."

"Why would he do that? What's in it for him?"

"Fucks us up. Takes her out of the game?"

"Or, to make a deal. What if they have one already?" Jay asked.

"I think it's time we got Alfonzo to use his government contacts. It's time I met my long-lost father."

***

Alfonzo arranged a rare slot with Duke Ormond Delissi, Dante's father and ambassador for the Atlantean Nation. But in order to meet, Dante had to go down to Washington DC. That's what had brought him to this brooding state whilst sitting on his private plane.

The occasion of meeting his father should have been a momentous one, but all Dante could think of was getting information on getting Tia back. He also felt a certain amount of resentment towards the man who had left him to deal with the shit, Dubonnetti, all his fucking life; and not to forget, leaving his mother to marry someone with his bastard child.

He made his way to the arranged meeting place immediately on landing. They were due to meet at the Smithsonian Museum. Jay had offered to go with him but he thought this was something he should do on his own. Plus, he could do with leaving him and Keenan in Montana in case any news was received up there. Today he just took two guards with him, so looking inconspicuous between the exhibits, with him looking like he did and flanked with two six feet six vampires, was nigh on impossible.

He asked them to hang back while he looked at the

exhibits of African art at the place he'd been told to go to. He killed some time by allowing his mind to reach out like he'd done so many times to see if he could contact Tia telepathically, but he got nothing. He was sure she must be unconscious.

"The ceramics are beautiful are they not?" A deep Italian voice rumbled to the left of him.

Dante stole a sideways glance at the stranger. "They are." And he turned squarely to look straight at his father.

The man in front of him had the overall appearance of a distinguished aristocrat. His look from his lively mahogany eyes was direct and confident. In fact they looked like they'd seen many things so nothing troubled him much. His hair was peppered grey and slightly long and wavy to his shoulders. He was tall and slim, dressed in a navy blue conservative suit with a beige raincoat over the top. He had a smart cane held in one of his gloved hands.

He allowed Dante the few moments to study him, as if he knew that he needed to process any genetic similarities, or not as the case may be. "Hello at last, Dante." And he held out his hand to him.

Dante took his hand, and shook it. He didn't feel like he expected to feel. In fact he didn't feel much at all. Maybe it was because all he'd ever known was Dubonnetti. Perhaps if he'd known about Delissi from childhood, this meeting would have held more import than it did.

"I am Ormond. Ormond Delissi. Perhaps we could

walk awhile," he said quietly, in his beautiful accent.

Dante walked in step with him.

"I hear from my friend and cousin, Alfonzo, that you are experiencing troublesome times?"

Dante nodded. He could have said, my whole life has been fucking troublesome times, but he kept shtum. He honestly couldn't think of anything constructive to say.

Ormond broke the uncomfortable silence. "I want you to know, Dante, that I loved your mother very much. She was the love of my life."

Dante just raised his eyebrows and looked at him.

"We are all earmarked for different things in our Atlantean lives. Mine was to be a diplomat and help ensure our place in the Human world. Secret service was my destiny, Dante. Marriage therefore, even to such a rare beauty as your mother, was out of the question. She had already been promised to Christian, my first cousin."

His father was obviously an excellent reader of people. "You want me to get to the point of the visit?"

Dante had stopped walking. "Do you know I am married?"

"I know everything. It is my place to know."

"Then you know she has been taken?"

Ormond took a piece of paper out of his inside breast pocket and passed it to Dante. "There is the name of the military base I believe she was taken to, and a map of the layout. You must be there at 0600 tomorrow. There will be a ten minute lapse in security in the route on the map marked in red."

Dante nodded and put the piece of paper in his

pocket.

"This is the one opportunity Dante. She will be moved soon, and I may not be able to locate her after that."

"I understand. Thank you." And he meant it. This was the only time he'd called on his father for help and he'd come through for him.

"One more thing," Ormond said, touching Dante gently on the arm. "I can't be sure, but there have been whispers of someone else ... someone other than your wife. There may be two held captive."

Dante thanked his father, realising that the meeting was drawing to a close. "Do you ever come to Ireland?" he found himself saying. "I have a presentation ... when I get her back." His voice was trailing off.

Ormond smiled at Dante. "I will try. I have to be a ghost in my own world, Dante. But if at all possible I will be there."

Dante took a deep breath and nodded.

Ormond turned and walked away. Then was gone in the crowd as if he'd never been.

***

When Tia awoke she was under water. She tried not to move while she got her bearings and alert anyone to her being awake. Was she in the Dubonnetti tank? No, the lighting was too bright. The tank also had no metal frame. It appeared to be all glass or perspex. She rolled her eyes and could see it was a rectangle about eight feet long by six high, and about three feet wide, suspended about three feet off the ground.

When she went to move she found that each of her

limbs was restricted as well as her head. She manoeuvred slowly and found she had enough slack to sit up. The bastards had stripped her though. Thankfully, they'd left her knickers on. She couldn't even move her arms enough to cover herself.

A muffled speaker in the water began crackling. "Specimen B is awake ..." she heard. "Hello there," came from a man in a white coat and small glasses – a kind of old-looking cliché of a professor. She gave him the finger.

"My name is Dr Smidt." He waited again for a response. "I would like to make sure your stay here is as comfortable as possible. Is there anything I can get you?" he said slowly, like people talk to foreigners having trouble with English.

She mouthed. "Get me the fuck out of here!"

He noted on his clipboard and mouthed, "Speaks English."

The radio device was switched off and she just heard the surges of the water and a humming of some sort of electrical equipment. Probably all the monitoring devices she was plugged into.

Now left alone she began to survey the room. She started from one end to the other. Nothing remarkable. A lab. Soldiers in uniform walking in and out. Military, she decided.

As her vision went left she could see another tank just like the one she was in. Fuck, there was someone in there. She started to struggle and tried to bang on the glass to get her attention.

Alarms began to beep outside her tank. The doctor came up close again. "Please relax, specimen B." She continued to look over at the other tank. There was someone in there. Unconscious. She could just make out long fair hair and white skin. Stripes. Yes, stripes like her own. She struggled again.

"Partition quickly," the doctor shouted.

Two soldiers wheeled over a large screen so she could see nothing after that.

She pointed to the doctor.

He came up close to the glass. "Shh!" he said, to those around him. "She is trying to communicate."

She looked at him with as much hatred in her eyes as she could muster and made a gesture of a thumb across her neck, and mouthed. "You. Are. Dead." Satisfied when she saw him swallow hard, she lay back down to make him think she was shutting herself down to all outside influences. She wracked her brains. *Fuck! Fuck! Fuck!* How was she going to get out of this one? She had been in some shitty places in her time but this was the scariest. She had no way of knowing if she'd ever get out.

She tried to relax herself; being stressed was not going to help. Gently, she sent out a mental feeler. She'd never covered any distance before but Dante had reached her a couple of nights ago, so she had to give it a go. She began by projecting out in circles that got wider and wider. It was methodical and less likely to miss anything.

Dante ... Dante ... where are you? Please hear me ... I need you. She said, like a mantra.

Tia ... is that you? came after a few moments.

Beeps began to sound all around her. She was aware of a commotion going on outside of the tank. People began rushing over to her.

"She is communicating. Record her brain activity. Then cut it off. She could be guiding others here."

Quickly Dante, they know I'm talking to you.

Are you okay? his psychic voice replied in anguish.

Yes, I'm under water. I can't move ... aghh! An electric current shot through her. Her brain shuddered. She became disorientated. Her head hurt.

Tia ... Tia! Dante called, over and over.

It hurts. She passed out.

Chapter 31

The military helicopter was speeding along low to the rendezvous point when Dante grabbed his head and shouted at them all to be quiet. Everyone shut up and looked at him. He looked like he was staring into space until eventually he let go of his temples. He hit his forehead with the palm of his hand in frustration.

"Was it Tia, Dante?" Jay asked, giving his arm a shake.

"Yes, but I could hardly hear her. They're keeping her under water … then they knew she was speaking to someone. They did something to hurt her and she just went."

Jay bit down his feelings of impotent rage. Of course she would contact Dante and not him. He stared ahead in blank focus.

"Jay!" Dante called.

He ignored him.

"Jay?" Dante called again.

Jay turned his head to him and tried to keep the anger off his face.

"It was me because I can reply … that's all."

Jay looked eyes front again. It didn't matter; just

another reason why he shouldn't be with her.

***

The helicopter landed at the furthermost corner of Milestorm Air Force Base. Three army vehicles were parked there with keys in the ignition and uniforms on the seats.

Jay and Dante changed and took the first vehicle with two of the guards. Cash and Sean took the next with two more, and Keenan with three of his guards took the last.

Despite being asked to stay behind, Dante insisted on coming to find her. He wasn't having any of that 'king must stay in safety' shit. And when he pointed out his psychic link with her, no-one could argue with that. Plus, Keenan and the guards were the trained muscle in case anything went pear-shaped. Delissi's instructions, if they went according to plan, should mean they'd be in and out before anyone knew she was gone, with no agro.

They drove along, not too fast and not too slow, so as not to draw attention. They went through a barrier that went up as soon as they reached it, with a nod from a soldier in the kiosk.

They followed the road around to zone F, as directed on the map.

They all got out of the vehicles and swept up to the building as one unit. In Dante's uniform pocket was a universal prox card, which hopefully would gain them access through every door. One swipe and they were in the building. They stuck together, moving down a corridor till they found a lift. Half went in the lift and half went into the stairwell.

They held their breath at the bottom as the lift doors opened. No-one was there. The corridor was dark and deserted as the others joined them from the stairs. This part of the base was obviously rarely used or off limits to the average squaddie.

They hid in an office as they heard voices approach until they went by and out of hearing.

They crept out one by one.

"Try to speak to her again, Dant," Jay said.

"Wait till we're right there. I only want to do it once as they shut her down last time."

Jay nodded and pointed and they all crept along the corridor in their crouched positions.

Eventually they came up to some huge, steel double doors, more at home in a bank vault than an air base.

"This must be it," Dante said.

Keenan came forward and looked at the door. "Try the card."

Dante swiped it down the monitor. Nothing.

"We'll have to blow it. Means it's gonna get messy," Keenan said.

Dante nodded. "Let me speak to her first. Make sure she's here, okay?" He closed his eyes, *Tia baby ... Tia ... can you hear me?*

Dante! It was like a shout in his head. Buzzers were heard going off on the other side of the door.

"Blow it now!" Dante said.

Keenan quickly shoved a blob of what looked like putty with a fuse on the door. "Stand well back!" And he lit it and ran flat out to join the others.

The explosion was noisy but effective. Dante hoped the remoteness of the building meant not too many soldiers would come.

They piled in. Keenan and his men went in first, heavily armed to cover everyone. Cash and Sean went running through to secure everyone's way out after they had Tia. Dante ran straight to the tank.

Tia was struggling. Her body writhed in pain, going taut with strain and then thrashed when it released her muscles. Jay ran around the outside of the tank and pulled out all the plugs from the monitors. All the while Keenan and his men watched through the barrel of their guns.

Two soldiers ran in from another door. Keenan and his men picked them off in seconds, then another two, then another. The noise was like little firework pops.

Then one of Keenan's men pulled a doctor out from behind a bank of computers by the back of his neck. Jay strode straight over to him.

Dante had climbed up to reach the top of the tank and managed to get the lid off. It clattered to the floor. He jumped straight into the water and plunged immediately below the surface and tried to pull all the wires off her, but her hair had become wound around all the leads and restraints. He couldn't free her no matter how hard he pulled.

Tia's body had gone limp and Dante began to really worry for her. He stood up in the tank. "Keenan! Get me a sharp knife or scissors or something."

Keenan came jogging over and handed him one of his sharpest daggers. Dante could do nothing else than shear off great chunks of her hair. Then he heaved her up and passed her to Keenan's waiting arms. Dante quickly climbed out and took her from him.

Tia started to struggle as the water evacuated her lungs.

"It's okay Tia. It's me, Dante."

She continued to struggle. *Let me look ... Let me look!*

Confused, he put her down. She ran to the other side of the partition, but the tank was empty. It no longer even had water in it. *Where's she gone?* She projected, with her hands on the glass.

"Come Tia, we must go," Dante said, picking her up again.

She was in there. Tia projected again.

Dante called over to Jay who stood holding the doctor. "Ask where the other one went."

***

Keenan marched over and took hold of the doctor for Jay.

Jay wasted no time and pulled out the doctor's hand and stabbed him once through the palm. The doctor screamed at the top of his lungs.

"I won't ask you again, where is the other one?" Jay said, slowly and quietly.

The doctor's breathing was ragged and uneven. "Gone ... she's gone."

"Gone where?" Jay asked and pushed the knife back through his hand without so much as a flinch in his expression.

Keenan watched his actions closely, all the while aware of the time.

"Gone ... swapped for this one."

"Who?" Jay asked.

"I never met him. They called him a ghost or the ghost ... I had little to do with it. Are you one of them?" the doctor asked, turning his head slowly to look into Jay's eyes.

"No. You're not that lucky," Jay sneered.

"What shall we do with him?" Keenan called over to Dante, trying to hurry things along. Dante was wrapping Tia in a lab coat.

"It's up to Jay," Dante shouted over his shoulder, as he began to walk Tia out of the lab.

Before Dante had even finished saying Jay's name, Jay had the barrel of a gun at the doctor's temple and fired it at point blank range. No hesitation or second thought. The body fell to the ground like a sack of potatoes and he and Keenan were on the way and out of there.

Keenan touched Jay on the shoulder as they walked briskly and caught up with Dante with Tia in his arms. Cash and Sean had cleared the way ahead and made their exit smooth. They tumbled out of the lift and along the last corridor. They breathed again when they made it outside, without challenge, to the waiting vehicles with their engines running.

Jay helped Dante carry Tia's shivering body into the back of one of the vehicles. Jay sat in the front next to one of the guards who drove, while Dante sat with her lying across his lap in the back. He wasn't saying anything out loud but Jay knew he was talking telepathically to her the whole time.

She looked in a bad way. Her skin was grey with heavy black bands all over her. She was rigid and shaking – probably from shock. And her once beautiful hair looked as if rats had gnawed it off.

***

Dante stroked back her hair and talked through his mind to her quietly until she calmed and stopped shaking.

The journey in the cars was short and before long they transferred to the helicopter, which made the short ride off the base where they changed again to a convoy of waiting SUV's. Then they made the two and a half hour journey back to Cash's ranch.

Jay escaped Dante and Tia and rode with Keenan for this part of the journey.

Dante huddled down with Tia and swaddled her in his coat. He put another blanket over them and then pulled her into his body as they lay across the back seat. *Hey babe. How ya doing?* he projected, when she lay awake and still next to him.

You came for me, she thought, smiling up at him.

His heart nearly broke as he looked down into her now completely ruined eyes. The constant confinement in water had dilated them beyond their capacity. He'd get her help, contacts or something like that.

Of course I came, you're mine aren't you? he projected back.

There was another one, Dante.

Another one like you?

She nodded.

We'll find her.

This seemed to satisfy her as she smiled. *Where's Jay?* she asked, with a look of worry on her face. *Is he okay?*

Yes, he's fine. We are all fine. No casualties. He pulled her to him and hugged her tight. *Sleep,* he said, *I'll wake you when we get there.*

I don't think I can.

Dante leant down and put his lips to hers and gently blew into her mouth, until she smiled in the warm orange glow of his cocooning essence. He gradually felt her breathing deepen and slow down and he knew she'd gone off.

He sat back from her slightly and thought that he should be angry at Jay right now for not being here when she needed him, but he couldn't help but feel grateful for these wonderful moments he could spend with her privately, as if they were a real couple.

He breathed a sigh and nuzzled into her rats' tails of hair and fell into a contented sleep with her.

***

Keenan drove along with Jay in the passenger seat. The two guards in the back were already getting some shut eye.

"You would make a good soldier, you know that?" Keenan said, glancing sideways at Jay.

Jay nodded once to acknowledge the compliment. "Thanks … I just did what needed to be done," he said, eventually.

"Yes, but you don't let emotion make you do anything stupid."

Jay looked at Keenan for an explanation.

Keenan continued. "I am a trained soldier, but I would have been tempted to give the doctor a lingering death for hurting my woman ... but you – quick dispatch and then out of there. Job done, and no-one put in danger unnecessarily," Keenan nodded appreciatively.

Jay raised his eyebrows in surprise. "I didn't think much at all, just that there couldn't be any witnesses." Uncomfortable with the attention, he changed the subject. "You will be pleased to get back to Lacy?"

Keenan paused for a second. "Yeah ... I want to get this presentation and pledging out of the way. Then I hope to get to work on getting her to remember some things ... I don't know how I'm gonna feel about her getting in the water with Dante though."

Jay totally understood that one and just nodded. "Has she breathed with you yet?" Jay asked.

"No, it has to be with Dante first ... She'll pledge, be married and then her power will pass to him. After, she can breathe with me, but her power will be his ... it has to be that way for princes."

"It's fucking hard man, I don't envy you."

"At least she won't have a sexual relationship with Dante."

"You hope," Jay said, but couldn't keep a straight face, when he saw Keenan's stone cold look. "No, that bollocks is just my shit to deal with," he added.

It was Keenan's turn to change the subject to

something happier. "Tia has breathed for you, though."

He nodded and smiled at the memory.

Keenan smiled back. "She has bound you to her then."

He nodded again. "She's scared though."

"Of hurting you?"

"Yeah."

"Give her time, she loves you man. Don't forget you're not dealing with a Human female here. Giving is as much a part of them as their music."

"Thanks man. You've probably saved the king's life."

They both laughed.

"How you don't kill him half the time I have no idea," Keenan said.

"I know, but I love to hate him and he knows it."

They laughed again.

Jay really appreciated the new friend he'd found in Keenan. Sometimes it was good to get another perspective on things. Whether he liked it or not, he was in this Atlantean nation for keeps.

***

The cars pulled into the yard at Cash's ranch at around lunchtime in brilliant sunshine. Dante woke first and sat up as they swung into their parking space. "Hey," he said gently to Tia, "we're here."

Reeve, who was sitting in the front passenger seat, passed back his sunglasses. "Put these on her, the sun is bright."

"Thanks man." Dante said.

He arranged the lab coat around her for her modesty and popped the glasses on. "Not bad, considering," he said, smiling.

"Thank you, Dante." Emotion wobbled her voice, which was barely a rasp.

Outside they could hear the slamming of car doors as everyone started to get out of their vehicles.

"Ready?" he asked.

She nodded.

He opened the door, got out first, and then helped her out. Then he surrounded her with his body to protect her from the light, and well, just to be near her for whatever short time he had left with her.

As they walked along the little path up to the back door, she started to call out. "Jay! Jay! Are you here?" She tried to run towards the house.

Dante grabbed her quickly. "No Tia, he's over there." And he turned her body to face the car that stopped behind theirs. Jay was getting a holdall out of the boot. She was looking all around but Dante could tell she couldn't see very much. She just kept calling in her little cracked voice.

Dante got down to her eye line and pointed her arm to where Jay was. He stood up as she ran to him. Her feet were bare, but she seemed oblivious to the stones as she slammed into Jay.

Dante was forced to watch as Jay slowly and stiffly let his arms come around her. He held her while he ran his fingers into her hair that was one tangled knot.

Dante walked over slowly. "I'm going to go straight back," he said to both of them. "I'll give you a few days, but then can you bring her to Ireland, Jay? I'll take

Keenan and Lacy back with me now."

"Sure," Jay said, nodding.

Tia was still clinging onto Jay.

"Tia," Dante continued softly, "I'll see you just before the presentation, okay?"

She nodded against Jay's chest, still unwilling to let him go.

Dante looked at Jay. "Thank you. Look after her?" he said to his old friend, hoping his pain didn't leech out too much into his face.

"No worries, man."

His heart was heavy as he walked back to the car and watched Jay walk her into the house. He got in the car and waited while Reeve got his pack and told Keenan that he and Lacy were going as well. Several of the Guard would stay and the rest would head back to their New York headquarters. Then they would come later to the presentation.

Dante took a last look at the house. *This is how my life's going to be*, he thought. *Better get used to it.*

Chapter 32

On the journey back, Jay had convinced himself that Tia was better off with Dante. It was a growing conviction since he'd left and gone back to London. So when Dante had saved her, it seemed right somehow. Whichever way he looked at it, it was best all round.

Living without feeling was what he did best. Whether it was endless one night stands with faceless women, playing hardball in business or blowing the brains out of some sick doctor-type. It didn't matter.

So when he'd seen Dante wrapped around her leading her to the house, he was already insulated against that. But then when he saw her struggle in Dante's arms calling for him, and then Dante pointing him out and her running blindly to him, it was a shock.

As she slammed into his chest it was as though a defibrillator had whacked his heart back into action. All he could do was comfort her despite what his logical brain was telling him.

Her hair had been hacked off, her eyes were shot to pieces and her skin was grey. She was a mess. He was filled with an overwhelming instinct to protect her and give her anything she needed.

When Dante had said goodbye, he felt for him, knowing how much this woman meant to him. And with his usual grace he was bowing out and leaving them to it. Perhaps there was a way forward after all. The way she'd clung to him was sobering.

As they walked in and reached the living room, Keenan was heading back out with Lacy. The girls stopped in front of each other.

"Hello, Tia isn't it?" Lacy said, tentatively and then looked at Keenan for reassurance.

"Hello Lacy," Tia managed, though her voice was barely audible. "I can't see you that well today."

"We'll see each other in Ireland though, won't we?" Lacy reassured her and looked at Keenan while she said it.

Tia nodded.

"Good luck, and thanks, Keenan," Jay said, holding his hand out to shake.

"Likewise," Keenan said, firmly shaking Jay's hand. "We'll see you in a few days." Then he ushered Lacy out the back way, through the kitchen.

Sean and Cash came over to them next and hugged her in turn. "Welcome home darlin'," Cash said.

She had no trouble identifying them. She breathed them both in as she hugged them, and sobbed into them at the comfort.

Jay was about to lead her up the stairs when Sarah, stood on the first landing, barred their way. Jay stood still with Tia.

"I'm so sorry Tia," Sarah said, horror all over her face as she took in the state of her.

"Don't worry Sarah, please. It's not your fault, okay?"

Sarah blinked back her tears and stood aside.

Jay helped Tia stumble slowly up the stairs to their bedroom.

***

Tia flopped down on the edge of the bed and felt her hair all over.

"Do you need anything?" Jay asked.

"Can you get some scissors and even up my hair a bit?"

"Me? I'm no Nicky Clarke you know."

"Please," she said, quietly.

She heard him disappear out of the room and come back through the door and close it after a few minutes. She could make out shapes, light and dark. That was about it.

Jay pulled a stool over and showed her where it was and she sat down on it. Gently he picked up what was left of her beautiful, lustrous hair and cut it slowly into similar lengths. The rasp of the scissors sounded hypnotic.

As the hair curled around itself now the weight was removed, it didn't look half bad.

"You look like a pixie version of Marilyn."

She smiled. "Thank you."

"Do you want some food?"

She shook her head. "I want to wash my hair. And I want to feel you naked with me."

"Come with me," he said.

She shrugged out of the lab coat and stepped out of

her knickers on the way to the bathroom.

He switched on the shower and guided her over the step and under the spray. She faced ahead, her blank eyes neither seeing nor blinking. She felt the most miserable person alive. Until she felt his skin brush hers as he stepped into the shower with her ... mmm.

Gently, he made sure her hair was completely wet and squeezed lemon-smelling shampoo into his hands and gently worked it through her hair. It felt wonderful to her. It was the best therapy, washing it all away with beautiful, soft, loving hands.

He rinsed it off, making sure all the soap was out, and then picked up the shower gel. He lathered it in his hands and moved them over her neck and back and then made sure he was gentle over her grazes and bruises on her arms and legs. Slowly, he made his way down to her ankles and feet.

She stroked his hair and back as he bent down in front of her. As he stood back up she put her hands on either side of his face and guided his mouth down to hers. She brushed her lips softly over his and coaxed him to open with her tongue. A small murmur escaped him as he complied and gently kissed her.

He broke their kiss gently, and, as soft as butterflies, glided his lips down her neck to her shoulder and lower till his mouth closed around one beautiful peak and then the other. She was already breathing hard. Her skin was so sensitive. She looked down at Jay and then her body. Even in her blindness she could see the stark black bands on her skin against her paleness. "I'm ugly," she said, and went to pull away from him.

He stood up and held her shoulders. "You could never be ugly," he said, quietly.

She could feel his eyes roaming over her. "It's what you are, and you're what I want."

He bent down and kissed her again, more urgently this time. "I can't help myself."

"Yes... please Jay." At that moment nothing was as important as feeling him near her, on her and in her.

He lifted her as he'd done so many times before and she leapt up and gripped him with her legs around his waist. "I don't want to hurt you," he murmured, against her mouth.

"I won't break."

"Neither will I." And he pulled her down onto him in one ruthless thrust.

She gasped and gripped onto the muscle on his shoulder with her teeth and bit him hard. The overwhelming need to suck his lifeblood through his skin overcame her. Salt and copper mixed with the water on his skin and seeped into her mouth. This drove him into the ferocity of rhythm she wanted, on and on, over and over.

When his arms could no longer hold her he sank down the wall of the shower onto the floor, shifting his back against the tiles. She straddled him, completely lost to sensation. Her temperature soared but she revelled in the feeling she could have lost forever. She bit, scratched and scolded him for leaving her. He took it all in his quiet self-assured way and concentrated on giving her the upmost pleasure.

They moved together – he with one hand on her waist while the other pulled her to his lips by the neck. "Please Tia..." he whispered with his mouth moving against hers.

It felt so good. She was so close. She licked him to gain entry to his mouth and moved her body with him as she kissed him deeply. She could feel he was so close too. "Aagh..." She pulled away from his mouth. He pulled her down, tighter onto him, merciless in his strength, battering her resolve. "No ..." she cried.

"Please Tia," he whispered again. "I need ... I need you in me ..."

Those words of need ripped away the last of her willpower and she put her lips on his and his mouth parted. A gasp escaped him as she felt him almost there. She blew very gently at first and heard his wonderful groan of pleasure. She felt it bubbling up in her – her light and her climax at the same time. She just blew her essence for one second in a blast and stopped and pulled away from him to stop herself from completing the flow.

He clamped down on her shoulder and came, wave after wave, shudder after shudder, and pulse after pulse. She followed him on the first wave of his pleasure. His words made holding off any longer hopeless. Her orgasm shot through her nervous system and tingled her lips to her toes and buzzed like electricity. The feel of him in ecstasy totally did it for her as she ground down onto him and clutched him to her with all her might.

She sagged her weight onto him. He slowly relaxed and shuddered every now and again until he sat still.

His arms were still around her and he sucked gently on her shoulder.

She sat back slightly and felt his face. "I can't see you," she said. "Do you feel okay? Be honest."

"I feel fucking brilliant."

She could feel his lips smiling against her skin. "Really?"

"Yeah. Give me a minute though, I feel like I just ran two hundred metres."

She held him until his breathing got back to normal. Then they stood up together and he gently put her back onto her feet. Her hands felt up to his cheeks again to see if he felt hot. A bit. "Are you okay really?"

"Yes, Keenan gave me another shot of that stuff, just in case."

"Oh ... thank God," she sighed.

Somehow between Jay's wobbly legs and her blindness, they made it to the bed. After rubbing each other dry, they slid between the sheets. Tia felt safe, cool and content, lying in Jay's arms. "Back where I belong," she whispered on a sigh.

He kissed her forehead.

They were quiet for a while and just enjoyed the moment.

"Dante will only give us a couple of days before he has to do the presentation," Jay said, half-asleep.

"I know." She was trying to think of a way of broaching the subject, which had preoccupied her mind since before she'd been taken.

"He said you have to pledge again when your sister

does it for the first time?"

"Yes."

He roused himself and turned onto his side and looked at her. "Are you okay ... you're very quiet."

She swallowed a lump in her throat. "I just can't believe I'm back here with you and the people I love," and a tear escaped the corner of her eye.

Jay caught it with the pad of his thumb. "Why not think about what you want us to do after the ceremony? We can go anywhere you want in the world."

She latched onto his neck and cuddled him hard as if someone would rip him away from her.

"Hey, what is this?" He pulled her back and shook her slightly and searched her face.

"I have to go away, Jay," she said, eventually.

"Away ... you just got back?" he said, not understanding.

"I've got to do something only my mother can help me with."

Jay was quiet, then frowned. "You can't tell me?"

"No, Jay I can't. Not yet."

His expression hardened. "Do you have to be with Dante, is that it?"

"No, I don't think so. I'm going away from him too. You've just got to trust me ... I can't tell you what I don't know."

"Does he know yet?" he said, still cautious.

She shook her head. Then she reached out and felt his hot face and ran her thumb softly across his lips. "Do you not feel my love in you now?"

He nodded and kissed her fingers.

"That can't lie."

This seemed to satisfy him. "When will you go?"

"I'm not sure – straight after the presentation, probably."

***

The bombshell she'd dropped put a bit of a dampener on their last few days together. Jay became her eyes, but studied her and worried about her. She coped without her sight, wasn't eating but seemed happy enough. She was certainly insatiable in the bedroom – or the bathroom, should he say, breathing into him now every time. She'd become confident that he could survive it, so there were no complaints there.

He'd had niggling doubts in the past that she didn't want to breathe into him because Dante would know, and she didn't want to hurt him, but the last couple of days blew that theory out of the water. Maybe he just had to chill out and take her at her word. After all, she'd never lied to him so far.

The day came for them to go back to Ireland. He told her to go and say goodbye to her horse, as they were leaving soon, and took the opportunity to ring Dante.

"Dant?"

"Jay! You on your way?"

"Just leaving."

"What's up?"

"Has Tia said anything to you about leaving?"

"Last night."

He was about to ask how, when he realised. "In her

head?"

"Yeah ... sorry mate. If it is any conciliation, that ability ain't all good news."

Then realising what Dante meant. "Oh yeah, suppose not."

"I think you get the better deal."

Jay heard the smile in Dante's voice and conceded. "Good point. Do you know where she is going?"

"I think so."

"But you're not sure."

"No... she just asked me to tell her mother, that what she spoke to her about, was happening and she needed her."

"What did her mum say?"

"She said she will make the arrangements for after the presentation."

"That was it?"

"That was it."

Jay cut to the chase. "Where do you think she is going, Dant?"

"Murrtaine."

Chapter 33

Four days after Tia had been rescued, she and Jay arrived at Ballygowan Castle with Sean, Sarah and Cash. Dante welcomed them all warmly.

The castle was a hive of activity, getting ready to host the important bash the next day. Dante had taken up permanent residence there, so Ballygowan had become the centre of the Atlantean world that important Atlanteans flocked to.

They were all shown to their bedrooms below sea level. On their way Tia bumped into her sister Lacy coming in the other direction with Keenan. They all stopped to greet each other. Keenan pumped Jay's hand as well as Cash and Sean's.

Tia touched Lacy's arm lightly as she went by and whispered. "I'll see you later. We'll talk, away from the men, okay?"

A flicker of worry crossed Lacy's face, but she whispered back, "okay."

Jay led Tia along the rest of the corridor and into their bedroom. He took her bag and put it out of the way.

There was a knock at the door.

"Come in," Jay said.

Dante came in a moment later. "Hey, I just wanted to see you privately because I've got something for Tia."

She looked over in his direction. "What is it?"

"As soon as I came back, I sent a message to my cousin Vionne in Murrtaine, and asked whether there was anything that could be done about your eyes."

"Really?" she said, hope blooming in her face. "Did they have something?"

"I have it here."

Jay walked over to Dante to look.

"They are eye drops," Dante explained, "like liquid lenses. Then when you are in water they dissolve."

"Can we do it now?" Tia asked.

"We can try. You sure you don't want to rest first?"

"No Dante, I want to see."

He walked nearer to her. Jay came close as well.

Dante gently smoothed her hair out of her eyes. "Can you look up and open your eyes wide? Try and relax."

She did as he asked.

He put two drops in each eye as Vionne had directed.

She shut her eyes tightly. Her hands came up to them immediately. "They're stinging."

Dante tugged her hands down and pulled her into his arms. "Don't rub them. It's important Tia. Let it work."

Jay frowned. "How does it work?"

"Fuck knows," Dante said. "I don't know if it mends them or covers them. All I know is it's supposed to change them to look and work like they're supposed to."

After a few minutes she was able to unclench her

hands and relax. Dante put her away from him slightly. "Can you try to open them?" he said.

She very slowly flickered her eyelids and opened them a bit at a time. Everything was blurry at first, but gradually colours were visible and then shapes, then everything became clearer as she opened them fully.

"Fucking hell Tia, they're beautiful," Dante said, laughing.

"Wow," Jay said. "They look great. Look in the mirror. Can you see?"

"Yes. Let me look."

She rushed to the long mirror stand and touched her face. She had the most beautiful Human-looking eyes; maybe slightly larger than Human in moss green, but they had lovely small pupils and white around the irises – something she hadn't seen in a long while.

She turned round and hugged Dante hard. "Thank you," she whispered.

Dante stroked her hair, and she let him hold her for a while. Then he seemed to sober himself, probably because of Jay, and he put her away from him. "I'll see you in a while, when you're settled in."

"I'm going to go and see my sister next," she said, happily.

Now she could see and they were alone, she made short work of getting Jay naked and wet. He was exhausted, replete and under the sheets of their bed and she thought the timing was good. "I'm going to find Lacy."

"You sure you don't want to rest for a bit? It's going to be a long day."

Plenty of time for resting when she'd gone. "Might do ... in a bit." She slung on some jeans and a vest top and trainers, bent down and kissed him in the bed. "I won't be long."

"Mmm," was his goodbye, and she went off down the corridor.

When she got to the door she guessed belonged to Lacy and Keenan, she knocked.

Keenan opened the door and raised his eyebrows when he saw her. "Nice eyes."

"Thank you. Is she there?" she said, trying to see around Keenan's large body. Then when she saw her ... "You coming?"

"Yes," Lacy said, and walked straight out of the room and followed her.

They left Keenan unsure whether they should be left alone together so he followed along as well. He stopped quickly at Jay's door and put his head round. "You'd better come." Then both of them were following; Jay semi-naked in his jeans and barefoot.

When they got to the Great Hall, Dante noticed them.

"Shit, they'll never give us time together alone."

Lacy nodded. "I know."

Both girls turned around and began to push Jay and Keenan away. "Go!" they both said.

Dante excused himself and came running over. "What's going on?"

"I want to speak to my sister alone!" Tia said moodily.

Dante looked at Keenan and saw his trepidation. "You gonna be okay with her?"

Tia felt exasperated and poked her finger in Dante's chest. "I want to test my own sister my way, after the pig's ear you made of it last time ... Decks! Where are they?"

He pointed to the small stage in the bottom left-hand corner of the Hall. "They're setting them up over there."

"Right. Out. The lot of you," she shouted, clapping her hands.

The men all looked at Lacy for back-up. "You heard her. Out!"

The three of them went to walk back down the corridor towards the living quarters. As they disappeared from sight, Tia collapsed in peals of laughter. Lacy began to laugh as well and they high-fived.

"For fuck sake. They won't let us breathe. We'll so have to do something about that."

Lacy nodded enthusiastically. "What now?" Lacy asked, intrigued.

"I know Dante, he'll get them to run around to this entrance here," she said, pointing to another exit to the right of the little stage. "They'll try to listen ... give them a minute and then we'll let the music do the talking. If we are sisters, then we'll know."

Lacy nodded sagely, "So DJ'ing is your thing?" she asked.

"Yes. Dancing is yours?"

Lacy nodded.

"It will be interesting to see how in sync we are, being sisters," Tia said.

They heard the clatter of something being knocked

over behind them.

"Show time," Tia whispered, and fired up the decks.

Sifting through the records she asked, "Do you have a type of music or do you just want to follow my lead?'

"I can follow you," Lacy said, finding a pole dance pole already set up on the stage. She made a 'what the?' face.

"Dante is such a pervert, so fuck knows," Tia said, extra loud.

They both laughed knowing full well they were being watched and probably heard.

"Are you ready?" Tia called, and dropped *Can You Dig It* by Ramon Tapia.

Tia began working her magic with her earphones on one ear. And Lacy hoisted herself up on the pole after shedding her jeans and hung upside down. Then she worked the pole with strength and grace. Tia nodded in time to the beat and watched her sister from behind the decks.

***

"Fuck! Out of the way and let me look," Keenan said, struggling to get a look around the corner of the service entrance to the Great Hall. Dante had taken them to the doorway to try and eavesdrop on the sisters.

"She's good," Dante said, nodding and smiling at Keenan.

Keenan gave Dante a dirty look that would wither a lesser man.

Dante just laughed. "Chill. She's bound to be sexy … they all are."

Keenan looked at Jay. "How do you let him live?"

Jay smiled sympathetically. "The night is young." And they all laughed until ...

"Whoa!" Dante said, "did you see that?'

The other two had missed it.

"Wait until the music drops again," Dante continued.

Then they saw it: a sonic pulse coming from both girls at exactly the same time. It was a coloured mushroom cloud emanating from them outwards. Tia's was green and Lacy's was yellow. The girls both laughed after it happened. Then it happened again and again. They were totally in sync.

Eventually the record ended and Tia switched off the decks, and Lacy came down off her pole and bent and stretched at the waist and caught her breath.

"You can come out now," Tia shouted.

The girls walked over to each other and high-fived again.

The three men came out like a group of caught red-handed schoolboys. Tia and Lacy walked over to them.

Dante was smiling. "You knew we were there?"

Tia shrugged. "Of course. We needed to get to know each other, and you lot weren't going to let us. Did you see? It was a bit kinder than drowning her."

Dante nodded and hugged her to him. "There's absolutely no doubt ... you look great," he said, pointing to her eyes.

She smiled and swallowed back her welling-up emotion, and then turned to Keenan to change the subject. "Just so as you know ... I don't know what's going on with you two," she said, whilst pointing at him and Lacy, "and she may be your compatible partner and all that, but she's her own person and so am I," she said, directing the last statement to Dante as well. "And we're not on our own anymore."

And the two girls high-fived again and walked off back to their rooms arm in arm, leaving the three men gawping after them.

***

The testing and marriage was due to take place that evening. It was just an intimate affair, to be witnessed officially by Alfonzo, Sebastian and Naomi.

Jay had primed Keenan what he was in for, should he not want to watch. But Keenan had told him where to go in no uncertain terms, mainly to do with Dante and keeping his balls.

Jay laughed, but suspected that the guy really wasn't prepared for how intimate the process was.

It was a ceremony to bond a husband and wife after all.

Dante had said that it was up to Lacy to choose whether she wanted to bond herself to Keenan. He thought it was their own business to do in their own time, but he urged Keenan privately not to hang around. The idea was that each bonded prince should sit on his council, with Dante at its head.

The time came. Tia stood next to the fountain with Lacy. Both of them were looking super-hot in their bikinis.

Jay felt sorry for Lacy not being able to be tested in the

Dubonnetti's tank, as she would have to go into the sea and be viewed through the big panoramic window of the Hall – way more scary.

Lacy stood bewildered as everyone made a big fuss of her before she went into the fountain, so Jay used the opportunity to pull Tia to him for a hug, more for his benefit than hers. "Don't forget me," he whispered next to her ear.

She looked up into his face lovingly. "Never."

He let her go but kept hold of her hand, as everyone started to move towards the fountain. Naomi had offered to go in as well, as she feared for her daughter, as, unlike Tia, Lacy had never breathed the water before. Tia had been relieved at the news. Jay was pleased she had another female close to her.

Dante stood in the fountain first. Then as he turned to step down into the depths, and so typical of the bastard, he winked at Keenan before he went down.

Jay had to grab Keenan's arm. "Let it go, man ... let it go."

Keenan fidgeted as Naomi stood in the fountain next, keeping hold of Lacy's hands as she followed her in. Tia was to be last.

They had to swim the tunnel under the floor of the Hall before they were visible in front of the window. There they would be about sixty or seventy feet below the surface. Fucking scary.

As they disappeared, Jay pulled Keenan over to the window. Dante was already out and treading water. Jay found it fascinating watching his oldest friend in the world turn into this other-worldly being in front of his eyes; taking in water, producing paler markings similar to Tia's.

Naomi was next to come into view. She looked the most alien of all. Her legs appeared to grow below the knees, at least another foot long. Her skin took on a bluer tinge and her bands were black and vivid. Her eyes were huge and her hair floated around her like a mermaid. She held on to Lacy who was obviously still holding her breath and looking very scared.

Jay touched Keenan's shoulder. The guy was dying a thousand deaths watching Lacy panic. Tia came out and helped her mother try to calm her down.

"Naomi can communicate with her, so she'll be trying to reassure her," Jay said, trying to allay some of Keenan's worry.

It was agony to watch Lacy get to the point where she could no longer hold her breath and Tia and her mother having to restrain her.

Dante thankfully stayed back, probably more for Keenan's benefit. There was a time for joking and this wasn't it.

Eventually Lacy went limp. Keenan rushed to the window and banged on the glass.

"It's about a foot thick, mate," Jay said.

"Fuck!" Keenan shouted, beside himself.

Then, thankfully, the telltale bubbles began to rise from behind Lacy's ears and her eyes opened. Tia and her mother hugged her.

Just when Jay thought he could relax, he thought

Keenan would internally combust when Dante beckoned Lacy to him curling a finger. "Fucker," Keenan said.

Keenan was forced to watch impotently as Lacy swam to him. Dante looked so big and tall in comparison. She looked like a little girl going innocently to the big bad wolf. Yeah. Wolf was the right word.

Tia and Naomi stayed back so as not to interfere in the ceremonial transfer of power and pledging.

Lacy stopped and trod water about a foot away from Dante. He then took her shoulders and pulled her gently to him.

Jay looked at Keenan. "Close your eyes mate."

Keenan looked at him in a daze ... then did as he was advised and turned away from the window. "Tell me when it's over... Fuck no! I have to watch," and he turned back again, just in time to catch Dante putting his mouth on hers. They stayed still for what felt like ages. They stopped and then started again. Then eventually they saw a light emanating from her chest. It glowed orange.

The glow travelled upwards to her mouth and then transferred to Dante's where he closed his eyes. Jay knew how that felt and touched Keenan in support again. At least he didn't know yet.

Then when it hit Dante's chest, he let go of her and they drifted apart. Dante appeared to be stunned. Everyone was looking at him waiting for him to move.

A few seconds later he shook his head and grinned and curled a finger again for her to come to him.

"What the fuck?" Keenan said, about to lose it.

Jay touched Keenan on the shoulder again. "He's just got to do it back, then it's over."

"What's he got to do it back for? He's got her power."

Jay shrugged. "I dunno. I think it's the link. He has to be able to join with them all."

"Fucking hell," Keenan said, and passed his hand over his brow and exhaled.

Dante held Lacy again and breathed gently for about five seconds.

Like a pro, Jay thought, not without a certain amount of resentment at never being able to do that for Tia himself. "That's it," he said, as Lacy drifted and they all gathered around her to make sure she was okay and to congratulate her. They could all communicate now – that was evident.

Jay watched Dante gently touch Lacy on the shoulder and say something to Naomi – probably to bring her back inside. "Come on mate. She's coming out. She'll be in pain for a while with breathing, so she won't be able to talk, okay?"

"Fuck Jay, that was intense."

"I know, I can't watch anymore."

Keenan looked at Jay sympathetically.

"Don't," Jay said, pointing at him. "Don't make me have to punch you."

Keenan nodded and swallowed, knowing exactly where he was coming from.

As Jay went back to the bedroom he shared with Tia, he stole a quick glance back at the window as Dante pulled Tia out to sea and out of view.

Chapter 34

When Tia watched the exchange of breath between Lacy and Dante, it was with a strange detachment. She wasn't sure if it was because the last time it was with imposters and this was her sister, and therefore meant to be, or what. But she didn't feel like stabbing her after, which was progress.

She hugged Lacy after it was over. *We can speak like this now Lacy, any time you want.*

Thank you, Lacy replied. She seemed a little overwhelmed.

Dante dismissed her and asked Naomi to take her back inside. Tia felt him waiting patiently for her to turn her attention to him.

Tia! He projected, eventually.

She looked over at him. She was stalling and he knew it.

He held out his hand. *Come and say goodbye to me.*

She swam over to him and put her hand in his and he pulled her out to sea, away from the window and prying eyes.

They came across a crop of rocks and he pushed her

up against them and immediately pulled her up into a kiss. She was swept up in it for a few moments before she could break away.

This is our goodbye Tia, he said.

She nodded and looked down and away from his eyes. She couldn't help but notice that they were both fully transformed – the same.

He seemed to read her mind. *If you'd never met Jay, we would have been together wouldn't we?*

Maybe ... but you're too much of a scoundrel for me.

Scoundrel? he thought, in mock horror and drew her to him. *How long will you be away?*

She nestled in his arms. *I'm not sure ... a few months maybe.*

You've not told Jay?

I've only told him I'm going. I don't know many details myself.

He touched her cheek. *I would come with you if I could.*

She looked up into his eyes. *I know you would.*

He bent down and kissed her tenderly. *I love you, Tia. I want you to know that. Whatever I'm doing, whoever I'm with, however much of a scoundrel I'm being, I do love you.*

They both laughed into another kiss.

This is it then, babe, he said, afterwards.

She just looked up at him, motionless.

He pulled her around and swapped places with her. *Do you want to go first or shall I?* He said, leaning back with one foot flat on the rock behind him.

She swam up to his mouth and put her lips over his.

He parted his mouth. *Fuck, I want you, Tia.* He bit

her lip.

She couldn't help herself, instead of breathing into him, she full on kissed him and he took the cue and pulled her tight against him. He pulled one of her legs up around his waist, held her there by the backside and kneaded her with his fingers.

He pulled her up to his level, kissing her the whole time.

Now, she thought, and she felt him. His light blinded her for a second – stronger than she could remember. He'd become so powerful her heart stopped for a few beats.

His hand dipped beneath the material of her bikini and he stroked her and felt her fire. She grabbed his hair. He loved her roughness and bit her lip again. She opened her mouth and he blew again. His light hit her hard. It seeped down into the centre of her and nestled in her heart and bound her to him tighter. Forever.

There was no going back now, as he positioned her over him. She was still delirious in the afterglow of euphoria his essence gave her, so he inched into her, inch by glorious inch. He went so slowly to prolong the exquisite torture, and to give her every opportunity to stop him. He smiled in triumph when she did not.

Instead she grabbed his face and let her essence loose and free, in full stream as she could never do, and dug from her toes.

Externally, they glowed red-hot, emanating a warm light which flooded their whole bodies. They looked like they were glued together in a tight embrace with very little movement at all. But inside, in their minds eye, they cavorted and plunged and drove each other in wild abandon.

Suspended in the sea, where they were meant to be, their nervous systems were a riot of sensations. Their bodies were fused and the breath they had propelled into their bodies spliced them together as never before.

Her mind received pictures of love like a movie, which replaced his words, as his state of *ecstasy* was so profound that any projected words arrived in a jumble. A blast of her breath hit his heart in a starburst of light and their climaxes arrived simultaneously. They clamped onto each other and dissolved and floated in the same position for an age.

Rarely did Tia give in to Dante's advances, but sometimes she just couldn't help herself. The pull from him was too strong as if everything was just so right – so as it should be. And the longer she knew him, and the more she gave in, the stronger the pull. They were damned.

They continued to float, still joined, in the water. Dante kissed her neck and murmured how much he loved her. Neither wanted to let go.

I'm sorry Dante.

For what? he said, looking down at her with concern.

That things couldn't be different for us.

He hugged her to him. *It's no-one's fault. We just make the best of what we've got.*

Reality was slowly sinking in. *Oh God, Dante. He'll hate me when I get out. I'll hate me.*

No Tia. Never hate yourself for us. Besides, he never hates you. It'll be me, and I can't blame him. He may have you but he can never share what I can with you, and that's what kills him. He gave her a last lingering kiss. *Let's breathe for each other one last time and I'd better get you back to him before he wears my guts for garters.*

It was late when they made their way back to the tunnel under the fountain.

***

When they stepped out of the fountain, dripping, everyone had gone and the Hall was deserted. Tia guessed it was probably late.

After expelling the water from their lungs, Dante grabbed two towels left for them nearby and wrapped her in one.

He escorted her back to her room. *Do you remember the first time, Tia, when I took you to my room after you were tested?*

Yes, she smiled back at him but with a heavy heart.

Will you be okay? he asked, as they reached her room.

She nodded.

He kissed her on the cheek for a long moment and then left her without saying anything further. She waited for him to disappear, and then she opened the door and slipped inside.

Jay was still awake, sitting in a chair with a glass of scotch in his hand.

"Hey," he said quietly, as she walked in.

Hey, she projected back.

"Are you okay?" he asked.

Are you?

She knew her face was red with self-loathing and guilt and he could read her like a book. She hurried past him into the bathroom and showered off Dante and the seawater quickly, and despite wanting to stay in there all night, she came back out.

Jay was sitting in the same position – new drink though. "Come here," he said.

She felt scared, but swallowed and went over to him slowly.

He pulled her down to sit on his lap. "Tonight is our last night, so I don't want to argue with you, okay?"

She nodded, gratefully.

"But the next time you have to do this shit, I'll bring you, but I won't stay."

Her heart felt like it would break for him. *I understand … was Keenan okay?*

"Not really. But at least it's quick for him."

A stab of guilt pierced her heart. *I don't know what to do to make you feel better?*

There was a beat of silence. "Breathe for me, Tia," he said, looking at her with soulful eyes.

Saying nothing, she took his shirt off so she could straddle his hips in the chair and feel his skin against her. She ran her hands over his many tattoos, which were so much a part of him. The lettering may as well have said, 'it will all end in tears'.

He allowed her to study him while he leant back in the chair and put his head back. His arms lay limp over the sides.

She moved forward slowly and put her mouth on his and gently kissed him and blew. Instead of a quick blast, she slowly streamed into him and sat back. She ran the tip of her finger over his face and along his lips and into his mouth, still slightly open in the bliss that followed. He looked like he'd taken a hit from a crack pipe.

She cupped his face with her hands. Although Jay was drunk he would feel her bone-deep love for him, but would also feel her turmoil and know she loved Dante as well. A love whose tendrils where riddled inside her like bindweed and threatened to break them all apart.

Feeling wretched, she stood up and pulled him to stand with her. *Come and hold me in bed, Jay, it's our last chance.*

He allowed her to lead him and flopped onto the bed. She pushed him to lie down, undressed him, covered and got in with him. She snuggled up close and he fell into a deep sleep immediately, his body awash with scotch and Siren breath.

***

Tia stayed in bed most of the next morning with Jay, nursing him through the mother of all hangovers. Eventually she had to start to dress and he joined her when he started to feel Human again.

Sarah had brought with her the purple dress which she had chosen, in what seemed like a lifetime ago. Which was a good job since she hadn't given a thought to what she would wear.

Her hair was in big lustrous curls almost to her shoulder. She felt too glam – so unlike herself. So for her own entertainment, as everything was going to be majorly dull, she put her trainers on underneath her dress. And instead of the pearl earrings Dante had sent her, she found her silver skull and crossbone studs.

Satisfied she had defied convention enough, she helped Jay choose his suit – a steel grey Valentino with a black tie and crisp white shirt. She helped him with his tie. "Like butter wouldn't melt," she said, tightening it.

"What? Mothers love me," he said, flashing his shy grin.

"Mmm … you Mr Gardiner are a truly dangerous guy. My dad should've warned me about boys like you." She felt her eyes tearing up and blinked them away.

"How do I look?" she asked.

"Beautiful." He stood and looked down into her eyes and held her hands. "Did you wear the earrings Dante sent you?"

"Nope." And she showed him the skull and crossbones she was wearing.

"That's my girl." And he kissed her, probably for the last time in a long while.

The door knocked, jolting them out of their moment. It was Keenan and Lacy. She looked beautiful with her long brown locks coiled on top of her head like Audrey Hepburn and a sea-green figure-hugging jersey dress that skimmed her to the floor.

Keenan looked smart too, but she thought too many muscles always showed through a suit and made him look like a soldier. But Lacy must love them.

"We've got to take them to Dante's study and leave

them with him. The families will come in and officially meet them and sign the charter and then go down to the party. We're supposed to meet them there," Keenan said.

"Let's get it over with," Jay said, and he held out his hand to Tia.

Tia held Jay's hand tightly till they reached the study, with Keenan and Lacy following along behind. She wished she had more time to know what was going on with those two.

When they reached the study, Reeve was standing at the door working, as so many of the Santalini family were that day. He nodded at Jay and Keenan in greeting. "I will escort them from here."

Jay looked over at Keenan who nodded, "It's okay."

Tia grabbed onto Jay's arm as if it was the last she'd see of him. In a way it sort of was. It felt like the end of something somehow; the edge of a precipice.

"Don't worry, I'm only at the bar."

She looked at him and laughed. Those simple words grounded her like nothing else could. She blinked away her tears before her lenses dissolved and pulled his head down and kissed him. "Thank you, Jay."

She looked over at Lacy standing really awkwardly waiting. She'd forgotten things were still weird between her and Keenan. She held her hand out to her sister who grabbed it gratefully.

"Ready," she said to Reeve.

He waited for Jay and Keenan to get into the lift and go back down to the Great Hall, then he knocked and

Tia and Lacy stepped into the room.

Nothing ever prepared her for the visual impact of Dante. It was always like being punched in the stomach. It was probably the whole compatibility/fate thing. She would have loved to have the chance to ask if Keenan had the same impact on Lacy. Every cell in her body lit up when she got near him. Oh her traitorous body.

Dante was standing talking to Alfonzo and a very tall man; even taller than regular Atlanteans, she remembered him from their wedding celebration. Dante was dressed in his trademark black, his hair left loose to his shoulders, wearing an expensive watch and his ring. He turned and looked at her as soon as she came into the room as if someone had told him she was there.

His eyes locked with hers and he smiled and held out his hand for her to join them. He kissed them both chastely on their cheeks, smelling delicious, and introduced them to the mysterious man who didn't speak. He was, she found out, the Prince of Murrtaine, called Vionne.

She and Lacy took their place on either side of Dante and he introduced them, one by one, to all the representatives from the five families; well four, discounting the Dubonnetti's.

Her father signed the charter for the Bonaci, Vionne for the Borge, a very serious Italian prince called Sandro for the Florianna, and Marius, Keenan's oldest brother, for the Santalini. Then the room was cleared.

"There will be a representative for the Dubonnetti after all," Alfonzo whispered to Dante discretely.

Tia looked over at Lacy who shrugged.

Reeve opened the door a few minutes later, still talking into the mouthpiece attached to the earpiece he was wearing, like the secret service. A moment later an aging gentleman with a cane walked into the room, with all the bearing of a prince.

Dante immediately went to leave his station from behind the desk but the man held up a gloved hand. "No Dante. Today I have come to pledge to my king like everyone else."

He sounded Italian, but then again, all the older members of the families did. He bent down and signed the charter. Dante, she noticed was very quiet – with emotion she realised.

"I didn't think the Dubonnetti were pledging today," Dante said, quietly after he'd signed.

"I couldn't let that happen because of the foolishness of my cousin."

As if he'd read her mind, the man faced Tia and added, "Christian and I share a grandmother. As you know the female line is very important to Atlanteans." And he smiled a beautiful familiar smile at her. Straight away she knew who he was, and inclined her head accepting the compliment.

Dante introduced them to the Duke Ormond Delissi and held his hand out to him to shake. Ormond held it, turned it and kissed it instead. "Your Highness ... we have waited a long time."

Dante remained quiet and solemn. Tia had never seen him so serious and composed. He amazed her. Then he came out from behind the desk and walked Ormond to the door, where Reeve waited to escort him back to his waiting limo, ready to whisk him off to wherever.

Lacy mouthed. "Who was that?"

"Real dad," Tia mouthed back.

"Oh."

They returned eyes front again.

Dante turned, came back into the room and shut the door, deep in thought. The girls just watched him, not knowing whether to try and lighten the mood or stay sombre. He walked towards the pair of them, stopped, and then looked squarely at Tia. "Don't think I didn't notice you didn't wear the earrings I sent you."

Tia grinned.

"What shoes have you got on, dare I ask?"

She pulled her elegant dress up slightly so he could see her scuffed Adidas®.

"Fucking hell, Tia!"

"Ha!" Lacy barked.

Dante and Tia both snapped their heads around at her. Lacy lifted her dress to show a pair of flip-flops. Tia put her hand to her mouth. "Fuck, we didn't even confer." They high-fived.

After Dante looked upwards to the heavens for strength, he held his arm out for each of them to hold on to. "Ladies. Let's go get a drink and piss off those blokes of yours." And he was back to frivolous Dante, just like that.

Reeve and another guard escorted them down to the party. Everyone turned, looked and clapped as they descended the stairs into the Great Hall. She looked over and searched the bar area straight away and spotted Cash, Sean, Sarah and Jay and blew them all kisses.

Tamping down the urge to run to them, she circulated the room with Dante, who was loving the two of them on his arm. The whole thing really appealed to his sick sense of humour. She was having such a nice time that she almost forgot that it was her last night. She was jogged out of her reverie by the sight of her mother sitting demurely on the edge of the fountain. Her soulful eyes nodded to say she was ready as soon as she was.

She looked over at Jay laughing with Cash and Sean and then she looked at Dante in animated conversation with other cousins she hadn't even met yet. Then she looked at Lacy, her poor little sister she hardly knew, looking lost and bewildered. She'd forgotten how hard it must be for her with a huge chunk of her memory gone.

Do you wanna go to the ladies? she projected to her.

Lacy nodded.

As soon as they got in the loos, she pulled Lacy into a hug. They stood and held each other for ages. Ladies came in and out smiling. They must have thought they were mad or drunk or something.

"Lacy, I just wanted a chance to speak with you before I go."

"Keenan said you were going away for a while. Where are you going?"

"I'm going to spend some time with mother in Murrtaine. It's something I have to do. You will too when the time comes … when being on land isn't enough."

Lacy just nodded and looked a bit bemused.

"I can't say any more than that, okay. I just want you to know that when I'm back we'll spend some real time together … be real sisters, and tell each other stuff."

Lacy started to cry.

"Please don't cry Lacy. I promise I'll come back and Keenan is a good guy, I promise."

As if on cue, Keenan barged into the loos. "Keenan? This is the ladies!"

"I thought you'd fucking gone …" he said and paced up and down. "We're outside." And he smacked the door open and walked back out.

Tia shook her head and faced Lacy once more. "Don't take no shit off him, Lace. Before I go, remember our mental bond. Because of Dante we can speak to each other, okay? I don't know, but I reckon it works under water."

Lacy hugged her. "Good luck Tia … come on, we'd better go before I start blubbing again." She pulled herself together and opened the door to Keenan and Jay hovering outside.

Tia walked up to Keenan with Lacy. "Please look after her for me, Keenan. I don't want to lose her now I've found her," and she squeezed her hand.

"No problem," he said, and took her hand possessively. "Good luck," he added. Then he whisked Lacy away. She was still looking over her shoulder at her when the crowd swallowed her up.

Jay was leaning casually against a wall, in his usual understated way, not showing any emotion on his face. Tia walked over to him and made sure she stood in his personal space.

"Won't you get in trouble being Dante's wife?" he said, looking down into her eyes, a small smile playing on his lips.

"I'm more worried about being Jay's woman right now." And she stood on tiptoes and bit his lip. "I love you Jay Gardiner, always."

He kissed her softly, lovingly. "Be careful."

"I will."

"I'm going to go."

Her heart went up into her mouth in panic. She held onto his arm. He leant back to her and kissed her again, then he turned and walked briskly into the crowd. She was left standing alone.

She pushed her way back through the crowds and made a beeline for the fountain. No point putting this off any longer. Her mother stood when she saw her coming. Her father stood with her and hugged Tia when she neared them. "Good luck my daughter. I am so proud." And he kissed her on both cheeks.

Are you ready daughter? her mother projected.

Tia nodded. She didn't know what prompted her, but at that moment she looked across the crowded room, straight into Dante's eyes. Terror flickered in them for a brief moment and then he seemed to gather himself. *Safe trip my love,* sounded in her head.

"Let's get out of here," she said to her mother.

Instead of giving in to the almost overwhelming urge to ball her eyes out, she pulled her dress over her head, raising more than a few eyebrows, made sure she stood on the fountain wall giving everyone a really good eyeful, swung her dress around her head three times and let it go. Then she jumped into the deepest part of the fountain.

Dante's laugh rang through her head. *Love you babe…*

And she swam away with her mother.

Chapter 35

It was a sombre evening at the Dubonnetti Estate. Christian and the four brothers sat in the sitting room in the dim light.

"How much longer do I have to wait father? He's going to fuck everything up if he's allowed to carry on much longer."

"Patience," Christian said sternly whilst he leant on an arm and stared into the old fireplace. "We had to wait to learn how the fates fell with the rings. You could have been meant for a Siren legitimately."

"I should have had her while I had the chance," Marco said, shaking his head ruefully.

The other brothers just brooded over their drinks.

"If he can't even keep his most compatible mate, what hope is there for his kingdom?" Christian smirked and turned to face his sons.

"I want him to pay for Joselle," Stephan said, low like a growl.

"No offence bro, but didn't she and her sisters try to con us all with their Siren routine? Antonio said.

Stephan snapped his head round to him and spoke

through gritted teeth. "He would have known instantly that she wasn't. He didn't have to suck the fucking life out of her for months."

Antonio shook his head, accepting that this was an argument he was never going to win.

Christian nodded and sighed. "Simmer down. Our time will come, never fear. I have sent feelers out to all the other families. There are many cousins and sons, from lesser branches of their families or born the wrong side of wedlock, all champing at the bit for their chance."

"What if the Bonaci won't back us? What about the Borge?" Marco whined.

"The Borge will be with the Bonaci. One will not come without the other."

Marco stood and begun pacing impatiently. "Then surely it is in our interest to help the bid crumble and take our chances with the Human factions?"

Christian looked up at his son disgusted. "Humans? Never," he spat. "No, everything is going according to what is written."

All the brothers looked up, suddenly interested. "How so father?" Paulo said.

Christian sneered. "I doubt whether the Delissi brat has done his homework, but if he did he would know that when the Soul Breathers are amongst us at the time of the end, so is the Darkly Begotten."

"What is the Darkly Begotten?" Marco asked, his eyes narrowed.

"It is a cancer that starts from within. It contaminates, it corrupts – it does the job for us."

"What do you mean, time of the end?" Antonio asked warily.

Christian downed his drink, "When the Soul Breathers appear for the last time, the sky chariot will be on the move. Atlas will return, son. And when they do, they will find the Dubonnetti ready."

Epilogue

Several months later

Jay had been in Barbados for three weeks taking a well-earned rest. After Tia had gone he'd thrown himself into his work. But recently he'd become exhausted. Dante had lent him his bungalow on the beach and told him to use it before he burned himself out.

The time off had allowed him to do much soul-searching for the first time. She'd been away for months, about ten in all. But every time he'd thought of cutting his losses and maybe trying to start a new relationship with someone, it was always an empty, hollow experience. It didn't help when Dante reminded him that he could never really leave Tia as he was physically joined to her through the Siren's bond, which was why he felt so tired. He still didn't fully understand it.

Today he sat on a sun lounger reading a British newspaper on his veranda, which was only about fifty feet from the sea front. It was a glorious day.

His phone rang. It was Dante.

"Hey man. How ya doin?" Dante asked.

"Hey. I'm fine. Rested up … looking forward to coming back. Is that female voices I can hear in the background?"

Dante laughed, as if busted. "I'm sampling the pleasures of water nymphs. Two of them."

"Water nymphs? What the bloody hell are they?"

"We are not the only water folk, you know … why don't you come and join me?"

"No thanks man. I think my wingman days are over."

"Good. Glad to hear it," Dante said in mock seriousness. "I'm sending you something today, so don't go out."

"This had better be something good, Dante, and not one of your sick jokes."

Dante laughed, and then sounded very preoccupied. "Look, I've got to go. Ring me when you get it, okay?" he said, through staccato breaths.

"Okay," Jay said, smiling. "Later." He clicked off his phone and looked out to sea.

He'd woken up thinking about her this morning. She was an ache in his chest that wouldn't go away, and he rubbed it absently where it hurt.

He got up, went in to the kitchen and got himself another orange juice from the fridge and came back outside. He stood and looked out to sea while he drank it.

There weren't that many people on the beach yet as it was still early; just locals single-line fishing and diving. He put his hands over his eyes like a visor … what was that?

It looked like six people swimming in over the reef. As they got closer he could see they were definitely people. Then four – one larger and three small – turned and waved to two other large people, who waved and turned and dove down and disappeared. *Murrs?*

His heart started to pump. Could it be? He put his orange down and took a step forward onto the sand from the deck. Then he ran to the edge of the sea. Still they came nearer. Yes, definitely one adult, he squinted, and three kids; one a lot younger compared to the other two.

The adult – a woman – reached shallower water and began to stand up and threw the little one on her back, who linked his arms around her neck. The two others swam along next to her.

As they got nearer Jay started to wade in, cautiously at first. He couldn't be sure it was her, as she was still a way off. When the water was just half way up her legs she bent down and began rubbing the little one's back, who appeared to be sick. She then did the same with the other two, who could now stand up.

He studied the children. The little one looked like a toddler and the other two he guessed to be around three or four years old; but then how would he know.

When he was close enough to witness her release the water from her lungs, he was in no doubt who she was and began to run into the water to meet her. As she finished coughing she stood up and saw him. She handed the baby to one of the others and began to run towards him.

As she reached him she threw her body weight at him and knocked him backwards into the water and kissed him for all she was worth.

She tasted cool and salty, but it was her. She kissed and kissed him and he kissed her back hungrily, forgetting to breathe in his desperation. She blew a little of her essence intermittently with her kisses and that wonderful warm familiar glow began to flood him. He'd tried to remember this feeling so many times but it had been too long. Now it was real and happening in the flesh.

Jay! Jay! I've missed you so much, she projected through her bond.

When he opened his eyes and she allowed him to take a gulp of air, he saw three new pairs of eyes staring down at him. Seeing that he'd spotted them, Tia got up slowly and allowed him to get up.

He looked down, studying the little ones one by one, who each looked up at him expectantly. "Aren't you going to introduce me, Tia?"

Tia grinned and stood behind the bigger two. "This is Xavier and Alexia," she said, putting a hand on each of their heads.

Jay decided they were obviously Dante's; they couldn't be anyone else's. They had the tell-tale black stripes covering their bodies, Tia's beautiful green eyes, and Dante's olive skin and jet black long curly hair.

They say hello, Tia relayed to Jay. *And this little one,* taking the youngest one from the little girl's arms, *this is JJ. Jay Junior. He is a miracle.*

Jay looked at the fair-skinned, fair-haired boy, with

faint grey stripes and beautiful eyes the colour of aquamarine, and then back to Tia, then back to the boy again in confusion. His face must have been a picture.

She handed the baby to Jay, who immediately touched his mouth and tried to prise a little finger inside.

"How is this even possible?" Jay asked, looking over at Tia in wonder.

I know, crazy isn't it? That's why I've been so long. It's a miracle he's even alive.

"But you ... you didn't even look pregnant when you left?"

I know. On my wedding to Dante, all my mother said was that when I felt like I need to be in the water and it became all-consuming, then I must seek her out. I had no clue this was the reason. Well ... till right near the time. Dante guessed I think. But I was scared that my being pregnant would hurt you, as it should have been impossible for us, as I should only be able to conceive under water. The doctors explained that my body just stored the foetuses until I could be in water. I think when I was held in the tank it must have set things off. It became urgent then...Then little JJ was born. And she tickled his face making him give a huge grin. *Doctors had to get his little gills working, just like a Human premature baby. Then he needed help swimming and everything.*

"How are they all so big, Tia?"

They told me Murr children grow really fast for the first five years. It's a survival thing. These two are almost pure blood; that's why the little guy is smaller. The doctors said Sirens could store more than one pregnancy, so hey presto

– three.

Jay kissed the little fingers still trying to invade his mouth. He leant over and kissed Tia. "I wasn't expecting this, Tia … I need a drink. Let's go inside."

They all need to learn to speak as well. They've never used their vocal cords, Tia continued animatedly.

Jay put an arm around her whilst cuddling little JJ, who already clung to him. The other two ran in circles, bickering like kids do.

It's going to be difficult with Dante and the kids and everything, Tia said when they got inside.

He pulled her to him. Little JJ squealed.

His first noise! Tia thought in surprise.

They both laughed.

Jay passed JJ to Tia, and bent and picked up the other two, and sat them both on the counter top so they weren't left out. And when he pulled Tia in close for a hug, he put an arm around the little girl and little Xavier joined the hug as well. A little family.

"You never cease to amaze me, Tia." And he kissed her again.

As their kiss ended, a distant voice echoed in his head, *Congratulations brother!*

Coming soon: **DIABLO,** The new standalone by T Stedman.

To find out more, visit:

www.tstedman.com

www.facebook.com/TStedman1author

www.twitter.com/AuthorTStedman